STUCK ON YOU

PATTI BERG

STUCK ON YOU

AVON BOOKS
An Imprint of HarperCollinsPublishers

AVON BOOKS
An Imprint of HarperCollins*Publishers*
10 East 53rd Street
New York, New York 10022-5299

Copyright © 2003 by Patti Berg
ISBN: 0-7394-3169-2

Printed in the U.S.A.

For Lucia Macro—
many, many thanks for your guidance,
your editorial flair,
and your unfailing patience.

And, as always,
for Bob.

Chapter 1

"*Powdered sugar drifted down, down, down, settling lightly on the dead man's chest, speckling the hideous words carved deep in his skin.*

"*'Lust—your seventh and very last sin!'*

"*'Interesting.' I popped the last of a lemon bar into my mouth and chewed thoughtfully, studying the depth of the letters, their width, the spacing, and the insidious exclamation point that followed.*"

"Ridiculous. Absolutely ridiculous." Ida Mae slammed her book shut. "Forensic pathologists do not eat lemon bars during an autopsy."

Scarlett O'Malley's gaze drifted up from her novel and settled on the elderly ladies who were supposed to be listening to the riveting Jayne Mansfield-Smythe story she was reading.

"Quiet, Ida Mae," Mildred muttered. "We don't interrupt you when it's your turn to read."

"I'm sorry, but Jayne Mansfield-Smythe is too stupid to live."

"Yes, yes, I agree she is—at times. But if she didn't do crazy things on occasion, if she didn't get herself in risky situations, the books would be dull, not to mention boring, and not one of us would buy them. Now"—Mildred smiled at Scarlett—"where were we?"

Undaunted by her friends' interruption, Scarlett's gaze slid back to the pages of *Seven Sins,* and once again she began to read.

"*I circled the autopsy table, licking powdered sugar from my fingers as I considered the meaning of the words, particularly the first: Lust. The dictionary described it as an intense or unbridled craving for bodily pleasure. My own definition of the word would be Detective Dylan MacLeod—naked and in my bed. Wishful thinking. After working three homicides with the blue-eyed cop, he's yet to touch me.*

"*But I digress. It isn't my sins I need to deal with at the moment; it's Councilman Tamblyn's.*

"*Had the politician lusted too much and as a consequence been killed? Had he lusted after the wrong person, in the wrong place, at the wrong time?*

"*So many, many questions.*

"*I took a sip of Diet Pepsi to wash away the last bits of the tangy lemon and powdered sugar, snapped on a pair of gloves, and picked up my scalpel. 'Don't worry, Councilman. If it's the last thing I do, I'll find your killer.'*"

"Sweet merciful heavens! Please tell me I'm not seeing what I'm seeing."

Once again Ida Mae's tormented cry ripped Scarlett out of Jayne Mansfield-Smythe's fictional world and back to the reality of her cozy, antique-laden bookstore. But when she looked up this time, her three elderly companions had abandoned their Louis XIV chairs, their delicate china teacups, not to mention Scarlett's recitation, and huddled in front of the shop's display window, staring outside.

"Poor, poor Opal!" Mildred gasped, her angst yanking Scarlett from the table. Tugging at her blue leather miniskirt, Scarlett strode toward Mildred, Ida Mae, and Lillian, with her Scottish terrier, Toby, waddling behind.

"What on earth's happened to Opal?" Scarlett asked, peeking between two stout bodies to see what was going on outside.

"*Him!* That's what's happened to her." Ida Mae pointed a pudgy finger across the street, at the male half of the odd couple exiting the white clapboard building that had housed the Plentiful Bank and Trust since 1892. "That' man's after Opal's jewels and God knows what else, and fool that she is, she's bound to give him everything he wants."

Mildred clapped a hand over her ample bosom. "You don't think he's out to have sex with her, too, do you?"

"Give me a break. Opal's old enough to be his grandmother," Ida Mae declared. "I tell you, the man's a gigolo, a no-good, dirty rotten scoundrel who wants nothing more than Opal's fortune."

"But you have to admit," Lillian said, "he's a very handsome, no-good, dirty rotten scoundrel."

It was hard to argue with that, Scarlett thought,

squeezing between the ladies of the Tuesday Morning Sleuth Society to get a better view of the man they were talking about. She studied him as she studied most everything else in life—with a keen eye for detail.

Broad-shouldered and narrow-hipped, he towered over poor, dear Opal, as well as the few tourists meandering past them on the nineteenth-century boardwalk. His thick, wavy hair was the same blackish-brown color of her special-recipe dark chocolate brownies. It was streaked with burgundy, the autumn wind had whipped several stray locks over his brow, and, as if his slightly shaggy mane wasn't splendid enough already, it had the audacity to shimmer in the Wyoming sunlight.

Scarlett coiled a springy strand of her unruly mop around her index finger. It wasn't quite fair, she decided, for a man to have hair that looked that fabulous, when the color of her own rowdy curls fell somewhere between boiled carrots and pickled beets.

"He *is* gorgeous," Scarlett said, puffing at a corkscrew that unwittingly fell over her left eye, "but what makes you think he's a gigolo?"

"Just look at that smile." Ida Mae's nose moved precariously close to the window. "Only seducers and debauchers smile like that."

Scarlett squinted to get a better look at the stranger's smile. Granted, it was far from plain and ordinary. It was one of those Kodak-moment smiles, the kind that could make a woman get all weepy for no reason at all, or make her heart go pitter-pat, if she was so inclined.

Scarlett wasn't. After watching her mother suffer through two lousy marriages, after she herself had wasted too many years looking for Mr. Right, going so far as to date Plentiful's cold-as-a-corpse mortician not once but twice, she considered herself a woman who couldn't be hornswoggled by a man, not even a tall, dark and handsome one with a to-die-for smile and heaven-sent hair.

But that didn't mean she wasn't curious about the great-looking guy.

Who was he? she wondered. Why was he in town?

He wasn't a local. The population of Plentiful and the surrounding area was only one thousand four hundred and forty-four, give or take a few, and she'd definitely remember this guy if he lived anywhere near. His boots weren't clumped with mud. He wore black jeans instead of faded blue, and they looked like Levi's—a sin to wear in Wrangler country. To top it off, the weathered black leather bomber jacket he wore over a black polo shirt made him look more like a *GQ* model than a rough and tough cowboy.

She was on the verge of asking the Sleuths if they knew the man's identity when Mildred, in her usual fashion, clasped a hand to her chest and gasped, "Look! Look! Oh, my God, I think he's going to kiss her."

All four women held their breath as they watched the stranger bend his tall, muscular frame toward the richest widow in town and go in for the kiss.

It was quick. It was chaste. It was on the cheek instead of the mouth.

Scarlett let out a deep—and quite unexpected—sigh of relief.

"Pretty poor excuse for a kiss, if you ask me," Mildred huffed. "If a gigolo wanted to get something from me, he'd have to do a lot better than that."

"They always start out slow," Ida Mae said. "This one's doing all the right things. Just watch him."

All eyes stayed glued to the episode playing out on Main Street, in the quaint old west town turned tourist mecca. The stranger, in typical Don Juan fashion, helped Opal into her silver Mercedes, closed the car door easily, then braced his hands on the open window and shared a last laugh or two with his elderly companion.

"See. He's smiling again." Sarcasm oozed from Ida Mae's every word. "He's got the role down pat. A flirtatious word here, an enticing smile there, a bit of friendly banter to butter Opal up before he zooms in for the kill."

"What do you suppose they're talking about?" Mildred asked.

"Opal's stocks and bonds, more than likely," Ida Mae said. "Maybe her will, or her quote-unquote cottage that's worth seven mil, if not more. I have half a mind to go out there right now and talk some sense into that woman."

"Too late," Scarlett said, watching the Mercedes screech away from the boardwalk with Opal, in her usual speed demon fashion, tearing up Main Street and leaving a trail of dingy gray diesel smoke in her wake.

Ida Mae shook her head. "Well, I suppose I'll have to talk to her some other time. Maybe go out to her place tonight or tomorrow and set her straight. But right now, considering all the commotion"—she fanned her red-cheeked face—"I need tea."

Lillian and Mildred followed their leader back to the table, their chatter turning to a low drone as Scarlett continued to study the fascinating stranger, wondering what he'd do next.

His back was turned to Scarlett, but what she could see was still rather divine. Muscular legs. Great tush. Powerful shoulders, not that she took much stock in a man's appearance or physique. It was what was inside a man that counted, and so far Scarlett had found most men rather hollow.

When the silver streak that was Opal's car disappeared behind the enormous pines at the far end of town, he twisted around slowly. Through the almost black lenses of his sunglasses, he scanned the windows facing Main Street. First the Misty Moon Saloon, the java and ice cream shops, and the Elk Horn Café. He took a cursory glance at the art galleries, posh boutiques, and fine jewelry stores that catered to rich tourists, as well as rich widows like Opal, Lillian, Ida Mae, and Mildred. And finally, he fixed his stare on Scarlett's stately Victorian, on the blood red words scripted in Old English across its picture window: A Study in Scarlett—Mystery Book and Tea Shoppe.

Scarlett shuddered. Whether it was trepidation she felt or a twinge of excitement, she wasn't sure, but she stepped back a few inches and pulled the sheer, white ruffly curtain in front of her to veil her face and body. Jayne Mansfield-Smythe—a goddess of cunning and derring-do, even if she was fictitious— wouldn't hide. Oh no, she'd want the man to know he was being watched. But Scarlett opted for stealth and secrecy. Until she was sure what the stranger was up to, she didn't want him to know she was curious, didn't want him to know that she'd be observing his actions, keeping track of his activities. If he was out to scam someone in town, she darn well planned to prevent it.

How she'd do that was questionable, since her skills in that department had been pretty hit-and-miss in the past, but she figured she'd deal with that when the time came. For now, she kept her eyes on the man in black, watched him turn his attention away from A Study in Scarlett when supermodel-wannabe Miranda Green strutted by him in her tight designer jeans and her zillion-dollar lizard boots. The stranger fixed his eyes on Miranda's tight little be-hind and its decided wiggle, and he didn't stop watching until she slipped into her zippy gold Porsche and whizzed out of town.

As if he sensed he was being watched, the stranger faced Scarlett's shop and glared once more at the dis-play window. A shiver fluttered up Scarlett's spine when he smiled. It was a sly smile, a knowing smile that seemed to say "I'm watching you, too."

Suddenly he was on the move, heading toward her shop. Did he plan to give her a piece of his mind?

Was he going to check her out, see what kind of bank account she had, then put the make on her, too?

An out of the blue pitter-pat fluttered in her chest. A lump of dread caught in her throat. She wanted him to walk through her door; then again, she wanted him to stay far, far away so she wouldn't be tempted by his obvious charm.

All of a sudden he stopped, something in the window of the Mischievous Moose Emporium catching his eye, and without so much as a wave good-bye, he disappeared through the swinging doors of Plentiful's biggest souvenir trap.

Scarlett let out the breath she'd been holding for heaven knows how long. She wished she could ignore the man, as if he were any other visitor in the wannabe-Aspen tourist town, but he made her nervous. He also piqued her interest, and she needed to know more about him.

Crossing the Victorian's parlor, she straightened a doily beneath a Tiffany lamp and picked a piece of lint from the burgundy velvet rippling over the small round table where she was displaying the latest Jayne Mansfield-Smythe novel.

At last she took her usual place at the table with Ida Mae, Mildred, and Lillian, while Toby crawled underneath and plopped on Scarlett's toes. A copy of *Seven Sins* sat in front of each lady, but all books were closed. Today, the women seemed more interested in real life than fiction.

Scarlett took a sip of Earl Grey with lilac, the preferred tea of the Tuesday Morning Sleuth Society, and finally got down to gossip. "So, who is this new man in Opal's life?"

"*Logan Wolfe.*" Ida Mae emphasized the man's name as if it were a dirty word. Poor Ida Mae. She looked like a plumper version of Oprah, with short, curly gray hair and a cowgirl's wardrobe. Hiram, her ex, had wanted her to dress like Diana Ross; Ida Mae preferred Dale Evans. In the end Hiram had run off with their slinky young housekeeper, and ever since, Ida Mae had made no bones about despising men.

With her gaze intent on Scarlett, Ida Mae plucked a scone from the platter in the center of the table and nibbled at the edge. "I'm surprised no one's clued you in on Mr. Wolfe yet. The man's all the gossip around town."

Mildred, the spitting image of Mayberry's Aunt Bee and more often than not just as sweet and sincere, spooned honey into a gold-rimmed cup and stirred her tea gently. "It's not like you to ask us what's going on in Plentiful. Land's sake, child, you've been holed up in this place much too much lately. Some of us"—Mildred eyed Ida Mae, then Lillian—"have begun to wonder if you've grown tired of spending time with us."

"Of course not. I've just been preoccupied."

Mildred's eyes narrowed with concern. "You aren't going through your mother's things again, are you?"

Scarlett took another sip of tea, staring at the variegated colors of the hand-painted pink roses inside the cup, rather than look at her friends. "I've been reading her diaries, and—"

"And no matter how many times you analyze her words," Mildred said, "you're not going to find proof that Adam had anything to do with her death."

"He's a low-down, dirty rotten bastard," Ida Mae said. "You know it, the three of us know it, but everyone else in this town thinks your stepfather walks on water."

Lillian rested bejeweled fingers over Scarlett's hand. "We've tried proving he's a snake—"

"Not to mention a philanderer, a cheat, a crooked cop, and a vicious man who caused your poor, saintly mother nothing but grief," Ida Mae interrupted.

"Yes, all of that, too," Lillian said. "But we have no evidence to back our beliefs."

"And the people in town think we're crackpots." Mildred heaved a frustrated sigh. "No matter how sound our accusations are, they only laugh when we hint that Adam's done something wrong. So, Scarlett, dear, don't you think it's time you put this aside and move on with your life?"

"Mildred's right," Lillian said. "This is causing you nothing but heartache."

Scarlett looked past her friends to the garden outside. Fall had just arrived, but the English roses her mother had planted when they'd come to Plentiful twenty years ago still blossomed with pink, red, and yellow blooms. The fragrant flowers and the hummingbirds that even now darted from one bud to another were the only things—besides her daughter's love—that had made Elizabeth O'Malley-Grant smile in the last years of her life.

There was no way Scarlett could give up her search to prove that Adam Grant had driven her mother half out of her mind, which in turn had led her to an early grave. But she didn't want her friends worrying about her own state of mind.

Putting a smile on her face, she looked from dear friend to dear friend and fibbed. "You're right. Maybe it is time I put the past behind me."

"That's our girl," Mildred said, drizzling a little more honey into her cup of tea.

"Now that that's settled," Ida Mae added, "you can help us keep an eye on *him*."

"You mean Logan Wolfe?" Scarlett asked, perfectly happy to have a change of subject.

"Exactly." Lillian grinned from behind her rhinestone-studded glasses. They were Coke-bottle thick, covered one-third of her face, and were bright green chartreuse, the same color as the polyester pantsuit and lace-up, ankle-high platform boots she wore. Bless her heart, Lillian was a dead ringer for Elton John.

"So"—Scarlett pinched off a piece of scone and popped it into her mouth—"what do you know about this Logan Wolfe? Who is he?"

"Who knows," Ida Mae said. "We dogged his footsteps for two days after we heard he'd put the make on Opal."

"You're sure he's putting the make on her?" Scarlett asked, figuring the man deserved at least some benefit of doubt.

Ida Mae frowned. "I've read enough mysteries to

know when someone's up to no good, and he meets all the criteria for gigolo."

"Which are?"

Scarlett's continued interrogation made Ida Mae roll her eyes.

"He's exceptionally handsome," Mildred said. "I hate to admit this, but that means he's far too perfect to be real, and that spells philanderer in my book."

"He took Opal out to dinner the other night," Ida Mae added, then hesitated a moment, glaring at Scarlett as if waiting for another question. When it didn't come, she continued. "Lillian, Mildred and I managed to get a seat at the booth right next to Opal's and we tried our darndest to hear every word, which wasn't always easy. You know how noisy it can be at the Misty Moon on a Friday night, but we kept our ears glued to the conversation and heard him asking Opal all sorts of questions about her finances."

"He also plied poor Opal with wine—the expensive stuff—and we heard her insist on picking up the check." Mildred shook her head. "Poor, poor Opal. She was tipsy when she left the restaurant—"

"And I'm sure he took advantage of her." Ida Mae clicked her tongue in disgust.

"Did you ever stop to think that Opal might be taking advantage of him?" Lillian asked.

"Never," Ida Mae declared.

"But his smile's lovely. He seems utterly charming, and . . . and . . . well, not that I could ever actually do this," Lillian sputtered, "but there are women who pay for a man to treat them . . . nice. Perhaps

Mr. Wolfe was doing exactly what Opal wanted him to do."

"Impossible." Ida Mae shook her head. "She would never do something like that."

"If she was lonely enough she would." Lillian sighed deeply. "I've been alone off and on for a long time. I'm not young any longer, but that doesn't mean I don't remember what it was like to be loved, that I don't remember what it was like to be held in a man's arms. Sometimes, late at night, when I'm all alone in bed, I . . ." Lillian grinned; her rosy cheeks turned crimson. "Well, that's neither here nor there, but let me assure you, I miss those things, and there are times when I'd be willing to give up everything— to do anything—to have a man in my life again."

Mildred's eyes widened. "You'd pay a man to do those things to you?"

"I'm rich. I'm lonely. Why not?"

"Because it's not right." Ida Mae chomped down on her scone, chewing with great annoyance as she glared at Lillian. "Because you could end up paying the wrong kind of guy, some jerk who makes you believe he loves you when, in truth, he's nothing but a devious, low-down bucket of lying, cheating scum. And in the end you'll wind up hurt or, God forbid, dead, like our poor, dear Elizabeth."

Tea sloshed out of Scarlett's cup. Ida Mae's sharp reminder of her mother's gullibility, her frailty, her death at the young age of thirty-eight, when Scarlett had just turned nineteen, shook her to the core.

Composing herself, Scarlett pressed her lace-edged

linen napkin over the spill before the amber liquid made too big a mess on the crocheted tablecloth, one her mother had made during those few happy years between lousy husband number one—Scarlett's father—and even lousier husband number two.

Adam Grant, Scarlett's stepfather, was one of those devious, low-down buckets of lying, cheating scum. Her mother hadn't paid him a penny for anything, not that Scarlett knew about, anyway, but she'd fallen hard for Adam's charm and good looks, and he'd ended up taking most everything she ever had— her self-esteem, her vitality, her heart and her soul. He'd hurt her dreadfully, and then she'd died. Suddenly. Tragically.

Some day, Scarlett vowed, she'd prove that Adam was at fault.

It had become eerily quiet in the room. Scarlett looked up slowly to see the Sleuths staring at her, sadness dimming their usually bright eyes.

"I'm sorry, Scarlett." Ida Mae attempted a smile. "I got carried away and said too much."

"But everything you said is true," Scarlett admitted. She dropped the stained napkin into her empty teacup and allowed herself to smile. "Adam Grant is the devil's spawn and my mother didn't stand a chance once he cast his evil eye on her. Unfortunately, I've got the feeling there are a lot of men like that in this world, and we've all got to be wary of them. That includes you, Lillian."

Mildred nodded in agreement. "She's right, Lil."

"All right." Lillian harrumphed. "Maybe I should

be wary. But what about Opal? It looks as if she's already fallen for that sexy Logan Wolfe. What can we possibly do now?"

The Sleuths aimed their eyes at Scarlett as if she had all the answers when, in truth, she had none. She didn't know a thing about the purported gigolo, other than the extremely annoying and perplexing fact that she found him fascinating. That was not going to help Opal, however, if she was, indeed, in need of help.

Best get down to the crux of the matter.

"So"—Scarlett picked a speck of scone from the tablecloth and dropped it on top of her napkin—"you've dogged Logan Wolfe's heels, you've assumed he's a cad, but what do you know for certain about him?"

"Not much," Mildred said. "He's renting that old cabin in Grizzly Hollow. You know, that place where Crazy Pete used to live."

"Crazy Pete who talked to bears?" Lillian asked.

Mildred nodded. "The very same."

Scarlett remembered the place quite well. Twenty years ago the cabin was nearly falling down and served as little more than a haven for wild animals and a mad old man who disliked trespassers of the two-legged variety. It was the perfect place for a young girl to hide from an overbearing stepfather. Not only that, it was a great place to play Nancy Drew, teenage spy. But why would a good-looking guy want to live there? Did Logan Wolfe have something to hide—or was he merely hiding? Frowning at this new possibility, Scarlett asked, "How long has he been living there?"

Mildred shrugged. "Two, maybe three weeks, from what we've been able to find out."

Scarlett began making mental notes of all the details, just as she did when she read a mystery, hoping she'd come up with enough information to solve the puzzle before she got to the end of the story. "Is he working in town? Is he vacationing?"

"We think he might be doing some odd jobs for Opal—hopefully not *too* odd," Ida Mae said. "He's paid cash for all his groceries and for the gas he puts in his pickup."

"There's more, too." Mildred opened her black patent handbag and dug around, apparently for other pertinent details.

The ladies weren't bad for amateur sleuths; they weren't all that good, either, and they did get carried away on occasion. Their detective skills came from the cozies they selected as their preferred reading and from reruns of *Murder, She Wrote*. They'd also taken a mail-order make-me-a-sleuth course but had failed miserably at Miss Marple 101.

Still, their antics gave them something fun to do, and it kept them from being old and alone and pining for the past, as too many other widows and widowers in town seemed to do.

"Here it is." Mildred withdrew a leather-bound diary from her purse and flipped through the pages, scanning dozens of scribbled notes. "To the best of my knowledge, Mr. Wolfe hasn't deposited any money in the bank and he hasn't used any credit cards." She gazed at the ladies sitting around her, and one carefully penciled gray eyebrow rose. "Makes him sound very much like a man with deep, dark secrets he doesn't want uncovered."

Ida Mae folded her arms on the table, leaned forward, and whispered, "We overheard him telling Opal that he'd hightailed it out of Vegas as fast as he could because he was tired of that hellhole."

Scarlett drummed her fingers atop *Seven Sins*. "Interesting."

"We thought so, too. Unfortunately," Mildred said, "we've hunted high and low to see what information we could get on him, using that one little detail we'd gleaned about his past, but we can't find anything more. Not a credit report, not a civil or criminal record, no marriage or divorce records. Nothing. It's as if the man didn't exist before he came here."

"Or he managed to erase all traces of his past," Scarlett said.

Lillian frowned. "Is that possible?"

"I suppose anything's possible, if you want it badly enough, and if you have the right connections." Scarlett thought of her stepfather again, of the way he always came out smelling like a rose, even though she knew, deep down in her heart, that Plentiful's chief of police wallowed in crap.

Ida Mae's spoon clinked against the sides of her cup as she methodically stirred her tea. "Scarlett, dear, do you have any idea how we can get Logan

Wolfe's birth date and Social Security number? I imagine we can find out much more about him if we have that information."

"There's always a way, but—" Scarlett again drummed her fingers atop *Seven Sins,* thinking of all that she'd heard about the connection between Opal and Logan Wolfe, which wasn't much. If she and the Tuesday Morning Sleuths jumped to conclusions, they could wind up in trouble. Not only that, but they could cause embarrassment to Opal and themselves.

Scarlett drummed a little harder while the Sleuths watched and waited for her advice. What would Jayne Mansfield-Smythe do? she wondered.

A light, melodious jingle came from the doorway, and four pair of eyes shot toward the entrance. The dangly crystal chimes swayed and continued to tinkle their tune as a tall, slender woman walked inside. Her cottony white hair was short and curly. Her face and neck were crinkled with age, and the lines next to her eyes and mouth showed nothing but sadness.

"May I help you?" Scarlett tugged at her skirt as she rose from the table to greet her first real customer of the day. Toby waddled after her, and in usual Toby fashion, snarled at the stranger.

The woman aimed angry, squinted eyes at the dog. Toby might be a pest, one Scarlett had inherited when her former neighbor—Art, the barber—was shipped off to prison, but the pooch didn't deserve the scorn of a stranger.

Next the woman grimaced at the stars and stripes

blazing across Scarlett's chest. Maybe she had over-
done it a bit when she'd designed the spandex top,
but she'd liked the glittery fabric. The lady didn't
seem to approve of her belly button ring, either. Or
her five-inch heels.

Finally the woman's eyes settled on Scarlett's unruly red hair, a mess she'd quit trying to tame ages
ago. She tilted her head slightly, studying Scarlett, siz-
ing her up. But why?

Scarlett cleared her throat, and once again asked,
"Could I help you with something? I have tea,
scones, and thousands of books."

The woman's eyes narrowed as she stared con-
temptuously at the Tuesday Morning Sleuths, who
were paying rapt attention to the lady's every move.
"Obviously you're busy." She turned back to Scarlett. "If it's all the same to you, I'll just browse."

The stranger wasn't making very many points, but
Scarlett flashed her best you're-not-very-nice-but-
I'm-determined-to-make-money-off-of-you smile.
"Take your time. Please." *And buy a lot.* "I carry all
the latest mysteries and try to keep the complete
backlist of the most popular authors in stock."

"I'm sure you do."

"Could I interest you in some tea while you
browse?"

"No." She turned her back on Scarlett and the
sleuths, stepped over Toby, and headed straight for
the children's section, with a guard dog hot on her
heels.

She didn't look the grandmotherly type, nor did

she look as if she still read Nancy Drew. Oh, well, she wasn't the first discourteous or peculiar character to walk into the shop. She definitely wouldn't be the last.

Except for the attention-grabbing stranger who'd come into town, this was a pretty typical early autumn day. Fairly quiet; fairly peaceful. In the next two months there'd be few tourists in town, which meant Scarlett could close the shop early if she wanted. She could open late. Maybe she'd re-paper the walls in her bedroom, hobnob with the sleuths, or dig for dirt on Adam, as well as Opal's gigolo.

The chimes jingled again. Actually, it was more of a clash of crystal against crystal. A gust of wind blew into the Victorian and slapped at the backs of Scarlett's legs. She spun around on her stilettos, and who should she see in her doorway?

The Big Bad Wolfe.

Chapter 2

The cool morning breeze whipped about the room, playing havoc with the pages of the few books that were open for display. It stirred the ruffled curtains and rustled the crocheted cloth on the table where the Tuesday Morning Sleuths perched on the edges of their chairs, staring at . . . *him*.

Be brave, Scarlett told herself. It's not like he's going to huff and puff and blow your house down. Jayne Mansfield-Smythe would laugh in the face of such menace, perceived or otherwise. Scarlett Mary Catherine O'Malley was determined to do the same—well, at least she could smile.

One step forward. Two.

Smile pretty.

Logan Wolfe, eyes hidden behind nearly black sunglasses, stared about the room. Was he looking for prey? A helpless innocent he could carry back to his lair?

He shut the door behind him, and at last the clanking chimes settled down to a serene tinkle. The curtains, the book pages, and the tablecloth stilled.

All was quiet except the rapidly beating heart within her chest. "Good morning." Amazingly, the words came out of her mouth as if she were calm and cool. For reasons that could only be attributed to the stranger's unexpected appearance in her shop, she was anything but.

Logan Wolfe removed his sunglasses and tucked them in an inside coat pocket. "Good morning."

She should have known he'd have a nice voice. Kind of George Clooney-ish, with that hint of laughter ready to break out at any moment. That same playfulness glinted in his eyes.

Big Bad Wolfe? Maybe. Maybe not.

"Mind if I browse?" he asked.

Browsing seemed to be the modus operandi of the day. "Not at all."

He headed toward the Agatha Christies. Not a bad choice, as far as she was concerned, but not what she pictured a guy like him reading. Still, it got him away from her, gave her a chance to think. She was rarely at a loss for words, but she found herself wanting to ask him questions like, Do you howl at night? or Which do you prefer eating? Little old ladies or short young women who have to wear five-inch heels just so they're tall enough to stare straight at your chest?

She asked neither. Instead, she headed toward the Sleuths, who didn't seem to want her anywhere near.

Ida Mae glowered at her and whispered through nearly clenched teeth, "Ask him what his intentions are where Opal's concerned. Ask him where he's from. Get his Social Security number."

"I can't do that and you know it."

"Then ask him anything." Mildred jerked her head half a dozen times toward Logan, hoping Scarlett would get the point that the Sleuths wanted her to get to know the man, not because he was hot stuff—which any red-blooded woman could see plain as day—but because they wanted to get the skinny on him.

Scarlett scowled. She wasn't an investigator, she was a book seller with snooping tendencies. But Ida Mae, Mildred, and Lillian were relying on her.

Working up the courage to face the man whose very presence left her tongue-tied, she turned on her spiked heels and marched across the room. She mounted the ladder that stretched to the top of the nine-foot bookshelves and finally stopped climbing when she stood eye to eye with his eyes. "Can I help you find something?"

"Just browsing, thanks."

Just browsing—ha! He'd begun to scrutinize her body. He started at her crimson toenails and strappy blue stilettos, worked his way up to her hip-hugging leather skirt, the belly button ring with an itty-bitty gold American flag dangling from it, and her midriff-baring star-spangled shirt. He didn't smile. He didn't frown. His eyes merely shot toward her hair and settled there. Long, flaming red corkscrews spouted every which way. This was her curse, a blight upon her very existence when she was a kid, but she made the most of it now. If she was going to look like an exploding firework she was darn well going to dress as if every day were the Fourth of July.

Absently—or maybe not so absently—she fluffed her curls. The calm, impassive look remained on his face, but she could swear a little tick worked away at the edge of his mouth, as if he wanted to laugh.

"Should I salute?" he asked, catching her totally off guard.

She fired back with the first thing that came to mind. "I prefer it when men bow down at my feet."

His gaze slid to her crimson toenails. "Nice feet. But"—he put a hand on the ladder and leaned in close, his eyes mere inches from hers—"I don't bow down to anyone. What about you?"

"I don't have a submissive bone in my body."

At that he grinned, some suggestive comeback tickling his tongue, but he kept it to himself.

Scarlett groaned deep down inside, yet she kept a cool façade in spite of herself. Had she really uttered those flirtatious words? Did he see them as a challenge? A come-on? Could she possibly climb inside one of the books on the shelf and hide? She came up with a better idea. Maybe she could run to the kitchen for some refreshments and come back out composed.

"Could I interest you in something to drink while you look around? I've got a black tea blend—Russian Roulette—that you might like. It's extra strong. Has a bit of a smoky taste." Something a sexy, albeit no-good, dirty rotten scoundrel might drink when he wasn't guzzling whiskey or seducing women.

"No thanks. I'm just interested in getting something to read."

Could have fooled her the way he gave her body the once-over—again—before letting go of the ladder and studying the books. He fingered his way through half a shelf, not looking at any book long enough to read even the spine.

Now what? He didn't want tea, so she had no reason to run to the kitchen. She shot Mildred, Ida Mae, and Lillian a quick I-don't-know-what-to-do-now glance. Lillian patted her romantic heart. Mildred and Ida Mae looked at her cross-eyed. What more could they possibly expect her to ask him, now that she'd made a fool of herself?

She climbed two more rungs on the ladder before she heard Ida Mae clear her throat. The ladies expected her to be the expert on surveillance, on interrogation, on anything spy related, which was absolutely ludicrous. She didn't know anything more than they did. Any success she'd had in solving the two piddly little cases she'd solved had been done on nothing more than sheer luck.

Maybe she should forget about quizzing him about Opal and just go back to being a purveyor of books, tea, and scones. That was something she did with ease. Offer him something else, just as you would any other customer, she told herself. Just don't become a pest.

"I have fresh macadamia nut and apricot scones."

He angled his head toward her, and for the first time she noticed the color of his eyes. Maple syrup brown. Not the artificial variety but the real thing, very dark and very rich. A woman could drown in those eyes, and she was sinking ridiculously fast for a woman who, for the most part, wanted nothing to do with men.

"No thanks," he said, once again.

She should give up. Maybe he found her annoying. Then again, maybe he just didn't like apricots or macadamias. "I have huckleberry scones, too, and they're absolutely delicious. Could I get you one? Two maybe?" She smiled sweetly, like a love-struck teen staring dumbly at some boy-band superstar, and wondered which book would be big enough to crawl into.

He didn't smile in return. No, he simply frowned as if she'd lost her mind.

"And milk. They go really well with milk." Oh, God, she was rambling now. "Not chocolate milk, of course. Plain milk. Non-fat, two percent, or whole. Take your pick, because I'm sure I have just about any kind you could possibly want in the refrigerator."

He latched on to the ladder again and hit her with those maple syrup eyes. "I prefer beer to milk. Cinnamon rolls to scones, and coffee to tea. Black and extra sweet." He smiled at last. Definitely a George Clooney-ish smile. "On the personal side, I'm thirty-six years old, never been married, don't smoke, have all my own teeth, and my name's Logan Wolfe. How about you?"

"Scarlett Mary Catherine O'Malley." As if he needed to know all of that. "Twenty-nine. Single, healthy and everything you see belongs to me."

His gaze trailed over her star-studded breasts to her belly button. "Nice flag."

If navels could blush, she was certain hers now matched the crimson polish on her toenails. "Thank you."

"I take it this shop belongs to you, too?"

She nodded. "A Study in Scarlett, after Arthur Conan Doyle's first Sherlock Holmes book, with a little play on the spelling."

"Cute."

"I try."

He focused on her face again. "I see that."

His charm was irrepressible. He exuded sex. A lady-killer for sure. She'd never thought of herself as gullible. In fact, she'd forced herself to be just the opposite, because gullible had gotten her mother into a world of hurt. But here she was falling right into his spell. Not good, and definitely time to climb out, before she got in so deep she couldn't get out again.

She stepped another rung higher on the ladder, grabbed the feather duster she'd been using earlier this morning, and swished it over the books on one of the shelves. "So, what about you, Mr. Wolfe?" she said, working toward a polite conversation, nothing more than bookshop proprietor to customer. "What do you do for a living?" There, she'd finally gotten a sensible, non-embarrassing string of words out of her mouth.

"I'm retired."

"At thirty-six?"

"Yeah, at thirty-six." He didn't sound too thrilled with the situation.

"In that case, I've got a lot of wonderful books that could help you while away the hours."

He pulled a brightly covered paperback from one of the shelves, stared at the parrot wearing an eye patch on the cover, then flipped it over and scanned the back copy. "This one looks interesting."

"It's a bit tame as far as mysteries go. But if you like cozies—"

"Never read a cozy. Never read a mystery, for that matter."

"What do you read?"

"The daily fishing report. Stock market quotes. The *Plentiful Gazette*." He pushed the cozy back into its allotted space, and his broad shoulder, encased in weathered black leather, brushed lightly over her hip. She forced herself not to enjoy the tingle that zipped through her. "Maybe you can recommend something," he said, his eyes level with her belly button when he faced her again.

"I need to know more about you before I can do that."

Slowly his gaze glided up her anatomy until it settled on her eyes. "What do you want to know?"

Your Social Security number. Your date of birth. What, if anything, you've got up your sleeve. That's what the Sleuths wanted to know, and over the top of Logan's head Scarlett could see them egging her on. But she couldn't blatantly ask any of those things. It didn't seem right or fair, considering that she had no proof that he'd ever done anything wrong in his life.

"I can usually tell a person's likes and dislikes as soon as they walk in the store," she said, although figuring him out was bound to be harder than most. "Could I have a moment or two to size you up?"

He hit her once again with a raised eyebrow that said you've-got-to-be-out-of-your-mind. "Do you size up all of your customers?"

"My customers, people in restaurants, absolute strangers. Everyone." She grinned. "It's my life."

He shook his head slowly, laughter tugging at one corner of his mouth. "All right, have at it." He leaned casually against one of the upright supports on the bookcase, folded his arms over his big, broad chest, and watched her intently as she studied him—a guilty pleasure, if ever there was one.

Scarlett climbed down a few rungs for a better view. His hair was definitely the color of dark chocolate brownies and definitely a bit on the shaggy side, which was completely understandable given the fact that he was retired.

His face wasn't quite as perfect as she'd thought at first glance, but it was undeniably interesting. He had a scar on his jaw. It was a good inch and a half long, shaped like a crescent moon. Jayne Mansfield-Smythe would probably examine it for a lengthy time and try to figure out what had been used to gouge his skin. Scarlett, however, found herself feeling his pain, wondering how the scar had gotten there and why. And then she wished it wasn't there at all, not because it marred his face, but because she hated to think of him—or anyone—suffering.

"It only hurts if I nick it with a razor," he said, jerking her away from her inspection as he skimmed an index finger over the scar.

"You read minds?" she asked.

"Expressive faces."

"What am I thinking right now?"

"That you wish I couldn't read expressive faces."

She smiled and reached out to touch his chin lightly. She tilted his head a little to the right so he faced the Sleuths, not her. "I'm supposed to be figuring you out, not the other way around."

The ladies wiggled their fingers at him, a silly, we're-watching-the-two-of-you kind of wave, which brought Scarlett back to reality again. The white-haired lady she'd basically forgotten all about dropped a book in the children's section. It hit the floor with a decided thud, and her eyes narrowed. Toby stared up at the woman and growled. Scarlett could almost hear the woman growling, too.

Sum Logan up before he thinks you're flirting with him, Scarlett told herself. Help him find a book and send him packing, because, heaven forbid, you've got another customer. The white-haired lady undoubtedly wasn't as interesting, but she was a patron, and an angry one at that.

Okay, so he had a scar on his jaw. That one small feature told a big story—unfortunately, she didn't know if it was good or bad—which didn't help when summing him up. He also had a heavy beard. It was closely shaved, but the dark shadow on his face told Scarlett he either took a razor to it twice a day or went for that old-fashioned *Miami Vice* look after sundown.

Every second that she scrutinized him, she got a better picture. Underneath his brazen charm was someone tough, a man who knew what he wanted and took it, a man who'd seen more than his fair share of fights, and even though he'd been injured a time or two—the scar on his jaw and the jagged one she couldn't miss on the bridge of his slightly crooked nose were proof of that—he almost always won.

"Still trying to figure me out?" he asked.

"All done." She climbed down from the ladder and skirted around him. "Follow me and we'll see how close I am."

She led Logan to the back room, where she kept two black leather arm chairs that had once belonged to her dad, the legendary suspense author Edgar O'Malley. They were worn but big and comfortable. His ancient Remington-Rand typewriter sat on the battered oak desk, where he'd written all of his books. Framed posters of his novels-turned-to-movies hung on claret-colored walls. A Casablanca fan whirled slowly above them, ticking lightly with each rotation.

The room had a seedy, underworld feel to it, and her hard-core mystery and true crime readers often sat here with their books, letting the atmosphere draw them more completely into the fantasy.

Logan circled the room, taking in every small object, all the big ones. He relaxed in one of the chairs, crossing one ankle over his knee, and she couldn't be-

lieve how comfortable, how right at home he looked
in the shady world she'd created.

She pulled a hardback from one of the shelves. Its
dustcover was black, and slashed across it in ruby red
foil was *Kiss of Evil,* with the author's name, Edgar
O'Malley, in large, embossed white letters across the
bottom. She could almost recite this book word for
word, having sat at her father's right side as he'd written it. His other companions had been a bottle of Jack
Daniels and a glass tumbler that had never been empty.

Her father had thrived on the underworld. Scarlett
wondered if Logan did, too.

"Have you ever read Edgar O'Malley?" she asked.

"Never even heard of him. Any relation?"

"My dad. He wouldn't have liked knowing that he
was unknown in some corners of civilized society."

"Could be I'm not all that civilized."

She grinned. "Exactly what I was thinking."

She handed Logan the book. His long, strong fingers moved tentatively over the raised letters, over
the embossed ruby red blood that dripped from the
title. He frowned deeply. "You think this is my
style?"

She nodded. "Hard-edged. Brutal. It's life on the
streets of L.A. as seen through the eyes of a bad-ass
police detective."

"Or as seen through the eyes of an author with a
creative mind."

"Edgar O'Malley was a bad-ass cop in the '50s.
Like Bud White."

"Bud White?"

"In *L.A. Confidential*."

"Never read that book, either."

"And you didn't see the movie?"

Logan shook his head. "Should I?"

"Do both." She walked across the room and pulled a paperback copy of *L.A. Confidential,* as well as a videotape and DVD of the movie, out of her James Ellroy section. She'd figure out later which format Logan Wolfe should buy.

When she turned, Logan was staring at *Kiss of Evil*'s back cover, at the picture of the burly Irishman with a crew cut. The photo was in black and white, so Logan couldn't see her dad's flushed cheeks or the red in his eyes. He couldn't smell the whiskey on his breath. But Scarlett remembered all those things, and so much more. The crude, loud-mouthed cops he drank and played poker with. The women who'd drop by the house when her mom wasn't around. The way she'd cower in her bedroom when her dad was berating her mom. The heavy makeup her mother often wore that didn't completely hide the bruises.

Scarlett sighed inwardly, trying to forget the bad stuff about her dad and remember only the good— that he'd instilled in her the love of reading, that when he was sober, which wasn't often, he'd tell her stories and occasionally give her a hug, and the fact that he had been a damn fine writer.

But that was history. Over and done with.

Turning her concentration back to Logan, she said, "*Kiss of Evil* is one of my dad's best books. I'm sure it's right up your alley."

"I think you've got me pegged all wrong." Logan shoved out of the chair and moved across the room, standing much too close, towering over her. "I'll give your dad's stuff a try. Same goes for *L.A. Confidential.* But hard-edged brutality does nothing for me, and I've known my share of bad-ass police detectives."

"Really?" Was a confession coming?

"Really." His answer was flat, with no explanation. "Got anything funny to take the edge off the rough stuff? Maybe a wisecracking female who uses her brains instead of a gun?"

Maybe he wasn't the seedy underworld type after all.

"Think you might like a busty blonde forensic pathologist named Jayne Mansfield-Smythe?"

His mouth cocked up on one side. "Sounds like someone I could take to bed with me."

For that crack she'd sell him the hardback rather than the less expensive paperback. She might even sell him all seven books in the series without a discount.

She stalked out of the underbelly of her shop, through a row of cherry wood bookshelves, and headed for the peaceful parlor, where feathery green ferns hung in baskets, a pair of yellow canaries chirped inside an ornate gilded cage, and muted light glowed behind fringed Victorian lampshades. Her heels clicked on the hardwood floors and thumped when she tread over the Aubusson carpet. The clomp of Logan's boots followed her at a more casual pace. He was probably staring at her butt. Typical male with nothing on his mind but sex.

The Tuesday Morning Sleuths had their heads bent over their open copies of *Seven Sins* when Scarlett breezed by. The ladies were breathing hard and trying to look inconspicuous. It didn't take a detective, however, to know that they'd been eavesdropping outside the Edgar O'Malley room or that they'd beat a hasty retreat back to their table so they wouldn't be discovered.

Scarlett was breathing hard, too. Logan Wolfe made her edgy. He was a little too brash for her tastes. Jayne Mansfield-Smythe might like her men a bit on the cocky side. Hell, Jayne Mansfield-Smythe liked sleeping with cops. That kind of man was fine in fiction or fantasy, but not in real life. In real life, that kind of man had hurt her mom—twice.

As far as Scarlett was concerned, if she ever again wanted to be with a man, she'd take nice and sweet—in spite of the boredom.

Logan—not boring; definitely not nice and sweet—stopped beside her at the Jayne Mansfield-Smythe collection and picked up a copy of *Seven Sins,* flipping the book over to stare at the author's colored portrait. Juliet Bridger. Rich. Blonde. Big boobs. Tan, gorgeous, and probably air-brushed— the spitting image of her protagonist. Logan grinned. "Looks good."

Scarlett ripped the book out of his hands. "It's what's inside that's important, not what the author looks like."

"You don't think that cover and that picture on the back sell books?"

"I know they do, but a poorly written story isn't going to keep readers coming back for more." She thrust a copy of Juliet Bridger's *One Is the Deadliest Number* in his hands. "This is the first book in the series. It's what started a multi-million-dollar success story, and notice there's no author photo on the back."

"Think I'll like it?"

"It's got laughs. Wisecracks. A smart-mouthed prostitute or two. A brainy, busty blonde protagonist. Murder, intrigue, suspense and sex. Everything a guy like you could possibly want."

Logan chuckled. "Fifteen minutes together, and you know me as well as I know myself."

"I'm sure I've just scratched the surface."

He leaned forward and whispered in her ear. "That's further than any other woman has gotten."

His breath was warm. It tickled her skin and made her tingle all the way to the tips of her crimson toenails. And then the sirens sounded. Warning! Warning! Danger ahead!

Somehow she pulled her senses together. What was she thinking? He'd had brushes with the police. That wasn't conjecture, it was fact—at least he'd given her that impression when they'd been in the Edgar O'Malley room. He was charming. Enticing. A wolf in sheep's clothing, and she'd darn well better remember that.

She picked up a copy of Juliet Bridger's second book, grabbed the first one out of Logan's hands, and walked behind the cash register. "Okay, we've got *Kiss of Evil, L.A. Confidential,* the book and the movie." She looked up through her eyelashes and

caught Logan's grin. "Which format would you prefer? DVD or tape?"

"DVD."

She rang up the price and shoved the goods into a
scarlet-colored paper bag. "Let's see, we've also got
copies of the first two Jayne Mansfield-Smythe stories, *One Is the Deadliest Number* and *Two Murders
Are Better than One.*"

"When did I decide to buy the second?"

Scarlett smiled her finest bookseller-knows-best
smile. "Trust me. The moment you finish the first
you'll be chomping at the bit to start the second. Before you know it, you'll be reading *Seven Sins,* just
like the rest of us." She flashed another smile at the
Tuesday Morning Sleuths, who, in unison, held up
their copies for Logan to see. "Maybe you'd like to
buy all seven now?"

"I think I'll wait, see if Jayne Mansfield-Smythe
pleases me. If I like her, I'll come back for more."

"You'll be back. I'm sure of it."

Out of the corner of her eye Scarlett saw Lillian
patting her romantic heart once more. She also saw
the white-haired lady glaring at her from the children's section, looking disgruntled, and rightly so.

It didn't surprise her when Logan paid with cash.
It did surprise her that he left with a simple "See ya
later," rather than an invitation to dinner, or at the
very least a whispered "Come to my den, little lamb,
and I'll show you my . . . etchings."

The crystal chimes clanked as the door shut behind
him. The nervous energy that had crackled through

the shop disappeared right along with Logan Wolfe. If only the pitter-pat in her heart would go away, too, things could return to normal and she could pretend to herself and the rest of the world that she hadn't enjoyed his visit, that she hadn't felt a small bit of lust, which could prove to be a very deadly sin.

Mildred scurried past her, stopping at the window to peek out. "Should we follow him?"

"Why would you want to do that?"

"To find the truth about what's going on between him and Opal. To find out what kind of odd jobs he's doing for her. And naturally"—Mildred turned around and stared at Scarlett point blank—"to find out if he is or isn't a dirty rotten scoundrel so we can protect *you*."

"Protect me?"

"Definitely." Ida Mae tucked her copy of *Seven Sins* under her arm and joined Mildred at the window. She peeked out quickly, then turned back to Scarlett, shaking her head. "I have absolutely no idea what got into you, but I swear, if the three of us hadn't been here you and that man would have had down and dirty *sexxxxx*."

The way Ida Mae hissed the word *sexxxxx,* one would think it was dirty. Forbidden. A sin.

"I haven't had down and dirty sex in so long I'm sure I wouldn't know how to go about it even if I wanted to go about it," Scarlett stated, then crossed the room and opened the door for the Sleuths. "I know you worry about me, but there's absolutely no need. Not where Logan Wolfe is concerned."

Ida Mae's left eyebrow rose halfway up her forehead as she walked to the doorway. "You mean to tell me you didn't feel a thing for him?"

"Not a thing."

Ida Mae huffed. "So you say." She pecked Scarlett on the cheek and bustled out the door. "See you next Tuesday, if not before."

Mildred scampered after Ida Mae. "Goodness, where's the time gone? If we don't hurry, we'll miss the beginning of fall half-off sale at the Gold Nugget, and I've been dying to see what kind of deal Ted will give me on that luscious sapphire that's been in the window for months." She waved on her way out the door. "Bye-eeeee."

Lillian took her time following her sister Sleuths, stopping in the doorway and putting a friendly hand on Scarlett's shoulder. "It's been a long time for me, too, dear."

Scarlett frowned. "Long time for what?"

In her own sweet and meek way, Lillian gave a little shrug, a little smile, then murmured, "Sex." She patted Scarlett's arm. "But don't worry, dear, you never really forget how to do it."

Scarlett smiled halfheartedly. "Thank you. I needed to hear that."

"I thought so. And"—Lillian leaned forward and whispered—"I really do think if you need reminding how to have down and dirty sex, Mr. Wolfe is the man to do it."

This conversation wasn't really happening, was it? "I'll try to remember that."

"Good." Lillian offered her a conspiratorial grin.

"Now, I'd best catch up with Ida Mae and Mildred before I get scolded for taking too long."

At last, Lillian was out the door and Scarlett had time alone to reflect on all that had happened in the past half hour or so.

"Excuse me."

Oh, my God! She'd completely forgotten her other customer.

The white-haired lady stood beside the cash register, a copy of Nancy Drew's *Haunted Bridge* clutched in her hands, Toby at her heels.

"I'm so sorry," Scarlett apologized. "I'm not in the habit of neglecting customers."

"Is that so?"

Scarlett ignored the woman's boorish remark, as well as her narrowed eyes, and gazed at the book in her hands. "*The Haunted Bridge* was one of my favorite Nancy Drews," she said, going into bookseller mode. "*The Haunted Showboat,* too. Actually, I devoured every Nancy Drew I could get my hands on."

"How nice. But . . ." The woman dropped her carpetbag-like purse, along with the copy of *Haunted Bridge,* on the counter beside the cash register as if they'd become too heavy to hold. She took a deep breath, then paced the room with Toby waddling right behind.

"Is everything all right?" Scarlett asked, suddenly concerned by the woman's actions.

"Everything's fine." Still, the woman paced. And frowned. Stopping at last, she stared at Scarlett through deep-set, bloodshot eyes. Her skin was a pasty gray, she looked frail and tired, and Scarlett worried that she might be on the verge of collapse.

"Could I get you some tea?" Scarlett asked. "I have a lovely Darjeeling—Tibet Royal Blend. It's one of my favorites."

The woman didn't answer. Instead, she walked to the cash register and gripped the edge of the counter. "It's not Nancy Drew I want to talk with you about. It's not tea, nasty little dogs, or whether or not you ignore your customers. There's something—"

The front door whooshed open and banged against the wall, startling Scarlett and her irritable, neglected customer. Their gazes shot to the front of the store as the door bounced again and again against the wall. A chilled wind gushed inside. Dry leaves whipped into the room and danced about until they fell to the floor and skittered helter-skelter across the wood. The chimes clanked and clattered.

And Logan Wolfe reentered the shop, looking big and powerful and . . . contrite. "Sorry about that." He caught hold of the door, closed it against the breeze, then smiled. She could almost see a twinkle in his eyes through his sunglasses. "I forgot my books."

"I knew I shouldn't have come. Try to do something nice and—" The white-haired woman spun back toward Scarlett, knocking her purse to the floor. "Damn it all."

Logan touched the woman's arm gently. "Here, let me get it for you."

"It's the least you could do, since it's your fault it's there in the first place."

Scarlett chomped down on the nasty words ready to spill over her tongue. She'd dealt with crotchety people before and could usually put them at ease, even make them smile. But this one was a real piece of work.

Getting down on hands and knees, Scarlett picked up a cherry ChapStick that had rolled out of the woman's bag. Through the opening underneath the antique oak buffet that served as a checkout counter she could see Logan's strong, powerful hands—*The better to feel you with, my dear.* She stifled a sigh and wished her heart's annoying pitter-pat would slow to a normal beat, but nothing seemed normal when Logan was around.

She plucked a bobby pin from under one of the claw feet, then went after a tube of lipstick. Her fingers and Logan's clutched the black cylinder simultaneously. They wove together and lingered. Their eyes met and held, and the musky scent of his aftershave wrapped around her. Her heart rose to her throat, and she willed it to settle back down, just as she willed herself to pull away from his powerfully magnetic hold.

With half a dozen miscellaneous items in hand, Scarlett climbed up from the floor, only to face Logan again. Was there no escape?

She dropped pencils and paper and pens into the open purse he still held, and watched his long, strong fingers snap it shut. There was nothing out of the ordinary in what he was doing, but all of his movements, no matter how simple, had the power to tease, to tempt.

At last he turned his charm on the white-haired woman. "It looks like we got everything."

"Thank you." The woman smiled feebly. "I get a little agitated at times. Sorry I was so brusque."

Scarlett watched the exchange, the way the woman softened in Logan's presence, the way he offered a gentle smile in return. Like any good gigolo, he had a way with the ladies—elderly ones and gullible twenty-nine year olds, too.

"Now, if you don't mind," the woman said, squeezing her arms as she turned from Logan to Scarlett, "could we talk?"

"Of course. Why don't you have a seat at one of the tables by the window, I'll get us some tea—"

"And I'll get out of here." Logan grabbed his forgotten bag of books. "See ya later."

He was gone in an instant, the door opening and closing gently behind him, the chimes tinkling lightly. Through the window Scarlett watched him look both ways, then dart across the street and stroll up the boardwalk. Nice shoulders. Nice tush.

Definitely a man worth watching—in more ways than one.

Turning away from the window, she headed for the kitchen to steep a fresh pot of tea, and . . . "Oh, God."

The white-haired lady lay crumpled on the hardwood floor.

Motionless.

Silent.

Dead?

Chapter 3

Logan caressed the sleek black fly rod that had caught his attention when he'd walked into Teton Outfitters. He didn't need another pole, but lately he'd become as big a sucker for fishing gear as he was for Elvis memorabilia.

He wasn't, however, a sucker for books or DVDs. He'd never had time for reading, and he'd rather sing along with the King than mindlessly sit in front of the boob tube. The only reason he'd had for buying nearly a hundred bucks' worth of stuff he might never take out of the bag was the woman. Scarlett Mary Catherine O'Malley had thrust her belly button ring in his face and rendered him powerless.

He would have bought anything she'd offered.

There was something about Scarlett that triggered his libido, made him act like some jewelry wearing, ultra-macho jackass when he was in her presence—but what? He liked tall, leggy showgirl types. Scarlett was anything but. Running his fingers through long, silky hair had been one of his favorite pastimes, be-fore he'd switched his leisurely pursuits from catching women to catching fish, but there was no way his fingers could slide more than an inch through Scarlett's tresses without getting tangled up in a jumble of curls.

But damn if he didn't find her cute. Not beautiful. Definitely not stunning. Scarlett, with her turned-up nose, bright green eyes, and a face full of freckles, was . . . well, cute.

Of course, that belly button ring, affixed to a Britney Spears stomach, made the infinitely cute Scarlett Mary Catherine O'Malley one hot little number.

"Find something you like?"

Logan's fingers stilled on the fishing pole. He looked at the guy hobbling toward him, a middle-aged man supporting his burly body on a pair of crutches. His head was bald, he had a tattoo on his right forearm that said MARINES KICK ASS, and his camouflage T-shirt sported a nametag that read HI, I'M JOE!

Assuming Joe was asking about rods and reels and not cute women with sexy abs, Logan turned his thoughts back to the subject at hand.

"Yeah. I like the detailing on this one." Logan slid his fingers lightly over the intricately wrapped teal-colored threads, the impeccably aligned rings, and the cork grip that fit perfectly in his palm. It felt good in his hand. Light. Flexible. Not quite as good as a woman's curves, but a far cry from the gun he was used to holding.

"It's handmade," Joe said. "Retired guy named Wes brings them in every so often to sell on consignment." He shifted his weight from one crutch to the other. "He makes some mighty fine flies, too. Want to take a look?"

"Sure."

Logan followed Joe toward the back of the store, checking out a variety of waders and boots until Joe pulled a clear plastic tray from under a counter and set it on top. "What do you think?"

Logan fingered through the brightly colored assortment of hooks, admiring the craftsmanship. "Nice." He set the pole atop the showcase and picked up a scarlet feathered fly, thinking about the fish it would attract, and the scent of rainbow or cutthroat trout sizzling over an open fire. Damn if the vision he'd just conjured didn't include little miss curly top in that short, tight leather skirt and midriff-baring top—and she was sizzling, too.

"Did you do much fishing in Vegas?" Joe asked.

Logan's eyes narrowed, the question catching him off guard. He looked up slowly. "Vegas?"

"That's where you're from, isn't it?"

"Once upon a time." He hadn't expected anyone in Plentiful to know his name, let alone where he'd spent the past fifteen years. Vegas was over and done with. He was starting a new life, and the less said about old and bitter history the better. "I started fishing five months ago—up in Canada."

"Whereabouts?"

"Bow River in southern Alberta."

"Been there a time or two myself. Heard you could catch trout up to thirty inches long, but the best I ever got was a twenty-six-inch rainbow. That's a hell of a lot better than what I got in Vegas." Joe shook his head in disgust. "Went there twice. Lost a lot of money the first time. Lost more the second."

"I lost a lot there, too." Not money, Logan thought. Things far more valuable: the job he'd loved, the respect of his friends, and his own sense of self-worth. But that's what happens when a cop rats on his fellow officers.

"I sure as hell don't plan to go back," Joe said. "How about you?"

"Don't think so."

"You plan to stick around Plentiful?"

"For now."

"The place has a way of growing on you. You'll see." Joe stuck out his hand. "By the way, I'm Joe Granger, owner of this place. And you're Logan Wolfe. Right?"

"Yeah." Logan shook Joe's hand. His grip was strong. Friendly. A guy Logan figured he'd like, in spite of his nosiness. "How'd you know?"

"Word travels fast in this town."

"You always listen to gossip?"

"I'm the town's mayor, president of the Rotary Club, and assistant leader for my daughter's Brownie troop. Even if I didn't want to listen, I can't escape it."

Joe grabbed a short fishing rod from the wall and shoved it under the cast that covered his right leg from big toe to mid thigh. "I lead hunting and fishing expeditions, too. This is what happens when some Hollywood hotshot shoots a bull elk in the butt instead of the head. Crazy animal was determined to get revenge, and I'm the one he took it out on." Joe rammed the rod further down the cast and wiggled it around. "You hunt?"

"A couple of times. Fishing's more my style."

"Soon as I get this blasted cast off, I'll show you the best fishing spot on the Snake, and if you don't mind freezing your ass off, we could head up to the Madison." Joe pulled the rod out from under the cast and frowned. "You wouldn't by any chance be interested in a job, would you? I could use a guide, someone who doesn't mind working with rich, over-confident city slickers."

"I'm retired."

Joe laughed. "I tried that once. Put in my twenty years, then quit the Corps. Took up gardening. Tried photography. Hell, I even took French cooking classes, and all of it was boring as hell."

Logan was getting pretty damned bored with retirement, too, but he wasn't sure he wanted another job right now. Didn't know what he wanted to do if and when he got another job. Didn't even know if he wanted to settle here. He wanted to start a new life, but how could he, when his old life still weighed heavy on his mind.

Fortunately the subject of careers dropped when another customer walked through the open front door. The guy looked like Robert Redford just past his prime—blonde, average build, dark tan, well-cut suit, a conservative pale blue shirt and a striped navy tie. Actually, he looked like a cop.

"Hey, Adam," Joe called out. "Come meet Logan Wolfe."

Adam crossed the room, the old wood plank floor creaking beneath his spit-polished black boots. "Heard a lot about you," Adam said, to Logan's dismay. "I'm Adam Grant, the town's chief of police."

Bingo.

"Nice to meet you," Logan said, shaking Adam's hand. The guy had a cop's grip and a cop's eye for detail. With a friendly smile plastered on his face, he gave Logan a quick once-over, trying to determine if he had a hidden agenda. That was a cop thing, too.

There was a time when Logan could sum someone up in an instant. He was trying to do that now, but Adam seemed a hard man to figure out. Charming? Yeah. But there was something beneath the surface that he couldn't quite peg. Not that it mattered. He wasn't a cop any longer, and it wasn't his job to sum up anyone, especially a cop.

"You like living out there in Grizzly Hollow?" Adam asked, picking up the rod Logan had been looking at.

"It's not bad." If you don't mind bears, squirrels, and dive-bombing ravens—the creatures that kept him company. "Quiet and peaceful most of the time."

"Same can be said for the rest of this town, at least in the off season. Of course, like any other place, we've got our assortment of oddballs and losers, you know, the drunks who spend most every Saturday night in jail and the couples who get into fistfights that we've got to break up."

"Beats living in a town where drug dealers, twelve-year-old prostitutes, and a murder every two or three days are the norm."

Adam raised a brow, and Logan knew that he'd said too much. "Is that why you left Vegas?"

"Yeah." Logan chuckled, anxious to change the subject again. "And the fishing's lousy, too."

"Fishing's pretty good around these parts. So's the hunting." Adam put the rod back on the counter. "You just vacationing here, or planning to stick around?"

"Sticking around—for now."

"You play darts?"

"Not lately."

"Some of us play a friendly game or two every night but Sunday. If you get bored, stop by the Misty Moon sometime between eight and midnight, have a beer and a burger, and we'll show you the ropes."

Joe laughed. "They'll take your money, too, if you're not careful."

"You win some; you lose some. Me"—Adam grinned—"I like to win."

"And you usually do," Joe added.

Adam shrugged. He looked away from Joe, and his gaze shot toward the scarlet-colored bag tucked under Logan's arm. "You a big reader?"

"A guy's got to do something after he retires."

"You married or single?"

Tired of Adam's obvious interrogation, Logan asked, "Why all the questions?"

"I'm responsible for everyone in town. I hear rumors—

I follow up on them. I suspect someone of being up to no good—I keep an eye on them. I see a stranger hanging around my stepdaughter, I get protective."

Logan frowned. "Your stepdaugther?"

"Scarlett O'Malley."

"Oh, yeah. The redhead from the bookstore." Logan managed a grin, even though he didn't like the idea that Adam had been watching him. "Nice lady."

"I don't know if your interest in Scarlett goes beyond book buying, but if it does, let me give you a bit of advice. Stay away from her."

Was that a threat he'd heard, or concern? "You going to tell me why?"

"I don't like to talk about her behind her back, but—"

The scream of a siren chopped off Adam's words. The white ambulance and flashing red lights whizzed past the window. Adam shot away from Logan and Joe, threw open the front door and stopped just outside on the boardwalk. Logan ran, too, stopping at Adam's side to stare a block up the road where Main Street Td into Yellowstone.

The sirens went silent when the vehicle stopped in front of A Study in Scarlett, and even though he kept his emotions in check, dread lodged thick and heavy in Logan's throat.

Without a word, Adam sprinted up the boardwalk toward Scarlett's shop. Logan followed, not knowing if it was instinct that drove him or a need to be sure that Scarlett was all right. He barely knew her, but she'd already burrowed under his skin.

A handful of people rushed out of the Misty Moon Saloon, crowding the boardwalk. Adam broke through, but Logan's path was blocked. He could skirt around them, but he decided to hang back, out of the way of the emergency team.

Over the heads of at least a dozen gawkers, he watched the paramedics throw open the bookstore's front door, watched Adam rush inside. Through all the commotion, he could see inside the shop and saw a head of springy red hair and a petite little body bending over someone on the floor.

A moment later Scarlett was pushed aside by Adam and the emergency techs so they could do their jobs. She backed into the sunlight streaming through the window, and Logan watched her clasp her arms, rubbing them for warmth, as she stared at the men huddling over the body. She looked cold and scared, and Logan felt an unexpected desire to hold her, to give her the comfort she so obviously needed.

He stepped down onto the street, but before he could head for the bookshop, a heavy hand clamped on his shoulder. Joe Granger stood at his side. "Was it curiosity that made you run, or Scarlett?" Joe asked.

Logan shrugged. He wasn't a man to wear his heart on his sleeve, and he sure as hell didn't share his personal thoughts with near strangers.

"She's a nice lady," Joe said. Apparently he didn't mind sharing his own personal thoughts. "Makes the best scones I ever tasted, and if you're into tea, well, she brews the best around. But . . ."

Logan angled narrowed eyes at the man beside him. "But what?"

Joe scratched his ear, then answered hesitantly, "She's neurotic. A bit of crackpot who hangs around with other crackpots." He shook his head. "Like I said, she's a nice lady, but she and her friends see a mystery behind every door. No one's safe from their prying, especially new people in town."

"You're saying I've already been targeted?"

"Oh yeah. You've been the major topic of discussion for the past couple of days. That's how I knew about Vegas, the fact that you're living in Grizzly Hollow, and your name. Give it a few more days, and I may know your age, weight and height." Joe grinned. "Nothing's sacred where those women are concerned. If you've got something to hide, they'll dig until they find it—unless something juicier comes along and catches their interest."

Logan frowned. He didn't want to be the topic of conversation. Definitely didn't want anyone snooping into his past and uncovering all the crap.

Turning away from Joe, he looked up the street, into the bookstore, and zoomed in on Scarlett. What was she up to? Why on earth was she digging into his background? Damn it all. He didn't know if he should get mad at the cute little redhead, or get even. The only thing he did know was that whatever he ended up doing, he planned to do it up close and personal.

Chapter 4

Scarlett stood at the display window, watching the ambulance speed toward the end of town, its screeching siren ripping to shreds the peace and serenity of the valley.

Shopkeepers, tourists and townspeople stood on the wide boardwalks and gawked. A mangy black cat skittered across the street and disappeared under the wooden steps leading to the Elk Horn Café. And Logan Wolfe stood in front of Teton Outfitters, his sunglass-covered eyes focused intently on A Study in Scarlett.

She spun away from the window, from Logan's magnetism, from inquisitive, prying stares, and drew in a deep breath, hoping she could relax, but that seemed an impossibility.

The ambulance was gone. The body was gone. But too many people remained behind. A few of the regulars from the Misty Moon Saloon huddled around the tea tables, eyeing her as if she'd murdered the white-haired lady. Molly MacGregor, the saloon's proprietor, short, stout, in kilt and neon orange

Nikes, frowned at her for the longest time, then dis-appeared through the swinging kitchen door. Even the Tuesday Morning Sleuths, suspicious of everyone and everything, had their eagle eyes trained on her.

She hadn't done anything wrong. Still, they stared. The only ones who didn't seem interested in Scarlett were Toby, who hid under the checkout counter chewing on a plaything, and Ted Lapham, who stood with the Sleuths in the far reaches of the children's section, keeping a watchful eye on the jewelry the ladies had been trying on when the commotion first began.

Outside she heard the thud of boots on the board-walk and turned to see if Logan had come to stare at her up close and personal. It was only Adam stand-ing in the doorway, looking tired and drawn, as if something weighed heavily on his mind. He'd been the first to arrive after the paramedics and, in his usual style, had tried to micromanage everything. She'd hoped he would leave along with the ambu-lance, but she rarely got what she wanted where Adam was concerned.

Except for the frown and eighteen years of aging, he didn't look much different from the first time he'd walked into the Victorian. He'd been new in town, a cop with a bright smile, sparkling eyes, and oodles of charm. The spitting image of Robert Redford in *The Way We Were,* at least that's how all the ladies in town had seen him. He'd raved about the Victorian's cherry wood banisters and moldings, the English rose wallpaper, the intricate gingerbread, and the colorful garden out back. He'd dreamed of owning a place just like this, he'd told Scarlett's mom. He'd imagined having the prettiest wife in town, the sweetest daughter, and the happiest family.

Scarlett had thought he was a jerk, but her mother had fallen in love. Scarlett had told him the house rightfully belonged to her, not her mom. Told him it had been a gift from her dad, hoping he'd go away, but still he'd hung around. Two weeks later Adam and Elizabeth had been married right here in this room; eight years after that she was dead, and deep down inside Scarlett knew he was responsible.

She just wished she could prove it.

She watched him as she did all too often. He circled the room, talking briefly to the Sleuths, to Ted, to the guys from the Misty Moon. At last he stopped in front of Scarlett and hit her with his usual critical glare. "Did you know her?"

Scarlett shook her head. "Not her name. Not where she's from. Nothing."

She blamed Adam for her mother's death, but the fact that she knew nothing about the white-haired lady and the fact that the woman was in an ambulance on the way to the hospital rested solely on her shoulders. She might have known about the woman if she hadn't spent so much time with Logan Wolfe, if she hadn't let her utterly foolish fascination with him distract her. If she'd been more aware of the white-haired lady, she might have sensed something was wrong, and maybe then she would have reacted sooner, been able to do something. Anything.

"Do you think she's going to be okay?" Scarlett asked. "Did the paramedics tell you anything?"

Adam shook his head. "It doesn't look good, but I don't know." He uncharacteristically massaged his right temple with three fingers. "Do you know what she was doing here?"

"Buying a book. She'd picked out a Nancy Drew and I told her it was one of my favorites." Scarlett hugged her arms, trying to rub some warmth into them. "She wanted to talk about something besides books, but we never had the chance."

"You don't know what?"

"She didn't say, and I didn't have time to ask."

The kitchen door swung open, and Molly came out with a cup of steaming tea. She squeezed between Scarlett and Adam. "Drink some of this," she said to Scarlett. "I put a wee bit of whiskey in it, something to calm your nerves."

"I'm fine. Really," Scarlett said, but the heavenly scent of lemon mixed with Jim Beam wafted toward her. She took the cup and, in spite of her protest, drank a healthy swallow. It burned her throat, and its heat slithered all the way down to her stomach. At last she felt something other than numb.

She took another sip and turned to Adam, frowning as if something odd had just dawned on her. "You don't normally respond to medical emergencies. Did you come for some special reason?"

"I was talking to Joe Granger when the ambulance went by. Figured I'd stop by and see if I was needed."

"But why all the questions? That isn't normal in a medical emergency."

"I've been a cop for a long time. Questions come natural." To make his point he turned to Molly. "You didn't talk to the woman, did you?"

"No. In fact, I don't think anyone here had seen her before."

Adam's fingers went back to his temple again, digging at the throbbing nerve. He faced Scarlett once more. "I'm going to head over to the hospital and see how she's doing. If you hear anything, let me know."

He didn't say good-bye to anyone, merely walked through the open door and disappeared out of sight.

"He's acting a bit odd," Molly said. "Like something's troubling him."

"Not exactly his style, is it?"

"I've only see him distressed once before, and that was when your poor mama, God rest her soul, passed away and that was what, eight, nine years ago?"

"Ten."

"Sometimes it seems like only yesterday she was lighting up this town, and then . . . well, that was a long time ago." Molly smiled her gentle, pudgy-faced smile, and cupped a comforting hand around Scarlett's arm. "I'd best get back to work, get out of your hair and take those nosy customers of mine with me."

Scarlett said her good-byes to Molly and the beer crowd. A few minutes later the Sleuths and Ted Lapham departed, all of them telling Scarlett to call if she needed anything.

What she needed was a rerun of the entire day, a chance to relive it and do everything differently. Most of all, she wished she'd paid more attention to the white-haired woman.

Taking a sip of now cold tea, she fixed her stare on the hardwood floor where the lady had fallen. Had she had a heart attack? A stroke?

What had she wanted to talk about? Her disgruntled but passionate "Could we talk now" rang through Scarlett's ears. Her nervous pacing and her frustration when Logan had come back into the store played over and over in Scarlett's mind. Something had been troubling the woman—but what?

Scarlett walked across the room and dropped into a chair, setting her teacup in the midst of all the clutter. Years of living under Adam's rule, under his fastidious need for perfection, had made her cringe at the sight of lint or dust. The mess should have bothered her, but at the moment, things far more important than a spotless shop occupied her mind.

Was the woman a friend of her mother's? One of her father's old flames? An Edgar O'Malley fan hoping to obtain a bit of memorabilia?

Scarlett shoved her fingers into her hair and stared numbly at the floor. Gold and amber leaves had skittered inside and lay crumbled on the rug. A few Jayne Mansfield-Smythe novels sprawled beside the display table, their pages twisted and bent.

Across the room she heard Toby's low, contented growl. He'd been at her side, barking while she'd called 911 and attempted to give the woman CPR.

When the ambulance had come he'd hidden under the counter. Poor thing. This day had been rough on him, too.

"Come here, Toby," she called, but not one bit of silky black fur peeked out from under the counter.

Scarlett crossed the room and knelt down to pick up the dog that could annoy her as well as make her heart melt in the space of five minutes, but Toby merely looked at her and snarled, his teeth firmly clenched around the handle of the white-haired lady's carpetbag, his body plopped down on top.

How on earth could she have forgotten to give the woman's bag to the paramedics?

"Come on, Toby," she pleaded, trying to wrench the bag away. "You know that doesn't belong to you, it belongs to that poor old lady."

Toby snarled again.

"I really do need to take it to the hospital."

Toby yapped.

Ornery little thing. It had been a test of wills since day one with the dog. If Art Steinman wasn't ensconced behind prison bars for selling prime pieces of Wyoming real estate that he had no right to sell, she'd give him a piece of her mind for dumping the dog on her doorstep.

"Off," Scarlet demanded. Toby's tail wagged, but the rest of his body remained smack on top of the purse.

"Come on, Toby, you know darn good and well that's not a chew toy."

Toby gnawed a little harder.

"All right. That does it." She was going to do

something absolutely devious and had the horrid feeling that she might rot in hell for being so underhanded, but it had to be done.

Scarlett strolled to the window, peered outside at the blue sky and puffy white clouds and exclaimed with glee, "Oh, my gosh, Art's come home."

Toby scrambled out from under the counter, his claws scraping on the wooden floor. He slid to a stop in front of the door and sat on his haunches, his tail wagging merrily while he waited for his master to step inside.

Before Toby caught drift of her mean and despicable ruse, Scarlett rushed to the checkout, grabbed the bag, and headed for the door. Guilt getting the best of her, she patted Toby's head. "I'm sorry, boy. I made a mistake. It wasn't Art at all."

The poor dog tilted his head one way and then the other, trying to make sense of what she was saying, then sprawled out in front of the door to wait as long as it took for the man who'd always be his master to return.

Feeling a bit sick inside, Scarlett flipped her OPEN sign to CLOSED, patted Toby's head and told him to be good, then walked out into the early afternoon sunlight, locking the door behind her.

Plentiful Memorial was a little over a mile away, a nice walk on a beautiful day. Today she scurried, but even in her rush she couldn't miss the old and familiar fragrance of pine that was a hallmark of Plentiful, the mouthwatering scent of burgers and onions frying on the Misty Moon grill, and the sweetness of cinnamon and sugar from the bakery.

There'd been a time when she and her mom had walked hand in hand along Main Street. They'd window-shopped, grabbed an ice cream cone, gone to the park and lain in the grass to do nothing more than listen to the wind whistle through the pines.

The last time they'd walked down this street together, Elizabeth had still wanted to look through windows, but it wasn't pretty things she'd been interested in. It hadn't been yummy food or a friend to wave hello to. She'd been looking for her husband, sure she'd find Adam with another woman.

Scarlett rarely window-shopped anymore. The bookstore kept her busy; so did baking for the PTA, the Elks, the Moose, the Oddfellows, the senior center and her store. But as she neared Teton Outfitters she couldn't help but glance through the open front door to see if Logan Wolfe had gone inside.

Sure enough, he stood behind a counter looking at . . . guns. Of all things, why did it have to be guns?

"What do you think?" Joe Granger asked, balancing his burly body on a pair of crutches.

"Don't know if any of these will do."

"I've got a couple of new Glocks and a Colt that came in yesterday," Joe said. "Haven't had a chance to get them ready for sale, but hang on a second and I'll get them out of the back so you can take a look."

Joe tottered through the far door and Scarlett continued to watch Logan inspect the lethal weapons inside the display case.

What use could he possibly have for a handgun? A rifle she could understand, since hunting was a prime business in Plentiful. But a handgun? Something that could be hidden inside his leather jacket?

As if he knew he was being watched, Logan raised his head slowly and stared right at her. A lock of hair had fallen over his brow. His eyes were dark and intense. Penetrating. He looked sinful, sexy, and with all of those guns and rifles around him . . . dangerous.

Her throat tightened. She couldn't swallow. Could just barely breathe. Logan frightened her; he excited her. She knew she should run, but she was paralyzed by the mesmerizing smile that touched his lips. And then he winked, a twinkle-eyed Big Bad Wolfe wink—*the better to woo you with, my dear.*

It was the same kind of wink Adam had flashed at her mother when he'd first walked into the Victorian. A wink that had made her succumb to a man who'd wanted total control of her.

But she was stronger than her mom. She wasn't as gullible. Through all that had happened to her mother, through a few dumb mistakes in her teens and early twenties, she'd learned that she had to be wary of men, especially someone sexy, like Logan.

Forcing herself to get a handle on the situation, she took a deep breath, smiled, waved politely, and went on her way.

There. That was easy.

Still, she found herself rushing along the board-walk toward the park at the far end of town. Her shoulder muscles bunched. Pain throbbed behind her eyes. Five-inch stilettos weren't as good for sprinting as tennis shoes, but in no time at all she was in the park, far away from *him*.

When she hit the gravel path she slowed to a jog, and when her legs could take it no more, she plopped down on a bench, crushing golden aspen leaves beneath her derriere. She took a deep breath, then another, massaging her temples, hoping the sudden, vicious pain in her head would go away.

She never had headaches.

Women didn't come into her store, act mysterious, then collapse.

Dirty rotten scoundrels didn't turn her on.

Yet all those things had happened in the past few hours. It was as if she'd stepped into a gothic romance and become its neurotic heroine, suspicious of the most gorgeous guy around, even though he made her heart go pitter-pat.

So much like her mother.

She wanted her own life to be different. She refused to fall for a man and let him drive her crazy. But . . . she longed to be cherished; to love and be loved. How would she ever experience those things if she continued to run, to hide, all because she didn't want to be hurt like her mom had been hurt?

Maybe she should act on that crazy pitter-pat she felt when she was around Logan. Maybe she should ignore all the innuendo and her instincts and take a risk.

Scarlett sighed heavily. Ignoring innuendo and her instincts might be a good idea, but risk-taking could be a very dangerous game—one she wasn't quite ready to play.

Chapter 5

Scarlett tiptoed through the hospital hallways. If she could keep her heels from clicking on the linoleum and sending out a signal that she was lurking about, she might be able to sneak into Emergency.

"Hi, Scarlett."

Caught.

Lucretia Laughton stepped out of a supply room, looking more like a prison guard than a kindly nurse.

"Hi, Lu." Scarlett smiled innocently. "Is Dr. Anthony around?"

"He's with a patient at the moment."

"Someone the ambulance just brought in? A woman?"

Lucretia nodded. "Chief Grant's in there, too. Apparently no one seems to know who she is."

"Any chance I can sneak in? I've got her purse."

"Why don't you give it to me. I'll make sure Dr. Anthony and the chief get it."

Scarlett clasped the bag against her chest, feeling as connected to it as she did to the crotchety woman it belonged to, a woman she needed to see, to know more about. "I know I'm not a relative. I don't even know the poor lady. But she was in my shop, she had something she wanted to talk with me about, and then this happened." She blew at a curl on her forehead. "Couldn't you let me give the purse to Adam and the doctor? I'd like a chance to see the woman again, maybe hold her hand."

Lucretia shook her head slowly, playing her guard role to the hilt.

"Pleeeeeze."

Lucretia shrugged, then added a defeated sigh. "I could get in trouble for this, but come on."

Scarlett followed the nurse through a pair of double doors, past ICU and a couple of empty rooms, then around a corner. Scarlett came within inches of smacking into Lucretia's back when the nurse stopped dead in her tracks. Peering around Lu's Amazon body, Scarlett saw Dr. Anthony and Chief Grant standing in the hallway talking like a couple of conspirators, totally unaware Lu and Scarlett were there.

Lu edged around Scarlett and backed away, waving as she disappeared. Lu was smart, sneaking off before getting caught. But Scarlett had no intention of leaving. She'd come to see the lady without a name and she was determined to do just that.

Peeking into the room on her right, she saw the usual hospital room equipment and an empty bed. She looked through the open door on the left. It was stark and white and filled with still and silent machines. Instead of a bed, a gurney sat in the middle of the room, and the white-haired woman who'd been in her store not more than an hour ago lay just as still and silent as the machines around her.

Tears threatened as regret wrapped around Scarlett's throat and squeezed. She went toward the door and stared at the lady. She hadn't been the least bit nice, but Scarlett hadn't been all that polite, either. She'd ignored the woman because she'd been too wrapped up with Logan. Now she wished she could say "I'm sorry." But it was far too late.

"What are you doing here?"

Scarlett twisted around. Adam glared at her over Dr. Anthony's shoulder. She couldn't miss the red in his eyes. Was it worry she saw there? Was it exhaustion? Sorrow? Or was it just the lights or the scents of alcohol and Pine-Sol?

"I wanted to see how she was doing," Scarlett said. "I've been worried since the ambulance left."

Dr. Anthony turned, smiling fatherly. "She was gone before the ambulance got here," he said. "I'm sorry, Scarlett. Adam told me you're the one who made the 911 call, that you gave her CPR, but it looks to me like she was dead before you picked up the phone."

Scarlett rested her shoulder against the doorjamb and looked at the woman's wrinkled face, at pasty skin, at long fingers on frail hands folded atop the white sheet that covered most of her body.

Dr. Anthony touched Scarlett's shoulder. "You didn't know her, did you?"

Scarlett shook her head. "I found her purse under the

cash register," she said to Adam. "I should have given it to the paramedics, but I'd forgotten all about it."

Adam took the bag out of Scarlett's hands. "Did you look in it already?"

"No. I brought it here as soon as I found it."

Staring at the bag, Adam hesitated a moment before popping the clasp, taking his time digging around inside. "Lipstick. Compact. Kleenex." He unzipped an inside pocket and an outside one as well, then shook his head. "Most women carry wallets, don't they?"

"Of course," Scarlett said. "Wallet. Checkbook. Credit cards. Pictures of their families. Why?"

"There's nothing like that in here."

"That's impossible." Scarlett plucked the purse from Adam's hands. "Sometimes men don't look quite as well as women, especially if they're digging through a purse. You know, they're afraid of finding something . . . hygiene related."

"My guess is she was long past the age of needing anything hygiene related."

"I'll look anyway."

Scarlett upended the purse on an empty cart sitting in the corridor and went through the contents. She inspected each inside pocket, ran her fingers along the bottom, and when she found no wallet, let out one more long-winded and frustrated sigh.

"She was going to buy a book." Scarlett shook her head as she looked up at Adam and Dr. Anthony. "She must have had some cash, or at least a credit card or checkbook."

Adam snatched the handbag, his jaw tightening as

he dropped one item after another back inside. "Did you see anyone going through the purse?"

"You mean, someone who might have stolen her wallet?"

"That's the general idea."

"No one was near the checkout counter while the paramedics were there. In fact, the last time I saw her purse—" Scarlett stopped short. Her eyes narrowed, deep in thought. The last time she'd seen the purse, Logan Wolfe had been picking up things that has spilled from it. Surely he wouldn't have pocketed the wallet when no one was looking?

Adam frowned. "You were saying?"

She couldn't implicate Logan, not when she had no proof that he'd taken anything from the bag. Her suspicions about him were based on hearsay and conjecture, and her personal feelings about him were a jumbled-up mess of want, need, anxiety and excitement. If she mentioned anything at all about Logan to Adam, he'd accuse her, as he had so many times before, of letting her imagination run wild, of reading too damn many mysteries, of being as neurotic as her mother.

If she wanted to find the truth, she'd have to search on her own.

"The purse was under the counter. It must have fallen during all the commotion," she said, telling Adam the truth, omitting a lot of other details. "Toby was laying on it, chewing on the handle." Scarlett ran her fingers over the claw marks. "I don't think anyone else touched it."

"I'll still have to talk to everyone again. Molly. Ted. The Sleuths. Someone may have seen something. Even you, Scarlett."

"But I just told you I didn't see anything."

"You might remember something later. If you do, I need to know."

And what would he do with the information? she wondered. File it away for posterity? That's what he'd done when she and the Sleuths had gone to him with information that Art Steinman might be scamming land buyers. They'd had no real proof, only suspicions. Adam had said he'd check it out, but he hadn't. It wasn't until the Sleuths had hired someone to pose as a buyer that the truth had come out. Adam didn't like having egg on his face, and ever since he'd tried to make the Sleuths look like foolish old women with a crazy lady as their leader.

Well, she and the Sleuths were through giving information. If Logan was guilty of something—and more and more she hoped he wasn't—she'd find out for herself.

"What do we do next?" Dr. Anthony asked, directing his question to Adam. "Do I keep her here until you find out who she is, or send her to the funeral home? What about an autopsy?"

"I don't see any need for that. You said yourself it looked like a massive heart attack." Adam tucked the woman's handbag under his arm. "Call Dan and have him pick up the body. I'll get someone over to the mortuary as soon as possible to take photos, get her fingerprints—"

"What about checking the missing person's database?" Scarlett asked. "What about asking around the motels? And then there are the campgrounds. She might have been vacationing with family and come into town for a change of scenery. What about her car? Obviously she didn't walk into town."

Adam glared at Scarlett, his annoyance growing by leaps and bounds. "I know what I'm doing."

Scarlett bit her tongue. There were a few retorts she could make about the validity of his statement, but it would only start an argument, and she could already sense Dr. Anthony feeling uncomfortable with the friction between them.

"You two want some coffee?" Dr. Anthony asked. "This woman's death and the fact that we don't know who she is seems to have made everyone a little tense."

Scarlett was too wrung out to want anything other than answers. "I'm fine, thanks."

"Sounds good," Adam said, "but I've got to get back to the office. I've got an officer on vacation and another one sick, so it looks like I'll be taking care of this case myself."

"I could talk to people in the campground."

Adam frowned at Scarlett, making it perfectly clear he didn't want her help, then turned back to Dr. Anthony. "How long do you think it'll be before Dan can pick her up?"

"Couple of hours, I'd guess. Sooner, if he's not busy."

"Good. When you talk to him, tell him not to do anything with the body until I give him the okay."

"No problem." Dr. Anthony tossed out a few good-byes, walked down the hall, and disappeared down a corridor on the right.

Once again, Scarlett leaned against the doorjamb leading into the room where the woman lay and stared at her forever silent face. The conversation between Dr. Anthony and Adam had seemed so impersonal, as if they saw the white-haired lady as nothing more than a dead woman without a name. Dr. Anthony might care a little, but as soon as Jane Doe was out of his hospital he'd put her out of his mind. More than likely Adam saw her as just another case, one that would take extra effort to solve.

Scarlett saw her as a lady who'd had something on her mind, something she hadn't been able to share. She'd died alone, without a friend or family to hold her hand, to say "I love you" before she took her final breath. Scarlett's mom had died in much the same way, only far more tragically—on a winding stretch of mountain road, when a drunk driver had forced her to swerve, straight into a tree.

Why she'd been driving that night, even though she was on medication, under a nurse's care, and confined to the house, no one could explain. Some speculated it was suicide. Some said it was an accident. Scarlett knew her mother would never kill herself, not when she had a daughter who loved her.

Something had driven Elizabeth from the house. Something had made her drive erratically. Ten years later, Scarlett still wondered what had happened that night, wanted to know what had been on her mother's mind.

Now she had a stranger to wonder about, too.

Stepping into the room, Scarlett walked to the gurney and rested a hand on top of the woman's. It was cold but soft. It would be easy to believe she was alive, if it weren't for the fact that she was lying so still.

"Why all the concern about someone you don't know?"

Scarlett looked over her shoulder at Adam, who stood casually in the doorway. "Someone's got to care. She doesn't have a family, not that we know of, anyway."

"I'll find one."

Scarlett's eyes narrowed. "Will you?"

"It's my job."

Scarlett shrugged off his comment and walked from the room. It had been Adam's job to care for her mother, too. And he'd failed miserably. Some day he'd pay.

Chapter 6

Scarlett kicked a pinecone that dared to get in her way as she walked through the park, eyes trained on the gravel path. She wished she could get rid of her anger, her distrust, her fear of being vulnerable, and her need for revenge half as easily. Those things had preoccupied too much of her time and were ruining her life, just as her mother's obsession with Adam had ruined hers.

But she didn't know how to let them go.

"Good afternoon."

It wasn't the words that stopped Scarlett but the broad chest she smacked into. Stunned, she pressed her hands against the leather jacket and took a step back before looking at the tall, dark, and imposing figure that had appeared out of nowhere.

Logan cupped his hands lightly around her arms. His thumbs drew circles over her bare skin. Goose bumps speckled her flesh, and the spicy scent of his aftershave, mixed with the fragrance of pine, engulfed her every sense.

"Are you all right?" he asked.

She wasn't the least bit all right. She was hopelessly captivated by the man, and when he was near, she seemed to forget the rest of the world existed.

"I'm fine. Thanks."

Everything about him, especially his sudden appearance, had taken her by surprise. She didn't want him to think she was weak or vulnerable, even though it felt as if her knees would buckle in his presence, so she took another step backward, took a deep breath, and forced a smile. "I wouldn't have pegged you as the stroll-through-the-park kind of guy."

One of his dark brows rose at what had turned out to be a rather insipid comment. "Summing me up again?"

"It's the mystery lover in me, always trying to figure out what a person's up to or what's going on in his or her mind."

"You could ask."

"But then there'd be no mystery."

"Maybe not, but assumptions leave you with questions. Worse yet, relying on assumptions without ascertaining the facts can make you think all the wrong things about someone." He grinned cynically, as if he knew that she and the Sleuths had been conjuring up any number of dreadful scenarios to explain his actions.

"For instance," he continued, "at this very moment you might be thinking I'm a stalker, a man who's been watching your every move, just waiting for the perfect moment to strike."

"I thought no such thing. I assumed you were out for a leisurely stroll."

"Your assumption would have been wrong." he reached out and brushed a windblown curl from her brow. "I was waiting for you."

"Waiting?" She swallowed hard. "Why?"

His eyes narrowed as he stared down at her. Was he mad? Angry? Desperate to get even for God knows what?

She thought about running, but at last the soft tilt of his lips returned. "Thought maybe we could get some coffee," he said. "Chat awhile. Get to know each other rather than making rash assumptions."

He was sexy as hell, and having coffee might have been nice if he'd bumped into her out of the blue. But the fact that he'd been waiting for her seemed rather odd. "How'd you know I'd be in the park right about now?"

"I watched you walk through here earlier. Saw you go to the hospital. Figured if I waited long enough you'd come back."

She eyed him suspiciously. "Why on earth would you be watching me?"

"Why not? You've got a great walk. A little sway. A little wiggle. Any man in his right mind would watch."

"Any man who's retired and has nothing better to do with his time, that is."

He shrugged, and Scarlett used that moment to skirt around the man who caused her constant confusion.

"Don't go," he called after her. As if the gentleness in his voice held some magical power that could reach out to her, she stopped. Turning slowly, she looked once more into his eyes and felt her blood heat near to boiling as it surged through her veins.

He troubled her. She was sure she couldn't trust him. But no man had ever made her burn, not like this.

He moved toward her, deliberately, methodically, his gaze never leaving her eyes. "You're afraid of me, aren't you?"

She trembled inside but stiffened her shoulders. "What makes you think that?"

"You shake when I'm near. Your eyes get dark. You ramble"—he grinned—"offering me scones and milk, two percent, nonfat, and even chocolate. You start breathing hard. Either you're afraid of me, or—"

"I'm not afraid of you. It's been a rough couple of hours, that's all."

Understanding and concern filled his eyes. "I heard what happened. Is the woman okay?"

"She's dead," Scarlett blurted. "I didn't know her, but that doesn't make it any easier."

"It's never easy," he said, as if he'd seen death up close and personal, and more than once. "You want to get that coffee? Talk about it?"

The gentleness of his offer tempted her, but she shook her head, not knowing if it was fear of getting to know him better that made her decline, or a need to get back to her store. "Thanks, but I've got a dog to get home to before he finds some unique way of getting in trouble."

"I'll walk you back, then."

"You don't have to."

He tucked his hand around her arm and drew her close to his side. "I'm retired, remember? I no longer do anything unless I want to."

As comforting as it felt to walk at his side, she couldn't help but wonder if he was up to something.

"Why the sudden change in attitude?" she asked as they strolled along the path.

"What do you mean?"

"A few minutes ago I had the distinct feeling you were angry with me."

"Not angry. Annoyed."

Scarlett came to an abrupt halt. "Annoyed? What on earth about?"

She could see the muscles tightening in Logan's jaw. He dropped her arm and stepped directly in front of her, aiming heated eyes her way. "I don't like being the talk of the town."

She feigned ignorance. "People are talking about you?"

"You know damn good and well they are."

"And you think I'm responsible, that I'm the one spreading rumors?"

"Aren't you?"

"I may have listened to some talk—"

"And then came up with all sorts of wild assumptions."

"I tried getting straight answers from you, but you weren't the least bit forthcoming."

"So you take what you've heard, put your own

spin on it, and even after you stare at me for God knows how long, trying to sum me up, you still decide that I'm some ruthless, brutal, hard-edged creep."

"Don't forget cocky and brash."

A horribly wicked grin touched his lips. "Want me to show you cocky and brash?"

"Isn't that what you're doing right now?"

"Kissing you right here, right now, so everyone in Plentiful can see us would be cocky and brash."

"I'm sure they'd find it totally insignificant."

"Why? Do you often kiss men here in the park for all to see?"

"Of course not."

"Then I'd be the first?"

"Yes, but you're not going to kiss me."

"I might."

"Why?" A lump settled heavy in her throat. "Just to prove a point?"

"Partially. Maybe I want to kiss you for no other reason than sheer pleasure."

"I doubt that."

She turned to walk away, but a strong arm fastened about her waist, spun her around, and dragged her decidedly short body up his exceedingly tall one, until her toes were far from the ground, until their eyes met. She struggled, but it was useless. How could a poor, innocent little lamb possibly fight off the big bad wolfe?

Instead of fighting, she glared. "What the hell do you think you're doing?"

"Giving the folks in town something else to talk about besides me." He grinned annoyingly. "What kind of things do you think they'll say?"

"That you're a brute."

"Maybe. Then again they might talk about how you were flirting with me this morning, how you flaunted that cute little butt of yours, not to mention the sweetest belly button I ever laid eyes on."

"I didn't."

"No?" His damn eyebrow rose again. "You climbed that ladder in your shop so I could get a better view."

"I climbed that ladder so we could talk eye-to-eye."

"Like we're doing now?"

"This isn't the same at all. This morning we were carrying on a civil conversation. Right now, you're holding me against my will."

"You're not struggling. Maybe you like it here?"

"You're bigger than me. What good would struggling do?"

"Not much."

"So are you going to kiss me or not?"

"Should I?"

"I thought that was your original plan. Kiss me. Embarrass me." She gritted her teeth. "Why don't you just do it and get it over with, then I can get to work."

"I've got the feeling people will talk more if I don't kiss you. They'll wonder when I'm going to kiss you. If I'm going to kiss you. And if I don't, they'll wonder why I didn't."

"Fine. Let them wonder."

"Maybe you'll wonder, too?"

"I'll be rejoicing."

He grinned, his eyes zooming in for a close-up on her face. "Have you ever counted the freckles on your nose?"

"What does that have to do with humiliating me?"

"Nothing. I was just thinking I might like to count them sometime."

"Then you'd better do it now, because you're never going to get this close to me again."

"Is that a challenge?"

"It's a statement of fact."

He chuckled. "I prefer challenges. The tougher the better."

"Just let me down."

He contemplated her demand for the longest time, his maple syrup–colored eyes twinkling. "All right . . . for now."

His hold on her relaxed slightly and she started to slide.

"Stop! Oh, God, stop!"

Logan's arms tightened about her again, keeping her flat against his chest. "Giving in already?"

"No. I'm . . . I'm stuck."

His brows drew together. "Stuck?"

"On you, damn it! My belly button ring's caught on . . . oh, crap! It's caught around the button on your jeans."

He laughed, the sound ringing through the park and up Main Street, dragging every pair of inquisitive eyes toward her struggle.

"I don't see this as a laughing matter." Scarlett swung her legs around his hips for extra support and dug her hands in between their waists in an attempt to free herself.

"You know, if I'm not mistaken," Logan said, moving one of his hands under her behind, which, unfortunately, wasn't covered by her short skirt, "we're closer together than we were before."

"Not for long," Scarlett bit out as she worked at his button and her belly button ring. "And if you do anything funny with that hand of yours—"

"Which hand?" he asked far too innocently.

"The one playing with my bottom."

"I'm supporting you, not playing, but while I'm holding you up, and since I'm so cocky and macho and brash, not to mention a brute, maybe I'll try figuring out if the panties I've accidentally come in contact with are silk, satin, or lace."

"Silk, and if your fingers make one more swirl over my derriere, so help me I'll . . . I'll—"

"What color?"

"What do you mean what color?"

"The silk."

She glared ferociously. Half a second later she freed her belly from his button. "Let me down. Now."

"I take it this means you're not going to tell me what color your panties are."

"Never."

He chuckled and let her body slide down his until her feet hit solid ground. "Never say never, Scarlett. Not around me."

She took one more look at the silly-ass grin on his face and stormed across the street, tugging her skirt over her red silk panties as she stomped along the boardwalk and through the gaping crowd.

She detested him. He was brutal and mean and, damn it, he was turning out to be just like every other blasted man on the planet. He was probably a thief, to boot.

Through angry, blinding tears, she managed to shove her key into the lock, trounced into her store, and slammed the door behind her. The chimes clanked, Toby barked, and Scarlett tripped over the big ball of fur, taking a nosedive into . . .

"Oh, Toby, what on earth have you done now?"

Chapter 7

Scarlett picked herself up off the floor, then picked half a dozen sopping wet scraps of paper off of her body and flung them into the trash can. She tugged her skirt back into place, then aimed a vicious frown at the Scottie.

Paws folded casually over an open book, Toby looked up from the pages he was chewing on. His dark brown eyes looked innocent, as if he were saying, "What, you think I knocked your delicate, hand-painted china cups and saucers off of the tabletop so they'd smash to smithereens and send cold tea slithering across the just mopped floors? You think I upset one of your precious Jayne Mansfield-Smythe displays and accidentally shredded some of the dust jackets? And really, Scarlett, you don't think I'd rip the pages out of four or five books and scatter them upstairs and downstairs, simply because you taunted me with the hope that my real master had finally come home? Oh, no, I would never do something like that."

Scarlett wiped the blasted tears from her face, got

down on her knees, and gave the pooch a hug. "Sorry Tobe. I shouldn't have said what I did. I shouldn't have left you alone."

Toby's tail wagged. He licked her face. He yapped twice, then went back to gnawing on the book.

If only her own life were so simple. She wished she could lie down in the chaos and forget everything—her mother, her stepdad, the dead woman, the missing wallet, and the foolish and embarrassing scene in the park with Logan. She wished she could forget the way her heart went pitter-pat when he was near, the heat that rushed through her body when they touched, and all the crazy, mixed-up emotions he made her feel—happiness, anger, frustration and lust.

But her life wasn't simple. It was one big mess.

Instinct made her want to clean up the chaos she was kneeling in, but the more immediate concern was the missing wallet. Find it, and some of the other problems might disappear.

Heading to the checkout counter, she latched on to the back of her skirt for propriety's sake, and got back down on her knees to search for the dead woman's identification.

She looked left. She ran the hand that wasn't holding on to her skirt under the far reaches of the counter, then got a ruler out of a drawer and waved it around the narrower spaces in the hope of finding something. Anything.

In the end she came up with nothing more than two paper clips, a dime and a dust bunny.

"Lose something?"

Scarlett peeked around the counter. The arrogant, brash, big bad wolfe stood just inside the shop, and only now did she hear the tinkle of the chimes.

"Just cleaning up some of the mess my dog made," she fibbed, getting up from the floor and readjusting her skirt. "There's a possibility I might have avoided some of this chaos if you hadn't detained me in the park."

"Look," Logan said, sweeping Toby into his arms without the pooch offering so much as a whimper or growl, "no matter what you might think of me, no matter what happened in the park, and no matter what you might have heard about me, I'm not some brash, arrogant, macho bore."

"Really?"

"All right." He shrugged. "I might be arrogant at times. God knows I can be a bore. But somewhere deep down under all that crap is a nice guy."

Scarlett swept up a handful of paper scraps from the floor. "And your point is?"

"You're not going to give me a break, are you?"

"You embarrassed me in front of half the town. They already think I'm loony-tunes, so that shouldn't bother me, but it does. You threaten to kiss me and then you don't, and on top of that, you nearly rip the ring out of my belly button. What do you want me to do, say I forgive you?"

"I was thinking you might let me take you to dinner."

She tucked the trash can under her arm, swept a gnawed, slobbery, and shredded hardback copy of

Seven Sins up from the floor and tossed the expensive tome inside. Gathering more paper and bits of crushed china, she tossed them into the trash as well.

Out of the corner of her eye she watched Logan cradle the Scottie in one arm, then collect some of the litter. He walked toward her in that slow, methodical way that made her extremely nervous, and dropped the mess into the trash can.

"You never answered me," he said softly. "What about dinner?"

Looking up into the dark, sparkling eyes of the man who caused her endless amounts of consternation, she smiled politely. "I don't think so."

"Lunch then? Tomorrow."

Scarlett sighed, then crossed the room and shoved the trash can back under the checkout counter. "Look, for all I know, you could be the nicest guy to ever walk into this store. Hell, Toby likes you, and he doesn't like very many people. But, the truth of the matter is . . ." She struggled to come up with a truthful statement, and at last settled on, "I don't date."

"Do you eat?"

"Of course I eat."

"Then let me take you out. We don't have to talk to each other, which means I won't have to worry about sounding like an egotistical lout, and you don't have to be nice."

"What, we just sit across from each other and stuff food in our mouths?"

"I've been on dates that weren't anything more than that."

"So have I. That's part of the reason I don't date."

"Maybe you've dated all the wrong men."

"And you think you're the right man for me?"

"We'll never know if we don't share a civil conversation."

"I don't think it's possible for the two of us to share a conversation that doesn't end up in an argument."

"You're assuming again."

"I'm acting on instinct."

"And your instinct says I can't be trusted."

"You've got it." The words rushed out of her mouth, and the look of disappointment she saw flash across Logan's face made her wish she could pull them back. But it was far too late. All the warmth and sparkle she'd seen in his eyes was gone, replaced by a cold, cynical smile.

He shook his head, dumped Toby into her arms, and went for the door. He opened it wide, and the chimes clanked as he stepped out onto the boardwalk. She thought he'd leave without another word, but he turned, looking at her over his shoulder. "You know, Scarlett, I've got pretty good instincts, too, and every single one of them is screaming at me to get the hell away from you and not look back."

"You're going to listen to them, aren't you?"

"I've already walked away from one thing I felt I couldn't do without. I'm not going to do it again." The twinkle returned to his eyes as he slowly closed the door. "I'll be back, Scarlett. Trust me."

Chapter 8

Scarlett immersed herself in *Seven Sins* and brownie batter. She licked the spoon; Toby licked the bowl. She read; Toby lay on her feet and kept her toes warm. She listened for footsteps, just in case Logan kept his promise of coming back; Toby snored.

It had been a far better way to while away the afternoon than cleaning up the mess Toby had made. She was breaking a pattern, doing something totally against her grain. Jayne Mansfield-Smythe would cheer her on for taking a risk.

The next risk would be trusting Logan, letting him get close. But she didn't have to attempt that until he came back—and he might not keep his word.

That, in itself, was another miserable thought.

She puffed at a wayward curl, and as the grandfather clock struck five, she licked the last speck of chocolate from her spoon, rose from the cluttered tea table, suffered through Toby's growl at being disturbed, and headed for the front of the store to flip the OPEN sign to CLOSED.

She was reaching for the lock when Mildred bustled past the window, threw open the door, and stepped inside. She huffed and puffed, staring at Scarlett as she tried to catch her breath.

"Everything okay, Mildred?" Scarlett asked as she locked the door behind her friend.

Mildred held up one finger. "Just a minute." She gasped between breaths.

Not wanting to take any more chances where an elderly lady was concerned, especially one of her nearest and dearest friends, Scarlett grabbed a chair from the tea table and positioned it behind Mildred's ample bottom.

Mildred scowled, ignored the chair completely, paced across the room *tsk*ing over the unsightly mess, then headed back to Scarlett. "What on earth happened in here?"

"Toby got a little playful."

Mildred shook her head. "Apparently he's not the only one feeling playful today." Her eyes narrowed. "What, may I ask, was that display in the park all about?"

"What display?"

"Don't play innocent with me, Miss O'Malley. I'm talking about what went on in the park between you and that man?"

Scarlett rolled her eyes. "Oh, that. Goodness Mildred, that was hours ago."

"It may have been hours ago but it's all the talk around town. If I'm going to clear up any misconceptions, I have to know the truth."

"The truth is simple. My belly button ring got stuck on one of Logan's buttons."

"So you say."

"You don't believe me?" Scarlett asked, turning away from Mildred to finally clean up the table. She'd tackle the trash later.

"That ring of yours wouldn't have gotten caught if you hadn't been in his arms in the first place." Mildred shook her head in dismay. "Didn't you hear anything Ida Mae and I told you this morning? The man's up to no good, and we don't want you getting caught up in one of his schemes."

"I can't get caught up in something that might not exist."

"Defend him all you want. I suppose that's only natural considering his good looks and all, but remember, Adam was good looking and charming, too, and look how he hurt your mom. Logan Wolfe is up to something strange, Scarlett. The sooner you believe that, the better off you'll be."

"The only thing we have proof of is the fact that he embarrassed me in the park." She refused to mention the fact that he'd excited her, too, or that he bewildered her. As for Jane Doe's missing wallet or ID, it was still missing. She couldn't discount Logan as the thief, but she couldn't prove anything, either.

"If that embarrassment wasn't enough to make you see the light," Mildred went on, "perhaps the dirt I got on him this afternoon will."

Scarlett flashed a curious but bothered frown at Mildred, then grabbed the trash can from under the checkout counter and started throwing bits and pieces of broken china inside.

Mildred followed her around the room. Toby waddled behind Mildred. "Aren't you at all interested in knowing what we saw?"

"Yes. No. Maybe." Scarlett stacked the few remaining pieces of unbroken china in her arms and headed for the kitchen, wishing this conversation had never started, because she really didn't want to hear anything dreadful about Logan, not after she'd spent the last few hours telling herself that underneath the charm was a rather nice guy.

She filled the sink with hot water and added a healthy dose of blue detergent, while Mildred grabbed a fresh brownie from a covered plate.

"I'd like to say what we saw today was conclusive, that it proved all our suspicions about Mr. Wolfe, but . . ." Mildred took a bite of gooey chocolate and chewed thoughtfully. "Actually, what we saw is all rather odd."

Scarlett drummed her fingers on a plate in the soapy water. "How odd?"

"Well, we were watching him—Mr. Wolfe—through the jewelry store window and saw him go into Teton Outfitters and come out later with a gun." Mildred dug in her handbook for her leather-bound diary, flipped through the pages, then tapped her finger on some notes. "Wait a minute. It wasn't a gun. It was a rifle. At least Ida Mae and I were petty sure it was a rifle, you know, long and thin, but it was wrapped in brown paper."

"Could have been a fishing pole."

Mildred huffed. "Playing devil's advocate?"

Maybe she was, but hearing the silliness of Mildred's suspicions magnified the silliness of her own. "Okay, what if it was a rifle? They're not illegal and I'd say ninety percent if not more of the people living here own one, two, maybe three or more."

"But they use them to hunt game." Mildred pushed the rest of the brownie in her mouth and chewed a few times. "Does Mr. Wolfe look like a hunter to you?"

"Not really. But you know, people buy guns and rifles for other reasons. Maybe he's a collector." Scarlett rinsed her hands, then grabbed a towel to dry them. "Purchasing a rifle isn't proof of anything."

"You're going to stick up for him in spite of what he did to you, aren't you?"

"I'm just giving him the benefit of the doubt."

Dropping the towel on the kitchen counter, Scarlett went back into the shop, with Mildred hot on her heels.

"Fishing pole, rifle, whatever it was," Mildred said, "he put it in the cab of a gigantic black truck. It was a Dodge, you know, with huge tires and 4 x 4 painted on the back." She flipped another page in her diary. "Want to know what he did next?"

Scarlett already had a pretty good idea what he did next. He'd waited for her in the park, he'd lifted her in his big, powerful arms, he'd come within a hair's breadth of kissing her—and then he'd let her go. But she decided to humor her friend.

"What did he do next?" Scarlett asked.

"Well," Mildred huffed, "you know perfectly well what happened in the park, I'm sad to say, but after that he went into Hershey's Interiors and came out not ten minutes later with a long, rolled-up carpet slung over his shoulder."

Mildred beamed, looking quite pleased with this revelation, although Scarlett couldn't see what it revealed. All Scarlett could say was, "And?"

"Don't you think it's odd that a man like Logan Wolfe would buy a carpet from Hershey's Interiors? They're expensive. They carry exclusive, one-of-a-kind items. More often than not you have to have an appointment to shop there."

"Maybe he had an appointment. Maybe he's wealthy. Maybe he likes nice things."

Mildred grunted. "Maybe." She flipped to the next page in her diary, shaking her head. "He put the carpet in the back of his truck, started to drive out of town, then stopped in front of Duffy's Ice Cream Parlor."

At last, the man did something quite common. "What kind of ice cream did he buy? Vanilla? Chocolate?"

"Strawberry." Mildred cringed. "I detest strawberry ice cream, but that's neither here nor there."

This whole conversation and all of this supposed proof was neither here nor there, too. Still, Scarlett listened to her friend.

"He stood out front, licked the ice cream a few times, then tossed it into the Dumpster, you know, that despicable one in the alley between Duffy's and the Mischievous Moose that the beautification committee's been trying to get rid of." Mildred slammed her diary shut.

"That's it?"

"No, no." Mildred opened her diary again, flipping through pages one more time. "I guess I got sidetracked thinking about that horrid Dumpster. Actually, Mr. Wolfe stood out front of Duffy's for several minutes, staring up and down the street, up and down, up and down. Most peculiar thing I ever saw. Then he got into his truck, acting quite mysterious, I might add, took something out, and threw it into the Dumpster."

It wasn't the throwing something into the Dumpster that raised the hairs on the back of Scarlett's neck, it was the way Logan had looked up and down, up and down, as if he wanted to make sure no one was watching, as if he had something to hide.

A wallet, maybe?

"You don't know what he threw away, do you?" Scarlett asked.

"Haven't a clue. Ida Mae, Lil and I might have taken a peek after he went to the park, but the Dumpster reeks of rotten banana peels and sour milk. I can't imagine anyone getting close to it."

"I can." Reeking or not, Scarlett had to know if Logan had tossed a woman's wallet into the garbage bin. She didn't want to believe it was possible, but she wouldn't rest easy until she knew the truth about the man who continually left her bewitched, bothered, and completely bewildered.

Chapter 9

Logan downed a gulp of Moose Jaw, feeling the dark, potent brew slither smoothly through his insides as he took aim with the dart. He was already down ten bucks and thinking he'd better call it quits, but the gang at the Misty Moon kept egging him on. Losing money was better than being home with nothing more than the grizzlies for company, but he was quickly losing interest in the game and the atmosphere everyone else seemed to find so fascinating.

With a quick flick of his wrist, he tossed the dart. *Thwap!* It smacked the wood plank wall about six inches from the board and vibrated for a split second before tumbling to the floor. Apparently his skill at darts was sorely lacking, but shooting darts wasn't exactly a marketable skill. If these guys wanted to take bets on target practice—stationary or moving—with a semiautomatic, he'd show them a thing or two.

Leaning against the booth where he'd been sitting when the match began, Logan bit into his double cheeseburger with bacon, grilled red onions and mushrooms, and watched Plentiful's chief of police step up to the line. Adam aimed with a practiced eye, his first dart hitting smack in the middle. Obviously there wasn't much crime in Plentiful if the town's head cop had time to become an expert at darts.

A burly guy named Larry patted Adam on the back and ordered another round of beer, as one dart after another flew across the saloon's back room.

"Wanna go another round?" Larry asked, holding three more darts out to Logan, but he wasn't crazy enough or rich enough to say yes. Instead, he shook his head and popped a hotly spiced French fry into his mouth, chewing thoughtfully as he listened to boasts about who was the best at darts and fly fishing and bagging elk, talk that segued into who could ride the longest, and what they rode covered the gamut from bulls to broncs to women.

Nice guys, Logan thought cynically.

Of course, how could he condemn them when he, too, had come off like a macho jackass earlier in the day? Scarlett might never forgive him, and he couldn't blame her if she didn't.

"You figure out who the dead lady is yet?" Larry asked Adam, then swigged down the last of his beer and grabbed a fresh bottle from his booth.

Adam aimed another dart. "Not yet."

"A local?"

"Nope." Adam wasn't half as talkative now as he'd been at Joe's place this morning. He frowned instead of smiled, and from the rapid way he threw the darts and the bluntness of his words, it was easy to see his patience with the game and what was going on around him had long ago worn thin.

"Got any clues?" Larry asked.

Adam concentrated on the dartboard. "Working at it."

"Better hurry before that stepdaughter of yours butts in." Larry laughed, guzzled down half his beer, and belched—one hell of a show of manliness. "How many of your cases has she solved now?"

Logan stopped eating fries and listened with more interest.

"Scarlett and her cohorts don't solve cases," Adam said, tossing a dart angrily at the target. "They get in the middle, get in trouble, and have to be rescued."

"Yeah, and after that you go riding in on your white steed and save the day." Steve laughed. He was a skinny guy with a big mouth, who dressed like a hotshot in skintight jeans and a plaid shirt with the sleeves rolled up. "We hear stories about you and your cops takin' all the credit. First there was Art Steinman and the land swindle. After that was the robbery at the gas station. Is this Jane Doe case gonna be their next bit of crime solving?"

Adam tossed another dart, and it landed just off center. He walked to the board, slowly pulled out each projectile, then turned and stared down his buddies. "You assholes keep shooting your mouths off like that and I'll have to take you out back and stomp you into the ground."

Adam grinned, grabbed his beer, and took a swig,

studying Logan over the top of the bottle. "Saw you in the park this afternoon."

"We all did." Steve laughed, and Logan wished he could kick himself for the asinine spectacle he'd created. "You got a thing going with Scarlett?"

"That's none of your business," Adam said, aiming a frown at Steve, then angling his head back to Logan. "Might be wise to stay away from her, though."

Adam's warnings were getting old. "So you said earlier."

"Adam's right," Larry said. "She's a crazy woman with an overactive imagination. Paranoid. Fanatical. Just like her mother."

Adam scowled, but Larry and Steve didn't back off.

"You know it's true, Adam," Larry said. "That wife of yours used to peek in bedroom windows to see if you were with someone else's wife."

"Hell, she even accused my old lady—"

Adam slammed the darts point down into a battered wood table, abruptly ending Steve's comment. His eyes blazed as he stared from jerk to jerk, then he turned on his heels and stalked out of the saloon.

"Touchy guy." Larry laughed and downed another long swallow of beer.

"Guess I'd be touchy too if I'd married a crazy woman." Steve joined in the laugher, grabbed the darts Adam had discarded, and tossed them haphazardly at the board.

Logan had to agree with Adam's assessment that potbellied Larry and emaciated cowboy Steve were a couple of assholes. He'd known his share of jerks like these two guys. Normally he'd walk out, leave them to their warped sense of fun and games, but they'd brought up Scarlett's name and he wanted to know more.

He ordered another round of beer for the gang and washed down what was left of his cheeseburger. "You know Scarlett well?" he asked.

Larry laughed again, the sound slushy, like too many bottles of beer were finally getting to him. "You live in this town long you know everyone. Course, some women it's better to stay away from."

"Scarlett fit in that category?" Logan asked.

"She ain't quite as crazy as that mama of hers," Steve said, "but give her a couple of years and she'll be just as paranoid."

"Everyone in town thought Elizabeth was going off the deep end," Larry snorted. "She even peeked through my bedroom window one night and caught me with some babe who was here on vacation. Started screaming and hollering right through the glass, called me a cheat and a womanizer. Adam ended up hiring a full-time nurse to make sure she didn't get loose and hurt someone."

Logan frowned. "Where is she now?"

"Dead." Steve started throwing darts again. "She went off her rocker one night, at least that's what the nurse said, got in Adam's car and plowed into a tree."

"Suicide?" Logan asked.

"Accident," Larry stated. "Drunk driver came at

her out on the highway and she swerved to get out of his way. Would have been dead whether she'd swerved or not, considering how fast both cars were going. Hell, she might have been dead if there wasn't some drunk headin' for her. Elizabeth was crazy as they come and there's no telling what she'd been planning to do when she took off in Adam's car."

"Don't listen to these two," Molly, the friendly-faced owner of the saloon, warned, eyeing Logan as she bustled across the room and picked up the empty bottles. "Elizabeth was a nice lady, but too fragile for her own good. You want to know the truth about her, ask the people who knew her a good long time, not the guys who hang around here. Same goes for Scarlett."

Sounded like wise advice, Logan decided. He'd never been one to judge someone based solely on word of mouth, especially when that word came from a couple of losers. He liked hard evidence, and so far he hadn't witnessed anything crazy about Scarlett other than the fact that she ran hot and cold around him. Truth be told, that was a turn-on. She played hard to get—he wanted her all the more.

Too bad it was late and A Study in Scarlett was closed, or he might pay her another visit. Maybe extend that dinner invitation again. Spending the past couple of hours with two of the biggest shits in Plentiful made him long for good company, even the company of a woman he couldn't figure out.

After paying the bill and leaving Molly a hefty tip, he headed out to Main Street and strolled the deserted boardwalk. A black tomcat scurried out from under the weathered wooden planks and pranced at his side.

Except for the saloon and a couple of other eating establishments, the town had pretty much rolled up for the night. Not at all like Vegas, he thought, which never closed and where you could always find something to do, if you were into gambling, getting drunk, or going to strip joints.

True, the place had its good sides, too. Friends. Barbecues out by the pool. He missed the good stuff, but he sure as hell didn't miss the cesspool he'd worked in. Didn't miss the crap, the corruption, the politics, or the rage-filled stares from guys who'd once been his friends. He'd wanted out of the place for years, wanted to settle somewhere else. It wasn't until he'd provided evidence that his partner and three other cops were dirty that he'd found the guts to call it quits.

But his self-imposed retirement had become a pain in the butt. How many hours could a man spend pulling rubbers up to his chest and standing in the middle of an icy river tossing a fly fishing line into the current before getting tired of it? How many fish could he clean, fry, and ingest without getting sick of eating fish?

How much longer could he stand being alone?

He thought this would be the perfect life; it was anything but. It seemed as if he'd counted every constellation in the sky, stopped to smell every flower, and hiked every mountain trail for miles around.

He'd even spent part of this afternoon reading a book—and he hated to read.

He'd hoped to fritter away his retirement years shacked up with some tall, big-breasted Scandinavian babe, but the closest he'd gotten to a woman like that was the fictional Jayne Mansfield-Smythe. She was luscious and curvy, but she felt like paper and ink. He preferred hot skin—and the softer the better.

Scarlett O'Malley instantly came to mind—again. Now there was one soft and curvy woman. Not to mention hot. And damn if she didn't have the sexiest belly button he'd ever been stuck to.

Thinking about Scarlett made him think about sticking around this place. He'd even given some thought to taking the guide job Joe Granger had offered. But he wasn't going to rush into anything.

The black cat rubbed against Logan's legs. He was about to pet the mangy thing, but it darted across the street to Duffy's Ice Cream Parlor. Apparently the cat found the smell of cream and sugar more enticing than the Tide embedded in Logan's jeans.

With nothing better to do, Logan followed the cat. They parted ways when they reached the far side of the street. The tomcat headed for the Dumpster in the alleyway and Logan pushed through Duffy's open door, where he ordered vanilla ice cream in a waffle cone. Unlike earlier today when he'd indulged in a strawberry cone, he let the kid behind the counter talk him into trying chopped gummy worms on the top. Tomorrow he might try the Grand Teton, eight flavors and four toppings, with real whipped cream, nuts and a cherry.

Bored. Sex-starved. And fat. That was going to be his lot in life if he didn't make some changes pretty damn soon.

He licked the big scoop of vanilla and thought about creamy thighs. Oh, yeah, there were better things a man could do with his tongue than lap up ice cream.

Logan paid the kid behind the counter and headed back outside. As he'd done a couple of other times today, he zoomed in on A Study in Scarlett. The lights were off downstairs, and only a dim light shone through one of the upstairs windows. He wondered if Scarlett was already in bed, and he pictured her dressed in skimpy red silk and lying on red, white and blue satin sheets, her index finger flicking her belly button ring.

He'd conjured up a pretty nice picture, but the real thing would be a hell of a lot better. That meant he'd have to pay another visit to the bookstore tomorrow. He'd use the excuse that he wanted to pick up the third installment of Jayne Mansfield-Smythe's adventures in murder and mayhem land, when what he really wanted to do was check out Scarlett Mary Catherine O'Malley's attire and hopefully see her belly button again.

But that was tomorrow. Tonight looked like a complete bust. He might as well go home and read. Falling asleep with a big-breasted, sassy-mouthed fictional sleuth in his hands was the closest he was going to get to fun . . . or sex.

Heading for his truck, he walked past the alley and chucked what was left of his ice cream cone into the Dumpster that mucked up the town's aesthetics.

"Oh, crap!"

Since when did Dumpsters talk?

Logan poked his head over the battered edge of the big gray trash bin, holding his breath to keep from inhaling the stench. A stream of light waved madly around inside, and then the beam hit him square in the face, blinding him until he grabbed the cheap red flashlight from the hand that had been clutching it tightly.

Aiming the pitiful excuse for a light into the Dumpster, he spied a pair of wide green eyes peering up at him through a wild cascade of flaming red hair—hair that was crowned by a glob of vanilla ice cream, a colorful variety of chopped gummy worms, and a waffle cone.

Scarlett looked like the Queen of Slime, and she didn't seem happy about it. He, of course, couldn't help but grin. "Fancy meeting you here."

She scraped the cone and ice cream from the top of her hair and stared at the mess in her palm. Slowly her head rose, and she squinted into the light. "I take it this is yours?"

Nice guy that he was, Logan aimed the light a bit to her left so she could see his smile. "Thought I'd share."

"I prefer chocolate, thank you." She shook the gunk off her palm, stared at her grubby hand, then wiped it on the back of her jeans. They were dirty, but they were tight and looked mighty fine.

"Anything interesting down there?" he asked, examining the pile of rubbish she stood in and the mountain of trash stacked on one side. Then he went back to examining Scarlett again.

"A few quarters, dimes, and nickles. Half a dozen pennies and a vast assortment of garbage."

"Do you supplement your income this way?"

She rolled her eyes. "I'm looking for something."

"Having any luck?"

This time she gritted her teeth. "If I'd been lucky I wouldn't still be here."

He grinned. "Testy thing, aren't you?"

"It stinks in here, I haven't found what I'm looking for, and you're smirking. Most people would be irritable under the circumstances."

"Most people wouldn't be scrounging inside a Dumpster."

"Look," she said, her hands going to her hips, "I lost my wallet. My ID's in it and so are my credit cards. I've got to find it."

"What makes you think it's in here?"

"It's a long story and surely you have better things to do than stare into a garbage pit and chitchat with me."

"Might have had something better to do, but you turned down my dinner invitation. So . . ." He swung up and over the Dumpster's side. The steel container rattled and clanked when his feet hit bottom. "Where should I begin?"

"I really don't need any help."

It was highly apparent that she didn't want him there, but he'd already climbed in and he planned to stick around. "All right, I'll look for nickels, dimes and quarters to supplement *my* income. But while I'm at it, I might as well keep my eyes open for your wallet. What does it look like?"

She rolled her eyes heavenward for the second time in a minute.

"It's rather nondescript," she admitted. It was a pretty lousy answer, but the kind he was used to getting when he interrogated someone.

"Leather? Vinyl?" He shrugged. "It might be helpful if you give me some idea what I'm looking for."

"It's a wallet, for pity's sake. If you find one, I'm sure it'll be mine."

"What makes you think it's in here?"

"It's a wild hunch. Okay? I lost it last night and now I'm just retracing my steps."

"You spend a lot of evenings in Dumpsters?"

She squinted. Her lips pursed. If he wasn't mistaken, that was an obvious look of annoyance. He had that effect on people. She followed the look with avoidance, bending over the debris and going back to work, gingerly sifting through the muck.

If you can't beat 'em, join 'em.

He kicked a black banana peel across the Dumpster and proceeded to examine the six inches of crap beneath his feet by moving bits of it aside with the toe of his boot. He'd been in Dumpsters before and knew what could turn up. He wasn't about to use his ungloved hands.

Scarlett wasn't as finicky. Obviously she hadn't spent much time in Las Vegas garbage pits.

He kept an eye on her, watching the way she cringed each time she picked something up with the tips of her fingers and tossed it aside. He also watched the way she watched him, as if she was afraid he'd pocket the wallet if he found it.

Maybe she *was* a bit paranoid. After all, she had one hell of a bad habit of looking at him as if he were the devil out to steal her soul. Truth be told, it wasn't her soul he wanted.

She picked up a McDonald's bag and peeked inside. After tossing that one aside, she grabbed another and went through the same examining process.

"You really think your wallet fell into a scrunched-up paper sack?" he asked.

"I don't know where it is, but I have to check everything. As far as I know, someone swiped it out of my shop, stuck it in a bag after he took out the important stuff, and tossed it in here."

"Yeah, I suppose that's a possibility. Of course, there's also the possibility that a pickpocket got it."

"A pickpocket? In Plentiful?"

"You never know."

"You rarely know anything for sure," she conceded. "For all I know, you could have pocketed it when you were in my store."

He chuckled. "Now why would I do a thing like that?"

"Who knows? Maybe *you're* a pickpocket. A thief. A no-good, dirty rotten scoundrel who preys on defenseless women."

"Maybe. Then again, I might be a nice guy with

nothing better to do at the moment than scrounge around a reeking Dumpster helping an unappreciative woman look for her wallet."

It took awhile, but a slight smile finally touched her face. "I suppose that's a . . . *possibility*."

She'd relented a bit, but he could see the doubt lurking in the emerald green depths of her eyes. Okay, so maybe he wasn't such a nice guy. Maybe he couldn't be trusted. He'd proved that in Vegas. But he was in Plentiful now, and he was trying to start a new life.

For some unknown reason, he was pretty well convinced that an itsy-bitsy redhead with a belly button ring might fit right nicely into his day-to-day activities.

"Go out to dinner with me Friday night."

Her slight smile turned to a frown. She stared at him good and hard. Hell, she seemed to find the invitation even more appalling this time around, as if he'd just risen out of a flaming hole in the ground and asked her to have his baby. At long last she shook her head. "I can't."

Paranoid and definitely stubborn. For some reason she'd made up her mind that he wasn't worth the time of day. Whether he was or wasn't, he could only take just so many rejections. He had better things to do than begging her to spend time with him, like going home to sing Elvis songs to his grizzly friends Yogi and Boo Boo.

Hoisting himself up on the side of the Dumpster, he tilted his head to look at her once again, to catch one more glimpse of the freckles bridging her nose, the stains on her clothes and cheeks, the remnants of a sticky ice cream cone plastered to flaming red curls.

Cute. Damn cute.

But he wasn't going to beg.

"See you around." He winked, and in one swift second leapt to the ground and headed for Main Street, trying not to think about the woman he was leaving behind, or the stench of rotten bananas and God knows what else that clung to his clothes.

"Wait."

A sudden grin touched his face. Scarlett must have changed her mind.

Wiping the smile from his face, he turned around slowly. All that was visible of the redhead over the top of the Dumpster were her fascinating green eyes, a thousand wild corkscrews springing every which way, and white fingers gripping the edge as she made a supreme effort to peer over the side.

Logan leaned against the brick wall on the west side of the alley and crossed his arms over his chest. "Need something?"

"No . . . well . . ." She heaved a gigantic sigh. "Oh, hell. Can you help me out of here?"

Chuckling, he headed to the Dumpster, reached over the side and slipped his hands under her arms. It wasn't intentional—well, maybe it was—but the tips of his thumbs pressed into soft, full breasts. Scarlett O'Malley felt awfully good, and he wanted to feel a whole hell of a lot more of her.

With barely any effort, and not too much struggle

on Scarlett's part, he lifted her out of the Dumpster. A big part of him was inclined to keep holding on to her, to suggest they go back to her place and shower together—just to get rid of the stench. Instead, he set her feet square on the ground, removed his hands, and once again headed for Main Street.

"Wait."

He kept on walking.

He heard her heavy sigh again. "Please."

She'd said the magic word. He turned slowly. "Need help with something else?"

"I just wanted to say thanks."

"You're welcome." He knew he should walk away because he really didn't expect anything more from her, but there was something about Scarlett that made him stay, made him want to know her better. "Need something else?" he asked.

She blew a red corkscrew away from her forehead; it fell back over her right eye. "I might be able to clear some time on my schedule for dinner Friday night."

His eyebrow rose. "Might?"

"All right," she huffed, as if it were a supreme sacrifice on her part to give in to his request. "I'm sure I can. What if I meet you at the Misty Moon at seven?"

"I'll pick you up at your place." He thought about giving her a different time—eight o'clock, maybe—just to be ornery, but they'd sparred enough for one night.

"All right. Seven o'clock. My place." Again she

blew at the unruly corkscrew dangling over her eye, but her effort was useless.

He couldn't stand to see a woman in trouble. Maybe it was only her hair giving her fits, but he felt this odd need to help her out. Okay, so maybe he felt an odd need to touch her.

He moved close and her eyes narrowed, but not before he saw a flicker of unease, possibly fear. She took a step backward as he advanced. Her paranoia was hitting hard, but he wasn't going to stop. All he wanted to do now was prove to her that she had nothing to fear from him.

One more step backward, one more, and she smacked into the Dumpster.

Logan stretched a hand out to her. She didn't flinch, she just looked uncertain, as if she had no idea what he was going to do next. Truth be told, he didn't know what he was going to do, either, not until he brushed his fingers lightly over her cheek and captured the disobedient red corkscrew between his fingers. He rubbed the surprisingly soft strands between his thumb and index finger, then swept the ringlet away from her face, tucking it back amongst all the other curls.

"Thank you," she whispered, a gentle smile forming on her lips.

"You're welcome," he whispered back. He thought it would be easy to touch her and leave, but he wanted more. He wove the fingers of both his hands into her mass of wild hair. It was softer than he'd ever imagined. Silky, just like her skin. In the dim alley light he looked down into her pretty green eyes. Doubt radiated up at him, but he saw even more in her eyes, something that scared even him.

Need.

Run, he told himself. But he'd been running for nearly a year and right now he didn't want to be anywhere else.

He looked at the freckles bridging her nose and the greasy smudge on her cheek and realized he'd been needing something in his life for a good long rime, and he had the strange, almost horrifying feeling Scarlett might be it.

He tilted her face up to meet his and her mouth parted slightly, just enough for her to lick her lips. They were wet and shiny and soft and, hell, he was wasting time thinking.

His mouth was on hers in less than a heartbeat. Gentle, he told himself. Keep it short and simple and gentle, and save the really good stuff for Friday night. But she sighed, her body relaxing into his as her hands swept up around his neck. Her hot breath spilled over his tongue. He forgot about gentle, forgot just about everything but the feel of her, the cinnamon and sugar taste of her mouth, and the high-powered electrical shocks ricocheting through his insides.

Their tongues claimed each other in a burning, lust-filled embrace and she purred, her fingers tightening about his neck as her little body rubbed up against his. Every one of his muscles tightened. He could barely breathe. And the damn buttons running up the front of his jeans almost groaned under duress.

Maybe they should go to her place for that shower after all.

"Scarlett?" he whispered against her soft, hot lips.

"Hmmm?" she murmured.

"Wanna go to your place, somewhere a little more private?"

Her fingers stilled. A second later they slid to his chest and shoved him a few inches away. Her eyes widened in sheer horror; her breasts heaved. "Oh, God, I can't believe I let you do that."

"You *let* me? Hell, Scarlett, you *encouraged* me."

"I'd never do such a thing."

"You did." He brushed his thumb lightly across her lips and she flinched, but she didn't move any further away. "I've got great hopes you'll do it again Friday night?"

"Maybe we should forget about—"

He tugged her toward him again and kissed away her refusal to go out with him. Gentle this time. Soft.

When he heard her resigned sigh he let her go, stepping back quickly before he took what he really wanted.

"See ya Friday." He winked, and the last thing he saw before walking away was a pair of bewildered green eyes peering at him through a veil of wild red curls, eyes that bewitched him—and bothered him, too.

Chapter 10

Scarlett tugged at her baseball cap to keep the denizens of the Misty Moon from seeing her sticky, ice cream-encrusted hair. She'd already doused herself with a dozen spritzes of Molly's cologne, wiped the smudges off her face, brushed some of the gunk off her jeans, and she looked somewhat presentable. Still, she pitied anyone who got too close.

Taking a quick, throat-stinging swallow of Moose Jaw, she balanced her elbows on the copper-topped bar, the place she'd been sitting for the past fifteen minutes, trying to recover from her astonishing, heart-palpitating brush with Logan.

"It wasn't just a kiss, Molly, it was a *kisssss*." Scarlett felt a strong need to reiterate this fact to Molly, who looked far too relaxed, as if she wasn't quite grasping what Scarlett had done by the Dumpster and the dire consequences of her actions. "Jeez, Molly," she whispered, leaning forward so everyone else in the bar wouldn't hear, "I have the feeling I might have rubbed up against him, you know, like I wanted more than just a kiss."

"Did you?" Molly asked, standing behind the counter drying a glass beer mug, still looking completely unruffled by Scarlett's confession.

Scarlett's eyes narrowed. "Of course not."

"Mind giving me a good reason why?"

"Because he's . . ." Scarlett sighed. "Because he might have . . ."

"Could you please speak in complete sentences?" Molly asked. "I'm having a wee bit of trouble understanding your reason for not wanting to kiss him."

"My reasons might sound irrational."

"If you're afraid they sound irrational, maybe they are."

"But what if they're not? What if he's . . . What if . . ." Scarlett sighed again.

"All right," Molly said, folding her arms on the bar and staring Scarlett in the eye. "Spill."

Scarlett ran her index finger around the ring of condensation her beer bottle had left on the bar. "Have you ever read one of those gothic romances?" she began slowly, watching Molly's eyes narrow. "You know, the kind of book where the heroine falls in love with the sexy owner of a dark and dreary yet fabulous castle but she suspects him of being a bad guy out to murder her?"

Molly plucked the beer from Scarlett's hand. "That's it, no more beer for you tonight." She shook her head. "Gothic novels? Castles? Murders? *Love?* Good God, Scarlett, what's gotten into you?"

Scarlett grabbed the beer back from Molly. "Nothing's gotten into me and it's not the beer talking, either. I'm just trying to explain why I feel the way I feel."

"You're telling me that you've fallen in love with Logan Wolfe, who you met just this morning?"

"No. I couldn't possibly fall in love that fast, even though he is gorgeous and charming and, heavens, Molly, I've never, ever been kissed that way, you know, where your heart goes pitter pat and your toes get all tingly. But in the back of my mind are all these dreadful thoughts that there's something sinister lurking behind Logan's handsome exterior."

"Such as?"

Scarlett sipped at her beer. It might be foolish saying anything more to Molly, but she'd gone this far, she might as well go even farther. "The Sleuths think Logan's a gigolo out to get Opal's money."

Molly laughed, exactly the kind of response Scarlett expected.

"I think the whole idea's pretty ludicrous, too," Scarlett said, "but I can't get those horrid little suspicions out of my mind."

"You read too many mysteries."

"Mystery's my life, it's how I make a living. I grew up with it, and let me tell you, Molly, any fictional sleuth worth his or her salt would suspect Logan, too."

"You're not a fictional sleuth."

"I realize that, but—"

"But nothing," Molly interrupted. "Your imagination's gone into overdrive and you've pushed everything you've heard out of proportion. For what it's worth, he seems like a nice enough guy."

"You've met him?"

"He was in here earlier with Larry, Steve and Adam."

"And that puts him in good stead with you?" Scarlett downed another swallow of beer to wash away the disgusting thought of Logan being with those three men.

"He threw a few darts with them, nothing more. He's a pretty lousy throw, if you ask me, but he didn't drink too much, didn't mouth off about women, he didn't fart or belch or swear, except for a few hells and damns. On top of that, he tipped good." Molly poured herself some ginger ale. "What's not to like about a guy like that?"

"That's just the problem, Molly. He's so close to perfect—well, maybe a little too charming and brash—that a woman could be totally overpowered by him. She'd lose all will, all thought, all . . . everything. *That's* what makes it so easy to think he's messed up in some way with poor, gullible Opal."

And it wasn't just his assumed involvement with Opal she was worried about. If she wanted to be really paranoid, she could bring up the missing wallet that he might or might not have stolen and the rifle he may or may not have purchased. But Molly would surely laugh, so she kept quiet and drank some more beer.

Molly sipped her ginger ale, staring at Scarlett thoughtfully, shrink to extremely mixed up patient.

"This might sound a little preachy, maybe a little condescending—"

"I can take it." Scarlett hoped.

"I know you and your friends, have helped solve a few scams here and there, and last year, even though you almost got yourself killed, you did thwart that holdup at the gas station." Molly popped a pretzel in her mouth. "The amateur detective work you do is all fine and dandy, as long as you're leading the pack, as long as there's real evidence about a crime. But sometimes there is no evidence."

Scarlett downed a hefty swallow of beer to make the ruler slap to her knuckles easier to bear.

"Sometimes," Molly continued, "those sweet old lady friends of yours dream up little intrigues because they have nothing better to do with their time. And bless your heart, Scarlett, you fall hook, line, and sinker for the stories those women cook up. If I'm not mistaken, they've cooked up this Opal story, too."

Scarlett swallowed a long gulp of beer, trying to digest all that Molly had said, when the shrink-slash-bartender decided to dish out more words of wisdom. "The way I see it, you like this Logan Wolfe and he likes you, but all your worries and suspicions are going to drive a wedge between whatever there could be between the two of you. You saw that same thing happen between your mother and Adam."

"Adam drove my mother mad," Scarlett bit out. "She had every reason to suspect him of . . . something."

"I know you believe that—"

"And one of these days I'm going to prove it."

Molly smiled, her concern evident. "I've said too much. I'm sorry."

Scarlett put a hand on Molly's when she started to wipe down the bar. "I know I obsess sometimes, that I get carried away, maybe even get worked up over nothing. I'm a lot like my mother in that respect."

"It drove her to an early grave, Scarlett. She invested all her time and energy into worrying about infidelities that didn't exist, and you've picked up where she left off. Sleuthing with your friends is perfectly fine as long as no one gets hurt, but you've spent far too many years trying to find something to pin on Adam so you can get even for what you feel he did to your mom. But you've found nothing. Don't you think it's time you stop, that you should put it all behind you and get on with your own life?"

Scarlett rubbed the back of her neck, feeling a horrid headache coming on. "The Sleuths said the same thing this morning. I know they're right. I know you're right." She sighed heavily. "I just don't know how to move on."

"Maybe you need something more important occupying your thoughts. Perhaps a man who's gorgeous and charming and makes your heart go pitter-pat? A man whose kiss isn't just a kiss, but a *kisssss?* You know, one of those gothic novel type heroes who seems a little suspicious throughout the book but always comes out shining in the end?"

Logan Wolfe in her life? Logan Wolfe a hero? He

had the to-die-for body. He had the thick wavy hair any woman would love to run her fingers through and he definitely made her heart go pitter-pat. But she wanted so much more in her hero. She wanted a man she could trust. A man who wouldn't hurt her—the way her mother had been hurt.

Could Logan possibly be the one? She'd never know if she didn't give him a fair chance, if she didn't toss all her suspicions about him in the trash.

She blew a curl off her forehead and took another swallow of beer. Okay, she'd do it. Tomorrow morning she'd be the new and improved Scarlett Mary Catherine O'Malley, who kept her nose where it belonged and didn't see evil lurking behind every door.

Well . . . at least she'd try.

Chapter 11

It had been twelve hours, thirty-seven minutes, and approximately forty-four seconds since Scarlett had given up being a snoop, and she was already bored to tears. She drummed her fingers on the stack of books sitting beside the cash register as she stared outside at the virtually empty street.

Molly, in white peasant blouse, tartan kilt, black knee socks and neon orange Nikes, lugged a box of Moose Jaw, her own special brew, into the Misty Moon. Ted Lapham swept leaves off the boardwalk in front of the Gold Nugget, and Adam walked out of the java café carrying a tall cup of coffee. He smiled and waved through shop windows at unseen people working or browsing inside. More than likely he was whistling as he made his morning rounds, playing his good cop role to the hilt.

Like him or not, Scarlett had the uncanny urge to run outside and talk to him, to ask him about the dead woman. Had he learned her identity? Had he contacted her family? But sleuthing, snooping, and getting involved in someone else's business were all a part of her past. She was turning over a new leaf and would no longer think about things like missing wallets, the identity of a dead woman, the fact that she thought Adam was a two-faced scumbag, and what, if anything, was going on between Opal and Logan.

Okay, so maybe she wouldn't stop thinking about Logan. Or his kiss. Or the fact that she wanted to taste his lips again, even though she wasn't quite sure he could be trusted.

In all honesty, it would be nearly impossible to forget any of her suspicions about anyone, but she would really, really try.

Sighing deeply, she grabbed the stack of books that needed to be shelved and headed for the miscellaneous mystery section at the far end of the parlor.

To keep from waking Toby, who was upstairs—hopefully sleeping and staying out of mischief—she tiptoed across the floor she'd scrubbed that morning, right after she'd dumped endless amounts of gnawed-on, shredded, and drool-doused paper, not to mention pulverized antique china, into the trash bin outside.

On a bottom shelf she filed a book about a modern day hunt for an immortal Jack the Ripper and a tome about an eighteenth-century pasha trying to solve the murder of twenty-two of his wives, then climbed the ladder to shelve a novel she'd ordered on an absolute whim. She stared at the words on its blazing red cover: *Come and Get It* by Rod Lichenstein. She checked out the spine and frowned. Where on earth could she file a book labeled "whodunit erotica"?

And what on earth was "whodunit erotica," anyway?

Peeking around the store to make sure no one had sneaked in and finding it all quiet, she opened the mystery to chapter one. A few lines should tell her if the book should be kept behind closed doors so her little old lady and gentleman customers wouldn't be appalled, in the hard-core crime section in the back room, or on the nightstand beside her bed.

A touch of guilty pleasure crept over her as she began to read.

> The panties were black leather. I'd seen them before, but the last time they were affixed to shapely hips. Now they lay at the bottom of the stairs, the crotch methodically cut out in a heart-shaped pattern. "Come and get it," they beckoned, and like the good dick that I am, I followed.

Not exactly the kind of stuff she was used to, but, totally engrossed already, Scarlett propped her elbows on the top rung of the ladder and kept on reading.

> I'd been trailing Jezebel Jones for days. She'd left her scent in a seedy motel on Wilshire and on one of the sound stages at Paramount. Jezebel got around. A whip here, a chain there. Some men liked her style and some men did a lot of talking while she took care of their humble little needs. Gordon Applebee was one of those talkative kind of guys, or so I'd heard. Now Gordon

Applebee was dead, throat sliced from ear to ear. He'd had the information I needed. I hoped Jezebel Jones had it now, and I was determined to find out . . . no matter what the cost.

A black leather bra lay just outside the bedroom, twisted and turned and shaped like an arrow saying "this way big boy." Naturally I complied, entering that room with only two things on my mind: a hope that someone else hadn't beaten me to Jezebel and that she was still alive.

I opened the door slowly and there she was, naked as the day she was born, spread-eagled on the bed. Her skin was pale against the black satin sheets. Her platinum hair—a sharp contrast to the brunette curls at the apex of her thighs—spilled over the pillow.

Wide eyes stared out from that cold, alabaster face. I was too late. Too damned late.

A soft laugh slipped between Jezebel's purple painted lips. "I'm not dead, darling. I'm alive. Very much alive and I have exactly what you want. All the secrets you've been looking for are here, deep inside me." She smiled wickedly. "Come, darling. The treasure is yours. All you have to do is figure out where I've buried it."

"Interesting reading?"

The nasty little book Scarlett was secretively devouring flew from her hands at the sound of Logan's voice. She grabbed for it, but it slipped through her fingers just as she toppled from the ladder. The book smacked to the floor; she plopped dead center in Logan's outstretched arms.

The Big Bad Wolfe winked. "You always greet your customers this way?"

"Not as a rule." She struggled—a little—then smiled. "Now that you've rescued me, maybe you could put me down."

"Do you have somewhere to go?"

"No, but . . . one wrong move and I could get stuck on you again."

Logan grinned. "I'll take my chances."

Scarlett breathed deeply as Logan's gaze scooted over her midriff-baring white T-shirt emblazoned with gold embroidered stars, the matching gold star clipped to her belly button ring, and her hip-hugging jeans. She wanted to push him away, yet she wanted to get even closer.

Slowly his eyes found hers again. "You always dress like the star-spangled banner?"

"I consider it my patriotic duty," she said proudly, but a sudden thought made her frown. "Why, don't you like it?"

Again he stole a glance at her hips. "I like it all— particularly your belly button ring. I also like the way your butt was wiggling when you were standing on top of the ladder."

Her eyes widened. "You were watching me?"

"I came in here to see you, and since you didn't bother turning around when the chimes rang out, I figured I'd enjoy the view."

"In spite of what you might think, I don't normally stand on ladders wiggling my butt in customers' faces, and if I'd known you were there—"

"No apologies necessary. If I didn't enjoy holding you like this, I might ask you to climb up the ladder and wiggle a little more."

"Are you always so blatantly honest?"

"You got a problem with honesty?"

"Only when it embarrasses me."

"You don't like flattery?"

"Of course I do. Behind closed doors where the rest of the world can't hear."

"We're behind closed doors now," he said, and began to nibble on the tip of her ear. Warm breath and tender kisses trailed across her cheek, and she found herself relaxing in the comfort of his arms, so content that a soft, dreamy sigh escaped her lips.

"You know, Logan," Scarlett said breathlessly, "someone could walk in at any second."

"Let them."

As if on cue, the chimes tinkled. Logan twisted to face the door, and Scarlett watched Jennie Appleton walk in, head down, deep in concentration. When her path crossed Logan and Scarlett's shadow in the miscellaneous mystery section, her head popped up. Her eyes widened when she spied them; her jaw dropped.

"Hi, Jen," Scarlett said nervously.

Jennie ducked her head. "Hello," she said nervously and scurried back to the true crime room, where she usually spent a part of every weekday.

Again, Scarlett was alone with Logan. His touch radiated through her denim jeans, through her spandex top. She could feel his thumbs making soft swirls over her thigh and the swell of her breast. Could feel his heart beating fast and heavy, just as hers was doing.

What did he want from her? Money? Sex? Everything?

Suddenly her gut instincts and all those apprehensions that had kept her from getting close to a man screamed at her to back away. "Maybe you should let me down," she said. "I've got customers to take care of—"

"Only one besides me, and I'm quite content with the service you're providing."

He was altogether too charming. "You're being a bit brash again."

"It wasn't bothering you before Jen walked into the store."

"A woman has a right to change her mind, doesn't she?"

"I suppose, but you seem to change yours every thirty seconds or so."

"That's just one of my little idiosyncrasies. Stick around me much longer and you're bound to uncover a whole lot more."

"That's a chance I'm willing to take."

Her eyes narrowed. "Why?"

"Maybe I'm lonely. Maybe I'm bored. Then again"—he kissed her lightly; she sighed once again—"maybe I like the way you feel in my arms."

Charming. So very, very charming—and she was falling much too hard. Pulling her senses together, she managed a weak smile. "I really do need to get back to work."

He shook his head and chuckled. "All right. You win."

Logan let her down easily, holding her until her five-inch heels settled solidly on the hardwood floor . . . right next to the nasty little book she'd dropped. Heaven forbid that Logan should see what she'd been reading when he sneaked into the store and took her by surprise.

"So, Logan—" She applied her toe to the edge of the book and pushed it an inch or two, hoping to secrete it away under the shelf without him noticing she was up to something. "What brings you here today?"

A silly grin formed on his face an instant before his gaze shot to the floor, to her crimson polished toenails, to the book that wasn't quite hidden. He swept it up and studied the cover, the title, and the words "whodunit erotica" on the spine. His eyes flickered up. "You weren't trying to hide this, were you?"

Her hand flew to her star-spangled chest. "Me? Why would I do that?"

"Maybe you didn't want me to know what you were reading, what had you so enthralled that you didn't even hear the chimes when I came in."

"Don't be silly." She tried to grab the book from his hands, but he gripped it tightly. "I read a broad variety of things." Again she tugged on the book, but to no avail. "It's all part of being a good businesswoman, making sure I know what's available so I can make recommendations."

"You discuss erotica with your customers?"

"It all depends on the customer." She yanked again. Logan let go, and she stumbled backward. Steadying herself quickly, she climbed the ladder and shoved the book in any old spot that was empty, then glared down at Logan. "Now, do you mind telling me what brought you here."

"Thought I'd stop by and see if you'd found your wallet."

Her wallet? She blew nervously at a wayward curl. What on earth was he talking about? And then it hit her. "Oh, the wallet." She chuckled weakly. "Would you believe I found it wedged between the cushions on my sofa?"

"So all that rummaging in the Dumpster was for nothing?"

She shrugged. "I came out with an extra dollar thirty-eight in my pocket and a new appreciation for trash men."

For sanity's sake and because she really did need to look like a busy bookseller, she climbed down from the ladder and walked to the checkout counter. She hid behind the cash register so Logan couldn't see her belly button ring.

Apparently Logan decided he should look like a book buyer and browsed the aisles, moving finally to the Jayne Mansfield-Smythe display. His long, powerful fingers stroked the covers, traced the embossed designs. His movements were slow, methodical, almost a caress, as if he were stroking a woman, not a book.

How easily she could feel those fingers whispering over her skin, dipping beneath her panties, driving her senseless.

She gripped the edge of the counter, fighting her imagination, her lustful thoughts. At last sanity returned. She became the businesswoman again. "You said you came in to ask about my wallet, but is there anything else you need?"

He looked up, and dark, spellbinding eyes settled on her face. "Thought I'd pick up the rest of the Jayne Mansfield-Smythe books."

"You've finished the first two already?"

"I'm only halfway through the first, but I'm finding the protagonist . . . interesting." He picked up a copy of *Three Penny Murder.* "Jayne's got a unique way of investigating. Not exactly legal, in most cases. Not exactly smart, either."

"Why do you say that?"

"She's got a bad habit of getting herself into sticky situations, ones most people wouldn't be able to get out of."

"The Sleuths—the three ladies who were here when you came in yesterday—say Jayne's too stupid to live, but that's what makes her intriguing to readers. She'd be awfully boring if she didn't get into trouble once in awhile, if she didn't make mistakes and then turn around and figure out how to solve her problems, as well as the case."

"But what she does would never happen in real life."

Scarlett walked out from behind the counter, took the book from Logan's hands, gathered up the next four in the series and went back to the cash register. "Some people need to escape from real life once in awhile." She opened one of the books and stared at the opening lines. "Sometimes I get so caught up in the world Juliet Bridger writes about that I forget everything else around me. Sometimes"—Scarlett laughed—"I find myself thinking like Jayne Mansfield-Smythe or wondering what she would do in certain situations."

Looking up from the words on the page, Scarlett saw a concerned frown narrow Logan's eyes, and she knew she'd said too much.

"Sounds crazy, doesn't it?"

He shook his head. "Actually, I was wondering what it is you want to escape from."

"A lot of little things." Doubts. Fears. Distrust. A whole lot of things that had messed up too many years of her life. "What about you? Don't you have things you want to escape from?"

"Yeah, but I've found I can't."

It was her turn to frown. "Want to tell me about it?"

He reached out and cupped her face, tenderly skimming her cheek with his thumb. "Not today."

"Don't you trust me?"

"No more than you trust your secrets to me, I'm afraid." He leaned across the counter and kissed away what would have been a halfhearted protest. "Besides, right now I need to get to the dump before it closes."

Scarlett rang up his books. "How about when we get together Friday night?" she asked, refusing to give up. "A little dinner, a little wine, a few confessions?"

"Maybe." He handed her cash and tucked the bag of books under his arm. "Then again," he said, walking to the door and opening it wide, "we might find other things we'd rather share."

"Such as?"

Logan winked. "Use your imagination, Scarlett. I'm sure you can think of something."

Logan strolled up the boardwalk toward his truck. He had nothing on his mind but red silk and creamy thighs, the weight of Scarlett's petite and curvy body straddling his hips, flicking her belly button ring with the tip of his tongue, then licking her flesh—all of it; all night long.

It would be hell waiting for Friday night, but wait he would.

With the mangy black cat who'd adopted him the night before prancing at his side, Logan strolled past Teton Outfitters. Only then did he think of something besides Scarlett and sex. He thought about sticking around town, maybe settling here permanently. The place had its quirks, but it also had that hot little redhead with the belly button ring.

Turning abruptly, leaving the cat waiting for him on the doorstep, Logan marched into Joe Granger's place.

The floorboards squeaked beneath his boots, and

Joe, standing behind the far counter, looked up from the catalog he was fingering through. "Didn't expect to see you back so soon."

"Me neither."

"Need another fly? How about that Glock I showed you?"

"No. Just wanted to find out if that job offer's still open."

"Yesterday you weren't interested." Joe frowned. "You always change your mind so fast?"

"Not often."

"I take it this means you plan on sticking around?"

Logan wasn't going to commit too easily. "Let's just say I don't have any immediate plans to pull up stakes."

"What changed your mind?"

"I like to fish and you know a lot of good fishing holes." Logan grabbed a Teton Outfitters baseball cap from the wall and tried it on for size.

"Scarlett O'Malley fit into the picture, too?"

Logan pulled the bill low on his brow. "Maybe."

Joe grabbed the fishing rod leaning against the wall, shoved it down his cast, and started to scratch. "Saw you and Scarlett in the park yesterday. Half the town saw you."

"So I've heard."

Refusing to get caught up in talk about himself and Scarlett, Logan dropped the cap on the counter and pulled out his wallet. "What about the job?"

"Six A.M. tomorrow sound like a good time to start?"

"I can handle that."

"Then put your wallet away. The cap comes with the job. So do the waders and any other gear you might need." Joe balanced his hands on the counter and leaned forward. "Got a couple of guys flying in tonight from Beverly Hills. Closest they've ever been to fishing is eating caviar off golden spoons."

Logan grinned. "In other words, I'm in for a rough day."

"Yeah, but I figure if you can handle Scarlett, you can handle just about anything."

Logan's eye narrowed. "What is it with you bringing up Scarlett's name all the time?"

"Just concerned."

"About her or me?"

"Both." Joe put the rod on the counter and hitched his arms over his crutches. "I've known Scarlett since she was a kid, when she pretended to be Nancy Drew and spied on everyone and everything. It was cute back then; it's not that cute any longer. People get annoyed, they complain." Joe shook his head. "She's the best baker in town, is sharp as a tack when it comes to knowing about books and authors, and God knows she's got a good heart. But getting involved with her could lead to trouble. You could hurt her; she could hurt you. Then again," Joe shrugged, "you might be just what she needs to make her forget the revenge-filled quest she's been on."

"Revenge?"

"Yeah, revenge. She's after her stepfather. Everyone in town knows it." Joe shook his head. "Scarlett and Adam never did see eye-to-eye, but things got worse when her mom died. It was an accident, nothing more, but Scarlett's spent the past ten years trying to prove that Adam was responsible."

"Was he?"

"Hell no. Adam's the best damn cop I've ever known. Keeps an eye on the people around town. Knows everyone's name, remembers birthdays and anniversaries. Hell, if someone's sick or needs help, he's the first one comes to their aid. I tell you, if he is or was guilty of *anything,* I'd know it."

Logan had thought the same thing about his last partner. Who would have guessed the guy had dealt drugs or killed a couple of guys who'd tried to stiff him? Who would have guessed that three other cops were also involved?

Logan shoved all the crap from his mind, chatted a while longer with Joe, thanked him for the job, said he'd see him at six in the morning, and headed outside into the cool afternoon breeze. The cat rubbed up against his leg and purred, then strutted along beside him as he headed for the truck.

He thought about Vegas again. He thought about dirty cops and dead cops and cops who hated his guts. He thought about Adam, all of his questions, his anger with Larry and Steve, and his warning to stay away from Scarlett.

He hadn't gotten good vibes from Adam, but in the end, Logan knew that whatever the guy did or didn't do—had or hadn't done—was none of his business. Even if he was curious about the chief of police, he'd never again pry into another cop's business.

As for Scarlett, he sure as hell didn't see her as crazy or revenge filled, although she was a constant contradiction, one moment sighing in his arms, the next moment pushing him away. Scarlett Mary Catherine O'Malley was definitely a hot little mystery, one he planned to unravel slowly, without help or advice from anyone.

Chapter 12

Ida Mae burst into A Study in Scarlett just as Scarlett flipped the OPEN sign to CLOSED. The chimes clattered and clanked as the door crashed into the dangling crystals, then slammed with a bang. Toby ran around the room, barking furiously, then dove into the pile of toys in the children's section and found something fun to gnaw on.

Obviously Scarlett's plan to hide away in her bedroom and let her thoughts run wild about Friday night's date with Logan had come to a screeching halt.

Ida Mae scurried to one of the tea tables and flopped her pudgy, cowgirl-dressed body into a delicate Chippendale chair. Considering the way Ida Mae was fanning her cheeks, it looked like Scarlett would have to put all of her personal plans on hold for quite some time.

"I need tea, Scarlett." Ida Mae's bosom rose up and down as she took several deep breaths. "Something strong, if you don't mind."

"What on earth's wrong?" Scarlett asked, locking

the door early, since customers had been few and far between all day.

"It's absolutely awful. Just awful, but I really can't talk until I've had some tea."

"Russian Roulette's probably the strongest thing I have."

Ida Mae's eyes widened. "Absolutely not. That's what you offered *him*."

Him? Ah, Logan Wolfe. What could he possibly have done to raise Ida Mae's ire now?

Ida Mae pressed a hand to her breasts and dragged in another deep breath. "If it wouldn't be any trouble, could you perhaps give me a cup of Jasmine Pearls? That private reserve you carry is awfully nice."

Not to mention expensive, but Ida Mae was obviously distressed and she definitely had something significant to share. Reformed snoops should not be anxious to hear all the low-down dirty details about anything, Scarlett thought, but curiosity got the better of her.

"Want to come into the kitchen with me while I fix the tea?" Scarlett asked, heading for the swinging door.

"I'd rather sit here, dear. I need time to catch my breath and to think about the ghastly things I saw this afternoon. It's so awful, Scarlett. Simply dreadful."

Now she just *had* to hear all the particulars. "I'll hurry with the tea," Scarlett said. "You just rest a bit, and I'll be back in a jiffy with tea and some of those lemon cookies you like so well."

Rushing into the kitchen, Scarlett haphazardly prepared the Jasmine Pearls. The water wasn't quite 184 degrees and she infused it for ninety-eight seconds rather than a full two minutes, but hopefully Ida Mae wouldn't notice. Throwing some cookies on a plate in less than her usual exquisite fashion, she raced back to Ida Mae's side. "Feeling better?"

"Much." Ida Mae munched on a cookie as Scarlett poured the tea.

"Now," Scarlett said, "are you going to tell me what happened?"

"It was so horrible, Scarlett. I still can't believe everything that I saw."

Patience.

"Take another deep breath, Ida Mae, and tell me everything."

Ida Mae's hand went dramatically to her chest once more. She took another one of her much-needed deep breaths, then a sip of the prized and pricey tea. She frowned as she stared into the cup. "Hmm, this isn't quite right, Scarlett. Maybe you didn't infuse it long enough."

"That's possible," Scarlett said in a rush. "Sorry."

Ida Mae waved off her apology. "Not to worry, dear. Perhaps you could give me a tad to take home, just in case I have nightmares about what I saw."

"Sure. I'd be happy to." Anything to get her to spill her guts.

Another sip. Another munch of cookie, and Ida Mae at last seemed ready to talk. "I suppose . . . oh, goodness, I almost forgot."

Scarlett heaved a sigh as Ida Mae dug around in her fringed, black-and-white cowhide purse and pulled out a handkerchief. "I picked this up from the floor yesterday, thinking it was mine. But obviously it's not, since the initials are E.G." Ida Mae dropped the hankie on the table. "Must have been one of your mother's."

"I don't think so." Scarlett examined the plain white linen and the roughly embroidered letters. "My mother edged her handkerchiefs in lace and embroidered them with roses."

"Then maybe it belonged to the woman who died." Ida Mae grinned. "There, we've solved that much of that mystery. Jane Doe's initials are E.G., just like your mother's. But, be that as it may, I've more important things to tell you right now."

Scarlett didn't want to think about anything but the initials and what they could mean, but Ida Mae plucked the handkerchief out of her hand, tossed it across the table, and leaned in close.

"Mildred told you about the rifle that Logan Wolfe character bought at Teton Outfitters?"

Scarlett nodded, concentrating on the current topic of conversation now that Logan's name was once again mentioned.

"*Well,* there was something fishy about that man's movements. I couldn't sleep all night. I just kept seeing that rifle—"

"It could have been a fishing pole," Scarlett said.

"Oh, no, I know a rifle when I see one."

"But it was wrapped in brown paper."

"You'll believe me after I've told you everything. Ghastly. Just ghastly." One more sip of tea. One more bite of cookie. "I got up this morning—well, I suppose it was closer to noon, since I tossed and turned most of the night and didn't get to sleep until five. Anyway, I drove over to Opal's to see if *he* was there, and sure enough, that monstrous black truck of his was backed up as close as it could possibly get to one of the side doors. Obviously I didn't want him to see me, so I parked in the trees, got my binoculars out—not my special night vision ones, of course, but my regular ones—and watched the house.

"I suppose half an hour went by before *he* propped open the door, and then he dragged out a carpet. It was long, and all rolled up, and it looked really, really heavy, like something was rolled up inside of it." Ida Mae paused for a sip of tea, her hand shaking as she lifted the cup to her mouth. She stared at Scarlett over the top. "What do you think could have been in there?"

Scarlett wasn't about to speculate. "I don't know. What do you think?"

Ida Mae's eyes rolled. "*Opal,* for heaven's sake. It was Opal—a *dead* Opal—inside that carpet. I know it as sure as I know my own name."

Sadly, that was the answer Scarlett had expected from Ida Mae. She didn't want to believe it. No, she *didn't* believe it, but still she wanted to hear more.

"What else did you see?"

"A dark spot on the carpet. Not a little spot, either. Must have been the size of one of those gigantic pumpkins Chuck Lee enters in the county fair. You know. *Huge*. It was a burgundy color." Ida Mae frowned. "No, that's not right. It was darker than that. Burgundy mixed with dark brown." Her eyes widened as she stared at Scarlett. "I'm sure it was blood."

This wasn't sounding good.

"What happened next?"

"He hoisted the rolled-up rug into the back of his truck, went into the house once more and came out again with a rifle, and this time it wasn't wrapped in brown paper. It was in his hand, right in plain sight and looking bigger than all get out and quite deadly through my high-powered binoculars."

Scarlett grabbed a lemon bar and plunged it into her mouth, chewing thoughtfully. Miserably. "Okay, tell me what he did after that."

"He closed and locked the door, put the rifle in the cab of his truck, and took off."

Another lemon bar found its way to Scarlett's mouth as she contemplated all she'd just heard. After she swallowed, she blew a stray curl off her forehead. It promptly fell back in place. "You didn't see any stains on Logan's clothes, did you? Something that might have looked like . . . blood?"

"He was dressed in black, so it would have been impossible to detect any blood. Even if he hadn't been dressed that way, he could have killed Opal, wrapped her in that carpet, cleaned up the mess and showered and changed clothes before lugging the body out to his truck." Ida Mae took another sip of tea, her hands still shaking. "Poor Opal. Poor, poor Opal."

Scarlett propped her elbows on the table and shoved her fingers into her hair. *Think,* she told herself. *Think.* There had to be other explanations for what Ida Mae had seen.

But what?

"Did you see where Logan went after he left?" Scarlett asked.

Ida Mae shook her head. "I didn't feel comfortable following him. Who would, under the circumstances? No, I just waited until he was good and gone, until I couldn't see any more of the dust his truck tires kicked up, and then I got out of the car and crept to the house to see what I could see through the windows, making sure I didn't touch anything—just in case."

"Did you see anything?"

"Nothing out of the ordinary. Everything looked neat as a pin. Too neat. You know—almost unlived in. I never did like Opal's decorating style, but it's really not fair saying anything negative about the dead."

"She might not be dead. We can't jump to conclusions."

"Maybe you can't, but I've already made up my mind."

Not surprising.

"After I peeked through all the windows I could get to and checked to see if there were any unlocked doors or windows," Ida Mae continued, "I went to the garage. Opal's car was there and you know as well as I do that she never goes anywhere without that Mercedes. But there it was, big and silver and expensive. And Opal was nowhere to be found."

Thump. Thump. Thump.

Scarlett jumped half out of her chair. Ida Mae sloshed tea across the tablecloth. Both women twisted around to see who was banging on the front door, and Adam Grant stared back.

"What's he doing here?" Ida Mae whispered.

"Probably wants a free scone or two. I can't think of any other reason for Adam to come calling on me."

"I guess we should let him in so I can tell him about Opal. We can give him that handkerchief, too."

Scarlett clutched Ida Mae's hand before the wannabe cowgirl got out of her chair. "Wait. Let me think about this a moment."

"Think about what?"

"About whether or not we should give him the handkerchief, but mostly, whether or not we should tell him what you suspect."

"Of course we should tell him."

Scarlett shook her head. "I think I should check things out first."

"This is murder, Scarlett. It's not someone being scammed. You can't walk up to Logan Wolfe and ask him if he killed poor, dear Opal."

"And if we tell Adam what you saw and it turns out to be something innocent, he's going to think we're crazier than he already thinks."

"I know what I saw."

Scarlett was sure Ida Mae had seen something. The question was, *What?* The immediate problem, however, was that Scarlett didn't trust Adam and never had. She couldn't possibly let *him* check this out. As for the handkerchief, she didn't feel comfortable giving Adam anything.

Thump. Thump. Thump.

Scarlett looked at Ida Mae. "Don't say a word. Please."

"You're sure?" Ida Mae asked, looking a tad skeptical.

"Positive."

Ida Mae sighed. "All right. But I'm not liking this."

Scarlett went to the door, unlocked it and let Adam in. "What the hell are you up to, Scarlett?" He barged into the room, eyes narrowed, his charming façade hard-edged and angry.

"I haven't got the faintest idea what you're talking about."

"Don't give me that shit. You're the talk of the town . . . *again.* Damn it, Scarlett, do you have to cause a scene everywhere you go?"

Scarlett shrugged, since she really had no idea which particular scene he could be referring to. She offered Adam a bit of an innocent smile as she went to the antique hutch, where she kept a few fresh scones, and lifted the glass lid covering the tray. "Would you like a scone, Adam? Huckleberry? Cinnamon raisin, maybe?"

"I'm not interested in the goddamn scones."

"Calm down, Adam," Ida Mae said. "You're going to have a coronary."

Adam turned on Ida Mae. "Butt out. This is between my daughter and me."

"Yeah, it *is* between you and me," Scarlett fired back. "So if you want to yell, direct your anger at me, not Ida Mae. And while we're at it, don't call me your daughter. Any connection you and I had died along with my mother. Remember her? The woman you pushed over the edge."

Adam shook his head and chuckled. "You're so like your mother. I loved her, but she was stubborn, meddling, and crazy. It took years for the talk about her to die down and now it's starting all over again. It's not just your meddling into anything and everything— even when it's none of your business—it's also crap like you pulled yesterday."

"Yesterday?"

"Those antics in the park and again last night in and out of that Dumpster."

Scarlett's eyes narrowed. She didn't think anyone had seen her escapade in the alley.

"Yeah, I know about that," Adam said. "People see things, they talk, and when it has to do with you it gets back to me. I hear you've been asking people about Jane Doe, too, when I specifically told you I had everything under control."

"I talked to Bill Rogers at the gas station and Nellie at the café, hoping they might have seen her around. But that's it."

"That's two people too many," Adam fumed. "Word spreads. Things get blown out of proportion and all of a sudden people in town are dredging up memories of your mother and the way she asked everyone if I was having an affair."

"Were you?" Scarlett asked bluntly.

"I told you. I loved your mother, and your antics are muddying her name—again. Is that what you want?"

"Is it my mother's name you're worried about, or your own?"

Scarlett could see the muscles working in Adam's jaw as he clamped his teeth together in anger. "I don't have time to go around defending your little sexual escapades *or*, for that matter, getting you and your cohorts out of trouble. So do me a favor." He stared down both Scarlett and Ida Mae. "Keep your private life private, and keep your nose out of things that aren't your business." With that, he turned on his heels and left the shop, slamming the door behind him.

Scarlett flicked the dead bolt and slipped the chain lock in place, then leaned against the door and stared at Ida Mae. "I think it was a good idea we didn't tell him your suspicions about Opal."

Ida Mae plucked a cookie crumb from the plate and popped it into her mouth. "Did you get the sense he was more uptight than usual? That it's not just our snooping that's getting to him?"

"Yeah, something's got him riled."

"You don't suppose . . . no, that's not possible."

"What's not possible?"

"Well, I have it on good authority that he was playing darts with Logan Wolfe last night at the Misty Moon, and yesterday, before Logan bought the rug and the rifle, I saw them huddled around the gun counter at Teton Outfitters."

Scarlett didn't want to hear this, but still she said, "Your point being?"

"Maybe, just maybe, Adam was in on Opal's murder and with the lot of us snooping around and asking questions, he's afraid he's going to get caught."

"I've never cared for Adam," Scarlett admitted. "I despise him, in fact. I'm sure he drove my mother crazy and I'm positive he did something that made her drive off into the mountains that night she died. But I can't believe he's a murderer."

"You're going to check out my suspicions, though, aren't you?"

Scarlett gave the question a second's thought. She'd sworn off snooping, but she'd known that promise could never last. "Of course I'm going to check into it."

"And what about Opal? You can't forget about her."

"I haven't forgotten about Opal."

"Or Logan Wolfe's involvement?"

Scarlett let out a hefty sigh, overcome with doubt and suspicion once again. "I definitely haven't forgotten about Logan Wolfe."

Chapter 13

The dump was ten miles out of town at the end of a remote dirt road. Tall pines, aspen, and groves of willow camouflaged the site, making the surrounding area as pristine as the rest of the valley. Leaves were beginning to turn amber, yellow and burgundy as late summer rushed toward fall. It was beautiful, serene, and a great place to go if you wanted to hide something—like a body.

It wasn't, however, a smart place to go at dusk. What the people of Plentiful considered garbage was manna for the wildlife population, especially the bears. Black ones. And grizzlies, too. They especially liked foraging through garbage.

At night.

In the dark.

And dark was coming fast.

Scarlett sat behind the wheel of her faded red Jeep, thankful she had bought a hard top instead of the rag top model, and that she was safely ensconced inside—for now.

Going to the dump might be pure folly, but Logan

had told her that he had to get to the dump before closing. His reasons for going could be entirely innocent. Then again, they could be wholly and completely appalling. Before she left this creepy place, she hoped to know which reason was the right one.

Why, oh why, weren't her thoughts about Logan a turnoff? Why did she like him even though he spent time with Adam? And why, in spite of her doubts and suspicions, did she still find him attractive and interesting and unbelievably desirable?

Worse yet, why did she want to hop in the sack with him?

Either she believed, deep down inside, that he was innocent, or she was missing a few screws for wanting to have down and dirty sex with a killer.

Sighing heavily, she drew Ida Mae's binoculars to her eyes and surveyed the area for anything that might be dangerous. When her surroundings looked safe, she scanned the dump itself. Old, ripped and dirty mattresses were scattered about, as well as discarded couches and broken-down recliners. There were thousands of black, white and dark olive plastic trash bags, and not for the first time she realized that coming here had probably been a huge mistake. Not only was it risky but finding one rolled-up carpet in a massive debris pit could be next to impossible, especially if the man who'd dumped it here didn't want it to be found.

After taking one more scan of the landscape and finding it reasonably harmless, she climbed out of the Jeep, zipped up her navy sweatshirt, and headed for the pit, clutching binoculars in one hand and a long-handled shovel in the other. It wasn't her intention to dig around in the slop—she'd had enough of that last night in the Dumpster. No, the shovel was the best defensive weapon she could come up with on short notice. And she'd use it if necessary.

A chill wind blew through the trees, and, as the sun dropped further in the sky, dark, eerie shadows crept across the land. She had half a mind to run back to the Jeep and get the hell out of there, but she was only a few feet from the edge of the pit and curiosity got the better of her. She had to know if Logan Wolfe had dumped a body here.

More than that, she had to know if she'd kissed a killer—and enjoyed it so much that her toes had tingled.

When she reached the perimeter, she started her search, hoping she could visually check out every square foot from this vantage point before darkness forced her to stop. Using the binoculars, she scanned the dump methodically from right to left to right. Two minutes went by. Five. She needed to be thorough, or at least as thorough as she could be without getting down in the trenches.

Behind her she heard the rustle of brush. *Swish-swish. Swish-swish.* An icy shiver ran up her spine. She tried not to breathe or move. Instead, she concentrated her efforts on trying to think of all those things she'd been taught to do if she ever encountered a bear. Unfortunately, she couldn't think of anything to do but twist her head slowly and peek over her shoulder.

The tips of the willows waved back and forth. *Swish-swish. Swish-swish.*

She could hear heavy steps on the ground. *Thump-thud. Thump-thud.*

The earth beneath her feet began to shake. Or was that nerves?

She swallowed hard. What now? She could run for the Jeep, but she'd been taught that running wasn't the smartest thing to do if you encountered a bear. The last thing she wanted now was to call attention to herself and make the bear's ears perk up. That could make him bare his teeth, and they'd be big and long and vicious.

Not a good idea to move . . . she hoped.

She could almost hear the seconds ticking by on her watch as the animal in the willows moved closer. Closer. *Swish-swish. Swish-swish.* Her eyes widened when something brown and furry lumbered out of the tall greenish-red reeds. Something big and ugly and—gawky—emerged from its hiding place. A bull moose. Huge, to be sure. Deadly if provoked, but he was only interested in the fresh tips of the willows, not in Scarlett.

Slowly she backed away, giving the moose plenty of room. She'd moved maybe twenty feet when the massive animal made his way back into the thick stand of willows, and Scarlett turned again toward the piles of trash.

Eyes right. Eyes left. It seemed useless, and then . . . she saw a roll of carpet behind a discarded, doorless refrigerator.

Once more she put the binoculars up to her eyes, moving a little further to the left for a better look. She stopped when a pair of bright red eyes stared back at her.

Oh, God.

A set of very sharp teeth appeared through the lenses. Then another set, snarling beneath another pair of bright red eyes.

Coyotes. Not too big but dangerous all the same, especially when hungry, especially when provoked.

One of them growled at her while the other buried his nose into the rolled carpet, trying to push it open to get at whatever was inside.

Scarlett saw the dark reddish-brown stain, the size of a prize-winning pumpkin, just as Ida Mae had said. One of the coyotes saw it, too, and sniffed at the spot, clawed at it, while the other continued to growl and snarl and kept his eyes on the crazy red-head who'd invaded their territory.

What were they so intent on getting? Scarlett wondered. A whole lot of horrid visions ripped through her mind, one in particular—a rich old lady who drove a silver Mercedes.

That did it. She was getting out of this place.

She ran for the Jeep, tossed the shovel into the back and climbed into the driver's seat, slamming the door behind her. She smacked down the lock and, with shaking fingers, grabbed onto the steering wheel and held on tight. She took one deep breath, then another, letting the air in slowly and out slowly, until she was somewhat calm. She started the engine, released the brake, and shoved the vehicle into first. An instant later she peeled up the dirt road, leaving a cloud of dirt and dust and gravel behind her. The sooner she got home, the better.

Night was just settling over the nineteenth-century town when she reached the city limits. Lights popped on right and left. The Mischievous Moose mounted outside his namesake emporium seemed to wink at her as she drove by, saying, "That'll teach you to go prowling through a dump two nights in a row." Music poured out of the Misty Moon Saloon. It was Patsy Cline singing "Crazy," and the title seemed pretty darn appropriate right now.

Another block and she saw her own pretty Victorian, its scallops and scrolls, its turrets and banisters and siding painted salmon, and teal, and cream. Home had never looked so inviting, but home wasn't where she wanted to be right now.

Pressing her foot on the gas pedal, she sped out of town toward Grizzly Hollow, toward Logan Wolfe.

Crazy? Definitely. *A snoop?* Oh, yeah. But both things ran in the family, so why try to change now? Fortitude ran in the family, too, and before this night was over she was bound and determined to find out what Logan Wolfe was up to—if anything.

Logan stood at the window, looking across the yard. He could have sworn he'd seen the flicker of car lights through the pines, but everything was dark. The moon and stars hid behind the clouds. The wind

was still. Even Yogi and Boo Boo, the bears who visited him nightly, were absent.

He'd come here for peace and quiet, for solitude
and escape, which was exactly what he was getting.
But tonight he no longer wanted to be alone.

Snagglepuss rubbed against Logan's pants leg. The
cat was a poor excuse for companionship. He was
male, for one; he was furry; and he clawed.

Logan wanted a petite woman with red hair. He
wouldn't even mind if she clawed or scratched—at
the right time, in the right place. Unfortunately, it appeared he'd have to settle for the cat.

The scrawny animal no longer resembled the
mangy thing that had followed him around in town.
Since finding its way into Logan's truck and sneaking
into the cabin, the cat had had a bath and developed
a taste for Moose Jaw. Now he wanted to be king of
the hill.

Snagglepuss stretched and purred. Logan swept
the tomcat into his arms and scratched the soft, per-
fumed fur on top of the cat's de-flea'd head.

"What do you think?" Logan asked his newfound
friend. "Was I imagining those car lights?"

Snagglepuss yawned, then burrowed his head
against Logan's palm and begged to be scratched and
petted a little more. So much for conversation.

Squinting, Logan stared into the darkness again,
hoping to see the lights. But he was alone, with only
the birds and the squirrels and other assorted animals
for company. Why they flocked toward him was a

mystery. The fact that some of the creatures liked his singing was a shock.

Logan dropped Snagglepuss on the end of the black leather couch, grabbed his guitar, and slouched beside his feline friend. "What do you want to hear? 'Jailhouse Rock'? 'Love Me Tender'?"

Snagglepuss dug his front claws into Logan's thigh and arched his back.

"I take it that means you're not a fan of the King?"

The cat narrowed his eyes. A moment later he leapt off the couch, sauntered toward the bedroom, and hid under the bed. "Some friend you are," Logan called after him. "Eat my pot roast, drink my beer, and scratch the hell out of me when I give you a bath. The least you could do is listen to me sing."

Wallowing in boredom that would thankfully end tomorrow at 6 A.M. when he started his new job, Logan picked at the strings of his guitar and warbled a lousy first line of "Heartbreak Hotel." He'd just gotten "down to the end of Lonely Street" when the phone rang.

He put the guitar on the coffee table and crossed the room to grab the cordless. "Wolfe." If it was a salesman hoping Logan would sign up for a blasted high-interest credit card, maybe that one word—growled—would scare him off.

"Brusque as ever, aren't you?"

The sound of his old friend's voice brought a smile to Logan's face. "Some things don't change," Logan said, going to the refrigerator and grabbing a bottle of Moose Jaw. "How ya doin'?"

"You know how it is. A stabbing here, a shooting there. Keeps me busy." Even through the phone, Logan could hear his first partner, Detective Nick Considine, chomping on a wad of gum, the bad habit he'd picked up when he'd quit the fouler habit of smoking. "How about you?"

"The bears haven't eaten me yet." Logan twisted off the bottle cap and took a swallow of beer, wondering what this call was all about. Nick wasn't a big talker, and he wouldn't be socializing if he didn't have something on his mind. "So, what's up?"

"When the hell you gonna come back to work?"

"Never."

"You gotta."

"Don't think so."

"Look, Logan, my last partner got promoted and they stuck me with a new guy who doesn't know shit. I swear he's gonna piss his pants the first time someone looks at him cross-eyed, and I'm gonna end up dead."

"I recall you saying the same thing about me fifteen years back."

"Nah, I said you were a mama's boy fresh out of diapers. Changed my mind first time you saved my ass."

"Yeah, well, I hate to break it to you, Nick, but I'm not saving your ass in the future."

Nick chomped long and hard on his gum. "You did what had to be done."

"You ever rat on another cop? You ever turn traitor on your friends?"

"Friends? They were assholes who got what they deserved."

"I was godfather to Jim Boone's little boy. You think that kid will ever want anything from me after I helped send his dad to prison?"

"Jim hurt his kid, not you. He hurt his wife, his friends, his family. Same goes for the other three guys. Bad cops don't deserve to wear a badge and good cops shouldn't quit the force."

Logan took another swig of Moose Jaw as he walked to the window and looked out into the dark. He wished he could forget what had happened, but the fact that he'd turned traitor was eating him alive. "Half the guys on the force don't trust me," he said, "and I'm not going to spend the next thirty years of my life trying to convince people that what I did was right when I don't believe it myself."

"You're a cop, Logan. The best damn cop I've ever known. Nerves are still a little raw since all the crap came down, but it'll settle soon enough. New guys will start. Old guys will forget."

"I'm not going back to Vegas. I'm not going back to being a cop."

The sound of Nick's gum chomping rang through the phone. "I give you another month of that sedentary life and you'll be bored as hell. By December you'll be on the phone to the chief asking for your job back."

"I already got a new job."

"Doin' what?"

"Fishing guide. I'm taking a bunch of city slickers out first thing in the morning."

Nick laughed. "You just learned how to fish yourself."

"You spend half a year doing nothing but fly fishing, you get to be pretty damn good."

"You're a cop, Logan, not a fishing guide. Always have been and always will be."

"Not any more. That life's over." And God how he missed it.

They chatted a few more minutes, Logan promising to send Nick a case of Moose Jaw, Nick swearing he'd check back in November to see just how bored Logan had gotten with his newfound career.

When the conversation ended, Logan walked back to the kitchen and hung up the phone. Snagglepuss rubbed at his pants legs again, his motor purring on high gear.

"What? You want some beer?"

The cat meowed loudly and pranced to his food and water bowls. Sitting on his haunches, he stared at Logan, his little pink tongue peeking out of his mouth, ready to lap up some brew. Logan dumped a speck of his Moose Jaw in a clean bowl, set it on the floor, and Snagglepuss dug in.

With the cat appeased for the moment, Logan went back to his guitar and sang "Are You Lonesome Tonight?" If he were to answer right now he'd have to say yeah.

He put down the guitar and picked up *Two Murders Are Better than One*. Maybe the antics of a busty blonde could get him out of his feeling-sorry-for-himself mood. But as he read he realized it wasn't a busty blonde that slapped him out of the blues but the memory of a cute little redhead with a damn fine belly button.

Scarlett parked in the thick copse of lodgepole pine that surrounded Logan's cabin and flipped off the parking lights. Climbing out of the car, she shut the door quietly behind her and set out for Logan's place. Aiming her flashlight at the ground, she crept through the dense forest, pushing aside prickly pine boughs and tiptoeing around anything that might go *snap, crackle,* or *pop.*

Coming out here like this was probably the craziest thing she'd ever done in her life, but spying seemed the best way to find out what Logan did in his retirement hours.

She reached Grizzly Hollow in just a couple of minutes but stayed under cover when she saw lights on in the rustic cabin. The place didn't look much different than it had twenty years ago when she'd wanted to be Nancy Drew and sneaked away from school to watch Pete Hall, the mysterious hermit who'd owned this place.

Some people said the only friends Pete had ever had were the wildlife. Rumors thrived that the house had mystical qualities, and that whoever lived there could commune with nature. Scarlett didn't believe a word of it.

When it came right down to it, the place was just

a cabin, like so many of the others that had been slapped together around Plentiful before the rich and famous had turned the town and its surroundings into a summer and winter tourist haven. It was built of logs, weathered now and in need of a face-lift. It had a river rock chimney, and a thin stream of pale gray smoke rose from it and disappeared into the nighttime sky. It didn't look at all mystical; it looked lonely and forlorn.

Scarlett shivered. The temperature had dropped, the wind had picked up, and the clouds were skittering away. It was going to be a cold night—but no one ever said detective work was a piece of cake.

Tucking her flashlight under her arm, she rubbed her hands together for warmth. If she were smart she'd knock on Logan's door, say she'd dropped by for a visit, and plunk herself in front of his fire. But tonight she was Jayne Mansfield-Smythe, braving the elements—no matter how foolhardy—so she could get the goods on her man.

Staying close to the trees, Scarlett circled the cabin to find the best location for her undercover operation. There were two small windows and a door on the front of the cabin, but clomping onto the porch would call attention to her surveillance. The best thing to do would be to stay on the dirt and pine needles, which softened the sound of her movements.

The back of the cabin looked identical to the front, without the porch. Through the window she could see a chrome-and-glass kitchen table, a shiny black fridge, stove and microwave, and a tiny glimpse of the living room. Definitely not a good vantage point, unless she wanted to determine Logan's eating habits.

The chimney side of the house had three windows, a small, opened one that looked like it might be positioned inside a shower stall, one looking directly into the bedroom, the other into the living room. Not only did that one offer a clear view of the main room in the house but through it she could also see the bedroom and its all-black king-sized bed.

That, she decided, was the perfect place to play Peeping Tom.

Moving silently, she made her way toward the house, keeping a sharp eye on the windows and front door for any sudden movement. What she was going to look for when she got to the house was anybody's guess. Jane Doe's wallet, of course. Maybe a rifle or a list of female suckers who could be hoodwinked with little effort by a handsome hunk. Then again, she might find Opal's will or an instruction book from Murder, Inc.

Scarlett laughed. Who was she fooling? She'd come here tonight hoping to find that the man who turned her on was a man she could trust.

A silhouette crossed between the window and the light from a table lamp, and Scarlett dashed behind the lone tree in the clearing. Swallowing hard, she peered around the cottonwood's trunk and stole a glance at the shadowy figure. Logan stood in front of the window, looking around as if he'd heard something. She'd tried to be quiet, but maybe he was trained to listen for near silent footsteps in the night.

Maybe that was in Chapter 7 of Murder, Inc.'s handbook.

She wondered if the black polo shirt that hugged Logan's chest and the black jeans he wore were recommended in Chapter 8. If so, a woman probably wrote the text, a woman who knew how to dress a good-looking thug.

When Logan turned and walked away, Scarlett sneaked out from behind the tree, taking one step and then another closer to the house.

Damn if Logan didn't come back to the window and damn if she didn't have to dart behind the tree again and sneak a peek around the trunk.

Logan swung a guitar in front of him, which was the last thing Scarlett expected. He swiveled his hips around and around and around, adding a wicked pelvic thrust here and there. Scarlett sighed. Logan's Elvis routine was very, very nice. Of course, what he was doing could be in Chapter 13: Sensual Ways to Distract a Spy. Maybe he'd sensed her behind the tree. Maybe he was trying to mesmerize her, to divert her attention until he could come up with his own plan of attack. If that was his intention, the slow, sexy roll of his hips was working quite well.

And then he strummed the guitar. He might as well have dragged his fingernails across a blackboard, Scarlett thought, as a shiver raced up her spine. Did he really think he could play? The second note twanged loud and sharp. A coyote howled in the distance. On the third strum Logan sang, sounding a lot like one of Ida Mae's old and warped records.

Scarlett frowned as she listened somewhat reluctantly to "Jailhouse Rock." A raven swooped down from the top of a pine and landed on the ground in front of the window, as if he'd come for the show. A couple of magpies winged their way over the house and settled on the telephone wire not more than ten feet from Logan's stage. Even a squirrel peeked over the top of the roof.

Maybe there were some mystical qualities to this place, after all. Or maybe it was Logan's animal magnetism, which had attracted her in spite of everything she suspected.

When Logan finished his tune—at last—he stared out the window and grinned. Then, as if the show he'd already put on hadn't been enough, he raised a fisted hand toward his mouth—was that supposed to represent a microphone?—and drawled, "Thank you. Thank you, very much."

Scarlett giggled. It was an accident. A completely ridiculous mistake for a spy to make, and she knew another giggle was ready to burst out. She clapped a hand over her mouth just as Logan flipped on the outside lights, pressed his nose to the window and stared out. He looked right. He looked left. Finally he shook his head and walked away.

She'd fallen for that walking-away ploy once before. This time she waited until the count of twenty. When Logan didn't return to the window, she hunched down low and ran toward the chimney side of the house.

Crouching beneath the window, Scarlett listened

for any sounds from inside. Except for the real Elvis singing "You're the Devil in Disguise," all was quiet. Slowly she stretched up just high enough to peek through the window and saw Logan lounging on a black leather sofa. He was barefoot, and his legs were propped up on a chrome-and-glass coffee table, ankles crossed.

Nice toes; nice feet, with just a sprinkle of dark hair atop the arch. They kept time with the music, and she couldn't help but smile.

Spying definitely had its up side.

A black cat leapt up on the back of the couch and stretched out behind Logan's head. It hovered over his shoulder, as if it, too, wanted to read *Two Murders Are Better than One,* which Logan read by the light from an Elvis Presley-does-*Blue Hawaii* ceramic lamp.

She tore her gaze from Logan and did a quick scan of the room. Nothing out of the ordinary, except for all the Elvis stuff—a *G.I. Blues* clock hanging on the wall, an Elvis sitting in a pink Cadillac cookie jar, and a massive green neon Elvis sign mounted over the fireplace. But she saw no rifle. No brass knuckles were displayed on the coffee table. And no Murder Inc. handbook sat out in the open.

The living room blended into the kitchen. Half a dozen empty bottles of Moose Jaw beer sat in a straight, orderly line on top of the bar; a few small bowls for the cat sat on the floor.

Other than that, the two rooms were fairly stark. Even the bedroom, which she could see from this vantage point, looked rather sparse. Obviously a man who liked to travel light, just in case he needed to make a quick getaway.

Five minutes must have gone by before Logan put the book down on the couch, stood up and stretched, making the fabulous muscles in his arms bunch and bulge. Scarlett held her breath and watched in awe.

He walked toward the bedroom, pulling his black polo shirt over his head as he moved. Scarlett took a deep breath and let it out slowly, fogging the glass as she stared. She quickly wiped a peephole-size portion of the window with her index finger, not wanting to miss a second of Logan's striptease.

Even though she'd cleared the condensation from the window, getting a perfect view was difficult, but what she saw of Logan's back side was utterly amazing. His skin was tanned a deep, intense bronze. His shoulders were broad, tapering down to slim waist and hips.

Like a basketball player, he tossed the shirt into a hamper on the far side of the room. Watching him was sheer pleasure, so blissful that the blood rushing through her veins turned to warm honey, heating her chilled nose and toes.

When Logan's fingers dove for the waistband on his Levi's, she knew what was coming next—he was going to slowly unzip his jeans, torturing her, teasing her, making the warm honey inside her boil and bubble. Maybe she shouldn't look. Okay, maybe she should. This was a stakeout, after all, and she couldn't leave any stone unturned.

Standing just inside the bedroom door, with the light from Elvis-does-*Blue-Hawaii* shining on his back, Logan pulled his jeans off one leg at a time. Just the right amount of dark hair was scattered over his thighs and calves, and, good heavens, the muscles in his legs were just as amazing as the ones in his back. It was all she could do to breathe. What on earth would come over her when he turned around?

Black boxers settled low on his hips, and when he twisted to the left she caught her first glimpse of a scar ripping from his shoulder blade toward his tailbone.

A lump caught in her throat as she thought of the unbearable pain he must have gone through when he'd been injured. She pictured the blood and Logan lying in a dark alley, close to death. If he was a killer she shouldn't care—but she did care, more than she ever dreamed possible.

He strolled toward the bathroom, and Scarlett quietly inched her way to the bedroom window for a better view—and what a view it was. Logan's shoulder and arm muscles flexed when he opened the shower door and turned on the water. She could picture him wet and slippery—black hair slicked back from his chiseled features, water swirling down his chest, over his belly button, and delicious places further south. It was ridiculous of her to want to steal into that shower with him, but she not only wanted to *see* that body wet and slippery but she wanted to *feel* it, too.

Steam filled the shower stall, and heat crept up

Scarlett's cheeks, turning into sizzling flames when Logan's fingers dipped under the waistband of his shorts. This was it. The moment when she really should turn away. She could get arrested for this, thrown into jail, but what a memory she'd take with her.

Thwack!

The bathroom door slammed shut, blocking Logan's naked body completely from view.

Disappointed, she sighed heavily and then got back to reality. Now was the time to make her move. Jayne Mansfield-Smythe wouldn't miss this opportunity to get inside a suspicious man's cabin and see what she could find. Maybe, just maybe, Logan had Jane Doe's wallet hidden somewhere, or evidence proving he'd done away with Opal, or, better yet, something that would prove he was just a nice guy, a normal guy—albeit a normal guy who had the body of Atlas and a scar on his back that left her wondering if someone had tried to cut him in half with a machete.

She shivered at the thought, then shuddered again when Logan's singing exploded through the open bathroom window. He was doing his Elvis impersonation again, ripping up the still and quiet night with "A Whole Lotta Shakin' Goin' On."

Before she could come up with a vision of what Logan might be shakin' in the shower, she made her way toward the front door, inching across the porch as quickly and quietly as her tennis shoes would allow.

One twist of the knob told her the front door was locked. A second later frustration hit when she tried one window and then the other, only to find them shut good and tight. Slipping off the porch, she crept to the window beside the chimney. She managed to work her fingers under the loose wooden sash and tried to lift it.

And then she heard the sound in the bushes.

Swish, swish. Swish, swish.

Her jaw tightened. The last thing she needed was another bull moose in her life, especially now. All it had to do was make some kind of horrid noise, bring Logan running from the shower to see what the hell was going on, and she'd be history.

"Go away," she whispered.

Swish, swish. Swish, swish.

She ignored the moose and worked on the window some more. Too many coats of old paint had pretty much sealed it shut, but it gave a little. With just the right amount of wiggle and pressure, she should be able to . . .

Grrrrrr.

Oh, God.

Scarlett swallowed hard. That growl hadn't come from a moose. She twisted her head and looked behind her. Two pair of beady eyes glared at her. Two sets of vicious, nasty, vile, flesh-tearing teeth gaped out of wide open and drooling jaws. Two massive brown bodies with humps on their shoulders stood on all fours in the clearing, and they looked like they just might charge.

Grizzlies. Gigantic, ferocious, man-eating grizzlies.

Scarlett tried to gulp, but nothing would go down; she was too petrified to scream.

What to do. What to do.

If she stood perfectly still they might ignore her and go back where they'd come from. Then again, they might charge, then devour her bit by tasty bit.

With her back against the cabin, with her green eyes attempting to stare down the beasts, she shoved her fingers under the window and tried to lift, but the window wouldn't budge. She tried again. Nothing. One more try and if that didn't work, she was going to plow her sweatshirt-covered elbow through the glass, scream at the top of her lungs, and hope and pray she could crawl through the broken window or that Logan would rescue her.

Open, damn it, open! She pushed, she shook, she pushed again, and at last the window broke loose and slid all the way up. Spinning around quickly, she hoisted herself up and flew through the opening. A second later she slammed the window shut and stared outside. The grizzlies hadn't moved an inch, their jaws were slack, their eyes not quite so beady. From the safety of Logan's living room they looked like a couple of big old cuddly teddy bears out for a leisurely stroll.

She took a deep breath, and one more for good measure. A slight smile touched her face. She was inside. The water was still running in the shower, which meant she could snoop. She'd worry about getting past the bears when it came time to hightail it out of Grizzly Hollow.

The bedroom seemed the best place to start. She'd scan it quickly while Logan was in the shower, then move on. She turned to her right, started to make her move, but a dark shadow blocked the doorway—and the barrel of a rifle stared her straight in the face.

Chapter 14

Scarlett screamed, the sound so loud and piercing that her ears popped. Logan and the big ugly rifle became a massive blur. Fear pulsed through her; she shut her eyes tightly to keep from seeing the explosion or her blood spurting everywhere.

She let out a second near window-shattering scream, and a wet hand clamped over her mouth.

The explosion never came. Pain didn't ricochet through her body. She didn't drop to the floor in a pool of blood. But she did feel the pressure of fingers on her face and heard hard breathing that wasn't her own.

Opening her eyes slowly, she saw Logan standing over her, tall, muscular, and menacing—sort of. Dark hair dripped over his narrowed, angry eyes, down the bridge of his nose and over his chin. Rivulets of water coursed over his body, and she followed one meandering stream through the hair on his chest, over his belly button, over . . .

Merciful heavens! He was stark naked.

Scarlett grabbed Logan's hand and tugged it off

her mouth. "If you're going to kill me," she lashed out through nearly gritted teeth, "you could at least have the decency to do it fully clothed."

Flames leapt in his eyes. "If I'd planned to kill you I would have done it long before now."

"Then why the hell were you pointing that gun at me, and in the nude, I might add?"

"To shoot the grizzlies I thought had broken in. If I'd known it was *you* breaking in, I might have gotten dressed first and I sure as hell wouldn't have gotten a rifle."

"So now that you know what's really going on"— she sucked in a deep breath, and even though he'd set the safety on the rifle and it was no longer pointing at her, she gingerly pressed a fingertip to the end of the miserable thing and pushed it much further away—"are you gonna get rid of that gun and get dressed?"

"Not until I know why you broke in."

"I didn't break in."

His brow rose. A drop of water slipped down his nose. "No?"

"No!" she lied. "I was escaping a couple of vicious and ugly bears."

Logan's head twisted toward the window. Another drop of water zipped down his body. In spite of her anger, she was tempted to keep watching the speeding drop to see where it landed, but she forced her eyes from his most impressive body and peered outside.

The bears wrestled in the well-lit clearing, tumbling, clawing and biting each other, grunting and snorting as they played in the dirt and pine needles. They looked perfectly harmless—now.

"Okay, so you were escaping the bears," he said, glaring at her again, "but that doesn't explain what you were doing here in the first place."

"I thought you might enjoy some company."

"Do you usually drop in on your friends—unannounced, I might add—at ten P.M.?"

"Not as a rule."

"Why me, then?"

"Most of the men I know work for a living and they're usually in bed by ten." She smiled weakly. "You're retired, I thought you might still be awake."

He glared at her for the longest time, and she glared back, watching another trickle of water slip down to his nose and over his chin before it dropped and splattered on the hardwood floor. Again he looked out the window to the bears in the lighted clearing. When he turned back, his eyes bore down on her. "This place is a good ten miles from town. You're not going to tell me you walked here, are you?"

If she lied, he'd certainly catch on sooner or later. "I drove."

"Where's your car?"

Scarlett threw back her shoulders, as if she had nothing to hide. "In the trees."

"The trees?" He chuckled. It wasn't exactly a cynical chuckle, sort of an I-don't-believe-I'm-really-hearing-this kind of snort. "The road up here leads to the front of the house. That's where visitors usually park their cars, so why on earth did you park in the trees?"

She smiled innocently, which seemed to be the best course of defense at the moment. "I thought I'd surprise you." Her eyes trailed down his body, settled for an instant on his hips and points in between, then moved slowly back to his still angry eyes. "Apparently I did."

Irritation replaced anger, but at last he set the rifle atop the fireplace mantel. With one more exasperated shake of his head, he turned his back on her and headed for the bedroom. "Don't go anywhere," he ordered and slammed the door behind him.

As if she could with two bears outside. Besides, she'd come here to snoop, not to run away.

Taking a quick look around the room, she rushed toward a desk, opened the lap drawer quietly and rummaged around for a wallet or anything remotely suspicious, like a handgun, Opal's jewels, a Murder, Inc. handbook. Fortunately, it was nearly empty, only some pens, paper clips, a couple of pencils, and a few maps of Plentiful and the surrounding area.

Closing it gently, she opened a small drawer on the side and found a stack of empty diary-type notebooks, a manila file folder with House Stuff scribbled in red ink on the tab, and—

"What the hell are you doing now?"

Logan's fingers clamped around her wrist as she spun around. His eyes were narrowed. Her own eyes widened in surprise. Staring at him now, dressed in only a pair of black jeans, she felt guilty, wary, and oddly exhilarated all at the same time. What would Jayne Mansfield-Smythe do under similar circumstances? Take him to bed, more than likely, but that wasn't going to work for her.

Think. Think. In an instant, an idea hit.

Scarlett smiled ingenuously, raised the hand Logan hadn't latched on to and wiggled her fingers in front of his face. "I broke a fingernail. I thought you might have an emery board somewhere around."

Logan gripped the hand she was wagging and stared at her short but nicely manicured and crimson-polished nails. "That worked in *One is the Deadliest Number,* but it's not working now. Want to come up with another . . . lie?"

She shrugged. "I'm fresh out."

"Yeah, but I've got the feeling you'll come up with a whole hell of a lot more before morning rolls around."

"What do you mean morning?" She tried to wrench her wrists from his tightening grasp. "As soon as the grizzlies leave, I'm out of here."

A slow, smug grin touched his face. "Yogi and Boo Boo camp here every night. *All* night."

"*Who?*"

"The bears."

She frowned. "You've given them names?"

"Yeah. The woodpecker that dive-bombs me every morning when I jog is Woody. The magpies are Heckle and Jeckle, the raven is Poe—they hog the bird seed. The squirrel that romps on the roof at night is Rocky." He nodded at the scrawny black cat standing on the couch, back arched, and hissing. "That's Snagglepuss, my latest guest. He doesn't like people who break in any more than I do."

"How many times do I have to tell you—"

"Yeah, I know. You didn't break in."

"That's right." Again she tried to twist free from his hold, but struggling was useless. She could kick him in the shins or plant a knee in his crotch, but that would make him angrier than he already was, and she couldn't exactly run out the front door, because then she'd have to deal with Yogi and Boo Boo.

"Could you please let me go?"

"Not until you can come up with a plausible reason for why you hid your car in the trees, why you climbed through the window instead of knocking on the front door, and why on God's green earth you feel the need to spy on me, to play Nancy Drew or Jayne Mansfield-Smythe or some other ditsy sleuth at my expense."

"I wasn't spying—and they're not ditsy sleuths."

His eyes narrowed as he shook his head in frustration. "Are you always this stubborn?"

"You haven't seen the half of it yet."

He tugged her toward the kitchen and grabbed the phone. "Maybe I should call the cops and let them figure out what you're up to."

"You wouldn't."

"Give me one reason why I shouldn't."

"Because . . ." She sighed as the dial tone buzzed in her ears. "Because I don't particularly care for the chief of police."

"So I've heard."

"From who?"

"Joe Granger, I believe. Word travels fast in this town, remember? I heard plenty of other stuff about you, too, and I'm kind of beginning to think it's all true."

"Such as?"

"You have a bad habit of sticking your nose where it doesn't belong, which gets you into all sorts of trouble, kind of like right now."

"What's happening right now has never happened to me before."

"You mean I'm the first naked man you've spied on?"

She gritted her teeth. "You're not going to back me into a corner with that little bit of trickery, thinking I'll say something like, 'Most of the men I spy on are polite enough to walk around fully clothed,' which would then lead you to believe that I really am a spy, when I'm not."

His silly ass grin returned. "Okay, in the interest of not going around and around on the subject of whether or not you're a spy, I give. You're not a spy." He gently twisted her arm up to look at her red, white and blue rhinestone wristwatch. "It's ten P.M. You've got about eight hours till the bears disappear and eight hours to come up with another explanation. Hopefully the truth."

What could she possibly tell him? That she was looking for evidence that he was a dirty rotten scoundrel, a thief, a murderer . . . or maybe a nice guy? She didn't think so.

"Okay, well . . ." Again she tried to jerk free, but he held on tight. "Eight hours is a long time, so why don't I just sit out here on the couch and think up a good answer to give you when morning rolls around." She smiled sweetly. "As for you, it's late. Why don't you go to bed."

His nasty little chuckle echoed through the room. "I've got a better idea." Gripping both of her wrists in one of his big and powerful hands, he reached into the desk's bottom drawer, pulled out a set of handcuffs, and clapped one on her wrist.

"What on earth do you think you're doing?"

"Making sure you don't snoop anymore."

"Why? Do you have something to hide?"

"I don't have anything to hide, but I'm sure as hell not going to let some little thief wander around my house all night long looking at things that are none of her business."

"I'm not a thief."

"Well, cuffing you is my insurance that you won't become one while you're spending the night with me."

"I'm *not* spending the night with you. Not now, not ever."

He dragged her against his bare chest and grinned. "Yeah, you are." That said, he hefted her up into his arms and headed for the bedroom.

"What do you think you're doing now?"

"Taking you to bed."

"No you're—" The air rushed out of her lungs when he unceremoniously dumped her on the mattress and clapped the second cuff to the chrome head-board.

Gasping for air and wishing her heart would stop its frantic beat, she stared him down. "And what do you plan on doing now?" She locked her ankles tightly together.

Logan's gaze settled on her protectively tangled legs. He frowned angrily. "You've got a real winning opinion of me, don't you?"

"Any man who handcuffs a woman to the bed without her permission is scum in my book."

Logan laughed, but there was nothing humorous in his face. "I could have handcuffed you to the drainpipe outside and let the bears have their way with you. But scum that I am, I've given you my soft, comfortable bed."

"And I should thank you for this?"

He shook his head. "What you should do is enjoy it for the next eight hours."

"I hope you mean I should enjoy it—*alone.*"

He stalked across the room. Halfway through the bedroom door he turned and grinned. "I haven't decided yet."

The door slammed behind him.

Suddenly she was alone, shackled to a man's bed. She was very much the victim of her own folly and distrust. To make matters worse, she had no idea what was going to happen next.

Beyond the bedroom door she heard Logan pacing, heard the floorboards creaking beneath his bare feet. The sound stopped. The doorknob turned a quarter of an inch. Her breath caught in her throat. The door opened half an inch, froze in place for several heartbeats, then closed again.

Logan's pacing began once more.

Scarlett's body tensed. Logan confused her terribly. In her head she knew she shouldn't want him; knew she should stay far away from him, especially now, when he'd handcuffed her to his bed. But her heart thundered in her ears, telling her to take everything Logan could give—because she'd never felt so alive as she had the past couple of days.

She stared at the door. It was shut tightly. The pacing outside went from heavy to soft, and Scarlett suddenly realized that she wasn't nearly as afraid of Logan coming back, of sharing the bed with her, as she was afraid that he wouldn't come back at all.

Damn fool woman!

Logan paced the living room, listening to the *G.I. Blues* clock tick past the minutes—ten, fifteen, twenty—and with every minute that passed, the headboard banged harder against the bedroom wall and the jangle of metal against metal grew louder as Scarlett struggled against her restraints.

Maybe he'd gotten too carried away. Maybe he shouldn't have clapped her in irons, but the woman was driving him mad. It wasn't so much the spying or her need to snoop that bothered the hell out of him, it was the fact that he wanted her so damn much in spite of her crazy antics.

He could take her easily. She was trapped on his

bed; she was little, he was big, and he could over-power her without blinking an eye. But that wasn't his style. Never had been and never would be.

He wanted Scarlett, but he needed her to want him in return. Unfortunately, he couldn't figure out what the hell she wanted. Had she, as she'd said, come by tonight just to say hello? He laughed out loud at that ridiculous thought. Hell, she'd hidden her car in the trees—a sure sign that she'd been out to spy on him. But why? Did she want to sneak a peek at his tax re-ports, checkbook or bank records to see if he was worth enough money to even bother getting involved with? Did she want to see him naked, to find out if his physical attributes suited her style?

If she'd come by simply to find out if he was a nice guy, he'd blown that. No doubt he wasn't winning any popularity contests with the sizzling little red-head by locking her away in his room.

Perhaps it was time to deal with the firebrand again.

Heading to the kitchen, he grabbed two bottles of Moose Jaw from the refrigerator, twisted off the caps, and strode toward the bedroom. The moment of reckoning had arrived—in the upcoming minutes he planned to find out if he and Scarlett were des-tined to be sworn enemies, bosom buddies, or red-hot lovers.

Scarlett yanked at her handcuff, twisted it and turned it and tried to free herself from this ridiculous en-trapment. She glared at the clock beside the bed.

Nearly half an hour had gone by since Logan had locked her up. Twenty-nine minutes ago she'd wanted him to come back, wanted him to press that big and powerful body of his against hers. But that was twenty-nine minutes ago.

Now she was mad. How dare he handcuff her to the bed and then walk away!

The bedroom door banged against the wall, and Scarlett jerked around. Logan stood in the doorway wearing nothing more than black jeans and a smug smile.

The moment had come. He'd returned. Now the only question that remained was whether or not he planned to share the bed. If he tried, she'd knee him good and hard.

Snagglepuss approached her first, a taunt devised by two ruthless males, more than likely. He pranced into the room, leapt onto the bed, narrowed his eyes at Scarlett, and hissed. She and that cat were destined to have a major run-in one of these days. The scrawny thing plopped down beside her, and with claws fully extended, pressed his rear paws against her leg. Obviously he wanted more of the bed; Scarlett refused to budge.

Logan came in next, his bare feet silent on the hardwood floor. He stepped over the tennis shoes and socks she'd kicked off and sauntered toward her, two bottles of Moose Jaw clutched in his fists. He looked like a sexy guy in a TV ad, the kind of unshaven, bare-chested stud women poked their heads out of office windows to gawk at.

Well, she refused to gawk. Instead of staring at Logan's incredible chest, she stared at the cat; Snagglepuss stared right back. She reached out her uncuffed hand to pet the feline; Snagglepuss hissed.

"Nice cat you've got," she said cynically, still staring at the motley beast.

"He's not mine. He's just spending time here until he wants to move on."

Her eyes narrowed; she looked up slowly. "It's nice to know you give your animals the right to roam free. Too bad you're not as generous with human beings—like me."

"Snagglepuss licks my toes; he curls up in my lap—"

"I don't lick toes."

Logan's smug grin turned wicked as his gaze shot toward her crimson-polished toenails. "Ever had yours licked?"

"Don't be ridiculous."

"I take it that's a no?"

"What I've had licked or haven't had licked is none of your business."

Logan shrugged. "For now."

Those words sounded ominous, making her muscles tighten as Logan walked toward the bed, holding out a bottle of beer. "Thirsty?"

"Are you hoping I'll say yes so you can ply me with beer, get me drunk, then have your way with me, licking anything and everything your heart desires?"

"You think there's some hidden meaning behind everything I say and do?"

"Isn't there?"

"No, damn it!" Logan smacked the bottle down on the nightstand. "I thought you might be thirsty—that's it."

Logan stormed toward the living room, bare feet thudding heavily on the floor. Halfway through the doorway he stopped. Scarlett heard his deep intake of breath, the way it gushed back out as his broad shoulders rose and fell. Slowly he turned around. She searched his eyes for anger but saw only frustration.

"If I'm not mistaken," he said, "you and I were getting along pretty good this afternoon. Remember? I was holding you. We shared a few kisses that you seemed to enjoy. We talked about Friday night—hell, I even thought we might have a good time. Then you show up here, sneak around like you're trying to solve some big mystery, and treat me like I'm an ax murderer. Mind telling me why?"

She couldn't possibly tell him that her friends thought he *was* a murderer and that she was trying to find out the truth. But maybe she could tell him a partial truth, just to get him off her back. "I don't have the most trusting nature in the world—"

"So I noticed." He folded his arms across his chest and stared at her, waiting for more of an answer.

"I thought if I came out here tonight I might get to know a little more about you before our big date."

"How? By peeping through my windows, trying to figure out what kind of music I like, what I eat, if I scratch myself when no one's watching?"

"I didn't see you scratch, and if I had I would have hightailed it out of here before the bears charged."

"So you *were* spying on me?"

"Okay, so I was, but don't go thinking it's something I do on a routine basis. Trust me, spying can be damn boring."

"But you spied on me in spite of the boredom."

"I didn't say *you* were boring." Jeez, she was making a mess of this, but what woman wouldn't if she were chained to a bed with a sexy, nearly nude man looming over her? "I mean, it's not every day that I encounter a guy with an Elvis obsession."

"It's not an obsession; it's a collection."

"Collection, obsession, whatever you call it, it took me completely by surprise. And I was even more surprised to find out that you play guitar and sing"— she grinned uncontrollably—"not too well, I might add, although your movements were pretty good."

He glared menacingly. "If you'd asked what I did in my spare time, I would have told you."

"But I wanted firsthand knowledge."

"That's something you get when you've known someone awhile. It sure as hell isn't something you get by spying."

"Do we have to go into that again?"

"We're going to go into it until you tell me the real reason you were looking through my windows, one that I'll believe."

"Okay, damn it! I came here to find a missing wallet." There, she'd admitted a little more, but that was all he was getting out of her.

His eyes narrowed. "Wait a minute. You told me you found your wallet wedged in the cushions of your sofa."

"That wasn't exactly true."

He plowed his fingers through his hair. "So you *didn't* find your wallet?"

She shook her head slowly. "I never lost my wallet."

"Then what the hell were you rummaging around in the Dumpster for?"

"Someone else's wallet."

"Whose?"

"The lady who died in my shop."

"Was there some particular reason you had to lie about that?"

She bit her lower lip and sighed loudly. "Yes."

"Mind telling me what that reason could have been?"

"You won't like it."

"Try me."

"I thought you might have stolen it, then tossed it into the Dumpster after you took out all of the money and credit cards."

He glared, long and hard and deep. Then he downed half of his Moose Jaw. Then he stared some more. The silence between them became almost deafening.

Snagglepuss climbed up her sweatshirt, stared her in the face, hissed, then leapt off the bed and went to stand beside Logan. Both of them stared at her now.

"Does all of this staring mean you can't believe I'd

suggest such a thing?" she asked. "Or does it mean you had nothing to do with the missing wallet?"

"Both."

"Then maybe you should give me some good reason to believe you're totally and completely innocent."

"Maybe we should start with you telling me why you would think I'd do such a thing in the first place?"

"Because you're the one person who had complete access to Jane Doe's purse before she died."

"Yeah, I had access. Her purse fell on the floor, and, gentleman that I am, I volunteered to pick up everything that fell out. Then I put the damned bag back on the counter and got the hell out of your store."

"Did you take her wallet with you?"

"What reason would I have for stealing someone's wallet?"

"I don't know. Maybe you're a thief. Maybe that's why you hightailed it out of Las Vegas. Maybe that's why you're hiding out here in the middle of nowhere with a couple of grizzlies named Yogi and Boo Boo for protection."

"I hightailed it out of Vegas because I hated the place, because I got tired of all the crazy people. I'm *living* here, not hiding, because it's secluded and quiet, but obviously I didn't escape the loonies because you're here now, and you're as loony as they come."

She gritted her teeth, ready to lash out at his accusation, but he turned on his bare feet and stalked out of the room, with Snagglepuss hot on his heels. Once again, he slammed the door.

Scarlett blew at a curl that had tumbled over her forehead, then grabbed the bottle of Moose Jaw from the nightstand. She took a long swallow. She wasn't crazy . . . or was she? What woman in her right mind would sneak into the cabin of a man she thought might be a murderer? What woman would feel nervous and anxious and tingle all over after arguing with a man who might or might not be a thief, a killer, a low-down, dirty rotten scoundrel?

Apparently she was totally out of her mind.

She took another swig of beer and called out to the man in the next room. "Logan."

All was silent on the other side of the door.

"Logan." Again she called his name, a little bit louder this time around.

The door opened slowly. Logan stood there, holding the cat, methodically petting the top of its head. "What?"

She fought back tears. "Do you really think I'm crazy?"

"One minute yes, the next minute no. Hell, Scarlett, I'm beginning to think I'm crazy."

"Why would you think that?"

"Because even though you don't trust me, even though you think I'm a thief and God knows what else"—he heaved a long-winded sigh—"I still want you."

"Why?"

"I don't know. Maybe it's the freckles on your nose. Maybe it's that damn belly button ring of yours."

"That's all pretty superficial."

He shrugged. "Maybe it's the fact that I'm bored out of my mind out here and even though you're rash, hot-headed and impetuous, you're also sexy as hell, and I find that a rather nice diversion."

"Diversion?" She sat up stiffly. "Is that all you want in a relationship? A nice diversion?"

"I haven't given a lot of thought to relationships."

"That's obvious, if you go around telling women they're a mere distraction, an insignificant toy to play with until something better comes along."

Setting Snagglepuss on the floor, Logan gave the cat a gentle shove into the living room and closed the door.

"I don't call sexy as hell insignificant." He strolled toward the bed, like a wolf stalking a poor defenseless lamb caught in a trap.

"I find you sexy as hell, too," she admitted, "but that doesn't mean I want to play with you, or that I want to be your diversion or anyone else's."

"What do you want me to tell you, Scarlett?" One of his eyebrows rose. "That I love you?"

She laughed nervously. "That's an impossibility."

He was standing over her now, staring down at the freckles bridging her nose, at her wild tangle of flaming red curls. "Why?"

"Because you have me handcuffed to your bed. Because we haven't known each other long enough. Because even though I want to trust you, I don't, and it's quite obvious you don't trust me either." She jerked on the cuff to show just how much he didn't trust her. "The way I see it, loving each other is completely out of the question."

He brushed a curl from her brow. His eyes flamed as he watched her. Her own body turned to hot lava beneath his touch. "Is making love out of the question, too?" he asked.

"Of course," she sputtered.

"Why?"

"Because we're in the middle of a major argument."

Callused but tender fingers trailed along her jaw. He caressed her lips with the pad of his thumb, so lightly and gently that her heart began to pitter-pat. "I thought we were making up."

"Maybe, but I still don't trust you."

He crawled onto the mattress and straddled her hips. "I'm not a thief, Scarlett."

"Are you a murderer?"

"No," he said slowly, his mouth inching ever closer to hers. "I'm just a man who finds you intriguing." He grasped her free wrist before she even thought about struggling, and held it beside her head. His lips feathered softly over her. "I want you to trust me, Scarlett."

"I don't know if I can."

"You can do anything if you want to badly enough." He kissed her softly. "Do you want to trust me?"

"I'd like to."

He reached into his pocket and pulled out a key. "Trust works both ways," he said. "You want to trust me, I want to trust you. Guess we'll start here." He clasped her cuffed wrist in one of his hands, slipped the key into the lock and popped open the restraint.

This was her opportunity to buck him off of her, to free herself and run, even if it meant hiding in the bathroom until morning. But he was right. Trust had to start somewhere. And this was where she'd longed to be since she'd first set eyes on him.

He drew her wrists to his mouth, kissing them both gently, slowly. His lips, his tongue glided over her open palms, tracing each life line, blazing a memory of this moment into her heart and mind.

When his hand slipped away and cupped her face, she threaded her fingers into his hair and tugged his mouth even closer. His warm breath mingled with hers, slid between her parting lips and teased her tongue, making her hungry for far, far more.

"This is crazy, isn't it?" she whispered.

"Yeah. Pretty damn crazy."

In spite of it, his mouth captured hers, hard, fierce and greedy. Her fingers sank into strong, muscular arms, holding him against her as their tongues mingled. He coaxed a sigh from her; stoked a fire inside her she hadn't known existed.

God, how he wanted her. Every breath. Every moan. Every speck of warm, sweet flesh. His fingers skimmed over her sweatshirt, sought out its zipper, then inched it down. Pulling reluctantly away from the tender heat of her lips, he spread the sweatshirt wide and cupped her heaving, silk-covered breasts in his palms. Soft. So damn soft.

Scarlett dragged in a shuddering breath, and he looked down into frightened eyes. Maybe he was moving too fast. Maybe she didn't want this at all. He'd stop if she asked him; but he hoped she wouldn't. Hell, he wasn't going to give her the chance.

Tearing his fingers from supple breasts that had swelled and tightened beneath his hands, he drove them into her wild, abandoned curls and captured her mouth once more, cutting off any protest she might cook up.

But it wasn't a protest that glided over his heated skin, it was Scarlett's fingers trailing up his spine, over his shoulders, and weaving into his hair, keeping him close.

They kissed endlessly. Mindlessly. Fear flew away; caution abandoned her, and Scarlett let the tingling, breathless sensations take over her body and force all thoughts of escape from her mind.

Logan tilted her head back and trailed kisses down the curve of her throat. He firmly licked one taut nipple through the silk of her bra, circling it, teasing her. Scarlett's breath caught and held. Her stomach muscles tensed, and she wanted to cheer when his tongue found her other nipple and gave it a repeat performance.

Expertly, he flicked open the front clasp on her bra and peeled it and her sweatshirt from her body, flinging them across the room. He sought one breast with his blazing hot mouth, its mate with his fingers.

Her body throbbed. She gasped for air as she gave in to the passion that frightened her, the excitement she knew she should fight, the need that was consuming her.

It was a wicked thing to want him so badly, but she couldn't help herself. Every touch, every kiss, every brush of his tongue drove her higher and gave her courage to seek more.

Her hand slipped between them, worked its way over his rock-solid belly, over the waistband of his jeans to his zipper and the hard, pulsing bulge straining to be free of everything but her grasp.

"Touch me," he growled, the sound vibrating against her breast.

She popped the button on his jeans, tugged down the zipper, and swept her fingers under his shorts. She took him in her palm, squeezed him, smoothed her hand up and down the long, thick, marble-hard shaft. Heat spread through her hand and radiated to all points of her body. A soft, contented sigh escaped her mouth.

Opening her eyes, she saw Logan looking down at her, lips tilted in a smile. "If you sigh like that when you're touching me, what are you going to do when I touch you?"

She buried her head into the downy pillows, gripped the headboard, and grinned. "Why don't we find out?"

It was an open invitation, and Logan wasted no

time acting on it. He tugged down her zipper, delved beneath her jeans, and into her silky panties. His fingers slid through curls he imagined were just as flaming red as the springy hair splayed across the pillow. He found soft skin. Slick, hot, velvety skin. He swirled his fingers over the needy little nub nestled secretly between her legs, and watched her eyes flicker beneath her lids.

He licked one nipple, then the other. They tightened and reached up to him for more, and he gladly gave everything he had while his fingers explored, seeking all Scarlett had to offer.

He slipped one finger inside her. Looking up, he watched her fists tighten around the headboard's chrome rails. Two fingers now. She sighed, purred, as his fingers swirled inside her hidden depths. Her breasts heaved; her hips rose from the bed, begging for more.

Logan smiled. With his fingers still seeking, playing, he stretched over her, kissed her warm, parted, wet lips, and whispered, "That's the way, Scarlett. Give me everything you've got to give."

Scarlett's eyes flew open. Hands that had clutched the headboard now pushed frantically at his shoulders.

"What is it, Scarlett?" Logan's eyes narrowed. "What's happened?"

"I've got to go." Scarlett rolled out of bed. "We shouldn't have gone so far," she mumbled, zipping up her jeans.

"We didn't go nearly far enough."

Logan shoved out of bed, managed to button up his pants, and tried to grasp Scarlett's shoulders, but she pulled away. She struggled into her sweatshirt, pushed her bra into one of its pockets, and sat on the floor to put on her shoes.

Sitting on the edge of the bed, Logan stared dumbly at the woman he'd been inches from making love to. "Can I get a straight answer from you, Scarlett? What the hell just happened?"

Scarlett tied one shoelace and then the other, never looking up, not bothering to acknowledge his question.

At last she stood, shoved her fingers into her mass of curls, and looked at him with tear-stained eyes. "I don't want to get hurt."

"Hurt?" he asked incredulously.

"That's right—hurt. I don't want you to burrow into my heart and then rip it out of me."

"So you just walk away without giving us a chance?"

Scarlett stared at the bed, silent for far too long. When he thought he might just walk out the door and leave her alone, her eyes flickered back to his. "My mother had two lousy marriages with two lousy men who hurt her every time she turned around."

"And you refuse to get close to a man because you're afraid the same thing will happen to you?"

"She told me it would. Year after year she told me to stay away from men. She said if I didn't, some man would take everything from me, and give me nothing in return."

"And you believed her?"

"I don't want to, but—"

"If you don't want to, don't."

She glared at him. "I can't snap my fingers and make the thoughts disappear. I've lived with them far too long."

"So you just snap your fingers and make me disappear instead?"

"If it were that easy I would have snapped my fingers the first time you walked through my door, that way I wouldn't have opened myself up to trouble or hurt."

That did it. He'd thought about fighting for her, helping her push her ridiculous doubts away, but she seemed to prefer wallowing in distrust and hatred of men to finding out that she might find happiness with a guy if she gave it a try.

"You know, Scarlett," Logan said, rising from the bed, "getting rid of me is pretty damn easy. You don't even have to snap your fingers." He clutched her hand, tugged her toward the front door and threw it open. "The bears ran off not long after you got here, and you know where you hid your car. If you really want me out of your sight—just start walking."

A tear slid down her cheek as she stared up at him, and he fought the urge to wipe it away. For a moment he thought she might ask to stay, might throw herself into his arms, but she turned away. She walked down the porch steps and across the clearing. He wanted to go after her, but he didn't need her kind of craziness in his life.

At last she disappeared into the trees, never once

looking back. He heard the car door open and shut, heard the engine roar, saw the headlight beams through the trees. And then she was gone.

Logan slammed the door. It was over. Finished. Tomorrow, right after the fishing trip he'd committed to, he'd pack up and move on.

Plentiful was history.

So was Scarlett.

Chapter 15

Scarlett closed her mother's rose-embroidered diary and placed it on top of the nightstand. She'd thought she could wipe out her headache by reading her mother's words; unfortunately, all the warnings, all the fear and hate scribbled inside had made the throbbing worse.

She switched off the light, pulled the cozy down comforter up to her chin, and fell back into the fluffy, lace-edge pillows on her canopied bed. Closing her eyes, she tried to sleep as soundly as Toby, who snored peacefully at the end of the mattress. But sleep hadn't come earlier; she doubted it would come now. Instead, she imagined Logan's arms around her again, thought about his lips trailing over her skin, and sadly, maddeningly, remembered how she'd pushed him away.

She tossed and turned and tried to shove away all thoughts, but her mother's cautionary words hounded her: *He'll hurt you—and you'll never be the same again.* And those words did battle with other words, ones her mother seldom used: *I was happy. Deliriously happy.*

Scarlett's eyes flew open and the combative words went away. Flipping on the bedside light, she grabbed the diary and fingered to a page that had always seemed so insignificant, but which bore those few significant words that had gnawed at her for the past couple of hours.

Edgar called me Princess. He brought me roses, always remembering that my favorites were the palest of pink. He told me he loved me in so many ways, and I was happy. Deliriously happy—in the beginning.

And now there's Adam. So handsome. So charming. In the middle of the night when he thinks I'm asleep, he'll come into this room where I've hidden away from the world and smooth a lock of hair from my face, or lightly kiss my brow.

Afterwards he goes to another woman's home and does the same to her—and much, much more.

If I could do it over again, I wouldn't marry. Men lie. They cheat. They're not to be trusted. A few good memories can't make up for years of anguish and pain.

Scarlett read the last sentence again and again. *A few good memories can't make up for years of anguish and pain.*

Damn it, mother! At least you had good memories! Scarlett flung the diary across the room. *At least you had a man to call you Princess. A man to bring you roses and kiss you and hold you in the middle of the night.*

Scarlett buried her head back in her pillow and cried. *I don't have any of that, Mother. None of it, because I've spent too much of my life heeding your warnings.*

Toby crawled up beside her, as if he sensed her loneliness. She wrapped her arms around him. But it was Logan she wanted to hold; Logan she wanted lying beside her. Damn her mother's warnings. Damn her own suspicions and doubts.

It seemed as though she cried for hours, but when she sat up and wiped the tears from her eyes, the grandfather clock downstairs tolled only three times.

She needed sleep. She didn't want to think anymore, not about Opal's disappearance, the dead woman's identity, the mysterious handkerchief embroidered with her mother's initials. She definitely didn't want to think about Logan, or the fact that she might never see him again.

She plowed her head back into her pillow and tried to drown out her thoughts, Toby's snoring, the tick of the grandfather clock, and the *click, click, click* of something hitting her second-story window.

Hail? Sleet? Did she need to run downstairs and cut roses to fill her vases one more time before winter buried them in snow?

Tossing back the covers, she tiptoed across the cold wood floor and peeked through the ruffled curtains. The garden was illuminated by moonlight. Logan stood in the center of the lawn, his hand poised to toss another little speck of something at her window.

Her heart leapt into her throat. Logan was giving her another chance. She didn't deserve it—but she'd take it just the same.

She raced down the stairs, ran through the kitchen, and ripped open the back door. To hell with her mother's warnings. To hell with giving up on life to keep from getting hurt. Tonight she was going to risk everything.

Her feet barely had a chance to touch the cold, damp grass before she launched herself into Logan's arms. She locked her legs about his waist, wove her fingers through his hair, and gave herself up to the power of his kiss.

Logan held her close, one hand splayed beneath her bottom, the other swept under her red satin camisole. His skin was warm. His lips were sheer pleasure, and her desire for him blazed.

The icy breeze rustled through the rosebushes, sending the sweet perfume to wrap around them. The moment seemed incredibly magical. She didn't want it to end, yet she wanted so much more.

"Please tell me you came here to finish what you started earlier," Scarlett whispered against Logan's mouth. "I'll be terribly embarrassed if you had something else in mind, like telling me that you just stopped by to return a book or ask for a free scone."

"I came to finish what I started." His voice was husky; his need abundantly evident as he let her body slide from his waist to his hips. She leaned back slightly, just enough to cradle his hard and needy arousal between her legs, then tightened the viselike hold she had on him so she could feel every inch of what lay hidden beneath his jeans.

Logan groaned, low, deep in his throat. Keeping her close, he bounded toward the house, yanked open the kitchen door, and slammed it behind him. "Where's your bedroom?"

"Upstairs. Second door on the right."

His boots thudded up the steps. His lips melded with hers and let her know in no uncertain terms that in just a few moments she'd be his—completely.

Toby barked when they stepped through the door. Logan inclined his head toward the bedeviled dog and slanted one brow, enough to show Toby that the bedroom was now Logan's domain. The Scottie trotted out of the room, his little paws padding rapidly down the hallway until the only things Scarlett could hear were Logan's heartbeat and her own, pounding in her ears.

Logan shut the door and locked it. Hot eyes burned down on her. Flames shot through his hands and set her body on fire. Scarlett breathed hard and deep as Logan carried her to the bed, threw back the comforter, and lay her in a garden of soft floral sheets and pillowcases.

Standing at the edge of the bed, Logan shrugged out of his leather jacket and tossed it over a wing-back chair. He ripped the black polo shirt over his head, and the pale, shimmering light from a fringed Victorian lamp rippled over hard planes and solid muscles.

Reaching out to her, Logan's warm fingers slipped under the spaghetti straps of her ruby red camisole. Rough, weather-hardened fingers skimmed her flesh. She shivered, yet burned, as his palms trailed over her breasts, and settled lightly on her tight, distended nipples.

"Do you have any idea how much I want you?" he asked, as skilled hands glided to the hem of her camisole. He drew it over her head and tossed it somewhere across the room. "Any idea how cold my bed felt when you weren't in it?" With hands gently cupping her arms, he pressed her gently into the pillows. Dark eyes were just inches from hers. "I want you in a way I've never wanted anyone or anything in my life."

Doubt flared, then ebbed. "You mean that, don't you?"

"I'm here, Scarlett. I don't want to be anywhere else."

Hot, moist lips kissed the curve of her neck, meandered over her breasts, suckled and teased one nipple, then the other. His tongue swirled around her belly button, caught the gold ring between his teeth and tugged lightly.

Scarlett's body quivered; goose bumps rose on her skin.

He looked up at her through thick, dark lashes. "Like that?"

Scarlett gasped when he tugged again. "I like it all." She took a deep breath. "So don't stop. Please."

He hooked his fingers over the straps of her satiny

thong. Slowly he peeled them from her hips. Like molten lava, his touch blazed down her legs, over her ankles, her feet and toes.

Scarlett watched the play of light on his skin; on her own needy flesh. His eyes had turned almost black; they were mysterious, yet they sparked with desire as his gaze scorched every visible inch of her body.

She wanted him, craved him. Inside, in that deep, dark place no one could see, her muscles clenched, begging to be touched.

At last, Logan shoved out of his boots. He popped the buckle on his belt and the buttons on his jeans, pulled a handful of condoms from his pocket and tossed them beside her on the bed. In another moment, he'd freed his body from man-made nuisances and stood before her, naked, strong, beautiful.

Kneeling on the end of the bed, he took her feet in the palms of his hands and raised them from the mattress. He pressed her cool soles against his hot steel rod. She could feel his pulse, his every desire, which mirrored her own. He dragged her feet over his stomach, over the mat of dark chocolate hair on his chest. At last, warm lips kissed each toe, pressed against each arch. His tongue swirled and teased, making her flinch and want to pull away, but he held them close.

"I'm not letting you go, Scarlett. Not again."

He rubbed the bottoms of her feet against his bearded cheeks, nibbled the very tips of her toes, and when she thought she might scream for him to take her, to make her his completely, he spread her legs apart and rested the backs of her ankles on his shoulders, holding them there so she couldn't move. He swallowed hard, his Adam's apple rising up and down. And then the Big Bad Wolfe winked: *The better to see you, my dear.*

Logan studied her; all of her, every nook and cranny, every fold of skin, every coil of flaming red hair visible in the lamplight. How was it possible to need someone so badly, when they'd only just met? When she'd pushed him away? When she'd thought he was a thief?

But he craved her, and God knows he didn't know what he'd do if she rolled out from under him again.

She beckoned him with her index finger. If this was a tease, heaven help her.

Logan reached for one of the condoms and rolled it on quickly. He'd take his time, but those long, drawn-out hours of pleasure would have to wait for another time. Right now, he aimed to claim her.

He leaned forward, slipped his fingers over soft, warm hips, under the tender flesh of her bottom, and held her tightly. He pulled her toward him, and his hard, almost painful erection pressed against the very center of her.

Scarlett's eyes slammed shut, and she sucked in a deep breath.

Logan froze. "Oh, God," he groaned. "Are you a virgin?"

Scarlett's eyes popped open. "Do you want me to be?"

"Hell, no."

"Good, because I'm not, but . . . it's never been good before. Well, not as good as I thought it should be."

Logan laughed, trying to control his desperate need to plunge all the way inside her. "How good do you think it should be?"

"One un-faked or un-self-induced orgasm would be nice."

"How about five to ten—for starters?"

"Is that possible?" she asked, a not-so-surprising innocence ringing in her words.

"What do you think?"

Scarlett smiled. "That we should stop talking and go for a world record."

He sank into her, inch by slow, agonizingly pleasureable inch. Her eyes were closed; she breathed deeply. Her fingernails tore into his arms and dug even deeper when he slowly withdrew.

"Don't stop," she begged.

"I'm just getting started."

Again he pressed into her. She was small and tight, wet and slick and hot. Her muscles quivered and convulsed, beckoning him, seducing him, imploring him to take more and more.

He clutched her soft, curvy hips as he moved in and out, establishing a rhythm, a roll. Soon her body moved with him, her pelvis writhing, her sweet, blessed stomach with the seductively powerful belly button ring undulating before his greedy, want-it-all eyes.

Her breathing came in gasps; soft moans spilled

through her lips. Fingernails scraped over his back, his chest, down his arms. She cried out for him to stop, then begged him for more, driving him on.

One moment Scarlett was beneath him, the next above, looking down on a smile that was pure as sin. She pressed her hands against his chest and felt the rapid pounding of his heart. "Had enough?" she asked with a wink, rising up and down on him, up and down, taking him deeper inside her.

He shook his head. "Something tells me I'm never gonna have enough."

She rode him a little more, grinding down on him, swirling around and around until she could barely breathe. She gathered her hair into her hands and pulled it high over her head, then smiled at the man beneath her. "You told me earlier tonight that I was just a mere diversion. Do you still feel that way?"

"You're a diversion, all right," he said, inhaling and exhaling slowly as his thumbs teased her hardened nipples, "the kind of diversion that could keep me from thinking rationally."

Grinding her hips into his, she leaned forward, letting her curls fall over his face as he stretched up to kiss her. "What do you need to think rationally about?" she asked.

"Nothing but you."

Logan took over again, rolling her beneath him. His fingers pressed into her bottom, dragging her against him as he plunged deep.

Repeated sighs tore from her throat; she purred, moaned. She wrapped her legs about his waist and met him thrust for thrust. Her insides convulsed, a repetitive ripple of torturous delight. Part of her wanted him to stop, but she urged him on, needing him to push her over the edge again and again, to push away any doubts, any fears.

Capturing her mouth, he caught her scream before it could echo through the room. His tongue swirled hot and deep with hers; he was the master, she his student. Learning to enjoy this part of life that she'd denied herself far too long was paradise.

Her head fell back, and he kissed the length of her throat, then found her ear and whispered through gasps for breath, "I can't make it to ten, Scarlett."

She looked deep in his eyes and smiled. "One climax with you is worth a million."

Through his smile, Scarlett watched him grit his teeth. Felt his muscles contract beneath her hands. She clutched him, rising again and again to meet each rapid stroke. Once more he pushed her to the edge and then over the top—and he exploded with her in a climax that could have sent her skyrocketing toward heaven, if she wasn't already content in his arms.

"Do you really have to go?" Scarlett asked, kneeling in the center of the rumpled sheets, wanting desperately to pull Logan back into her arms so they could make love again.

"It's five-fifteen." Logan swept his boxers up from the floor and tugged them on. "Somehow I've got to get home, change clothes, pick up my fishing gear, and be at Joe's place by six."

"You could have picked a better time to come out of retirement," Scarlett teased. "Or, if you needed money, I could have given you a job."

Logan hit her with a frown as he sat on the edge of the bed to pull on his socks. "Money isn't a problem. I took the guide job because I was bored, because I wanted a good reason to stick around town, and because I like to fish." Socks on, he grabbed his jeans. "And what kind of work could I possibly do for you? I'm not a salesman, I can't bake, I hate tea, and I'm the last person on earth who could make book recommendations."

She smiled. "You could keep my bed warm at night."

"That's not a job, it's sheer pleasure," he said, his gaze trailing over her still swollen lips, over nipples desperate to be kissed again, to her belly, her thighs, then back again to her eyes. "If I worked for you, your shop would go out of business because we'd never get dressed and never unlock the door."

"I'm sure you'd want to come up for air sometime."

"Only out of necessity."

"Well," she said, when another thought hit her, "on the off chance that either one of us got bored, or tired, or found ourselves incapacitated for a few days, you could always play sleuth and help me find a missing wallet."

Logan stopped mid zip on his Levi's and stared at her. "You mean the wallet you think I stole?"

"*Thought.* And you know darn good and well I don't think that now."

"Yeah, but something made you think that last night, and I'd love to know what."

Uncomfortable now, Scarlett pulled the sheet over her breasts and hugged it to her. "Maybe we should discuss that some other time, you know, when you don't have to get to work."

Logan shook his head as he finished zipping his jeans. "Something tells me I should hear the whole story now."

"You're not going to like it."

He pulled his shirt over his head, and when his face reappeared, Scarlett couldn't miss the tightness in his jaw—or the wee bit of a twinkle in his eye. "Tell me everything, Scarlett."

She might spill her guts about the wallet, but not about Opal and the fact that she'd thought he might be a murderer. That might push him over the edge. "Well—" She swallowed hard. "I didn't want to believe you could have taken the wallet, but as I mentioned before, you'd had access to it and then when Mildred told me you threw something in the Dumpster—"

"What?" Deep furrows formed between his eyes. "I threw God knows what in the Dumpster and that makes me a thief?" His voice was loud, incredulous.

"There's more to it than that."

"I'd sure as hell like to know what."

"Just put on your boots and I'll tell you."

Logan plopped down on the bed and grabbed for his boots as Scarlett continued her story. "As I was saying, Mildred saw you throw something in the

Dumpster. She might not have thought anything of it, but before you threw away whatever it was that you threw away, you were looking up and down the street, acting suspiciously, like you didn't want anyone to see what you were doing."

Still pulling on his first boot, Logan jerked his head around and glared at Scarlett. "I was acting suspiciously?"

"According to Mildred." Scarlett smiled sweetly. "You didn't throw away some hazardous materials or something, did you?"

"If you call cold fries and a half-eaten Big Mac hazardous."

It was Scarlett's turn to frown. "You eat at McDonald's?"

Logan shook his head in absolute frustration. "Yeah. Sometimes three meals a day, but that's neither here nor there. Who's Mildred, and why the hell was she watching me?"

"She's a friend. A good friend, and after she saw what you did to me in the park—"

"I kissed you."

"You *threatened* to kiss me. There's a big difference, and when Mildred saw that, she was afraid you might hurt me. So she kept an eye on you." Scarlett's eyes narrowed. "By the way, why were you looking up and down the street so suspicious-like before you threw the McDonald's bag into the Dumpster?"

Logan grabbed his other boot and tugged it on. Standing, he pulled Scarlett out from under the sheet and into his arms. A slight grin tilted his lips as he

held her against him, eye to eye. "Maybe I was looking for an old lady to rob."

Scarlett's eyes widened. "You wouldn't?"

"There's no telling what I'm capable of."

Weaving his fingers through Scarlett's hair, Logan
dragged her mouth to his. His kiss was soft, warm,
sweet, and far too abrupt. In the space of a few heartbeats, he set her libido on fire, then set her bare feet
on the cold floor and grabbed his coat from the back
of the chair. Apparently he was going to leave, even
though that short-lived kiss shouted that he wanted
to stay.

Once more Logan's gaze raked over her body, and
Scarlett thought—hoped—that he might rip off his
clothes and make love to her again. "Have you decided to stay?" she asked softly.

"No, I was thinking how cute you'll look standing
outside on the boardwalk waving good-bye to me in
your birthday suit."

"I don't want to wave good-bye to you at all,"
Scarlett said, then scrambled into her closet and
struggled into a pair of old jeans and a cropped
T-shirt. "I'd really like you to stay."

"I can't. Not this morning," he said, taking her
hand when she emerged from the closet, leading her
down the front stairs and out of the house.

Far too soon they were back in the real world
again, standing by his big black Dodge. The street-
lights shone down on them through an early morning
mist. A touch of frost had settled on the boardwalk,
and the wooden planks were icy cold beneath Scar-

lett's still bare feet. The autumn breeze whipped about her, raising goose bumps on her skin, until Logan kissed her.

"Have dinner with me tonight," he whispered against her mouth. "A little bread, a little wine—"

"A soft bed?"

Scarlett could feel Logan's lips tilt into a smile. "Can't think of a better way to warm up after a long day sloshing around in an icy river."

"Eight o'clock?"

"I'll be here."

Reluctantly, Scarlett peeled herself from his body, stepped back into her doorway, and didn't take her eyes off Logan until he and the truck disappeared into the dark. She rubbed her arms, feeling cold seep through her insides now that he was gone. She felt something else, too. A kind of calm, a peace with herself and with everything else in life. If Adam Grant walked by, she might even offer *him* a smile.

Slipping back into the shop, she closed and locked the door, then headed into the kitchen to make a cup of chamomile, the perfect way to begin a perfect morning. A batch of fresh scones sounded good, too. Lemon, maybe. Drizzled with a combination of dark and white chocolate.

Scarlett reached for a teapot just as Toby's doggie door swung inward. A pair of wet paws poked through, followed by a set of jaws clamped over a scrap of paper. Once in the kitchen, Toby shook out his long, silky fur, and drops of water sprayed about him. The Scottie sat, obediently raised his head, and offered his treasure up to Scarlett.

"What have you got, Tobe?"

Toby barked once, and the ragged piece of paper fell into Scarlett's outstretched hand. It was gnawed on and damp. What had once been pale yellow linen stationery was now spattered with mud, but Scarlett couldn't miss her father's name, Edgar, scrawled in blue ink.

Placing the paper on the counter, she took a soft rag from a kitchen drawer to wipe away the grime— and something horrid stared back at her:

Edgar O'Malley planned the perfect murders . . . and then we carried them out, one after another after another . . .

Scarlett trembled as her perfect day came to an abrupt and horrible end.

Chapter 16

Scarlett flipped on the porch light and flew into the backyard to see if she could find more pale yellow stationery marked with blue ink scrawl. The words she'd read had to be part of a joke, some sick brand of humor that made her stomach churn. Hopefully she could put her hands on another wisp of paper that said *Ha! Ha! Just kidding.*

She didn't have to look far to find paper—lots of it. Scraps from books and magazines fluttered about in the breeze. Soggy paper littered the lawn. Scraggly paper wove through her rosebushes.

Toby ran out of the house, barked and danced around in the muck, then plopped down in the center of the lawn. If Scarlett wasn't mistaken, he had a smile on his furry little face.

"Oh, Toby." Scarlett shook her head and sighed, her breath fogging the air. Walking back into the kitchen, she shoved her feet into a pair of old boots, slipped on an old sweatshirt, then barreled back outside, grabbing one piece of paper after another. None of it was pale yellow, yet all of it was mushy, sticky, chewed on or spit out. She flung a handful into the trash bin and went toward the roses for more. She plucked scrap upon scrap from the thorns and leaves, until a pale yellow piece glared up at her.

I'm sorry.

Sorry for what? Scarlett wondered. For committing murder? For writing a vicious note?

Scarlett stared at the two simple words. The handwriting matched what she'd seen on the other piece of paper—the scrawl unfamiliar, shaky, and almost illegible.

Scarlett looked for Toby, hoping he could show her where the paper had come from, where the rest of it might be, but the Scottie had his nose buried in a flowerbed, where he was happily digging up a chrysanthemum. Scarlett sighed. "You're a lot of help."

Toby continued to ignore her.

She set about freeing more paper from the bushes, none of it pale yellow, none of it with handwriting or even blue ink. As the sun peeked over the horizon, she at last found another piece of the puzzle.

atone for my sins

What sins? Whose sins?

Curiosity pushed Scarlett through the yard, snatching at scraps in the bushes, digging into the soil to pull out fragments of pale yellow paper too spoiled to read.

The sun rose higher, brightening more of the yard and the bits of paper Scarlett had tossed away yesterday when she'd seen them as nothing more than a mess. Yesterday she could have salvaged everything; yesterday the puzzle pieces might have been easier to find and put together. Now it could take hours, maybe even days.

By the time she'd picked the last of the paper scraps from the bushes it was nearly noon. She hadn't brushed her teeth, showered, had a cup of tea, or opened the shop. But with those horrid, incriminating words about her father hanging over her head, she didn't care. Edgar O'Malley had been a womanizer, a drunk and a brute—not a murderer. She couldn't believe that, and she wouldn't set aside this new mystery in her life until she knew what was going on.

She slogged through the rubbish, separating paper from everyday household garbage. With that chore done, she got rid of the trash bin, brewed herself some good, strong Russian Roulette to go with a plate of dark chocolate brownies, and hunkered down on the floor to begin the tedious chore of sorting pale yellow linen stationery from the rest of the muck. Handwritten scraps went in one of the boxes she'd brought from the storage room, book and junk mail scraps in another, and in a third she tossed miscellaneous, almost unrecognizable pieces soaked with tea and water or gunked up with food crumbs.

Toby came inside, feasted on dog food, slopped water on the floor, and left a trail of slightly muddy paw prints from one end of the kitchen to the other. He found a chew bone under the table and sprawled out on the floor to gnaw on his toy, his beady little eyes following Scarlett's moves.

"You're just dying for me to leave you all alone, aren't you?" Toby's eyes slammed shut. "I know you're not asleep, Tobe," Scarlett said, ruffling the Scottie's black fur, "you're plotting, deciding which box you'll hop into first if I leave the room. Well, I've got news for you, boy. I'm not letting you out of my sight."

Toby yawned. Moments later, he started to snore, and Scarlett buried her head back in her work.

At ten minutes till three, with everything sorted, the wet pieces of stationery blow-dried, and Toby cleaned up and sound asleep atop Scarlett's bed, she sat down at the kitchen's claw-footed oak table and began the task of piecing together the ragged bits of the jigsaw puzzle she'd been able to salvage.

By three-thirty she'd matched only four pieces, in two separate segments:

I can't help but wonder . . . but the doctor tells me . . .

And:

I'm giving you this letter . . . I want you to know it all.

Scarlett sighed. *Know it all?* Ha! She didn't know anything more than she'd known at 6 A.M.. She was confused, frustrated, and tired. She pressed her fingers to her temples and stared at the hard-to-read writing. It wasn't poor penmanship; if the strokes weren't so shaky, the letters would have been perfectly formed, fancy even, as if the person who'd scribbled the words had once written beautifully scripted letters—the kind her great-grandmother had sent her when she was young. This was the writing of an elderly person. Jane Doe, maybe?

Memories of the conversation Scarlett had had with Jane Doe resurfaced. The woman had desperately wanted to talk, to tell Scarlett something. Had she written those thoughts down, just in case she wouldn't have the chance to meet Scarlett face to face?

Scarlett again studied the scraps of puzzle she'd pieced together: *but the doctor tells me* . . . Had the woman been dying? Scarlett wondered. Had she needed to tell Scarlett something in order to *atone for her sins,* sins that must have involved Scarlett's father as well?

The knock at the front door tore Scarlett away from the mystery that nagged at her. Pushing up from the table, she shoved her fingers through her tangled hair and headed to the front door.

Ida Mae's nose pressed against the door's window. She rapped on the glass and mouthed, "Let me in!"

The last thing Scarlett needed was company, but she couldn't tell her dear friend to go away.

Scarlett opened the door and Ida Mae bustled inside. The crystal chimes jangled as Scarlett locked the door behind her.

Ida Mae glared at Scarlett, the toe of her purple cowgirl boots tapping rapidly on the floor. "It's nearly four o'clock, Scarlett. What on earth is going on?"

"What do you mean?"

"The shop's closed, for one, and you're never closed this time of day."

"Business has been slow. I thought I'd take a day off."

"Obviously you've taken the day off from *everything*." Ida Mae scowled at Scarlett's hastily thrown on and dirt-spattered attire. "You're barely dressed, your hair's a disaster—"

"It's always a disaster."

"It looks like you just got out of bed." Ida Mae snorted. "But that's neither here nor there. I've come by to find out what you've learned about Opal."

Opal? Heaven forbid, with everything else going on, Scarlett had pretty much forgotten the Opal intrigue.

"Actually"—Scarlett shrugged—"I don't know anything more about Opal today than I did yesterday, but I'm positive she isn't dead."

"Then where is she?"

"I haven't a clue. Of course, if we looked at everything rationally, we'd probably come to the conclusion that she took an unexpected trip—"

"Of course she took an unexpected trip—wrapped up inside a carpet and hauled off in *that* man's truck."

"Maybe Logan did haul off a carpet and maybe it did have a stain on it that looked an awful lot like blood," Scarlett said, "but I'm sure Opal wasn't inside."

Ida Mae folded her arms dramatically over her bosom. "That man's got you bamboozled, hasn't he?"

"No."

"He spent the night here. I call that bamboozling you—and God knows what else he did to you in addition to his bambooziling."

"How do you know he spent the night?"

"It just so happens I had breakfast at the Elk Horn Café this morning and the two of you were all the buzz." Ida Mae shook her head, her lips pursed in absolute dismay. "First there was talk about the two of you fooling around in the park, then the incident in the Dumpster, and then, the pièce de résistance came from Bill Spradling, who said he got a good look at the two of you making out on your doorstep before sunup this morning."

Scarlett rolled her eyes. "Okay, Logan did spend the night. But he's a nice guy, Ida Mae. He's not a murderer, not a gigolo—"

"Your dear, sweet mother thought Adam was a nice guy, too, and we all know that's not the truth. In fact, he proved that just this afternoon when I bumped into him in front of the Mischievous Moose."

Thank goodness the topic of Logan being a gigolo had been dropped. Scarlett wasn't crazy about discussing Adam, but at least her sex life was no longer the focus.

"So," Scarlett said, brushing one of far too many

specks of dirt off her jeans, "what did Adam have to say?"

"Not much, and you know how that annoys me." Ida Mae sauntered toward the kitchen, but Scarlett stopped her before her cowgirl friend gained entry.

"Did you say anything to him about Opal?"

"Of course not. I promised I wouldn't and I always keep my word. But I did ask him what he'd found out about the Jane Doe who died in your shop. In typical Adam fashion, he said, 'Nothing that would be of any interest to you.' " Ida Mae laughed cynically. "Obviously he knows more about her than he wants us to know."

"You think so?"

"You know as well as I do that Adam's got tons of secrets, things he's been hiding for years. Not that we'll ever be able to figure out what they are." Ida Mae scurried around Scarlett and pushed through the swinging kitchen doors. "Sweet merciful heavens." She clutched her chest. "What happened in here?"

"It's a long story."

Ida Mae tromped across the room, glowering at the mess. She plopped down in a kitchen chair. "I have nothing but time, Scarlett. I want to know everything."

Scarlett stared at the jigsaw puzzle on the table. "I want to know everything, too." She sighed. "And I have the strangest feeling that somewhere in the mess you see before you are the answers to all our questions."

Chapter 17

He was late. Damn late. After midnight, to be exact. Not exactly the way to impress a woman or make her trust what you say.

Logan eased his achy body out of the truck and looked for some sign of life through the front windows of A Study in Scarlett. But all was quiet and dark.

Heading to the side of the Victorian, he opened the gate and tromped down the narrow, gravel-lined passage between the bookstore and the barbershop. Last night, moonlight lit the way; tonight, clouds hid the moon and stars, and the backyard was illuminated only by the light coming through the kitchen window and the bedroom upstairs.

He'd had one hell of a day. Bad luck had been his bosom buddy through the entire fishing trip; hopefully, the grim reaper who'd been palling around with him had at last found another friend. Scarlett was the only one he wanted to hang around with tonight.

Crossing the backyard, Logan climbed the three wooden steps leading to the kitchen door and peered through the curtained window. Scarlett was there—pretty as ever, but sound asleep. Her arms were folded atop a mass of papers on the tabletop, her cheek cradled in the crook of her elbow. Wild red curls spilled over her brow. Tomorrow morning he wanted to wake with those curls spilled over him.

He tapped lightly on the window. Scarlett's eyelids fluttered open. At first she seemed dazed and confused, and then her gaze trailed toward the door. Their eyes caught and held. A soft smile tilted her lips.

So far, so good.

Pushing back her chair, Scarlett stood. She was an absolute knockout, and Logan couldn't help but study every inch of her. She had on mile-high red stilettos, something easy to kick off. An amazingly short red leather skirt rested low on her hips and hugged her bottom. A trio of gold stars dangled from her belly button ring. And her breasts were just barely encased in a strapless, red leather bikini top. Pretty nice attire for a date.

If he wasn't so damn tired, he'd burst through the door and take her on top of the table. But giving in to fatigue, he took a deep breath and merely concentrated on her sexy stroll toward him.

With her hand on the knob, she stared at Logan through the window, tilted her head to look at the clock on the far wall, then looked at Logan again. Her eyes narrowed slightly as she opened the door—not all the way, just a crack. Apparently she wasn't ready to let him come in from the cold.

"Rough day at the office?" she asked.

Logan leaned his shoulder against the doorjamb. "Derek Beauregarde the Fourth refused to listen to me when I told him where to fish, and in my attempt to rescue him from the rapids, he dragged me with him over a relatively short waterfall. Shortly after that, Tad Alexander accidentally shoved me into a beaver dam. To make matters worse, Erika Alexander pinched my butt every time her husband wasn't looking, and then took an expert swing with her fly rod and caught her hook in the crotch of my pants." Logan shrugged. "All in all, it was a fabulous day."

A smile touched Scarlett's lips. "Did Erika help you get the hook out?"

"Oh, yeah. She attempted to play touchy-feely, too, until Tad peeled her off of me, threatened to sue me for all I'm worth, which isn't a hell of a lot, and for good measure, kneed me in the groin."

Scarlett's concerned frown shot to Logan's zipper. "You're all right, aren't you?"

"Tad was the size of a pea and packed just as much punch. But I'm sore, I'm tired, and I tried like hell to make it here on time, but"—Logan shoved his hand into his hair—"my water heater broke, I had to take a cold shower, and when I finally thought I could leave, I had to change the flat tire on my truck."

Scarlett giggled. "You could have called and I would have come to you."

"Yeah, well, my cell phone is resting somewhere at the bottom of a beaver pond and I got some strange kind of static instead of a dial tone on my home phone. So I decided to drop by late." Logan smiled. "I thought you might have enough sympathy to take me in, take me to bed, and curl up with me while I sleep off a bad day."

"That's all you want?" Scarlett opened the door to let him in at last. "No sex? No food?"

Logan curled his fingers under her chin and tilted her face to his. "I want a lot of things, but right now, all I need is to hold you the rest of the night."

Closing and locking the door behind him, Scarlett slipped her hands up his chest, over his shoulders, and wove her fingers into his hair. "I'm awfully glad you don't want food, because the salad's wilted, the lemon chicken dried out hours ago, and Toby buried the asparagus somewhere outside. As for sex, well, I was afraid you'd hate me if I said I had a headache or told you I was too tired, and—"

Logan kissed away the rest of her words. She was warm and soft, and with the last of his strength, he lifted her in his arms and carried her upstairs.

Toby ran out of the room without any coaxing, and Logan kicked the door closed behind the dog. The covers had been turned back on the big canopied bed. Rose petals sprinkled the sheets, and unlit candles were scattered over end tables, the highboy, and the chest of drawers.

"I'd planned a romantic evening," Scarlett said. "Champagne, strawberries dipped in chocolate." She cupped his face in her palms. "I suppose most of it will keep until tomorrow, unless . . ."

She kissed him gently, making him forget the rocky

ride over the rapids, the prickly logs in the beaver pond, and the hook that had come within inches of rendering him weak and totally useless.

He forgot his aches and pains and thought only of soft flesh, of hot, rose-scented skin, and the taste of Scarlett's lips. Their kiss deepened. It burned, as did his body. Their tongues danced feverishly. Blood surged inside him; strength returned with a power he never knew he had. He wanted this woman desperately. All of her. Now.

Stalking toward the bed, he lay her down. She tasted so damn good that it was torture tearing his mouth from hers, but he wanted to taste even more.

Trailing his fingers down the length of her body, he shoved her little leather skirt up to her waist, ripped the tiny scrap of red satin thong down her legs, and with no further adieu, slid between her silky thighs and swept his tongue up the very heart of her.

Scarlett whimpered. Her body writhed, and her hips rose up for more. Another lick; another. Her fingers grasped his hair. At times he didn't know if she was trying to shove him away or draw him closer. He refused to leave—ever. Getting closer was something else entirely.

Somehow he rid himself of his clothes, while he watched Scarlett flick the button on her bikini top and toss the small scrap of leather to the floor. The skirt went next, and she tumbled back into the downy pillows.

Her body shimmered in the lamplight. Her eyes sparkled.

"I imagine this isn't quite as romantic as you'd wanted, is it?" Logan asked, his breathing hard as he entered her body.

Scarlett's fingers dug into his back. Her pelvis swirled and thrust, until he was deep, deep inside. "You're here, you're holding me, and you make me feel better than I've ever felt in my whole entire life." She smiled, joining him in a hard, rhythmic dance that Logan wanted to go on forever. "The way I see it," she said, kissing him lightly, "nothing's more romantic than that."

When morning came Scarlett saw the scar. She'd seen it the night she'd spied through his cabin window but had paid little attention to it each time they'd made love. Now it was vividly clear as the sun cast its first golden rays across the man in her bed. Lying on her side, Scarlett traced the thick gash across Logan's back, wondering who had done this to him, and why.

"Find something interesting?" Logan asked, rolling over and dragging her against him.

"The scar on your back." She reached around him, drawing her hand down the gash as she looked into his sleepy eyes. "What happened?"

"An accident." Logan pulled her hand away and kissed the tips of her fingers.

"It doesn't look like the result of an accident." Scarlett sensed from the way his jaw tightened that he didn't want to talk about it, but she needed to know more. "It looks like someone went after you with a machete."

"It *was* a machete." His words were just as sharp as the blade that had cut into him. He flung back the covers, swung out of the bed, and went to the window.

His tall, strong body was silhouetted against the pink and orange morning sky, but Scarlett could see the muscles bunch in his shoulders and arms, his tension palpable.

Dragging the sheet around her as she trundled out of bed, she crossed the room and drew her fingers over the vicious wound that stretched from his shoulder to tailbone. She kissed the swollen flesh and felt Logan flinch. "The guy who did this must have been out of his mind."

"He was out of his mind a long time before he did it." Logan sighed heavily. "Can we change the subject now?"

"You say that as if you knew him," she said, slipping in front of him, lightly kissing his hard, bronzed chest. "He wasn't a friend, was he?"

"Once upon a time." His gaze flickered downward. "End of discussion."

Scarlett curled her fingers over his jaw. She could feel his muscles tense as she traced the half-moon scar nearly hidden beneath his dark, heavy morning stubble. "Will you at least tell me about this scar?"

He chuckled lightly. "Awfully nosy, aren't you?"

"We established that fact a couple of days ago. Now please, tell me what happened."

Warm hands slipped down her back and cupped her bottom. It wasn't sexual—well, maybe a little. It was comforting, loving, and Scarlett rested her cheek against his chest, to feel the beat of his heart while he divulged a secret she was certain he didn't want to reveal.

"I was playing basketball with some neighborhood kids," he said. "We were young and stupid and competitive as hell, especially this one guy named Dave. God, it's hard to believe it was twenty-five years ago."

"You were eleven?"

"Yeah. Dave was twelve or thirteen and towered over me. I figured I needed a competitive edge to win, so I elbowed him just as he was getting ready to take a shot. Needless to say, he missed, and he wasn't happy about it."

"So he got back at you?"

Logan laughed. "I scored the winning points, and Dave got even with a broken bottle." He drew his index finger over the scar. "It's a C—for cheat."

"Let me guess. Dave's a hardened criminal now, and serving at least two life terms for murder."

"Last I heard he was an oncologist in Dallas."

Scarlett frowned. "Did he do *any* jail time?"

"Not that I know of."

"But he hurt you."

"I had it coming."

"That's the most ridiculous thing I've ever heard. I suppose next you're going to tell me you deserved to get whacked with a machete."

Beneath her hands Scarlett felt Logan's body tighten again. "That's not something I want to talk about."

"Please don't make me wonder." She curled her fingers around his neck and let him see her concern, her need to know the truth. "I've got this terribly overactive imagination and I can come up with all sorts of possibilities, none of them pleasant."

"It wasn't pleasant," he said bluntly. "But it's history, over and done with."

Pain radiated in his eyes, something deep, horrid, and intense, and she desperately wanted to see his smile again.

She stretched up on her toes and kissed his chin, then feasted on his hot, delectable flesh, nipping the vicious little C on his jaw and the stubbled skin stretching over the taut muscles of his throat. Her tongue roamed around the hollow of his neck, through swirls of dark chocolate hair, and dipped into his belly button, which seemed a nice place to play—for a moment.

Logan's fingers curled under her chin, and he tipped her face up so she could see his lighthearted frown. "If you think what you're doing right now is going to make me spill my guts about that blasted scar, you're wrong."

Scarlett smiled at the man looming over her. "I wouldn't dream of coercing you." She licked his belly button. "Of course, if you want to talk, I'm more than willing to listen."

"I'm not talking."

"That's what you say right now."

The kiss she pressed against his stomach made him sigh. Maybe it was more of a moan, something needy and eager. Again he sighed when she teased his belly button, then captured his ready and willing erection in her hand, kneading him, kissing the very tip, circling her tongue all the way down, all the way around, as if she were following the red stripe on a candy cane.

Who would have thought the Big Bad Wolfe could taste so yummy.

With his hands caught in her tangled curls, he held on tight. If he thought she might let go, he was sorely mistaken. He was wet and slippery, and she loved the feel of him in her mouth, the salty taste against her tongue, the texture of his skin, the distended veins, and his throbbing, heated desire.

She doubted if she could ever get enough of him.

In one fell swoop he lifted her in his arms, letting the sheet fall to the floor as he carried her to the bed. He kissed her, a soulful, searing kiss filled with longing and desire; a kiss to savor, to remember forever and ever.

His heart beat against hers; her whole body throbbed, and when his fingers slipped between her legs and touched that one special pulse point, she gripped the sheet beneath her and tried to hold on to her sanity.

Hot lips found her breasts. He sucked and licked and teased, then nipped the very tips of her nipples. Pressing her head back into the soft, downy pillows, she gave herself up to him—heart, soul, mind, and body.

Grasping her wrists, he imprisoned them above her

head, sank his hips between her legs, and thrust into her. A moan ripped from his throat. He stilled for only a moment, adjusting himself within her, until he felt just right, and then he kissed her softly, contorting his long, tall body to touch her lips tenderly.

"You feel so damn good," he whispered. "So damn tight. So sweet."

Suddenly he let go of her wrists and sank his fingers into her bottom, holding her against him. And then he moved, bringing into action, up close and very personal, those slow, sultry, pelvic rolls and thrusts she'd seen him do through the window, when he'd been imitating Elvis. Only this was far more entrancing, much more powerful. There was no guitar between them, no air, nothing but heavy breathing, sweat, and pulsing hearts.

She followed his undulating moves, craving his closeness, luxuriating in the heat of his body, the constant throbbing and friction deep inside her that set sparks flying through her blood. He made her cry out once, twice, a third time, as he continually carried her to the highest peak and pushed her over the top, only to pick her up and start all over again.

Once more. Once more. Higher and higher, her mind reeling, spinning, wanting everything and more, but mostly wanting to please him, to make him as happy as he was making her. And then he cried out, muffling his labored breaths, his intense pleasure, against her mouth, kissing her, holding her tight, softening the fall as they both came back down to earth.

Chapter 18

Logan sat at the kitchen table, studying the gentle sway of Scarlett's jeans-clad hips as she stirred sugar into his coffee. She wanted him to analyze the taped-together scraps of paper she'd carefully set in front of him, but detective work was part of his past; he much preferred scrutinizing Scarlett's curvy anatomy.

"It's bad enough having people think your mother was a nutcase," Scarlett said, walking toward him, cup in hand, "but my life's going to be a living hell when people find out that my father wasn't just a writer, but a murderer, as well."

"You're jumping to conclusions."

"Am I?" Scarlett set the cup of coffee in front of him and dropped into the chair at his side. She carefully picked up one patched-up piece of stationery after another, staring at the handwriting. "If some gossipmonger got his hands on this stuff, he'd have a field day."

Logan was having his own field day, concentrating on Scarlett's curls, still wet from their shower. Taking a drink of coffee, he let his gaze drift to her white

T-shirt, to her braless breasts, to hard, dark pink nipples thrusting out under thin knit fabric that was damp and clung to her skin. The hell with puzzles and murder mysteries, he wanted to sling Scarlett over his shoulder and take her back to bed.

But, gentleman that he was, he forced himself to stay put in the chair.

"Listen to this," Scarlett said, her pretty green eyes focused on the papers in front of her.

"Dear Miss O'Malley,

I'm sorry.
You're probably wondering why a complete stranger would begin a letter to you in such a way. There is a reason, of course. A good reason, which you will understand when you've finished reading this missive.
As I write, I can't help but wonder if I'm doing the right thing, but the doctor tells me my days are numbered and I feel the time has come to atone for my sins. It is time to talk of the past, to relieve myself of the burden that has weighed heavily on my soul.
It is always best to begin at the beginning, but I've rarely done what is best or what is right. So I'll begin by saying that the lives of three women came to abrupt endings because . . ."

Scarlett looked up from the page, eyes narrowed. "Lousy place for that part of the letter to end."

"Any idea what comes next?"

"The incriminating part." Scarlett shuffled through the papers. "I told you about this part before, but let me read it to you."

Logan got up from the table, poured himself more coffee, and stirred in three heaping spoons of sugar. He leaned against the counter, swallowed some of the strong, hot brew, and watched the pretty little redhead.

"Here it is," she said, and began to read once more.

"Edgar O'Malley planned the perfect murders . . ."

"There's a big piece of paper missing here, probably not too many words, though, and then it goes on to say . . .

. . . and then we carried them out, one after another after another . . ."

"Stop right there," Logan said, at last paying attention to what Scarlett had been reading.

Scarlett tilted her head up and glared at Logan. "I have to. I haven't pieced any more scraps together."

"Yeah, well what you have pieced together doesn't say your father killed anyone. It says he *planned* the perfect murders. It says *we* carried them out, and God knows who *we* could have been."

"*We* had to have been the old lady who died in my shop the other day. You know—Jane Doe."

"But you don't know that for sure. There's no sig-nature. You don't know if this was written by a man or a woman—"

"But I have a handkerchief that Ida Mae found on the floor when the paramedics were here. I'm sure it belonged to the woman." Scarlett retrieved the han-kie from the box on the kitchen counter that she'd marked Evidence, went back to her place at the table, and smoothed it out next to the letter she'd been reading from. "Look at this."

Logan put his empty cup in the sink and went to the table. Hands braced on the back of Scarlett's chair, he peered over her shoulder. "Okay, what am I supposed to look at?"

"The initials. E.G. Ida Mae thought the handker-chief might have belonged to my mom, since her ini-tials were E.G., but my mother would never have done work as shoddy as this. Her letters would have been entwined with ivy and roses. These are fancy, but nothing out of the ordinary. However, if you look at them closely, you'll see the E and the G are struc-tured just like the Es and the Gs in the letter."

Logan studied both the handwriting and the em-broidery on the cloth. "Okay, I admit, they look the same; I'll even admit that the letter must have been written by Jane Doe, because it seems the best expla-nation for now—but there's still nothing connecting your dad with any murders."

"But all of this looks convincing."

"A lot of things can look convincing if you want them to."

"What do you mean?"

"Just the other day you were convinced I'd stolen Jane Doe's wallet, just because I'd had access to it."

"Okay, so maybe I did jump to conclusions about a whole lot of things—"

Logan frowned. "A lot of things? You mean you've suspected me of even more?"

Scarlett laughed nervously. "Of course not." Her eyes dipped back to the paper, and Logan couldn't help but wonder if she was hiding something from him, something that made her uncomfortable. But he wasn't going to pry. Not now. If he pried, she might ask more questions about the scar on his back, which would lead to talk about Vegas, to his life as a cop, and how the job he'd loved had come to an abrupt end.

Someday he might share that nightmare with Scarlett, but not yet.

Logan flipped a chair around at the table and straddled it as he watched Scarlett attempt to piece together more puzzle pieces, her frustration evident as she blew at a curl falling over her brow.

"Why don't you give up?" Logan said.

Scarlett's eyes narrowed as she tilted her head to look at him. "Why don't you help?"

"I've never been any good at jigsaw puzzles."

"That's a lousy excuse."

"I'm much better at other things." Logan wrapped his finger up in one of her curls. "If we cleared off the table, maybe even one of the countertops, I could show you."

She smiled and sighed all at the same time. "As much as I'd like to have mad passionate sex right here in the kitchen, I can't, not until I get this mess straightened out."

"Why don't you give this mess to the cops and let them figure it out?"

"Because my dad's involved."

"You *think* your dad's involved," Logan said adamantly. "There's no proof of that, just as there's no proof any women were killed. For all you know this could be some hoax. But if it's not, the cops need to check it out."

"If I give this to Adam he'll tuck it away in a drawer somewhere. He'll think it's all part of some little intrigue I've conjured up."

Logan didn't want to get involved in this mess. He didn't want to go to the cops; but he didn't want to play detective, either—that life was over. What he wanted was Scarlett, and if the only way he was going to have her was to humor her, so be it.

"Tell you what, let's put all this stuff in an envelope, get dressed, and *we'll* take it to Adam. I'll make sure he doesn't tuck it away in some drawer.

"You'd do that for me?"

Logan cupped Scarlett's soft cheek in his hand and nodded. He kissed her gently and realized he'd do anything for the little redhead—he might even fall in love.

A flood of memories hit Logan when he entered the police station. Those memories, however, had nothing to do with the physical aspects of the place. Plentiful's two-story brick structure bore no resemblance whatever to the massive building he'd worked out of in Vegas. There were no uniforms in sight, no detectives, no derelict-disguised undercover cops, only a middle-aged clerk with short gray hair busily working away at a desk littered with picture frames and stuffed teddy bears. Even the smells were different, right down to the kind of coffee brewing on top of an old black file cabinet. In Vegas it was Folgers; the coffee here smelled like cocoa.

It was the underlying atmosphere of law and order that was similar, reminding him of his first day as a cop, when he'd walked into the briefing room all spit polished and raring to go, determined to be the best police officer Las Vegas had ever had. He'd put on a badge and sworn to uphold the law, to preserve peace—a tough job in some parts of Vegas. For fifteen years, even on the worst of days, he'd never faltered in doing his duty the best he could. A man couldn't do that without the trust of his fellow officers. When he'd lost that, he'd quit.

But damn if he didn't miss being a cop.

It felt good standing within the brick walls of Plentiful's police station. It was as if he belonged in this place, as if the door with *Adam Grant, Chief,* painted on it should have borne the name Logan Wolfe.

But it didn't and it never would. He wasn't a cop any longer, and he didn't plan to be one ever again.

The click of heels on the linoleum drew his eyes to the petite redhead. Scarlett paced the floor as she'd done for the past ten minutes, her cute little bottom sashaying back and forth in a short, blue leather skirt. Watching her wiggle kept him from concentrating on Adam's door and wondering if the guy was ignoring Scarlett or was taking care of business, but it didn't block out the familiar chatter coming through the monitor mounted high on one wall. Some cop, somewhere, was going 10-7 at the Cozy Cup, a dive Logan had seen out in the middle of nowhere, about thirty miles south of Plentiful. Most of the time he'd gone 10-7 at home, occasionally at his friend Charity's, sometimes at Denny's or the Krispy Kreme. Through the static he couldn't miss the dispatcher's cool and calm voice sending someone out to check on a couple of wayward cows plodding along the highway and holding up traffic. Not exactly a call to a 7-Eleven because the clerk had been blown away during a robbery.

In Vegas the dispatch center was a hubbub of bumper to bumper people. Here, dispatch came from some invisible man or woman working in a fairly quiet place a long way away. They probably looked out a window at mountains or prairies, maybe even at elk or pronghorn. In Vegas they stared at white walls and computer monitors, and went home with migraines.

A cop would probably be bored to tears in a place like this.

Maybe.

Logan turned his mind back to Scarlett's pacing, to her belly button ring. He'd rather be behind closed doors flicking the little gold firecracker dangling from her stomach and setting the cute little redhead ablaze, but since he was stuck here, he tore his thoughts from sex to the frown on Scarlett's face. She stared up at the black-rimmed clock on the wall and watched the minute hand tick to 10:45. They'd been here eighteen minutes, and she was growing restless.

She stopped her pacing in front of the counter, stood on the tiptoes of her sky-high blue heels, plopped her arms on the smooth wood countertop, and cleared her throat. The woman sitting at the desk on the other side rolled her eyes as she looked up from her computer.

"Sorry to bother you again, Janice, but could you please remind Adam that I'm out here. That I need to talk with him?"

"He's still on the phone, but if you're in a hurry, you could make an appointment and come back later."

Scarlett's sigh nearly echoed through the room. "That's okay. I'll wait."

Although Scarlett's back was to him, Logan had a pretty good idea that she was glowering at Adam's door. She'd crossed her arms over the chest of her firecracker emblazoned shirt, and the toe of her right high heel tapped repeatedly on the black-and-gray speckled linoleum floor. Patience was not one of her strong suits.

He, on the other hand, simply leaned against the wall, staring at Scarlett's leather-covered fanny, until Adam's door finally opened. The police chief stood in the doorway looking from Scarlett, to Logan, and back to Scarlett again. "Thanks for waiting." He turned to the clerk. "Buzz them in, Janice."

Not more than thirty seconds later they were seated in Adam's office. As planned, Scarlett didn't hand over the papers immediately. She'd wanted to—in her words—grill Adam first. She wouldn't hand over her potential evidence until she was positive he'd use it and not shove it down some dark hole.

"So," Adam said, sitting down at his desk, "what brings the two of you here this morning?"

Scarlett wasted no time getting down to business. "I wanted to know if you'd identified the woman who died in my shop?"

Adam leaned back in his chair. "As a matter of fact"—he grinned triumphantly—"I have."

Scarlett's eyes narrowed, a pretty good sign that she didn't believe what Adam had just said. "When?"

"Last night." He took a file folder from the OUT basket sitting on the corner of his desk, opened it, and stared down at the report inside. "Edna Grace. Age 83." His gaze rose just long enough to catch a glimpse of Scarlett's questioning eyes, then he recited a few more details. "She was from California. Chowchilla, to be exact."

Chowchilla set bells off in Logan's head. There was a woman's prison there—and not much else. He'd comment on that, but he figured he was better off keeping his mouth shut and just soaking up information.

"Did she have family?" Scarlett asked. "A husband? Children? Grandchildren?"

Adam didn't raise his eyes from the paper he stared at. "The police there told me she was living on welfare. By herself; no family."

Scarlett sighed in frustration. "How'd you identify her? From her fingerprints?"

"Nothing popped up fingerprint wise. Her name was on the ID in her wallet."

"You found it?"

"It found me, or I should say Tom Victor turned it in. He found it lying beside the ATM machine outside Wyoming First."

Another bell went off. The woman was on welfare, but was able to get money from an ATM? It was possible, Logan thought, but it sounded odd all the same.

Scarlett folded her arms on top of Adam's desk. "You didn't by any chance find out why Edna Grace came to see me, did you?"

"I found out everything the Chowchilla police could tell me, which wasn't much," Adam said. "They didn't have any missing person's report on her. They might never have known she was missing if they hadn't heard from me."

"How'd they know she didn't have any family?" Logan asked, figuring he should add something to the conversation.

"They checked out the address I found on her driver's license. Wasn't much of a place, just an old single wide in a senior park. Her neighbors and the doctor they located from records in her home provided the rest of the information."

"Such as?" Scarlett asked.

"Said she was a recluse; did nothing but read mysteries all day." Adam grinned. "Edgar O'Malley books, in fact."

Scarlett's eyes narrowed. "Do you think she knew my dad?"

Adam shrugged. "It's a possibility. She could have known him; she could have been an obsessed fan, but since we can't ask Ms. Grace, we'll never know for sure."

"Maybe her doctor knows," Scarlett said.

"The cops in Chowchilla already talked to her G.P." Adam flipped open the file again and stared at his notes. "Dr. Ferguson's his name. Didn't say much more than she had a bad heart and that she refused to go under the knife." Adam looked up from the paper. "Dumb move if you ask me, but people make dumb moves all the time."

Adam shoved out of his chair, crossed the room and looked out his window. It faced tall pines and the snow-capped Tetons. Nice view, Logan thought.

Some cops had all the luck.

Scarlett turned in her chair and stared at Adam's back. "Any idea how she got here?"

Adam tilted his head over his shoulder, a barely perceptible annoyance narrowing his eyes. "She rented a car. I found it parked on Yellowstone, a couple of blocks off of Main."

A rental car? The bells were ringing loud, now. How in the hell could someone on welfare get a rental car?

"Can I take a look at it?" Scarlett asked. "See if—"

"The rental agency had someone pick it up this morning," Adam interrupted. "I found an overnight bag inside it, a half-empty coffee cup, some cough drops, a fairly threadbare coat and a couple of maps, all of which is locked away, in case any questions ever come up."

Logan had a lot of questions, none of which he felt he could ask until he dug a little deeper.

"What happens next?" Scarlett asked, heaving a sigh. "Will she be buried in Chowchilla?"

Adam shook his head. "Cremation. Sometime tomorrow."

"Cremation?" Scarlett's eyes narrowed. "What's wrong with a burial? And what's the rush?"

"She's been around for days waiting to be identified." Adam kept his cool in spite of Scarlett's nagging questions, but Logan sensed the man was seething underneath the calm façade. "The woman's indigent," he continued, "she has no family, and the county she came from doesn't want to deal with her body. That leaves her in our hands. Cremation's no hassle and it's the least expensive route to take."

"I'll pay for a funeral."

"Don't be ridiculous, Scarlett," Logan said, coming to Adam's aid. It was a ploy to get on the guy's good side, to hopefully find out the real truth about Edna Grace. His scheme could easily backfire, but he had to give it a shot.

"I'm not being ridiculous." Anger radiated in Scarlett's words, in her narrowed green eyes. "You know how important this is to me."

"Adam's told you everything. The woman's dead, you didn't know her, so let him take over from here."

"She died in my shop. I gave her CPR and I've thought about her almost constantly for the past few days." Scarlett's jaw tightened. "If I want to bury her, I will."

"Funerals are expensive," Adam added. "The plot, the upkeep, the headstone."

"I've got the money and I'm going to do it."

"Fine." Adam laughed, shaking his head. "I'll call the funeral home and tell them to give her a modest burial—"

"With a service. And flowers, too."

"Tell you what," Adam said. "I'll tell Dan to call you for details."

"Good. By the way—" Scarlett reached for the envelope in her lap, but Logan stilled her hand.

"Was there something else you wanted to say?" Adam asked.

"Let's hope not." Logan laughed, not surprised to see the anger building behind Scarlett's eyes. "If she keeps this up she'll want to build the woman a marble mausoleum."

At that insensitive comment, Scarlett shoved out of her chair and went to the door. She glared at Adam. It was impossible to miss the loathing Logan saw in her eyes; it was exactly the same look she shot at him, right before she beat a hot and hasty retreat out of Adam's office and slammed the door behind her.

Logan chuckled, even though he was feeling pretty damn miserable inside. "She gets a little touchy at times," he said to Adam. "Gets a bit carried away, too."

"She's been that way since she was a kid." Adam walked to his desk and picked up the phone. "I sure as hell don't know why she's all hot and bothered about some dead woman she's never met, but maybe once the funeral's over, she'll put it behind her and move on."

"I sure as hell hope so. She's been driving me up the wall with all her little intrigues." Logan laughed. "Right now she's convinced that you knew Edna Grace, that you're hiding something."

"She's convinced I killed her mother, too." Adam grinned and shook his head. "Most people in town think she's a bit off her rocker, so they ignore her."

"You, too?"

"She's cried wolf one too many times in the past. She might be my stepdaughter, but I find it hard to get excited when she cries foul play. You might be wise to ignore her, too, before you become the pawn in one of her little mysteries."

Adam stuck his hand out and shook Logan's, bringing the conversation to an end. Logan looked deep in Adam's eyes, trying to find the truth about Edna Grace and about Scarlett's mom, but there was a void in Adam, an emptiness—as if the man didn't have a soul. Something was definitely wrong, and Logan—even though he wasn't a cop any longer, even though he really didn't want to get involved—couldn't help himself.

He was determined to help Scarlett, as well. All he had to do was catch up with her. Hopefully by then he'd have some kind of plan in mind.

Scarlett was at the far end of the park, jogging awkwardly in her sky-high heels when Logan was able to grab her arm. "Slow down, Scarlett, and listen to me," he said, somehow managing to spin the angry little ball of fire around, only to face red eyes rimmed with tears.

"How could you make a fool out of me in front of him?" she asked, jerking out of his grasp.

"I had my reasons."

"Mind sharing them with me?"

"Slap me first."

Her eyes narrowed. "What?"

He lowered his voice and spoke through almost clenched teeth. "Slap me across the face. As hard as you can."

"Are you out of your mind?"

He gripped her shoulders. "Damn it, Scarlett, slap me."

Her hand lashed out, striking him across the cheek. For a moment he thought his head might fly off his neck and roll across the park, but somehow he managed to yank her little body against him. "You didn't have to do it quite *that* hard."

"I'll do it again if you don't tell me what the hell you were doing in Adam's office."

"Trying to get on Adam's good side."

"Why on God's green earth would you want to do that?"

"So I can figure out what the hell he's up to."

Scarlett stared in disbelief. "You think he's up to something?"

"Yeah, don't you?"

"I've always thought he was up to something, but except for the Sleuths, no one has ever believed me."

"Well, I believe you. Hell, Adam was dishing out information about Edna Grace right and left. A lot more information than he had to. It's as if he thought we might check out everything he said, and if he lied about even one little detail, we'd check further."

"And he's hoping that if we checked just the stuff he told us and found out it was the truth, we wouldn't dig any deeper."

"Right."

"You think he's that conniving?" Scarlett asked.

"*You* think he's that conniving—and I think you're right. Too many things he said don't add up."

"Such as?"

"Edna Grace is indigent, she's on welfare, but she can rent a car, for one. Any *good* cop would have questioned that, but he just glossed over the whole thing."

"I didn't pick up on it. How did you?"

"Because I used to be a good cop."

Scarlett's jaw nearly dropped in shock. "A cop?"

"Yeah, and don't ask me any more questions right now. You're supposed to be pissed at me, so slap me again, turn around and storm off, and stay away from me until I tell you it's okay to be nice to me again."

"You can't just dump that cop thing on me and then tell me to get lost."

"I can and I did, which gives you a really good reason to be angry."

"Oh, I'm angry all right. How dare you let me believe you could have been a thief when you used to be a cop? How dare you—"

"Slap me"—Logan grinned—"and I'm sure you'll feel better."

Scarlett's eyes narrowed. "I'll slap you, all right. But first off, tell me what you plan to do while I'm busy fuming over this little secret you've sprung on me."

"I'm gonna get drunk."

"What?"

He didn't want to stand here all day explaining things, but maybe explaining it to Scarlett would make the hastily hatched scheme make more sense to him. "I'm going to the Misty Moon to play darts with Larry and Steve. I'm going to buy a lot of beer, and I'm going to see if they know anything about their good buddy Adam that they'd like to share with their new good buddy—me, the louse that everyone in this town will be talking about within five minutes of you slapping me again."

"Oh." Scarlett frowned. "And how long are we going to keep up this pretense?"

"Not long, hon, cause I prefer sleeping with you to sleeping without you." Logan grinned as he tugged her against him. "Now, I'm going to kiss you, and I want you to struggle."

"Do I have to?"

"Just do it, Scarlett."

He kissed her hard, his heart beating heavily as he soaked up her sweetness. For a moment he thought he might scrap the plan and take her to bed, but he had to get to the bottom of Adam's possible lies.

Scarlett struggled against him, her fists shoving at his chest as if she really meant it. Yet underneath her violent resistance he heard a purr down deep in her throat. And then she shoved away. The flat of her palm hit his cheek, and his teeth knocked together.

"Damn it, Scarlett." His hand clapped over his soon-to-be black-and-blue jaw.

"I hate you!" she screamed, the sound far too real for comfort. "Stay out of my store, stay out of my home, and stay out of my life."

If she could put on a show, so could he. "Come on, babe, you don't mean that."

Scarlett seethed. Her breasts rose and fell. Anger radiated from every pore in her little body. And then he saw the sparkle in her eyes. "So help me, Logan, you come anywhere near me again and you'll pay. Trust me, you'll pay big time."

With that said, Scarlett turned on a dime and stomped out of the park, her cute little bottom swaying as she walked. Fake or not, they'd just had one hell of a fight, and making up was going to be one hell of a good time.

Chapter 19

Logan walked into the Misty Moon before the Friday lunch crowd hit. The place was dimly lit, warm, and smelled like whiskey, peanuts, and burgers and steak grilled over mesquite. Someone had plunked quarters into the jukebox, and The King was wailing out "Stuck On You," which brought back vivid memories of a sexy belly button ring and the little lady who'd nearly knocked out his teeth just over an hour ago.

After the charade in the park, he'd killed time peeling out of town in his truck, driving around till he figured the rumor mill had done its thing, then screeching back into Plentiful and parking up the street from the saloon. All eyes turned on him now, but he ignored everyone in the place, ordered a rare cheeseburger, a mountain of spicy fries, a side order of Molly's special coleslaw, then got a Moose Jaw from the bartender and carried it to a booth close to the dart-tossing crowd.

Larry and Steve were nowhere in sight. He didn't know anyone else. But he'd wait as long as it took for the bigmouths to appear.

Molly dropped a platter-sized plate in front of him and whacked a second Moose Jaw beside it. Folding her arms over her ample breasts, she stared him down. "You disappoint me."

Apparently the word had spread.

Logan took a swig of his beer and let arrogance drip from his voice. "Is that so?"

"Yeah, that's so. I thought you were gonna be good for that little girl, thought she might have found herself a real humdinger, but I changed my mind after seeing what happened in the park a bit ago."

"That was a private discussion."

Molly's eyes narrowed. "Look, buster, Scarlett's been hurt enough in her lifetime without you sashaying that butt of yours into our town and hurting her, too."

He shrugged. "Seems to me she brings it on herself."

Molly shook her head. "Just leave her alone." She marched away, leaving no doubt in Logan's mind that his game plan was working.

He took a few more swigs of beer, checking to see who came into the saloon each time the door opened. Larry and Steve had both told him they spent their lunch hours at the Misty Moon, so he expected them any time. He had no idea what he was going to say to get them talking, but he'd winged stuff like this before; he could do it again.

Before the gang arrived, he ducked into the head when no one was watching, dumped the remains of both beer bottles, and headed back to his table to order more. Getting drunk wasn't part of his game plan; faking it was.

At last, the front door swung open. A skinny dude in a cowboy hat and his loudmouthed buddy swaggered into the saloon, grabbed a couple of beers, and headed toward Logan. Through their upturned bottles, Logan could see their grins. Apparently they'd heard the gossip.

Both jerks sat across from Logan. "Saw the walloping you got in the park awhile ago." Larry snickered as he grabbed one of Logan's fries and popped it in his mouth.

Logan chuckled as he rubbed his still stinging cheek. "I shoulda listened to you guys the other night. You were right—that woman's loco."

"Hope the piece of ass you got from Miss Scarlett made the rest of it worthwhile."

Logan shoved his bottle of beer in his mouth, clenched his teeth and shrugged. If he hadn't, he might have punched Steve clean through the booth and out the front door. And then he might have stomped the bastard's face into the boardwalk.

Maybe this wasn't such a good idea after all.

Molly walked by and shot half a dozen darts at Logan with a scowl aimed directly at his face.

"How about a round of Moose Jaw, Molly?" Logan said. "On me."

"Want me to dump it on you, or what?"

Logan laughed. "You aren't gonna be mad at me the rest of my life, are you, sugar?"

"Thinking about it. And if you call me sugar one

more time"—she leaned in close—"I'll hack off your balls, fry them in butter, and serve them to your pals. Is that understood?"

"Yes, ma'am." Logan saluted Molly as she stomped away. God, he loved the feisty lady. When this mess was over he'd send her roses.

Larry reached across the table and snatched another one of Logan's fries. "Heard you went to work for Joe Granger."

"Yeah," Logan said, fighting the urge to stab Larry's hand with his fork. "Get to go fishing all day and get paid for it, too." Of course, considering yesterday's disastrous trip, he should have been paid ten times as much.

Steve downed a swallow of beer. "You didn't ask Joe to pay you under the table, did you?"

"Didn't think about it," Logan answered. "Why?"

"Pisses Joe off if you ask him to do anything that isn't open and above board," Steve said, "as if cheating the government out of a few tax dollars is gonna hurt anyone."

"Shit," Larry said, chomping on another fry, "the guy's a damn Girl Scout leader. Too squeaky clean if you ask me."

Logan took a bite of hamburger. "I take it he runs a squeaky clean town, too."

"The guy may be mayor"—Steve laughed—"but he sure as hell don't run this place."

Logan's brow rose. "No?"

"Hell, no," Larry added. "Adam Grant's in charge. Some folks, like Joe, just don't realize it."

Just as the talk was getting good, Molly slammed three bottles of beer on the table. She aimed another frightening scowl at Logan. "I've got a tab running. Don't leave without paying."

When Molly was gone, Logan folded his arms on the table and leaned forward. "Do you guys help Adam run the town?"

Steve frowned, and Logan was afraid he might have asked that question far too soon. "He don't rough nobody up, if that's what you're thinking."

"He don't?" Logan said, trying to sound innocent—gullible even.

"Nah, it's just that way Adam's got about him, you know, like a snake oil salesman. Slick, real slick," Steve said. "He wants something around here, he asks, and most people give it to him. He wants something done, it gets done."

"Charming guy, huh?"

"Yeah." Larry laughed. "Couldn't ask for a better pal. We drink together. Shoot darts together."

Logan swallowed a gulp of beer. "Womanize together?"

"Adam ain't into that," Steve said. "Never has been as far as I can tell."

"Yeah, but remember when he used to go out of town every so often?" Larry aimed his question at Steve. "Said something about going to cop conventions, but I ain't never heard of cops holding conventions once a month."

"We thought he might have a girlfriend," Steve added. "Adam denied it. Got pissed anytime we brought it up. Then, of course, that crazy wife of his started asking the same kind of questions."

"Adam get pissed at his wife, too?" Logan asked. "Hit her, maybe?"

Larry shook his head. "Never heard him raise his voice at her, even when she was crazy as a loon."

"Think he loved her?" Logan asked.

Steve shrugged. "Could be. He used to parade the family around when Elizabeth was alive—before she smacked her car into the tree. Used to show up at all the town events with the wife and Scarlett. He ain't had no personal life—you know, females—since then, not that I know of."

"Don't know much about his life before he showed up in town, either," Larry volunteered. "Just kind of drifted in one day. Drove the women in town crazy."

"They thought he was Robert Redford at first." Steve laughed. "Course, he didn't have no money. Said he'd been a cop somewhere—L.A., I think—and got a job as a deputy here right off the bat. Then he set his eyes on Elizabeth O'Malley."

"I think he set his eyes on that Victorian first," Larry said. "Fanciest place in town."

"Course everyone in Plentiful knew that Edgar O'Malley owned the place. Used to come up here every so often to write—"

"And drink."

"Yeah, that too. A lot. Got a bad liver and croaked not long after the divorce. Willed that big old house to Scarlett. Bunch of money, too." Steve grinned.

"Too bad you screwed up with Miss Scarlett. I hear she's worth a small fortune."

"Out!" Molly appeared out of the blue, aiming her glare at Larry and Steve. "Both of you. Out! Now!"

The guys downed the rest of their beer and scooted out of the booth and out of the bar without putting up an argument, as if they'd tangled with Molly before.

An instant later Molly took their place, sliding her kilt-covered bottom onto the shiny red Naugahyde seat. She leaned fleshy arms on the table and stared at Logan. "What are you up to?"

"Not a thing," Logan said, munching on a fry.

"You a cop?"

"Nope."

"You're asking a lot of questions."

Logan leaned forward, too. He smiled. "Actually, I'm getting a lot of answers to unasked questions."

Molly's eyes narrowed. She bit her lip. "You out to hurt Scarlett?"

"You seem to be a good judge of people. What do you think?"

"I think you're up to something. I don't know what, but let me tell you something, buster. I don't like subterfuge." She shoved out of the booth. "I'm going to keep my eye on you," she said, looming over Logan. "One bad move, and you're gonna wish you wore armor on your balls."

Okay, so he couldn't fool everyone, Logan thought as Molly scuttled away. Larry and Steve were pushovers; Molly wasn't. He only wished she'd given him a few more minutes with the guys. He wanted to know more about all the cop conventions Adam had attended. Hell, he'd been a cop for fifteen years, and he'd never been to a one. He wanted to know more about Adam running the town—if there was more to know. Wanted to know more about Adam being interested in the Victorian, and how he'd felt when he'd found out Scarlett owned the place and not her mom.

He hadn't learned nearly as much as he wanted, but this was a start.

Logan was just about to leave the booth and head for home when he saw Scarlett's three old lady friends walk in. What had Joe called them? The Sleuths? He laughed to himself. Might be interesting to eavesdrop on some of their gossip—see if they might accidentally shed more light on what was going on behind the scenes with the chief of police.

Logan slid to the far side of the booth just as the Sleuths slid into the one next to his. Popping a now cold fry into his mouth, he listened to the scuffling of the ladies' shoes and their noisy chatter, which nearly drowned out the music on the jukebox.

"I can't believe the size of these booths," one of them complained. "I swear, Molly's squeezing everything in to make room for more tables."

"What makes you say that, Ida Mae?" another one said.

"Because last month I could sit here and my boobs didn't touch the table. Now I have to lift them up and set them on top."

Well, that was a bit of conversation he could have gone a lifetime without hearing. Maybe he'd be better off minding his own business.

"I tell you," one lady gasped, "that Logan Wolfe— scoundrel that he is—is responsible for everything."

Logan's ears perked up. Okay, so maybe eavesdropping had its merits.

"She wasn't herself yesterday. Not in the least."

"I noticed it, too, Ida Mae."

Who wasn't herself yesterday? he wondered, listening closely, trying to attach a name to each voice he heard.

"It's all *his* fault, I'm absolutely certain." Southern drawl. Definitely Ida Mae. "Ever since *he* showed up in town, poor sweet Scarlett has been in a dither, and it's not like her to get nervous or agitated."

So, they were talking about Scarlett. Good thing he'd started listening. And *he,* emphasized like a nasty word, probably meant him. What the hell had he done to raise the wrath of three elderly ladies?

"*Well . . .*" Logan strained to hear the women's sudden whispers. "Scarlett tells me *he's* a fishing guide," Ida Mae said. "As if a man like *that* could be interested in fishing."

Logan frowned. What the hell? What kind of man did they think he was? A thief?

"I tell you," Ida Mae said, "He's interested in one thing and one thing only—*sex*—and he's got our poor, sweet, misguided Scarlett all hot and bothered—"

"She's not!" Mildred gasped. Pretty much everything Mildred said came out as a gasp.

"She *is*," Ida Mae confirmed. "In fact, he's got her so bamboozled that she's completely ignored Opal's disappearance . . ."

What? Logan nearly choked on his beer. *Opal disappeared? When?*

"And I'm sure I told you that Scarlett wanted me to hide the fact from Adam and everyone else that our poor, dear Opal is *dead*."

Dead?

"*He's* responsible, you know," Ida Mae added. "I discussed that with Scarlett, too."

Shit.

"I don't believe any of this nonsense," the lady he still hadn't identified said. "He's not a murderer. I know it."

Damn right!

"Yes, yes, we all know what you think, Lillian," Ida Mae said in her imperious Southern drawl. "But I'll tell you this right now. Opal has not been paying *him* to . . . well, you know, to make her feel good, and I mean really, *really* good. No woman in her right mind would do *that*."

Logan gagged on his beer. Of all the lamebrained, idiotic ideas.

"That's not exactly what I think or even said—"

"Close enough, Lillian," Ida Mae interrupted. "He's a gigolo, he could easily be a thief, and even Scarlett agrees that he may have killed our poor, dear Opal."

She does, does she?

"Of course, the fact that he's a murderer isn't all

that surprising," Mildred added. "I mean, he is a little on the odd side."

What now? This conversation was going from bad to worse.

"Would you believe he has two pet grizzlies?" Ida Mae said. "He's even given them names: Yogi and Boo Boo. Can you believe that? Next thing you know we'll find out he serves them huckleberry pie and drinks home brew with them on the porch."

Were these women out of their minds?

"He has to be demented," Ida Mae continued. "And there's absolutely no telling what demented men will do."

Finally they got something right.

Logan downed the rest of his beer, dug in his pocket for a couple of twenties, which he hoped would come somewhere close to covering the bill, slapped them on the table, and shoved out of his seat. A second later he hovered over the booth full of loonies.

He cleared his throat. Three elderly ladies looked up. Three pairs of eyes widened. Three mouths fell open.

"Afternoon, ladies." Logan plastered a wide grin on his face, gave them a two-fingered salute, and said, "Have a nice day."

Before they could sputter, apologize, or even shut their mouths, Logan marched out of the Misty Moon headed for A Study in Scarlett.

The hell with his plan to get information on Adam. It was time to teach Scarlett Mary Catherine O'Malley a thing or two.

Chapter 20

Scarlett was dusting the Jayne Mansfield-Smythe display in the front window when she spotted the commotion up the street. If she wasn't mistaken, it looked like a lynch mob hot on the heels of a bad guy dressed in black, a man stomping up the boardwalk, his boot heels thudding so loud on the old wood planks that she could hear them a block away.

The rapidly approaching man was definitely Logan Wolfe. The rabble bore a remarkable resemblance to the Tuesday Morning Sleuths.

This didn't look too good. What especially didn't look good was the fact that Logan's heated gaze was aimed at Scarlett's window, and it wasn't love or desire she saw in his eyes—it was rage.

For some odd reason, she didn't think that look had any connection with the farce they'd executed in the park.

Her first thought was to run upstairs and lock herself in the bedroom where Toby was sleeping, but considering the look on Logan's face, he'd kick the door in and not bother to pay her for the damage. On second thought, she figured the safest course of action for herself and her house was to stand out in the open where, with any luck, she'd be protected by the masses.

Stepping outside, Scarlett listened to the merry tinkle of her crystal chimes, figuring it might be the last sweet sound she ever heard. Three rapid heartbeats later the Big Bad Wolfe stood before her, looking like he just might bite her head off. Hopefully this was all part of the plan he'd hatched in the park. And since Logan had specifically told her to keep up the ruse until he called the whole thing off, she was darn well going to play up her end of the farce.

Folding her arms tightly over her chest, Scarlett glared up at the man she was supposed to despise. "Didn't I tell you to stay away from me?"

Logan's jaws ground together. His eyes narrowed. "The game's over."

Scarlett swallowed hard. "In that case," she smiled sweetly, hoping that might calm down his heated temper, "maybe I should say good afternoon."

"Like hell!" Logan latched on to her poor little wrist and dragged her back into the shop. He slammed the door behind him, twisted the dead bolt, and fastened the chain lock.

Suddenly she wished she'd run to the bedroom. Just as suddenly, real anger shot through her. "What do you think you're doing?"

"Ensuring privacy. I've got a bone to pick with you—"

"About what?"

"About my reputation; the one you've done your best to shoot to hell."

Her shoulders stiffened as they faced off. "If anyone's hurt your reputation, it's you. You're the one who insisted we argue in the park; you're the one who insisted that I slap you. Then there was your little masquerade in Adam's office, making the king of all louses think you're a louse, too. And then there was the incident in the park where, in an attempt to further mess up *my* reputation, you had the gall to get my belly button ring hung up on your jeans. Surely you haven't forgotten that."

"I haven't forgotten a blasted thing. You're the one who seems to have forgotten—"

"Scarlett!" Ida Mae's thunderous Southern drawl ripped through the closed door, bringing the not-so-pleasant conversation to a rapid end. Scarlett spun around at the sound of Ida Mae's repeated "Scarlett!" and her hard-knuckled ra-ta-tat-tat on the window. "Are you okay in there? He isn't going to kill you, is he?"

"She's perfectly fine, and if I was going to kill her, I would have done it by now," Logan barked, flipping the OPEN sign to CLOSED.

Scarlett flipped the CLOSED sign back to OPEN. "You may be mad at me for God knows what reason, but you can't close my shop."

"I can and I will." Logan's eyes narrowed as he flipped the sign again, then tugged Scarlett away from the window.

"Should we call the police?" Ida Mae shouted, her pudgy nose now pressed against the window.

"Don't call anyone, especially the police," Scarlett hollered back. A lot of good it would do calling the police anyway, since Adam and Logan were now bosom buddies. Besides, Adam would merely rejoice at this latest pickle she'd somehow gotten herself into.

With another tug on her arm, Logan dragged her not-too-eager-to-go body out of the room, her five-inch spikes clattering on the hardwood floor right behind his thumping boots. "Where are you taking me?"

"Someplace where the loonies in this town can't see us."

"And what do you plan to do?" she asked as they reached the seedy underbelly of her store, otherwise known as the Edgar O'Malley True Crime room. "Handcuff me again? Slap me around, maybe?"

Logan's eyes blazed as he pushed her—gently—up against a bookshelf in the windowless room. He clasped her shoulders and leaned forward, standing just a hair's breadth away. Blazing eyes bore down on her. "Do you really think I'd beat you up?"

"I don't know what to think. An hour ago you told me to slap you. You told me to be mad at you, and now you've done this big flip-flop and are obviously ticked off at me." She drew in a deep breath. "Damn it, Logan, this morning you were sucking on my toes and telling me in great detail what you had in mind for our date tonight."

"The date's off."

"Mind telling me why, because I'm totally clueless here."

"Because I thought we had this trust thing going. Because I thought we had everything out in the open, but apparently we didn't. Apparently you neglected to tell me that in addition to thinking I was a gigolo and a thief, you and your cohorts also think I'm a murderer."

That was the last thing she'd expected him to find out about. She stared over his shoulder, afraid to look into his pain-filled eyes, and said softly, "That was a mistake."

"You're damn right it was a mistake." He cupped her face in his hands and forced her to look at him again. "Do you have any idea what that kind of rumor could do to someone, or how hard it is to live down something like that? And while we're at it, do you even care?"

"Of course I care. The last thing I want to do is hurt you or anyone else. As for that ridiculous murder suspicion, I wanted to tell you last night, but I'd already told you about my other suspicions and I was afraid if I heaped that one on top of all the others you'd walk away from me."

"So instead I get to hear about it in a crowded bar?"

"You shouldn't have heard it from anyone, anywhere."

"But I did, and God knows how many other people in the bar heard it, as well."

Scarlett reached out to touch him, but he jerked away. "I'm sorry," she said, sighing miserably, desolately. "I should have told you."

Logan shoved a hand through his hair. "Is there anything else you should have told me? Any other suspicions, any other rumors about me that you and your little old lady friends might have spread around? You know, like maybe I'm a terrorist, a hired assassin, or a drug lord out to corrupt everyone in town?"

"Contrary to what you might think, I haven't been spreading vicious lies about you. I did tell Molly that your kisses nearly knocked my socks off, and I told Ida Mae that you were the nicest guy I'd ever met. And . . . and in spite of all the yelling you're doing right now, I still believe that."

Logan shook his head, crossed the room and slumped in Edgar O'Malley's old leather chair. "If you think I'm such a nice guy, how come you thought I was a murderer?"

"If I tell you, you'll be even more upset."

His eyes narrowed. "That's impossible, so spit it out."

"Well . . ." She took a deep breath. "There was all this evidence. Start stacking one piece on top of another and after awhile it's pretty convincing."

"Evidence or speculation?"

"Speculation, mostly."

"Damn it, Scarlett. Good investigators—and I mean *good* ones—don't go jumping to conclusions. Make a bad arrest, one without all your ducks lined up in a row, and you can blow a perfectly good case. Or you can ruin a person's reputation. Hell, you can get them killed."

"No one meant to harm you, but you're the one who was hauling around a bloody carpet."

"Bloody carpet?"

"Yeah, a bloody carpet. The one you lugged out of Opal's house."

Logan laughed, the sound so loud and so full of anguish that it reverberated through the room. "Don't tell me you were spying on me when I was at Opal's."

"Actually, Ida Mae was spying on you."

"Mind telling me why?"

"She hadn't started out to spy on you; she'd gone to Opal's to warn her about you."

His brow furrowed, and Scarlett was afraid those horrid frown lines in his forehead might stay there forever. "Warn her about what?"

"That you might be a rip-off artist. That you might be out to steal her money—"

"Or have my way with her—*if* I got paid for those services, of course."

"Well, yes, that did come up in the conversation, too." Scarlett nervously drummed her finger on one of the bookshelves. "I didn't want to believe anything bad about you, but when Ida Mae told me you'd hauled a bloody carpet out of Opal's house—"

"And," Logan interrupted, "probably told you that Opal's body was rolled up inside."

"Ida Mae did strongly hint that that was a possibility, and when we started adding everything up, like you coming out of the bank with Opal, you kissing Opal, you having dinner with Opal and letting her pay the tab for everything, including an expensive bottle of wine, well, it all looked rather convincing."

"Only because you put a negative spin on what you saw; only because you assumed the worst about me."

"I'm sorry, Logan. You know I have trouble trusting people—"

"Maybe you should limit that distrust to people who deserve it, instead of heaping it on everyone who crosses your path."

"I've said I'm sorry. It's over and done with. If you want me to stand on the rooftop and tell everyone within earshot that you're a nice guy, that you're not a murderer, I will. But . . ." Scarlett wiped an unwanted tear from her cheek. "Can't we start over; try to put this behind us?"

Any of the warmth she'd once seen in Logan's eyes had faded. "If I could laugh this whole thing off, I would. I left that bar thinking all the ridiculous crap I'd heard about me was nothing but fun and games, that we could yell at each other about it, get it out of our systems, then hop in the sack and pretend nothing had ever happened. But . . ." He shook his head, sighing hard. "It goes a lot deeper than that."

Pushing out of the chair, Logan walked to the door, defeat heavy in his steps. Just outside the room, he turned slowly and focused sad eyes on her. "Relationships are built on trust, Scarlett. If you don't trust me, if every time I turn around you suspect me of doing something wrong"—he shrugged—"we've got nothing."

"So you're just going to walk away, as if I don't deserve another chance; as if what we've shared meant nothing?"

"It meant too damn much. Unfortunately, it seems our relationship has been a little too one-sided, and that's not what I want."

Turning on his heel, Logan walked from the room, the dull thud of his boots on the floor keeping time with the spike being hammered into her heart.

The front door opened and closed; the chimes seemed to toll farewell. Another tear slid down Scarlett's cheek, and she realized that just when she'd started to trust someone, she found out that she was the one who couldn't be trusted, and it hurt like hell.

Chapter 21

Scarlett dropped into her dad's chair and wiped away the blasted tears sliding down her face. She'd made a mess of things. Such a big, huge mess.

How could she possibly get Logan back? How could she make him understand that she trusted him, that she wanted to be with him, that she'd do anything to make up for all that had happened?

She rocked back and forth, seeing the pain in his eyes all over again. Hearing his words: "Relationships are built on trust, Scarlett. If you don't trust me . . . we've got nothing."

Nothing didn't hold you close all night long. Nothing didn't wipe away your tears when you talked about your fears. Nothing didn't laugh with you or share your silly secrets.

She'd shared so much with Logan. So very much. Obviously they had *something*.

Wait a minute. Logan expected her to trust him—and she did, damn it. She'd told him that again and again, in a whole lot of different ways. Truth be told, he was the one who currently had trust issues, he was the one who didn't want to share his secrets with her.

The louse.

He'd made her feel guilty; lower than low. Yeah, she hadn't been totally honest with him, but when had he ever been totally honest with her? He'd ducked her questions about what he'd done before coming to Plentiful, and even when he had finally told her he'd been a cop, he'd refused to tell her why he'd quit the force.

Was he hiding something? Didn't he trust her enough to tell her the truth?

Scarlett shoved out of the chair. It was time she gave Logan a piece of her mind.

She stomped off but got only halfway across the room before Ida Mae, Mildred, and Lillian bustled through the door.

"Well, *he* sure left in a snit." Ida Mae huffed and puffed as she circled Scarlett. "He didn't hurt you, did he?"

"Oh, Ida Mae," Mildred gasped, "does she look hurt?"

"She looks mad," Lillian said, staring at Scarlett through fuchsia-colored Elton John glasses. "If you ask me, she looks like she's ready to go another round with Mr. Wolfe."

"Damn right," Scarlett said, then turned her heated eyes on the Sleuths. "I'm about ready to go a few rounds with the three of you, too."

"And what, pray tell, have we done?" Ida Mae tipped her cowgirl hat higher on her forehead as she glared at Scarlett.

"If I'm not mistaken, you were telling everyone at the Misty Moon that I thought Logan was a murderer."

"Actually," Mildred said, gripping her black patent purse, "we were talking amongst ourselves and much to our dismay, we learned, quite unexpectedly, that Mr. Wolfe was lurking at the table behind us, eavesdropping on our every word."

"You don't think he's going to kill *us*?" Lillian asked. "I mean, now that he knows we know the truth."

"He's not going to kill anyone." Scarlett marched out of the room with the Sleuths stomping right behind her. She spun around when she reached the parlor. "Let me make this clear to all of you, right here and now. Logan hasn't killed anyone."

"He might have told you that, Scarlett," Ida Mae said, folding her arms across the bosom of her fringed cowgirl shirt, "but that doesn't mean it's true."

"He's not a murderer," Scarlett repeated, but her words seemed to fall on deaf ears.

"You believe that because he's got you bamboozled," Ida Mae stated. "But I know what I saw—a bloody carpet. I know that Opal's disappeared and her poor, bullet-riddled body is probably wrapped up in what was once a beautiful Aubusson. The way I see it, it's high time I go to the police and let them know that Mr. Wolfe murdered Opal."

"Maybe you should."

All heads spun toward the door. With the sun shining behind him, Logan's big, dark silhouette cast a shadow that spread forebodingly across the floor. "If you've got evidence against me," he said, his voice thunderous, "good, solid evidence, give it to the police. And if you don't trust giving it to Adam, call the State Police. Hell, call the attorney general."

Mildred and Lillian cleared a wide path for Logan as he stalked into the room. His eyes were hot—again—but his rage seemed to have subsided a bit, slowly being replaced by what looked like a mixture of frustration, hurt, and some strange kind of determination.

He was within feet of Scarlett when Ida Mae stepped between them, steeled her shoulders, and stated in no uncertain terms, "I think you should leave."

"I have every intention of doing just that." Logan sidestepped Ida Mae's short, stout body, latched on to Scarlett's hand, and tugged her across the parlor and out of the shop.

"What are you doing now?" Scarlett demanded, her heels clipping out a rapid tattoo on the boardwalk and across the street as she tried to keep up with Logan's hurried pace.

"Taking you away from here."

"I can't go anywhere. I've got a business to run. A dog to feed."

Logan stopped dead in his tracks, turned around and hollered over her head at the Sleuths standing in the doorway of A Study in Scarlett, their faces all aghast. "You ladies take care of the shop and the dog."

"Should we call the cops?" Ida Mae yelled back.

"No!" Scarlett shouted, once again scrambling after Logan.

"When will you be back?" Mildred's voice echoed off the clapboard buildings.

"She'll be back when I'm damn good and ready to let her come back," Logan bellowed.

It was like something in a movie. Logan the tall, stalwart and frustrated cop, she the petite, wacky woman who'd been making a mess of his life, as well as her own, rushing up the street, past friends, acquaintances, and tourists—all of them watching in awe.

"Do you think you could slow down a bit?" Scarlett asked. "I'm having trouble keeping up."

"Either you keep up or I fling you over my shoulder."

"You wouldn't."

"I would."

"Do you mind telling me how much longer I have to run? And while we're at it, do you mind telling me where we're going?"

"To Opal's place," he said gruffly.

"Why?"

"To prove I'm innocent."

Scarlett jerked on his hand and somehow got him to stop, right in front of the Misty Moon. Molly pushed through the swinging doors, folded her arms across her chest, and glared at Logan. Ted Lapham, broom in hand, came out of his jewelry store to stare. The Mischievous Moose bronze standing in front of the emporium seemed to frown, as did the patrons who barreled out of the souvenir trap to see what was going on.

"Since we have an audience," Scarlett stated, standing on her tiptoes in an attempt to stare Logan in the eyes, "I'll repeat what I said earlier. I know damn good and well you're innocent. You're not a murderer, you're not a thief, and you're not some slick and devious lothario out to take every little old lady in this town for her money. I don't even think you want *my* money—and let me tell you, I've got oodles of it."

Logan gripped her shoulders. "You believe all of that now, but how long is that going to last? Until one of your friends puts another nasty little bug in your ear about me?"

"No, damn it. I'm through listening to rumors."

"I'd like to believe you, but I don't."

"And you think that comes as some big surprise to me?" Scarlett's jaw tightened. "You accused me of not trusting you, but you don't trust me either."

"Damn right, I don't."

"Then why the hell are you bothering with me?"

"Because . . ." His breathing was hard. His teeth ground together; his eyes narrowed. "Because for some stupid ass reason I haven't yet figured out, I think I've fallen in love with you."

"Thank God!" Molly slapped Logan on the back. "Now that you've got that out in the open, could you please take this little love spat somewhere else. You're ruining my business."

Molly shoved her plump, kilt-wearing body back

through the swinging doors. Ted Lapham disappeared inside his shop. The Mischievous Moose grinned. And Scarlett glared at Logan.

"What do you mean you *think* you've fallen in love with me? And why is that such a silly ass thing in the first place?"

"Because a man would have to be mad to fall in love with you." Logan tugged on her hand, and once again she had to jog to keep up with his angry movements. "Because I came to Plentiful to fish, not to fall in love. Because I haven't known you long enough to fall in love."

"Well, excuse me for making your life so damn difficult."

Logan halted when he reached his big bad truck, threw open the door, and just barely stopped short of picking her up and tossing her inside. "You need some help getting in?"

"Thanks for the offer, but I'd rather do it myself." She grabbed hold of the steering wheel with one hand, the back of her baby blue leather skirt with the other, hefted one spiked heel toward the cab of the truck and didn't come anywhere close to getting a foothold.

Half a second later Logan's hands were on her waist. He boosted her up and into the truck. "There, now sit down and fasten your seat belt."

"Where would you like me to sit?" she bit out, getting darn fed up with his prickly little mood. "The middle or the passenger side?"

"Take your pick. Contrary to what you might think, I don't bite."

"Ha!"

Logan swung into the truck, shoved the key into the ignition, and gunned the engine as he peeled away from the boardwalk and tore up Main Street. When they were just out of town, he hit her with a scowl. "What was that '*Ha!*' supposed to mean?"

"You do too bite, and I've got the marks to prove it."

"Yeah, well, you did your own fair share of biting." She folded her hands politely in her lap and stared out the front window at the clouds thickening over the Tetons. "I'd planned to do more biting. Hell, I'd planned to bite you in places you've never even dreamed of being bit, and I'd planned to do even more, but that's over. Done. Kaput. I don't care if you did make some lamebrained attempt at saying you love me, you called off our date and it's still off."

"Fine. I'll sing my off-key love songs to Yogi and Boo Boo. I'll sleep with Snagglepuss. I'll—"

"Wait a minute." Scarlett flashed a suspicious frown in his direction. "Are you still ticked off because I thought you were a murderer, or because you cancelled our date and now you're going to miss out on hours and hours of hot, no-holds-barred sex?"

"I can do without sex if I have to."

"Is that right?"

"Yeah. I'm completely self-sufficient and can take care of myself when the need arises."

"And how much pleasure does *that* give you?"

His knuckles whitened on the steering wheel. "Not as much as you did."

Well, that was nice to know, Scarlett thought, staring through the windshield. "If it's any consolation," she said softly, "I can take care of myself, too, *when* the need arises."

He shot a quick glance at her out of the corner of his eye. "And which do you prefer? Your hand or my body?"

"I think I've made it pretty darn obvious what I prefer, but since it's apparently not going to happen again, maybe we should change the subject or just be quiet."

"Fine. Quiet works for me."

Quiet was all fine and dandy, but quiet gave Scarlett too darn much time to think about Logan's half-hearted confession of love. Did he mean it, or didn't he? And how did she feel about him? She'd never been in love before. Hadn't wanted to fall in love. But heavens, he made her feel as if she could dance on the clouds. And it wasn't just during sex—it was every second he was around.

Even now, when her anger was simmering, she didn't want to be anywhere else but at his side. It was the craziest thing; maybe when this day ended, she'd understand her feelings—and his.

They rode quietly for the next five minutes, at last reaching the winding road that led to Opal's hilltop home, nestled in the middle of one hundred and twenty acres of pristine beauty, with a fabulous view of the Tetons.

"So," Logan said, breaking the silence as he sped up the narrow gravel road. "*if* I was guilty of killing Opal, what was my motive?"

She'd rather discuss his statement about being in love with her, but that topic seemed to have been pushed aside. "Do we really have to discuss Opal, and motive, and murder?"

"Yeah, we have to discuss it. Every single solitary speck of it. If you're going to play Jayne Mansfield-Smythe, you might as well do it right."

"I'm through with that. I've gotten myself into more jams in the last few days than Jayne gets into in two or three books, so I think it's high time I give up my sleuthing. I'm even going to convince the Sleuths to give it up."

"You're not through and they're not through."

"What makes you say that?"

"You wanted to be Nancy Drew when you were a kid. Twenty years later you still want to play spy. Your father wrote mysteries; you own a mystery bookstore. It's in your blood, and nothing I say or do is going to change that."

She stared at him in disbelief. "You mean you don't want to change me, make me be something I'm not?"

"Why would I want to do that? I'm the one who keeps coming back for more of your zaniness. I don't do things I don't want to do, Scarlett. I'm here, now, and this is where I want to be—in spite of everything."

"Then why don't we just put this whole silly thing behind us, go to your place, and let me make up for all the trouble I've put you through."

"Later. First we've got to solve this Opal mess.

Then we've got to talk about Adam, and Jane Doe, better known as Edna Grace."

"That reminds me," she said, her anger slipping away, "I forgot to tell you that I've got Edna's funeral planned for the day after tomorrow—"

"We can talk about all of that later."

"But I'd like to talk about it now. And I want to know what, if anything, you found out at the Misty Moon."

"Later," Logan said flatly. "Right now I'm going to teach you the correct way to play detective."

She didn't want to play detective. Not now. "Couldn't I just enroll in a course or something?"

Logan's eyes narrowed. Apparently he wasn't going to let her off the hook. "Ninety-nine percent of the time, there's a motive for a murder. Occasionally it's just some stupid, off-the-wall killing for kicks, but that's rare. That means if I *had* killed Opal—which I didn't—I would have had a motive. Mind telling me what you think that was?"

Scarlett looked out the window at the beauty surrounding her. "Isn't it obvious? Opal lives in a multimillion-dollar home in a prime location. A lot of people would kill to have a place like hers."

"Okay, so I like the house; I like the view. I want it for my own and I decide to kill Opal to get it. But first off, I've got to make sure I'm in her will, that the house has been left to me." Logan's brow rose. "Right?"

"I suppose."

"So," he said smugly, "am I in her will?"

"I don't know."

"Why didn't you talk to Opal's lawyer?"

Scarlett began to nervously fidget with the end of her seat belt. "I didn't think about it."

"All right, so you didn't check out her will, but did you go to her bank and see if any large sums of money had recently been taken out, you know, to pay for my services? After all"—he grinned—"my services are worth a hell of a lot."

"No, I didn't check out her bank account."

"Why not?"

"It didn't cross my mind."

He turned into Opal's driveway. "A good cop would have checked those things when looking for a motive."

Scarlett blew a curl from her forehead. "I'll keep that in mind next time I'm faced with solving the disappearance of a friend."

Logan pulled his truck to a stop in front of Opal's home. It looked like it was worth a bazillion dollars, not just a multi-million, Scarlett thought, as Logan climbed from the cab. He went around to the passenger door and helped her out, his hands lingering on her waist after he lifted her to the ground. For one moment she thought he was going to kiss her. She even thought about closing her eyes in anticipation, but Logan's hands loosened, then drew away.

He leaned casually against the truck, arms folded across his chest, and stared at the fabulous log and river rock house sitting atop a bluff, at the lush green landscaping surrounding it, then tilted his head to look at her, his face void of expression. Nevertheless, she had the feeling a smirk lurked somewhere behind that nonchalant façade. "Where do you think we should begin looking?"

"What are we looking for?" she asked, not too sure how this game was supposed to be played. "A dead body?"

"I thought I hauled Opal away in a carpet."

Scarlett rolled her eyes. "That's right, I'd nearly forgotten. So what *are* we looking for?"

"Considering the lack of motive, I suppose we should look for some kind of physical evidence, you know, proof that she was murdered." Logan strolled up the black slate path leading to the front door, with Scarlett fast on his heels.

"Are we going to start inside?" she asked.

"If that's where you want to begin." He dug into his pocket and produced a key.

Scarlett frowned as he shoved the key into the lock. "Where'd you get that?"

"Good question." His mouth quirked into a grin. "I might have taken it out of Opal's purse after I killed her. I might have found it under the doormat. Then again," he said, giving her the silly evil eye, "she might have given it to me."

"And why would she do that?"

"Another good question. That's what a good investigator does. He asks questions. Lots of them."

That said, Logan stepped over the threshold and stopped in the center of a colossal entryway, where afternoon sunshine streamed in through the cut glass cathedral windows, scattering rainbow prisms across the black slate floor. The place was gorgeous and imposing—like Logan—but at least it wasn't eyeing her belly button ring, or grinning.

"Mind telling me what you find so funny?"

"That charm you're wearing."

"You mean this?" She flicked the little golden fish attached to her belly button ring.

"Yeah. You were wearing a firecracker earlier today."

"You noticed?"

"I'm an ex cop. I notice everything—your belly button in particular." His gaze swept to the golden fish again. "You didn't by any chance wear that for my benefit, did you?"

"As a matter of fact I did," Scarlett said, her stilettos clicking on the slate as she headed for the living room.

Logan caught her arm gently and circled her until they faced each other. "Why?"

"You like to fish." She shrugged nonchalantly. "Earlier today, when I thought we might be getting together tonight, I thought you might like to catch this one."

Reaching out, he curled a hand over her cheek and lightly stroked her lips with his thumb. "Keep doing nice things like that and I might reinstate our date."

"Keep being ornery and smug, and"—she smiled innocently—"I might not let you go fishing."

He smiled wickedly. "My frame of mind's improving rapidly. Who knows, I might be Mr. Congeniality by the time we finish our little investigation."

"One can only hope," Scarlett said. She dragged her fingernails lightly over his cheek and set about surveying the room.

Logan sat on the raised rock hearth, resting his forearms on his knees. "Okay," he said, "what should you look for now?"

Scarlett decided to play along with his silly game and took a stab in the dark. "Blood?"

"Maybe I cleaned it up."

"Then what did you do with the bloody rags?"

He smiled at her rapid comeback. "What do you think?"

"If you were smart, you'd take them far away from here and dispose of them. Burning them seems like the obvious thing to do. But . . ." She hit him with a self-satisfied grin. "You're not the smartest murderer in the world, and you're not all that good at hiding evidence. After all, you were seen buying a rifle at Teton Outfitters and you had it with you when you, um, disposed of the bloody carpet."

Logan smirked. "I did?"

"Didn't you?"

"Maybe I bought a fishing pole."

Scarlett threw her hands up in the air. "That's what I told Mildred, but she didn't believe me. Ida Mae didn't believe me, either. They insisted it was a rifle." Scarlett's eyes narrowed. "Was it *really* a fishing pole?"

"You could talk to Joe Granger, check out my story, or . . . you could trust me."

There it was again, that nasty little word called

trust that was causing so many problems for them. "I do trust you, Logan," she said for the umpteenth time. "But," she added with a wry smile, "a good investigator would check out the story."

"Damn right."

He shoved up from the hearth and paced the room, hands clasped behind his back, looking a lot like Sherlock Holmes might have looked if he'd been tall, dark, and handsome.

"Next question," he said, the sound of his boot heels thudding on the slate floor. "Did I get anything else when I was in town buying the fishing pole that you seem to think might have been a rifle?"

Scarlett had to think for a moment, remembering the way Mildred had flipped through the surveillance notes in her little black diary. "I believe you bought a carpet."

"Did you see a carpet at my place the other night?"

"No. Just wood and leather and"—her gaze trailed over his stunning body—"every inch of you. In fact, I wouldn't mind going back to your place right now and—"

"Don't change the subject, Scarlett. What did I do with the carpet?"

Stubborn. The man was definitely pigheaded. "I suppose you wrapped Opal's body in it."

He chuckled. "Why would I spend a few thousand dollars on a brand-new carpet when I could have shoved the bloody body into a cheap plastic trash bag?"

"Because you like to do things with pizzazz?"

"Think again."

Scarlett squinted; her jaw tightened. And then the obvious dawned on her. "To replace an already blood-stained carpet?"

"Not bad."

Ah, a compliment. Obviously her deducing was getting better. "You know, there's a possibility the floor beneath the carpet might be stained, or have traces of blood embedded in it."

Logan cocked a dark brow. "You think so?"

"It's a possibility." She looked around the room, but there were no carpets in sight. "I suppose the next step should be to look for a new carpet."

"Lead the way."

Scarlett proceeded methodically, Jayne Mansfield-Smythe at her best, studying the wide hallway first, then entering an immense library. Logan leaned against the doorjamb, watching her as she walked about. His gaze flickered most often to her belly button, and she wished they could get this whole thing over so something besides his gaze could flick the little gold fish dangling from her stomach.

Getting this thing wrapped up meant concentrating, and at last she saw the stained-glass patterned rug that sat between a grouping of forest green leather easy chairs.

"This carpet looks new," she said. "There's no wear on it. There aren't any impressions of shoes or a vacuum cleaner." She lifted the carpet and saw . . . nothing suspicious. "Well . . ." She shook her head in frustration. "It was a possibility, or it would have been if the floor was wood and could absorb blood, but it's slate, which isn't too terribly porous."

"So now what?"

"We either look for another carpet that could be new—"

"Why don't you pretend you've already searched the whole house."

"You think that's wise?"

"For this investigation."

She sighed with relief. "I suppose next I should operate on the assumption that you're a good housekeeper—something I gathered when I snooped around your cabin the other night—and you followed all of Heloise's hints for removing bloodstains from any kind of surface. However, I can't assume that you're smart enough to take the rags far away and burn them."

"Right. Good investigators don't operate on assumptions alone. They've got to look for facts."

"Okay, then next I look through the trash."

"Inside or outside?"

"Both. I can't leave any stone unturned."

"True, but for the sake of this investigation, and operating on the knowledge that I like to keep everything inside neat and clean, and that I'd never let trash spend more than one day in the house, why don't we look outside?"

She kissed her fingertips, then trailed them over Logan's cheek. "You could always tell me everything there is to know about the mysterious missing Opal, so we could move on to more pressing matters."

"I'd say a missing woman is rather pressing."

"But is she really missing?"

Logan shrugged. "You and your cohorts seem to think so."

"Darn it, Logan." Scarlett huffed. "Wouldn't you rather have sex than plan this game?"

"I'd rather have sex than just about anything, but right now you're paying the price for assuming far more than you ever should have assumed about me."

"Fine." Scarlett marched toward the door. "Where to now?"

"There might be a couple of trash cans out by the garage."

Stopping, Scarlett turned back to glare at Logan. "And I suppose I have to dig through them?"

"You dug through a Dumpster looking for a wallet you thought I'd stolen." He grinned. "What's one little trash can?"

Her eyes narrowed. "You're enjoying this, aren't you? You're getting your kicks by playing with me, making me suffer."

Logan clutched her shoulders and drew her up good and close to his body. "Did I ever tell you how pretty you are when you're angry?"

"No, you've been too busy making me play detective when I'd rather do something else."

He smiled down at her. "Did I tell you that I counted the freckles on your nose while you were sleeping?"

Thank goodness he was holding her, or her suddenly quivering body might slink to the ground. "Did you really?"

"This morning while you were asleep." He kissed the bridge of her nose. "There were thirty-seven on the right side."

Her toes tingled. "What about the left?"

"It was hidden in your pillow." Logan's lips whispered over her mouth. Soft, so terribly, terribly soft. Her heart went pitter-pat; the tingling in her toes rippled much further north. In another moment, he'd peel off her shirt and—

And his kissing stopped. "Okay, time to hit up the trash cans."

Fury hit her. "Damn you, Logan."

His laughter rang through the cavernous entry. "You're going to want me all the more when we're done here."

"Or I won't want you at all."

Logan slipped his finger through her belly button ring and tugged gently. "I'm in love with you, Scarlett. You might be fighting it, but I think you're in love with me, too."

"I'm not."

"You say that now, but once we're done here, once I get you back to my cabin, you'll change your mind."

"You think so?"

"I know so."

Scarlett tilted her head up and smiled. "Prove it."

"I will, Scarlett. Rest assured, I will." He grabbed

her fingers and tugged her out of the house. "But first things first."

"I am not going to dig through the trash."

"If you want to find the bloody rags you will."

"Oh, hell." She stomped away, leaving Logan behind to lock the door. When she reached the side of the garage, she saw three trash cans lined up neatly in a row, bringing back vivid memories of a stinky Dumpster—and other memories too. A kiss that wasn't just a kiss, but a *kisssss.*

"You going to check out the contents, or stare at the lids?" Logan asked, stepping up beside her and slipping a hand around her waist.

"I'd rather just stare, but since I'm anxious to find out what you plan to do to make me fall in love with you— which right now seems an absolute impossibility—I'll look inside."

Advancing on the row of old metal garbage bins, she lifted the first lid. The inside brimmed with grass clippings, but something hidden beneath reeked. She stared into the depths, wondering what might lurk there, then slammed the lid back down.

"You're not going to do a thorough search?" Logan asked, leaning against the garage, arms folded across his chest.

She wrinkled her nose. "It smells."

"A good detective would get out his plastic gloves and sort through the entire thing."

"As you may recall, I was dragged out of the shop in such a hurry that I somehow forgot my gloves."

He shrugged. "A detective doesn't always get fair

warning, and sometimes he—or she—has just gotta do what he or she's gotta do."

"You're enjoying this, aren't you?"

He grinned wickedly. "You got it."

"I suppose I deserve this, but that doesn't make me like it any better." Dragging in a deep breath, she lifted the lid a fraction of an inch, then stopped when Logan's hand swept over hers. He pushed the lid down.

"I thought you said I needed to look inside," she said, tilting her head up to catch his grin.

"I've changed my mind. I like you smelling like cinnamon and sugar, not rotting food. Besides, I know there's nothing in there besides grass clippings and a raw rib roast the cook took out of the refrigerator and then forgot to cook."

"How do you know all that?"

"Because I put the rib roast in the can, and I mowed the lawn yesterday."

"Why?" She shoved her fists against her hips. "And please, Logan, just give me a straight answer, one I don't have to go digging for."

"Because Opal's an old friend of my mom's. Because she's the one who said I might like the fishing in Plentiful. Because until I met you I was bored and I asked Opal if I could help out around her place— for free, I might add, because no matter what you choose to believe, I'm a damn nice guy."

Scarlett puffed at a wayward curl. She'd never even considered the fact that Opal might be a *friend*, which, next to relative, would have been the logical assumption. Oh, no, she and her friends assumed he was a gigolo.

Maybe she should climb in the trash can and hide.

Logan cupped her shoulders. "Does it surprise you that I could be friends with a woman, that I could have something on my mind other than sex?"

"Well, to be perfectly honest . . . yes."

"My best friend is a woman named Charity. She used to be a showgirl in Vegas and now she's married to a minister. She's stunning. Sings great, dances even better, and when I look at her I see *friend*. Nothing more."

"What do you see when you look at me?"

"Freckles. A damn cute belly button. Wild red hair that I want to bury my hands in. I see you naked and perspiring and straddling my hips—which you will be doing as soon as you get to the bottom of the Opal mystery."

"You're maddening."

He went back to leaning against the garage, a grin plastered to his face. "So are you, my dear."

Scarlett crossed her arms over her chest. "Since this is an investigation, there are a few questions I need to ask."

"Go right ahead."

"Did you buy a rifle?"

"I bought a fishing pole. I don't own a rifle."

"I saw you looking at guns at the sporting good store."

"I looked. Hell, Scarlett, I carried a gun for fifteen years and sometimes I feel naked without one. But I didn't buy a rifle."

"But you had a rifle the other night. A big one that you aimed right at me."

"It's Opal's. I borrowed it just in case Yogi or Boo Boo broke in." His eyes narrowed. "Need I remind you *who* broke in?"

"I know perfectly well." She paced the length of the garage, all her ridiculous notions slapping her across the face. But, ridiculous as everything seemed, Opal was still missing.

She stopped in front of Logan. "Do you think Opal's dead?"

His eyebrow rose. "That's for you to find out."

Damn, but he was exasperating. Latching onto the third can's lid, she tossed it into the grass and got walloped by another atrocious smell. "What on earth?"

"Smells like vinegar."

She sniffed cautiously. Definitely vinegar. "There's broken glass in here, too." She stared harder into the depths of the container. "It looks like it could have been a bottle, and there are a couple of rags, too, stained with something . . . dark." She turned to Logan, her eyes narrowing in question. "Wine, maybe? Red wine?"

"Merlot. Opal's favorite."

"Oh, God." Scarlett paced again, feeling totally and completely foolish. "I think I see the entire picture now."

"Do you?"

It was getting more vivid by the moment. "Opal, or someone, dropped a bottle of Merlot on the slate floor, the glass shattered, and wine poured onto the rug."

"You're getting pretty good at this."

"It's not too hard when the real evidence is staring you in the face."

"So, what happened then?"

Scarlett thought long and hard, trying to be Jayne Mansfield-Smythe and not a half-witted novice at the investigation game. "None of Heloise's hints for getting wine out of fabric worked, so Opal opted for a new carpet." Scarlett kicked a piece of gravel and sent it flying across the lawn, as she thought some more. "Since you're bored and doing odd jobs for Opal, you volunteered to pick up a new rug. You brought it here, rolled up the stained carpet, and took it to the dump. And the reason the coyotes were checking it out was because it smelled . . . interesting."

"You went to the dump?"

"Of course I did. You told me the other morning you were heading there, then Ida Mae told me about the bloody carpet she'd seen you put in the back of your truck, and I put two and two together."

"Which added up to me being a murderer?"

"Okay, so I have a vivid imagination, but if you'd seen the way the coyotes were sniffing at that rug, you would have thought there was a dead body inside, too."

"In spite of that, you still went to my place?"

"I had to know for sure."

"What if I *was* a murderer?"

"Then I'd probably be dead right now."

"Or maybe I've been toying with you. Maybe I brought you here to do the deed."

Scarlett grinned weakly. "You're joking . . . aren't you?"

"Am I? Opal's still missing, isn't she?"

"There's probably a very logical explanation for her disappearance, something that has nothing whatsoever to do with murder."

"You think so?"

"Damn it, Logan. You're not a killer!"

He chuckled. Anyone else might have stared him down and wondered if maybe, just maybe, he *was* a killer. But she'd slept with him, she'd let him do all kinds of things to her body and she'd done all kinds of things to his. No. He was not a murderer. She refused to believe it.

Pacing the length of the garage again, she started muttering to herself, because talking directly to Logan was getting her nowhere. "Opal could be staying with friends." Hmmm, now there was a thought. "She could have taken a vacation. But . . ." Scarlett stopped next to the window and peered inside the near dark garage. "Opal's car is parked where she always parks it." She faced Logan. "She never goes anywhere without that Mercedes."

"Maybe you should see if her body's inside."

Scarlett tensed. "Maybe you should."

"This is your investigation. I'm an *ex* cop, remember."

Okay, she could do this. She stretched her hand toward the doorknob and tried to turn it. *Locked.*

She shot a glance at Logan. "I don't suppose you have a key to the garage?"

He pulled the same key he'd used to unlock the house from his pocket. "It opens anything and everything around here."

Taking the key from his hands, Scarlett opened the side door, then crept in slowly. A stream of sunlight brightened the inside, but still it seemed eerie with the threat that Opal's body might be inside the car, with the possibility that Logan might have—

"I didn't kill her, Scarlett."

She spun around. "I know that."

Logan curled his fingers beneath her chin and tilted her face up to meet his eyes. "Do you?"

"Of course I do." She smiled, maybe a little half-heartedly, but at least she smiled, sucked in a deep breath, and moved cautiously toward the car. When she neared the door, she twisted around to look at Logan again. "You haven't by any chance hired someone to jump out at me and shout 'Boo!' have you?"

One of his dark brows rose.

"Okay," she said, giving in to his annoyance. "It was just a question."

She tried the handle on the driver's side door, and it opened without any resistance. The dome light popped on and illuminated the silver leather interior of the Mercedes. Empty, thank God! She crawled into the front seat, tugging on the back of her skirt so Logan wouldn't get too big an eyeful, and opened the glove compartment. Registration. Insurance papers.

A packet of Kleenex. A straw. A pen from the Plentiful Bank and Trust. A package of safety pins and a map of Wyoming, nothing to give any clue about Opal's whereabouts.

Needing to be thorough, she swept her hands under the seats. Clean.

She popped the trunk, climbed out of the car and walked around back, hesitating for a moment before opening it.

"Don't worry," Logan said, exasperation leaking into his voice, "no one's going to hop out of there and holler, 'Boo!' "

Opening the trunk, she immediately saw half a dozen travel brochures scattered across the gray carpet. She gathered them into her hands, carried them outside into the light, and looked at each one. "Tahiti. Walt Disney World. An Alaskan cruise. A European bus tour." Her gaze flitted toward Logan. "She's on a trip, isn't she?"

"With my mom. You know, her old friend."

Embarrassed, Scarlett turned away and fixed her gaze on the garage and the snow-capped mountains beyond. "I should have known. Shouldn't have made wild assumptions." She sighed heavily. "I should have trusted you."

Logan's hands, warm and gentle, slipped around her, resting on her belly. She breathed softly as his body melded against hers, and he held her close. "I've got faults, Scarlett, and God knows there are people who've trusted me when they shouldn't have. But I'm not like your dad. I'm not like Adam. I'm not going to lie to you. I'm not going to hurt you, and the last thing I want to do is change you. All I want"—he kissed her temple, and his lips whispered against her ear—"is to love you."

Scarlett turned in Logan's arms. She looked up into his tender, truth-filled eyes, and years of distrust and torment drifted away, replaced by some strange yet wonderful kind of happiness. "I want to love you, too. I want to love you more than I've ever wanted anything in my life." She threaded her fingers at the back of his neck and stretched up on tiptoes to kiss him softly. "Show me how."

Logan lifted her easily, strong arms gathering her against him, beating heart against beating heart. "I can show you how to fish. I can show you how to be the best damn detective Plentiful's ever seen. I can show you a lot of other things, too, but trust me, Scarlett"—his lips feathered over hers, his breath hot, his need smoldering and ready to burst into flame—"you already know how to love, and from here on out, it's just gonna get better."

Chapter 22

"Thank you," Scarlett whispered, licking a bead of perspiration from Logan's chin as she straddled his hips, "for teaching me to trust." She kissed the tip of his nose. "For showing me how easy it is to love you. And"—a grin touched her lips—"for showing me how to fish. I had no idea it could be so much fun."

Logan flicked the little gold fish dangling from her belly. "You just needed the right person showing you how."

Scarlett dragged her fingernails through the hair on Logan's chest, and winked at the man lying beneath her. "The right person plus a finely constructed pole. And yours is the best by far."

Logan groaned as she curled her hands around his hard-as-steel rod. He'd been using the same one all his life, but, he had to admit, it performed its duty a whole hell of a lot better when he went fishing with Scarlett—the woman he loved.

"You know, Scarlett, I was thinking all the fun of fishing was in finding just the right hole." Logan folded his arms behind his head, propping himself on a stack of pillows so he could get a better view of Scarlett's naked little body in the firelight. "The smaller the better, and I've always been partial to ones that are dark and mysterious."

"Hmmm," she purred, "how's this one?"

She took him in her mouth. Her lips tightened and slid down his shaft. Her tongue swirled, licked, and toyed with the very tip, and God if he didn't think he'd explode right then and there, but fishing was a patient man's sport, and if there was one thing he'd learned about himself in the last couple of days, where Scarlett was concerned he had all the patience in the world. Besides, there was another fishing hole he wanted to explore before he ran out of bait.

He was after the big one, and he knew where to find it.

Reaching for the candy dish beside the hearth, Logan latched on to one of the many foil pouches Scarlett had dumped inside, then he tossed it onto his belly. Scarlett's green eyes flickered up from the pole she'd been polishing. "Wanna put that on?" he asked, smiling at the pretty lady who was doing the most tantalizing things to his body.

Scarlett nodded slowly, then took her time getting to the chore, tormenting him with flicks of her tongue, languorously withdrawing, leisurely sucking and tugging until she reached the very top. He gritted his teeth; she, on the other hand, smiled up at him and wickedly licked her lips.

Plucking the pouch from his stomach, she tore it

open with her teeth, tossed the packet aside, then rolled the rubber down, down, down.

A second later Scarlett rose to her knees, her body undulating before his eager eyes, her golden fish dangling like a tempting piece of bait. She wrapped her fingers about him, guided him to just the right spot, then went down, down, down until she'd fully and tightly encased him inside of her.

Logan groaned as her cute, itty-bitty hips and her mesmerizing belly button started to sway. Around and around, up and down, her eyes closed, her breasts heaving as he watched. He ached to touch her, but he'd been given specific instructions that this time she was in charge, and the only thing she wanted from him was to enjoy.

Enjoyment had never felt so good or looked so fine.

With the King singing "A Big Hunk o' Love" in the background, Scarlett threaded her hands through her mass of curls, and her sweet, just-the-right-size-for-his-palm breasts rose high, tight, and her pebbled nipples looked ripe for sucking.

He'd obeyed long enough. He had to touch. To taste. He reached out and swirled his palms over the hard, pink nubs, loving the feel of her in his hands. He wanted more and pulled her down to him, capturing her mouth, sliding his tongue into her sweetness.

She was hot; perspiration beaded beside her nose, across her chest. One gasp from deep within her throat led to another; one moan turned to ten as she rode him higher and harder, keeping time with the pulsing music.

Gathering her into his arms, Logan rolled Scarlett beneath him, making sure she was comfortable on the blanket and pillows they'd tossed down in front of the fireplace. Still buried inside her, he slid his hands under her hips and lifted her up to meet his every thrust, sometimes afraid he was so big he'd hurt her, but sure of the opposite when she pleaded for more.

And it was more he gave her, again and again, until her fingers raked over his back, until her entire body quivered and her muscles tensed and she called out his name and begged him to come.

That was the easiest request he'd ever had, and he exploded deep inside her, losing himself completely to the cute little redhead.

One song ended; another began. Logan cradled Scarlett in his arms and lay there quietly, listening to the music and Scarlett's heart beating in time with his. Slowly she peeked up from her resting place on his chest and sang along with the King. "I will spend my whole life through, loving you, just loving you."

Logan smiled and dragged her little body up his big one until their mouths met. "I'm going to hold you to that," he whispered, and suddenly the music disappeared and all that remained was the love they shared, and the love they made—again.

"Are you ever going to tell me what happened at the Misty Moon?" Scarlett asked, flipping a pancake for her favorite man, as he walked toward her wearing nothing but black boxers and a smile.

"I can think of better things to talk about than Steve and Larry." Logan stepped behind her and ran his hands under the black polo shirt she was wearing. It was Logan's; it hung nearly to her knees and she wore nothing beneath it, which Logan seemed to enjoy. "While we're at it"—his palms cupped her breasts—"I can think of better things to do in the middle of the night than eat pancakes."

Scarlett tried to maintain control of her senses as his fingertips swirled over her nipples. "You said you were hungry."

"Obviously you misinterpreted my words. I wanted more of you, not food."

"Well," Scarlett said, taking a deep breath as she stacked six of her special recipe pancakes on a plate, "you may change your priorities once you've tasted these."

Logan nuzzled her neck. "I've tasted you. I know my priorities."

Scarlett thrust the plate into his hands. "Eat. The pancakes, that is, and while you're at it, tell me what you found out when you talked to Larry and Steve."

Grinning, Logan put his plate on the bar but continued to focus on Scarlett's anatomy as he doused his pancakes with butter and syrup. "To be honest, the guys didn't have a whole lot to share. I thought they were Adam's best friends, but I left thinking that Adam has hidden as much from them as he has from everyone else."

"So you didn't get any hint at all that Adam's in some way connected with Edna Grace, or covering something up that has to do with her?"

"No." Logan chewed thoughtfully on the maple syrup-saturated cakes. "They did tell me that Adam used to go to a lot of police conventions."

"Once a month."

"That often?"

"Thank goodness." Scarlett turned the fire off under the grill and carried her plate to the bar. "My mom hated it when he'd leave, but I loved it. I could eat in my bedroom if I wanted. I didn't have to dust everything in the house first thing in the morning. I didn't have to worry about doing something wrong, about not being perfect so Adam would look perfect."

"Did he ever talk about what he did at the conventions or tell you where they were?"

Scarlett drizzled a small amount of syrup over her 3 A.M. breakfast. "Adam didn't share anything about his work, not with my mother, especially not with me. I stood up to him too often, and I think he was afraid I'd get in his way if I knew too much."

"Do you think he might have been seeing someone else when he went away?"

"If he was, it wasn't someone he loved, or even someone who made him happy."

"Why do you say that?"

"Because he seemed relieved every time he came home, happy to see me, even happier to see my mom. It didn't last more than a day or two, but he wasn't so demanding, didn't stand over my shoulder while I did my homework, didn't come unglued if I wore something to school that wasn't exactly what he felt the stepdaughter of the chief of police should be wearing. He'd even hug me."

"Any idea why?"

"It wasn't out of some great love for me, I'm pretty sure of that." She thought back to those days, about the frown Adam would wear before leaving town, the way he looked ten years older when he came home. "At the time, it seemed like he had more important things on his mind than worrying about me being a good little girl."

"But you don't know what?"

"I haven't a clue." She pushed away from the bar and grabbed the coffeepot. "All I know is that he was really happy to see my mom when he got back." She filled Logan's mug and her own. "He'd walk through the door, swing her up into his arms and they'd disappear for hours." She grinned weakly, remembering how disgusted she'd been with her mother's sex life. "A few days later Adam would fall back into his normal pattern—telling us both how to act, how to think. We'd go to church and be the picture perfect family. He'd go to school functions with me and be the perfect dad."

"But he wasn't?"

"I suppose he was a better father than my real dad, but everything was superficial. When we were out in public he was all loving and caring; behind closed doors he became a demanding perfectionist." Scarlett sipped her coffee. "At times it seemed as if our home was the most important thing in his life."

"Larry and Steve told me they thought he'd married your mom for her house," Logan said, scooping three heaping spoons of sugar into his French roast and clicking the spoon around and around.

"I thought that, too, but he knew before getting married that the place had been built by O'Malleys and my father was determined to keep it in my name. Even though he knew it would never be his, Adam was always putting up new wallpaper, making sure my mom and I kept every speck of wood polished, and that the gingerbread outside was always perfectly painted."

"He must have hated moving out."

"After my mom died, I was afraid he'd sue to get a share of the place, or that he'd take everything that had belonged to my mom, but he just packed up and left. Next thing I knew he was fixing up this old junk heap of a Victorian a couple of miles from town. Turns out he'd bought it when he first came to Plentiful."

Logan frowned. "And it just sat empty all that time?"

"I suppose so."

"You don't think he entertained his supposed lady friends there, do you?"

"I have no idea what he did then or what he does in his spare time now. My mother's diaries said he used to leave the house in the middle of the night. She figured he was seeing other women—but there's no proof, only my mother's suspicions. He might have been going to that house, but I don't know."

Logan caressed her cheek, drawing his thumb lightly over her lips. "Getting tired of all my questions?"

"I would be if it wasn't for the fact that you're trying to help me figure out what Adam's been up to for so many years."

"What if the answer turns out to be nothing?"

"Then I'll try to put it behind me." She smiled and kissed his sugar-sweetened lips. "I'll fill my time obsessing about someone else."

Logan wove his fingers through hers and led her from the kitchen to the pile of blankets and pillows by the hearth. They curled up together in front of the leaping flames, her back pressed against his chest, his hot, callused fingers working their way under her shirt once again. He teased her nipples, nibbled her ear, then began the interrogation again.

"Adam was a cop in L.A., wasn't he?"

"So I heard."

"Your dad was, too, right?"

"Back in the fifties, right about the time Adam was born." She tilted her head to look at the man who was toying with her body. "If you're looking for some connection between Edgar and Adam, I doubt they ever met. Edgar was thirty years older than my mom, and Adam was a few years younger than she was."

"Maybe Adam is Edgar's son—a half brother you were never told about."

Scarlett laughed, stilling Logan's fingers so she could think straight. "Right, and maybe Edna Grace was married to my dad fifty or sixty years ago."

"It could be possible."

"There's no resemblance between Adam and my dad, and Edgar was married only once—to my mom—and he was through with her by the time she turned twenty-five. He liked women between the ages of just-past-jail-bait and legally old enough to drink."

"All right, maybe there is no connection between any of them. Truth is, we don't have enough pieces of that letter or any other evidence to figure out what's going on."

"You could call your cop buddies and ask them to do some checking?"

Logan's hands tightened on her breasts. "I don't think so."

Scarlett spun around, kneeling between his knees. "If we had some answers, we could stop coming up with all sorts of wild assumptions. Wouldn't it be better if we enlisted the help of someone who could tap into a police computer and come up with answers?"

"What am I supposed to use as a reason? That I need information because I think Plentiful's chief of police is covering up a murder?"

"You wouldn't have to be that blatant when you ask for help."

"I'm not going to ask for help. Let's just keep our suspicions between you and me."

"And what happens if we find out that Adam killed those three women Edna mentioned in her letter? Would we keep that a secret, too, all because you used to be a cop and you have some loyalty issues?"

Logan pushed up from the floor and walked to the window, staring out into the darkness. "Look, can we just drop this?"

"We've dropped too many things whenever the subject of you being a cop comes up. What's the problem, Logan, don't you trust me enough to share that part of your life?"

His shoulders rose and fell as he sucked in a deep breath and let it out slowly. He stood in silence, the firelight flickering across his back, over the vicious scar. At last he turned. He leaned against the wall; sadness filled his eyes. "My last partner dealt drugs. Not nickel and dime stuff, but big hauls with big dealers."

Logan dug his fingers into his neck, rubbing at tightened muscles. "He killed a couple of lowlifes who tried to blackmail him, and . . ." Logan sighed heavily. "When I figured out what he was up to I went to internal affairs, something I swore I'd never do, no matter what."

He stalked across the room, dumped the cold coffee out of his cup and filled it again. Steam rose from the mug as he stirred in the sugar. "I wore a wire to get more evidence on him. It worked for awhile, and then one night he figured it out."

Scarlett crossed the room and pressed a kiss to the scar on his back. "Did he do this to you?"

"Yeah." Logan laughed bitterly. "I told him to turn himself in, but he said he couldn't; he was in too deep. He told me that if he was going down, I was, too. Guess he didn't think I was tough enough to fight him after a whack with a machete, but he was wrong." Logan slugged down half his coffee, then put the cup in the sink. "When the whole thing was out in the open, four cops were in jail—four guys who'd once been my closest friends."

"Some friends."

"Glenn, the guy with the machete, and I were pretty damn close once upon a time. I was godfather to his little boy. Hell, I'm the one who took his wife to the hospital when she went into labor." Logan raked his fingers through his hair. "I did everything with that kid; now I'll never see him again. The guys I worked with had barbecues a couple of times a month, but suddenly I wasn't asked to show up. When I needed a new partner, no one wanted the job. I put up with it for six months, then I quit."

"And now you feel that you shouldn't have turned your partner in?"

"All I ever wanted to be was a cop. My dad's a cop. My brothers are cops. I was raised to believe that you don't squeal on friends, that you fight your own battles, and that a good cop is a loyal cop. I shot to hell everything I'd been brought up to believe."

"You mean to say that because your partner wore a badge he had the right to sell drugs, to kill a couple of guys, and take a machete to you?"

"I'm just saying that I wish I'd never found out what Glenn was doing. Turning him and his cohorts in cost me my job and my friends."

"What kind of friends take the side of a drug dealer who nearly hacks another friend to death?"

"They're not on his side; they just look at me now as a guy they can't trust. Like I told you before, Scarlett, if you don't have trust, you've got nothing."

Scarlett put her hand on his arm, felt the tension in his muscles. "They're the ones with nothing, and one of these days they'll realize—if they haven't already—what they lost when you left the force. One of these days most all of those guys will realize that they would have done the same thing if they'd been in your shoes."

Logan wrapped her in his arms and pulled her toward him; she could feel the rapid beat of his heart. "You're not going to let up, are you?"

"I never let up when I know I'm right." Scarlett caught Logan's fingers in hers and led him toward the bedroom. Climbing onto the mattress, she tugged the black polo shirt over her head and knelt before him, naked as the day she was born—except for a belly button ring. "I never let up when I want something, either."

Logan threaded his fingers through her hair. "What is it you want?"

"When the sun comes up you can make that phone call. After that, we can talk until we're blue in the face about mysteries and murders, but right now . . ." She pressed her lips against his and whispered, ". . . . I want to love you."

Logan pulled his fingers from the tangle of Scarlett's hair and rolled over in bed to look at the clock. Nine A.M. The sun was out, and through the window he could see Poe, Heckle and Jeckle dive-bombing the bird feeders in the clearing, while Snagglepuss crouched atop a weathered redwood picnic table, waiting for one of the birds to get close enough to pounce.

Nice morning. The best he'd had in years. Turning onto his back he looked at the reason the morning was so damn good—a pretty redhead lying beside him, breathing softly, with her hands tucked beneath her freckled cheeks.

Life didn't get much better than this.

He sat up in bed, stretched, then looked at the clock again. Nine here; eight in Vegas. Nick would already be at work, chomping on gum and making Sin City a better place to live and play. As much as Logan didn't want to make this phone call, he'd promised Scarlett. Grabbing the cordless, he punched in Nick's cell phone number. While it rang, Logan stuffed his pillow behind his back and leaned against the headboard. At long last Nick answered.

"I've got a favor to ask," Logan said. Scarlett woke at the sound of his voice, and he pulled her against him, letting her listen to the conversation.

"Yeah?" Nick munched on his gum. "And I need you as my partner again."

"That's not going to happen. I already told you I'm not going back to Vegas."

"Yeah, yeah, so what is it you want?"

"I need you to get some information on a woman named Edna Grace."

Nick laughed at the other end of the phone. "Let

me guess. Great breasts. A platinum blonde Marilyn Monroe type—"

"Eighty-three and dead."

"Doesn't sound like your type at all."

"I want to know whose type she was," Logan said. "Did she have a record? Relatives? Money?"

"I need more than a name."

"Can't give you much more than that, other than she lived in Chowchilla."

"In the prison or out?"

"Out, or so I've heard, but I've got the feeling she may have been an inmate at one time or other."

Nick chewed on his gum in thoughtful silence. "You changing your mind about being a cop?" he finally asked.

"No, just need to get some information."

"And loving every second of it. Once a cop, always a cop."

Scarlett grinned; Logan ignored the comment.

"I need to do a background check on an Adam Grant, too," Logan said. "He's the chief of police in Plentiful."

There was a long, deathly silence at the other end of the phone. Logan knew what was going through Nick's mind. He was wondering what the hell Logan was doing spying on another cop. But Nick was a friend. The one guy he'd always trusted, who'd always trusted him. They could rely on each other, and he knew Nick wouldn't question what he was doing.

"What kind of info you looking for?" Nick asked.

"Anything you can find."

"Pretty broad request."

"All right, see if you can connect him to Edna Grace. Maybe he arrested her once. Maybe they're related in some way—mother, aunt."

"You don't suspect him of killing her, do you?"

"I don't know what to think about him, that's the problem." Logan shoved his fingers through his hair. "Look, I know I should stay out of this, I know—"

"You weren't in the wrong the last time," Nick interrupted. "I told you that half a dozen times. So did a hell of a lot of other guys. If you want me to dig up some dirt on Adam Grant, I figure you've got good reason, so don't explain or apologize."

"Thanks, Nick."

"Now that I've kissed up, I'm gonna ask you again, one more time. You wanna come back to Vegas?"

"I'm staying here. Got a cute little redhead I'm thinking about settling down with. She's stubborn, impulsive, and—"

"Does she like to fish?"

Logan grinned. He swept his hand down Scarlett's belly and gently tugged on the golden fish hanging there. "Yeah. In fact, we're goin' fishin' as soon as I get off the phone. I've got a rod she's dying to try out."

Chapter 23

Except for the jangle of crystal chimes, all was quiet inside A Study in Scarlett when Scarlett and Logan walked through the door at noon. The message light blinked on the recorder. A vase of recently cut roses sat on the tea table in front of the window looking out to the garden. The books were all where they belonged; not a one lay on the floor, chewed on and spit out.

"Something's not right," Scarlett said, gripping Logan's hand as they looked around the parlor.

"You're imagining things."

"I don't think so." Scarlett marched toward the kitchen. "Toby," she called out as she pushed through the swinging door, but the Scottie didn't bark, didn't come flying down the stairs or through his doggy door to track mud on the floor. "Toby," she called again. Not a sound.

"He's probably with one of your lady friends," Logan said. "It looks like they took care of everything, just like I asked them to."

"And I have the horrid feeling that I'm going to

hear all about your request, not to mention just how well they took care of everything—all afternoon, all evening, and all night long—for the rest of my living days."

Logan grinned, his hands settling on her hips, pulling her close to him as he leaned against the kitchen counter. "I suppose that's the price you have to pay for having a good time."

"And what price will you have to pay for dragging me out of here and making a spectacle of me in front of half the town?" she teased.

His hands moved from her hips to her bottom. Warm lips tickled her ear. "I'm sure I've already paid you back for that, but if you feel I haven't given enough—"

"Oh, my God!" Scarlett's eyes widened when they set sight on the empty kitchen table. "The letter's gone. Somebody took all the pieces I taped together." She flew out of Logan's embrace, snatching the box that had been on the table yesterday but was now shoved underneath. "This is empty, too. All the scraps were in here."

"Are you sure you left everything in the kitchen?"

"Positive."

"Think one of the Sleuths might have taken it?"

"I don't know. Maybe." She stalked out of the kitchen and into the parlor, headed for the phone beside the cash register. "I'll call Ida Mae and see if she has any idea where the puzzle is. Then I'd better call and thank the other ladies for taking care of everything." She sighed heavily. "After that, I've got to call the mortuary and find out what time the funeral is, and—"

Logan clutched her arms. "Slow down, Scarlett. Take a deep breath."

"I should have come home earlier. I should have—"

"You didn't, and I'm glad you didn't," Logan said, kissing her softly. "Now, take that deep breath."

Scarlett smiled and inhaled deeply, letting the air out slowly as Logan held her against him. "Feel better?" she asked, grinning at him.

"Much."

"Good. I've got calls to make now. Later"—she winked—"I might let you find some other way to make me relax."

She grabbed the phone, then put the receiver down when she again saw the blinking light on the recorder. Punching the playback button, the first of four messages echoed through the shop.

"It's seven-fourteen in the morning," Ida Mae drawled. "Answer the phone, Scarlett." She was silent for a long moment. "Well, I suppose you're not there, which leads me to believe you're with *him*." Ida Mae snorted. "Be that as it may, I want you to know that Lillian, Mildred and I took care of your patrons yesterday afternoon. Actually, it was just one patron, Cindi Farmer, who bought absolutely nothing. Toby, bless his heart, was acting a bit fussy, so I took hm home with me after the Sleuths and I locked up. He's a little peaked this morning, too, and if he's not quite right in a little bit, I'll take him to see Doc

Sheridan—you know, the good-looking hunk you should have gotten involved with instead of getting involved with *him*. Well, Scarlett, dear, I'd best get going."

The next message was from Ida Mae, as well.

"Obviously you're still not home, but there is one thing I forgot to tell you in my last message. Dan Murphy called to confirm the time for Edna Grace's funeral. Heavens, Scarlett, you could have told me you had taken it upon yourself to give that stranger a proper burial. Needless to say, I coerced all the details from Dan and added a few special touches of my own. I'm sure you remember how lovely I sang 'The Old Rugged Cross' at Ben Butterworth's funeral. Well, I've decided to do it again." Scarlett groaned. "Oh, and I've contacted Lillian and Mildred to make sure they'll be there in their best mourning clothes. Molly said she'd try to make it, too, if it's not too busy at the Misty Moon. It'll be a lovely funeral, Scarlett. Just lovely."

Lovely, Scarlett moaned to herself. She'd thought it could be private, no big deal. Now she imagined the entire town would turn out.

The third message was also from Ida Mae.

"Merciful heavens, Scarlett. I just received a call from Opal. Can you believe that?"

"I can," Logan said, laughing.

"She's in Austria," Ida Mae's message continued, "trouncing around some big old castle. She tells me that Logan Wolfe is her best friend's son. And would you believe he used to be a cop? Good grief, I never!

Well, I suppose I owe him an apology. I suppose, too, that if you want to fool around with him more than you have been—not that you've ever asked for my permission or even wanted it—well, it's perfectly all right, given the current circumstances."

It wasn't at all surprising to find that the fourth and last message as also from Ida Mae.

"One more thing, Scarlett, dear, I've got that mysterious letter of yours. I agonized over it last night and couldn't piece together a thing. A little bit ago I tried again and came up with the most shocking thing. Listen to this: *'They say revenge is sweet, but to this day I hear your mother's tears as I divulged the truth. Maybe I was a better person than I thought, because I felt genuine sorrow for her. A few days later I called again. I wanted to tell her it was all a bunch of lies. But she was dead.'* "

Ida Mae sighed heavily. "That woman was involved in your mother's death. I'm so sorry, Scarlett. So very, very sorry. I'm sick about this, just sick, and I've decided not to sing at her funeral after all. If I did, I might have to sing 'Ding Dong the Witch is Dead' and I'm afraid that wouldn't be very Christian of me. So I'll just keep quiet and while my head is bowed in prayer, I'll ask that Edna Grace rot in hell."

After the tears, after the anger over the way Edna Grace had hurt her mother, after Logan went home to wait for a call from Nick, Scarlett spent the rest of the afternoon taking care of a rush of weekend customers, baking her dark chocolate brownies for a

shindig at the senior center that night, and while trying to pretend that her life was somewhat normal,
she wished that Edna Grace had never existed. The
woman had made her life miserable; worse yet, it appeared the white-haired woman had pushed Elizabeth O'Malley over the edge.

What the hell had Edna said to Scarlett's mother
on the phone that night? What lies had she told? The
mystery continued to go from bad to worse, and
Scarlett felt she was no closer to knowing the truth
about her mother's death than she had been a week
ago.

Adding to her frustration, she'd tried getting in
touch with Ida Mae, but the woman seemed to have
dropped off the face of the earth.

At 6 P.M., Scarlett flipped the OPEN sign to CLOSED.
She was just about to lock the door when Logan
stepped out of the darkness and into the light cast by
the streetlight. She fell into his arms when he walked
into the shop, feeling relief and comfort spread
through her, making a lot of the day's worries vanish.

"Rough afternoon?" Logan asked, sliding the
chain lock in place and turning the dead bolt.

"I've tried to keep my mind off of everything, I've
tried to go about my work, but it's been awful. Now
Ida Mae seems to have disappeared." She pulled away
from Logan and paced the room. "I've called her
house. I've called Mildred and Lillian. I called the vet."

"No one's seen her?"

Scarlett stopped her pacing and puffed at a coil of
hair that had fallen over her brow. "The vet told me

she'd never called about Toby, never dropped by his office. Nothing."

"What about Mildred and Lillian?"

"They had lunch with Ida Mae at the Elk Horn, since they allow dogs and the Misty Moon doesn't." She paced again. "They both told me that Toby was fine, that he'd had a bit of an upset stomach, but Ida Mae said it wasn't serious enough to take him to the vet." She pinched a wilted petal off one of the roses sitting on top of the tea table, and angled her head to look at Logan again. "She didn't tell Lillian or Mildred she was going anywhere else."

"Does she usually?"

"Well . . ." She rubbed her arms. "No."

"Neither does Opal." Logan moved toward her; warm hands cupped her shoulders. "You're worrying over nothing. More than likely Ida Mae's out running errands."

"Or try this scenario on for size." Scarlett looked into Logan's tolerant brown eyes. "What if she found something really awful in Edna Grace's confession letter and decided to do some snooping on her own? What if she's gotten herself in trouble?"

Logan shook his head, a soft grin on his face. "What if she went to Jackson or Idaho Falls to visit friends?"

"What if she didn't? What if she's had a heart attack, or accidentally run her car off the road? What if—"

"Tell you what," Logan interrupted. "We'll go by her place, see what we can find inside—"

"I don't have a key."

"I can pick locks."

Scarlett frowned. "You can?"

"I can do a whole lot of things." Logan cocked a wicked grin. "So, to make you happy, let's head over to Ida Mae's. If necessary, I'll show you a thing or two about picking locks, then we'll come back here and I'll show you a few other things that I'm good at."

Scarlett's smile was just as wicked. "Will those things make me happy, too?"

"Happy, blissful, overjoyed. Pick your adjective, Scarlett, and I'll make it come true."

The door squealed as Scarlett and Logan stepped inside the sprawling, one-story ranch on the edge of town. They searched each room for Ida Mae or Toby, but not a Southern drawl or a bark could be heard anywhere.

"It's nearly seven," Scarlett said, flopping in a chair at the kitchen table. "Ida Mae doesn't drive in the dark. Never. She says it scares her. So where could she be? Why hasn't she bothered to call me?"

"Maybe she thinks you're still at my place," Logan said, hoping something would calm Scarlett's nerves. "Maybe she's got a lot on her mind getting ready to sing 'Ding Dong the Witch is Dead' when tomorrow rolls around. Maybe she went shopping for new cowgirl clothes, something black and funereal."

"Your maybes sound a whole lot better than the miserable conclusions my brain keeps coming up with. Ida Mae likes to skulk around more than I do.

She says Jayne Mansfield-Smythe is too stupid to live, but she swears by Jessica Fletcher and isn't above putting her nose where it doesn't belong." Scarlett sighed. "I'm worried sick that she's gotten herself into trouble this time—kidnapped, tied up and gagged and shoved in some dark room, or . . . murdered, even."

Logan slipped his hands over her shoulders and massaged her tightened muscles. "She's not dead. Put that out of your mind."

"If only I could."

Scarlett's head fell forward, and Logan moved his fingers to her neck, kneading gently. This whole mess with Edna Grace was wearing on his nerves, too. It was hell having a mystery to solve when you didn't have the legal right or the proper tools to investigate everything on your own.

"Think I could use Ida Mae's phone to call Nick?" Logan asked, hoping the detective might have some news by now.

"I'm sure she wouldn't mind," Scarlett said, wandering through the kitchen when Logan picked up the phone and punched in Nick's number. His friend answered on the second ring.

"Got any information yet?" Logan asked, watching Scarlett move about, looking beautiful tonight—not just cute—in spite of her worry.

"Yeah, a little. Adam Grant was a cop in L.A. in the seventies. Clean record, but no commendations." Nick gnawed on his gum. "What the hell's all that static?"

"Must be the phone system up here," Logan said. "I'm using someone else's phone, but I've got the same problem at home."

"Yeah, well, that's a small town for you. Don't have that problem in Vegas."

"You've got a hell of a lot of other problems there," Logan said, then didn't give Nick a chance to go on again about Logan moving back to Vegas. "So, what about Edna Grace? Got anything on her yet?"

"I'm working two homicides, my so-called partner's home sick, and the couple of calls I've managed to make have turned up nothing. But nice guy that I am, I ain't gonna give up."

"I appreciate that. Call me at home tomorrow and let me know if you find anything else. Just leave a message on the recorder if I'm not there."

Nick laughed. "Or otherwise occupied with that redhead who likes to fish."

Logan studied Scarlett's swaying bottom as she stood at the counter brewing some dreadful-smelling tea. "When you meet her, you'll understand the attraction."

After they said their good-byes, Logan hung up the phone and joined Scarlett in the kitchen. "Don't suppose Ida Mae has any beer in the house."

"That's the last thing Ida Mae would have around—other than men."

"And I thought it was only me she despised."

"Apparently you've forgotten that you're in favor now—at least for a little while. Do something to get on my bad side, and she'll change her mind about you right fast."

Scarlett strolled toward him carrying a cup of steaming tea. The silver stars in her belly button swished in time with her hips, and he wondered how he could have ever wanted a tall, voluptuous blonde, when he found everything about Scarlett so damn nice.

She settled in his lap and took a sip of tea. "I take it Nick didn't have any real information yet?"

"Not really. Just confirmed that Adam was a cop in L.A. and that he had a good record."

Again she sipped her tea; Logan swept the mass of springy curls from her neck and settled his lips on her warm, silky skin.

"Ida Mae wouldn't approve of what you're doing; I doubt she'd even approve of what you're thinking."

"Ida Mae's not here."

Scarlett set her cup on the table and wove her hands into his hair. "No, she isn't."

Her lips were soft against his; they tasted like cinnamon and sugar and he figured he'd better start liking tea because it was very much a part of the woman he loved.

He nibbled the edge of her mouth—

And the damn phone rang.

Scarlett bolted up; hell, she even jumped out of his lap, as if Ida Mae had walked into the room. "Should we answer it?" she asked, staring wide-eyed at the telephone.

"We've got nothing better to do," Logan spouted off as he fought to get his libido back in control.

Scarlett grabbed the phone; Logan punched the

conference button so he could hear, too, just in case it was something he needed to know. "Hello," Scarlett said.

"Scarlett?"

"Ida Mae?"

"What on earth?" the cowgirl drawled. "Did I call your number by mistake?"

"Actually, you called your own number," Scarlett answered, rolling her eyes at Logan.

"Then why are you answering?"

"I've been trying to hunt you down all day, and when I couldn't find you, I dropped by your house to see if you were all right."

"I'm perfectly fine."

"Then where are you?"

"In Jackson. I've been coming up here to get my hair done ever since Penny Schnetz retired. You remember her, don't you? Moved to Cheyenne a couple of years ago."

"Of course I remember her. Beehive hairdo, straight out of the sixties."

"That's the one."

"So . . . you're okay. Nothing's wrong at all?"

"I'm okay. Toby's okay, although the little pill threw up all over himself this morning. It was just ghastly, but he's feeling better now, especially since I took him to Peach's Pampered Pets to get his own little do while I got mine. And those nice groomers gave him a jaunty little red bow. He's just adorable now."

Toby barked in the background, a disgruntled bark if Logan had ever heard one. Logan's sixth sense told him Toby didn't like having a red bow in his hair any more than Logan would like it.

"Are you coming home tonight?" Scarlett asked.

"You know how I hate to drive in the dark," Ida Mae said, confirming what Scarlett had said earlier, "and even though it's not that far, I just hate that two-lane road. No, no, I'm going to stay here at the lodge, spend a little more time reading through that letter of yours."

Scarlett's eyes narrowed. "You have it with you?"

"Of course. I couldn't leave something that valuable laying around. By the way, I've pieced together a bit more of the puzzle, and it's quite interesting. Apparently there's a key to some storage shed somewhere, and all the evidence we could ever possibly want is there."

"Do you know where the storage shed is?"

"I haven't figured that out yet."

"And the key?" Scarlett asked. "Did you find that, too?"

"It was supposed to be enclosed with the letter, but we all know the letter is a mess. My guess is it's at your place somewhere, Scarlett."

"But I've scoured every speck of my place looking for more pieces of paper. I would have found a key if it had been anywhere in the house."

"Perhaps Toby buried it, which means we'll never find it," Ida Mae said. "My suggestion is that tomorrow, right after the funeral, we check out the storage places in town and see if Edna Grace rented a space."

"Tomorrow's Sunday," Scarlett sounded frantic again. "There won't be anyone working."

"Don't you worry about that. I know a lot of people in this town. One way or another we'll find that storage shed, we'll get it opened, and before you know it, we'll find all the answers behind this Edna Grace mystery."

Logan certainly hoped so.

"Now," Ida Mae continued, "will you do me a favor and hang up. And when the phone rings again, don't answer."

"Why not?" Scarlett asked.

"Because I called to leave a message to myself on the answering machine. I do it all the time. You know, record little reminders about things I'm supposed to do, since I have a habit of losing the messages I write down."

"Are you sure you don't want me to leave you a note? I could put it on the refrigerator."

"No, no. Just hang up, and I'll see you tomorrow. Which reminds me, I've decided to sing after all—and won't my song be a shocker to everyone."

The real shocker would be that they'd actually find the storage shed, Logan thought to himself. But they would. Come hell or high water, Logan was going to help Scarlett wrap up all the loose ends to this mystery and bring it to a close. He wanted Scarlett—bookseller, baker, purveyor of tea, and lover—in his life, not the Jayne Mansfield-Smythe wannabe. Although . . . he'd take Scarlett no matter what she wanted to do or be, as long as lover fit into the mix.

Chapter 24

There were flowers everywhere. Next time Scarlett planned a funeral service for someone she didn't know, she needed to be a little more specific when she told the florist, "Do it up nice."

Fortunately Dan Murphy had listened to Scarlett when she'd said don't go overboard on the casket. "Something nice but unadorned will do," she'd said, and he'd obliged. Cardboard would have been sufficient, or plain old plywood, but she hadn't known that when she'd made the arrangements.

"You okay?" Logan asked. He'd gone home early that morning to change into a suit, and they'd met up at the cemetery. He held her hand now as they walked across the grass to Edna Grace's final resting place. "If your jaw tightens much more, you're gonna wear your teeth down to nothing."

"I just wish this was over."

Scarlett puffed at two errant curls as she took her place next to the casket alongside Mildred and Lillian. Dan Murphy had said he'd officiate, for a price, of course, and he stood at the head of the coffin with an open Bible in his hands. Adam had come to the funeral, too, and stood on the far side of the coffin, holding one long-stemmed red rose.

Mildred, in her best black Aunt Bee dress, the one that sported the Peter Pan collar, leaned close to Scarlett and whispered, "Have you seen Ida Mae?"

"No. I talked to her last night and she said she'd be here this morning."

"Then she will," Lillian added, "although she's never late."

Scarlett tried not to worry. She'd spent far too many hours fretting yesterday, only to find out that Ida Mae was basking at the lodge, probably in a luxury suite. She might have overslept in one of the big soft beds, or decided to have a Swedish massage before heading home—and she was simply running late.

With those encouraging thoughts in mind, she listened to Dan Murphy clear his throat, read a passage from Psalms, and drone on about Edna Grace, the impoverished woman from Chowchilla, who'd had the good fortune of dying in Plentiful, where so many good people had come to wish her farewell.

So many people? There were only six.

Dan continued to murmur, doing the dust to dust bit, and asked everyone to bow their heads and say a silent prayer. Scarlett bowed hers and imagined Munchins skipping around the casket singing "Ding Dong the Witch is Dead." It seemed cruel and heartless, but it appeared from Edna Grace's letter that she'd been a cruel and heartless person.

At last, Dan said, "Rest in peace." He nodded at

Scarlett, which meant "I'll be sending you the bill post haste," then walked across the lawn toward his big silver hearse.

Adam stepped toward the casket and dropped his red rose on top. A slight smile tugged at his lips. He looked tired. Exhausted. Relieved that all of this was over. Without saying a word to anyone, he sauntered away.

The workers moved in to lower the casket into the ground, and Scarlett, Logan, Lillian and Mildred walked toward their cars. They stopped beside Lillian's VW bug, painted psychedelic orange, with hippie flowers and happy faces scattered here and there.

"Okay, it's my turn to worry," Scarlett said. "Where on earth is Ida Mae?"

"I have absolutely no idea." Lillian pushed her black rhinestone Elton John glasses up on her nose. "But I was leaving Gene Chaffey's place about three this morning, you know, after we played our usual game of Saturday night poker, and I saw Ida Mae zooming by in that pink Cadillac of hers."

"You're sure it was Ida Mae?" Logan asked.

"There's no mistaking that Caddy, and there's no mistaking Ida Mae," Lillian answered.

"Are you sure about the time?" Scarlett asked.

"Of course. Three A.M. That's when Gene has to take his heart medicine—every three hours, like clockwork. I left while he was swallowing his pills."

"But she told me she was spending the night in Jackson," Scarlett said. "And we all know how she hates driving in the dark."

"Well, something must have roused her out of bed," Mildred stated, "because I was up at three A.M., too, and I also saw her driving down the street."

"Did either of you go by her house this morning?" Logan asked. "Or talk to her?"

"I went by her place on the way here," Lillian said, "thinking she might want a ride, but her car was gone so I didn't stop."

"I did the exact same thing," Mildred said. "I'm certainly surprised she's not here. She was so looking forward to singing."

"I'm sure she's all right," Scarlett said, even though she feared that wasn't the truth, "but I'm going to go by her place just to make sure."

"We'll go, too," Mildred said. "In fact we'll leave right now. Lil doesn't drive all that fast so even if you leave five minutes from now, I'm sure you'll catch up with us."

Logan opened the doors for the ladies and helped them into the car. A moment later the bug sputtered, Lillian shoved it into first gear, and the old VW lurched up the road.

"Are you going to follow me, too," Scarlett asked Logan, "or do you want to ride to Ida Mae's together?"

Logan shook his head. "You go to Ida Mae's, I'm going to follow Adam."

"Why?"

"Some kind of sixth sense tells me I need to."

Scarlett frowned. "My sixth sense says you've got something else in mind."

Logan smiled, and Scarlett knew darn good and well that whatever he had planned, it wasn't the smart thing to do. "Maybe I should go with you just in case trouble comes up."

"If trouble comes up, I want you somewhere safe." Logan tugged her against him and kissed her softly. "Don't do anything crazy, okay?"

"I'm just going to Ida Mae's."

"That's what you say now, but there's no telling what can send you off on some other tangent. So do me a favor, please. Just go there and stay put, no matter what." His lips were warm against her mouth as he whispered, "Promise?"

It was childish, terribly childish, but Scarlett crossed her fingers behind her back, stood on her tiptoes, and kissed the man she loved. "I promise."

"Where on earth did you learn to pick a lock?" Mildred asked as Scarlett fumbled with the tools she'd bought ages ago but had never been able to master. They'd been in her Jeep for a year, buried under a pile of junk in the glove compartment, but after watching Logan use his own lock-picking tools last night she was sure this would be a piece of cake.

It wasn't.

"I read the instructions that came with the set," Scarlett said, trying to keep her frustration with the lock to a minimum.

"You know," Lillian said, "I keep a key under the flowerpot next to my door. Do you think—"

"Ida Mae would never leave a key under a flowerpot," Mildred said. "That's the first place a burglar would look."

"All the same . . ." Lillian bent over in her Elton John black-and-white-striped pantsuit, lifted the flowerpot containing a dead chrysanthemum, and, with a silly grin lurking behind her rhinestone glasses, held up the key. "Shall I give this a try?"

After one quick moment of embarrassment, Scarlett stepped aside while Lillian easily opened the front door and all three women tread inside.

"Good heavens!" Mildred gasped. "What is that smell?"

Lillian clapped a hand to her chest. "I hope it isn't our Ida Mae lying dead on the floor somewhere."

Scarlett hoped the same thing.

A search began from one room to another; they looked under beds, inside closets, shower stalls, and behind the sofas and chairs, but turned up nothing. Stopping in the kitchen, where the horrendous scent was the strongest, Scarlett bravely lifted the lid on the trash can. "It smells like someone threw up."

"Toby," Mildred blurted out. "He was sick yesterday." She shook her head. "Why on earth didn't Ida Mae throw that mess outside?"

"That's not the big question of the moment," Lillian corrected. "Where on earth can Ida Mae be? is more apropos."

And is she alive? Scarlett wondered miserably.

"Maybe she left herself a message on the recorder, something that might give us a clue," Scarlett said, looking at the blinking red light on Ida Mae's answering machine.

Mildred opened Ida Mae's Roy Rogers cookie jar and helped herself to an Oreo. "Why would she do that?"

"She told me she loses messages to herself," Scarlett said. "This is the way she keeps track of things."

"Obviously that woman needs a little black book like the one I carry around. It's the only way I can remember things," Mildred said, licking the cream filling around the edge of her cookie. "Just wait until you're older, Scarlett. You'll have to write things down, too."

"Well, let's hope she left something here," Scarlett said, pushing the play button, "because if she put it in a little black book, we'll never know about it."

The tape recorder clicked, and Ida Mae's drawl filled the room. "Reminder: pick up carton of buttermilk and can of smoked oysters." That message clicked off and another clicked on. "Reminder: tell Scarlett that Jayne Mansfield-Smythe gets far too carried away in *Seven Sins*. Maybe she did figure out that Councilman Tamblyn was killed by the wife of the male hooker who serviced the Councilman behind the Marquis de Sade display at the wax museum, but good God, she had to disguise herself as a male prostitute to figure that out. And then there's the sex bubble-brained Jayne had with Detective Dylan MacLeod—*at last,* I might add—when they were left to die in the trunk of his car. Ridiculous. Just ridiculous. Tell Scarlett that you refuse to read another one of Juliet Bridger's novels."

Scarlett shrugged at her companions as the tape clicked again. "I rather enjoyed that part of the book."

Mildred snickered; Lillian giggled. Both ladies blushed.

"Reminder:" Ida Mae's voice sounded again. "The key fits storage shed D-12 at Teton Storage."

Mildred frowned as Ida Mae's messages came to an end. "What key? What is that woman talking about?"

"It's a key that could lead to my future happiness." Or, Scarlett thought, I could find out that I'm too stupid to live. Either way, she scurried out the door, with two of the Sleuths right behind her, in search of storage shed D-12.

Chapter 25

Logan parked in the shade behind a ponderosa pine at the far end of the park and watched Adam pull his white Ford Explorer, with half a dozen antennas gracing the roof, up to the boardwalk a block or so from the Misty Moon. He fidgeted with the radio, then leaned against the headrest and seemingly closed his eyes.

That wasn't something Logan ever had the luxury of doing when he was a cop. But this was Plentiful, not Las Vegas.

Real crime didn't happen here. Or did it?

Logan let his gaze drift toward the Sunday tourists and shoppers who roamed the boardwalks, peering through windows, greeting friends, and carrying picnic baskets toward the park.

This would probably be the last weekend anyone spread a blanket on the grass and feasted on fried chicken and potato salad, Logan thought, as he turned up the collar on his leather jacket. It was getting damn cold in town. Soon they'd be knee deep in snow, yet Scarlett continued to romp around in barely nothing. Not that he was complaining. He liked her in barely nothing. He liked her in nothing at all.

Hell, he loved her. A week ago, he was ready to call this town quits; now he never wanted to leave. Who knows, he might even find himself working as a cop again, if Adam wasn't in charge.

His gaze shifting back to the Explorer, Logan watched as Adam finally climbed out and locked the door behind him. He chatted with one person after another as he strolled the boardwalk. It was a small town, but it still amazed Logan that Adam knew so many people, or found so much to talk about.

Steve and Larry came out of nowhere and clapped Adam on the back. They laughed together, as if sharing some raunchy joke, then ducked into the Misty Moon, hopefully for a few rounds of beer and darts.

That's what Logan had been waiting for. Now was the time to make his move.

He started the engine and headed north out of town, driving past one mini-ranch after another, past fields of tall golden grass, where horses and cattle roamed. Less than five minutes later he turned down a one-lane gravel road that meandered through thick groves of aspen until he reached the stately pale yellow and forest green Victorian that sat beside a stream.

Joe Granger had given Logan directions to Adam's place yesterday. Logan only hoped that Joe hadn't inadvertently mentioned anything about it to Adam.

Parking around back, Logan grabbed his flashlight

and climbed out of the car. He made his way up the brick-lined path toward the house. There were no other cars around. No sounds, except the wind rustling the aspen leaves and water trickling over rocks in the stream.

Peeking through the back porch door, Logan saw no movement, heard no sound. He tried the handle and, when he found it secured, jimmied the lock until he was able to get inside.

He had no clue what he was looking for, but he worked his way through the spotless kitchen, the immaculate parlor, and a neatly organized downstairs office. Nothing was out of place. Nothing looked unusual. Each room looked like it had been torn from the pages of some decorating magazine.

In the office, Logan went through Adam's unlocked desk and found nothing bearing the names Edna Grace or Edgar O'Malley, only the normal utility bills, folders marked Taxes, a dictionary, a thesaurus, and the controller for the small TV that sat in the corner of the room.

Taking the stairs three at a time, Logan searched the three bedrooms upstairs. Two looked like never-used guest rooms, formally decorated, spotlessly clean. Scarlett had said Adam was a perfectionist, but he seemed to have carried it to the extreme.

Finally Logan reached the master bedroom and stopped in the doorway. Hanging over the bed was a nearly life-size portrait of a red-haired woman in a flowing white gown. Not Scarlett, thank God, but her mother—Elizabeth. The painting looked as if it had been copied from a photograph similar to one Scarlett kept in her own bedroom. A wedding picture taken, as Scarlett had said, on one of the last days Elizabeth had been really and truly happy.

Photos in all shapes and sizes filled picture frames that sat on every imaginable surface in the room—a shrine to a woman dead for ten long years.

It seemed that Adam had loved Elizabeth after all. Maybe there had been no other woman. Maybe he had nothing to hide—except his obsession for his wife.

Leaving the bedroom behind, Logan went into the nearly empty attic, which was just as immaculate as the rest of the house, then made his way back down the stairs. He'd turned up nothing, and it was time he hightailed it out of the place.

Walking through the kitchen to the back porch he heard a faint whirring noise, like a motor churning slowly. Behind a rack on a mudroom wall, he found the door, nearly hidden by an odd assortment of coats and hats. Opening it cautiously, Logan clicked on his flashlight and moved slowly down the basement steps.

On the bottom step, Logan heard a woman giggle, and then the beam of his flashlight fixed on a wall of intricate wires and recording equipment.

"I'm telling you, Chery"—more giggles—"it looked like a stubby #2 pencil. The way Larry was spouting off about his manliness, I was sure I was in for the ride of my life. But once he unzipped his pants, all I could do was laugh." More giggles. "Oh, damn it all. My husband's home. Gotta go."

The phone clicked. The tape recorder stopped re-volving.

Logan moved close, studying the bank of sophisti-cated machines. It didn't take a genius to figure out that Adam Grant was bugging telephones. A lot of them.

In a three-ring binder Logan found an index of calls received and placed. The times and dates were carefully noted. The conversations were summarized in one or two lines. And beside each was a tape num-ber, which corresponded with the recordings Logan found in an unlocked file cabinet.

Scanning the thick index, Logan ran across entries for "Joe Granger: Home" and "Joe Granger: Of-fice." Similar notations had been entered for Molly. Steve and #2 pencil Larry hadn't been ignored, either.

Scarlett had numerous listings, and going back more than ten years, Logan found entries for calls made to and placed by her mother.

Even Logan's calls had been recorded.

Was anyone in town safe? Was nothing sacred?

Another click of the complex recording system caught Logan's attention, as did Nick Considine's voice. "Hey, Wolfe. You home?"

Logan wanted to grab the phone, but there was no phone to grab. All he could do was listen and hope that Adam wasn't sitting in his car or in his office, lis-tening, too.

"Got the information you wanted, Logan. Hate to leave it on your recorder, but you said it was impor-tant and I've got a shitload of work today. Since we might not be able to touch bases, here goes.

"Edna Grace got out of Chowchilla a few weeks back. Seems she has a history of petty theft and larceny, and this isn't her first round at serving time. She's lived in a couple of other correctional facilities—I can give you the names of those at some other time, if you're interested. She's lived in Florida and Texas, but grew up in L.A. She was living there about twenty years ago, too. Was married to a guy named Red Grace—a real piece of work; got shot robbing a liquor store.

"Edna disappeared off the records for a long time. Couldn't find too much until she ended up in Chowchilla. Can't tell you much about her except she was old, minded her own business, and once a month was visited by her son. You ready for this? The guy's name was Adam Grant.

"I got more info but I gotta get to work. Call me later."

Damn right I'll call you later.

Edna Grace's son? Logan shook his head. Why the hell had Adam found it necessary to hide that bit of information? Why the hell was he taping people?

And what was Adam going to do next?

Locker D-12 was the perfect size for storing a 1956 pink Cadillac, not to mention the body of a Dale Evans wannabe and a furry black Scottie, Scarlett thought as she pulled her Jeep to a stop in front of the twenty-by-twenty-foot garage. She only hoped that she had this whole scenario wrong; hoped that Ida Mae hadn't been here yet and, most of all, hoped that Ida Mae was safe.

Scarlett climbed out of her vehicle just as Mildred and Lillian, looking pale and panicky, arrived in Lillian's Bug. The two women shuffled out of the car and joined Scarlett next to the garage.

"You don't think Ida Mae's inside there, do you?" Mildred asked, her fingers gripping her black patent clutch.

"I don't know," Scarlett said, wishing she had something more positive to say. "Let's just hope the message meant absolutely nothing."

Taking a deep breath, Scarlett put her ear close to the cold, dirty metal door and listened for any sound inside. Nothing. "Ida Mae," she called out. "Ida Mae. Are you in there?"

Still nothing.

Scarlett grabbed her lock-picking tools from the passenger seat of her Jeep. She stared at the big metal lock hanging from the door.

"Please tell me you're better at picking padlocks than you are at door locks," Mildred said, "because there aren't any potted plants for us to look under this time."

"I've never tried a padlock and to be perfectly honest, I have no idea how to do this. But I've got to try." Scarlett stared at the monstrous thing dangling on the side of the roll-up door. It looked simple enough, but so had the knob on Ida Mae's house. This time, however, she had the feeling she was dealing with a life or death situation, and she had to concentrate.

Slipping the skinny metal instruments into the padlock, she hoped she could hear the tumbler sound that Logan had mentioned last night. She fidgeted and fumbled and fidgeted some more, and miracle of miracles, the padlock popped open.

All three women grabbed the bottom of the door and shoved it up. Sunlight bounced off of the pink Caddy, and Scarlett found herself saying a silent prayer as she, Mildred and Lillian rushed to either side of the car and pulled open the doors.

The dome light flashed on inside, and an instant later they saw Ida Mae lying on the backseat, bound and gagged. Her eyes popped open. Fear radiated in her pudgy face, and then a tear trickled down the elderly woman's cheek.

"Don't worry, hon," Mildred said, slipping her fingers under the gag, "we'll have you out of here in no time flat."

Toby peered up from the floor beside Ida Mae. His big brown eyes were sad and frightened. His little mouth and paws were bound just as tightly as Ida Mae's had been.

Scarlett lifted Toby from the floor and encircled him in her arms, gently pushing away the bindings. He didn't bark when he was freed; he simply whimpered and nuzzled against Scarlett's chest.

"Sweet Jesus, Mary and Joseph," Ida Mae drawled as soon as her mouth was unbound. She gasped for air, sucking in long, deep breaths and letting them out slowly, while Lillian and Mildred worked at the rest of the ropes.

"Are you hurt?" Scarlett asked Ida Mae.

"Only my pride. I can't believe I let some man

sneak up on me, but it happened. Took me completely by surprise."

"Did you see who it was?" Lillian asked, although Scarlett already had a pretty good idea.

"His face was covered with a black ski mask, like those hoodlums you see on TV. And he had this nasty deep voice—probably disguised so I wouldn't be able to identify him later."

"Could you see the color of his hair or anything?" Mildred asked. "What about his clothes?"

"I don't know. There might have been a bit of blonde hair sticking out from under the mask." Ida Mae's eyes narrowed. "It happened so fast. He didn't say much, he didn't . . . oh, as I live and breathe!" Ida Mae spun around, deep furrows in her brow as she looked at Scarlett. "It was Adam, wasn't it?"

"That would be my guess." Scarlett sighed. "I wish I could say it surprises me, but it doesn't."

"But why would he do such a thing?" Lillian asked.

Ida Mae shrugged. "I imagine he wanted the stuff inside this storage shed."

"But it's empty, except for your car," Mildred said.

"It wasn't empty when I got here. There were two boxes filled with papers and photos." Ida Mae walked around her car. "He must have took them, which is awful because I didn't get a chance to read any of the papers before he grabbed me. But"—Ida Mae grinned—"I know what was in them."

"What?" Scarlett asked, petting the frightened dog, who was still shaking in her arms.

"Proof that Adam killed a couple of women." Ida

Mae patted her chest. "It was in the confession letter."

"Please tell me you still have it?" Now Scarlett began to shake. "Please tell me Adam didn't get that, too."

"Oh, no, it's safe and sound in a plastic bag inside my bra. I let no man go there!"

For once, Ida Mae's distrust of men had paid off.

"Did the letter also tell you where the storage shed was?" Scarlett asked.

"No, no. The information was printed on the key."

Scarlett frowned. "Where'd you find it?"

"Poor Toby." Ida Mae patted the dog. "He was so sick. He'd throw up, then he'd feel better, and then he'd throw up again. Finally, about two o'clock this morning, he threw up the key, right in the middle of the bed I was sleeping in at the lodge. They're going to charge me an arm and a leg for that, but that's beside the point. As soon as I found that key, I hopped in my car, and darkness be damned, I drove here as fast as I could."

"Did you call anyone? Tell anyone where you were going?" Scarlett asked. "I mean, someone must have known you were coming here in order for Adam to find you."

"I left a message on my recorder, but that's it." Ida Mae frowned. "All I can figure is Adam must have guessed I was on to him."

How on earth did Adam always know so much about what was going on in town? Scarlett wondered. Did he have some sixth sense?"

And . . . who was next on Adam's list of people to get rid of? Fear swelled in her throat. Logan had set out to follow Adam; but was Adam really following Logan?

The basement contained a treasure trove of information on Plentiful's townspeople. It wasn't just birth dates and anniversaries that Adam kept track of in one binder after another. Logan also found detailed accounts of husbands cheating on wives; wives cheating on husbands; records of stock transactions; investment deals; what kid was smoking pot; and who was having sex with whom.

One complete journal was filled with nearly ten years' worth of information about Art the barber's numerous land swindles.

Scarlett's journal was inches thick, and so was the one on Elizabeth. That one, however, ended abruptly with the words, *How could you, Edna? How could you?*

Working quickly, Logan rifled through the file cabinet and pulled out all tapes containing Scarlett's conversations, as well as her mother's. Somewhere in those recordings he hoped to learn even more about Adam's connection to Edna Grace, find out what Edna had said to Elizabeth the night she'd died, and fill in the blanks about the murdered women mentioned in Edna's letter.

With the journals and tapes referencing Scarlett and Elizabeth in his possession, he headed out of the basement. Halfway up the steps he heard the whir of the tape recorder again. And then he heard Scarlett's voice.

"Be careful, Logan. Please. I'm afraid Adam might be following you. He tried to kill Ida Mae but failed. I've got Edna's confession letter and I'm on my way to your place so we can sort all of this out. With any luck, Adam will be behind bars tonight."

The tape clicked off. Logan's heart beat rapidly, and he ran up the stairs and out of the house, hoping that Adam hadn't heard that call, praying that Scarlett wasn't in danger.

Chapter 26

Scarlett kept an eye on her rearview mirror, watching for anyone who might be following her as she drove toward the cabin. She'd sent the Sleuths to Lillian's house, told them to lock the door and not let anyone in. They'd be safe there. Heaven knows they couldn't go to the police.

Logan's truck wasn't parked in front of the cabin when she arrived. Fortunately no other cars were around, either.

The front door was locked. So was the back door, but the window into the living room that she'd climbed through nearly a week ago was still open a crack. She shoved it all the way up, dropped Toby to the floor, and, in spite of her tight, black leather skirt, managed to pull herself up on the ledge and slither inside.

It didn't take more than a moment to search the few rooms, and when she knew it was safe and sound inside, she filled a bowl with water for Toby. Later she'd take him to the vet to make sure he hadn't suffered from swallowing the key, or being bound and gagged by Adam.

As Toby lapped at the water, Snagglepuss sauntered out of some mysterious hiding place to see what
was going on. Toby snarled when the scrawny black
cat got too close; Snagglepuss arched his back and
hissed. Toby, looking completely undaunted, lapped
more water, then trotted to Snagglepuss's food dish
and scarfed down every morsel, while Snagglepuss
looked on.

There was bound to be a fight any minute, but
Scarlett had other things to worry about now.

Where was Logan? She'd call him, but his cell
phone was at the bottom of a beaver pond. All she
could do was pace, her black heels clicking on the
floor as she walked back and forth, back and forth,
with a black dog and a black cat both giving her the
evil eye every time she got too close.

She went outside for a breath of fresh air, then
went back inside and plopped down on the sofa,
where she opened the plastic bag filled with Edna
Grace's letter and read through the newly pieced together pages.

*Your dear father, the great writer Edgar
O'Malley, wrote a book about a black widow,
a woman who married for money then did
away with her husbands by the most devious of
means. Your father—my favorite author—was
quite the clever man, giving step-by-step instructions on how to obtain false identities,
how to pick the perfect target and the perfect
method of death, without anyone being the*

wiser. He even described in great detail the way to cover the trail.

My dear, precious Adam read the book, too, and we spent hours discussing your father's words. Could such a perfect crime be pulled off? we wondered. Days went by. Weeks. I read the book again, and once more after that, taking notes . . . making plans. One night I told Adam we should give it a try. Money was tight. There were so many things I wanted, so many things he wanted, and pulling this off could make us rich.

There was only one hitch. Black widows should be young and attractive, not elderly women whose beauty long ago began to fade.

Adam, on the other hand, was young, attractive and charming, the perfect man to play the black widower game, and he didn't bat an eye when I asked him to give it a try.

It amazed us how easy it was to execute the first plan. Six months and it was over, and no one was the wiser. Adam even carried on his regular job as a policeman. Isn't that ironic?

The second was over and done with in four months. Practice makes perfect, they say.

And then Adam went to Plentiful because he'd heard the pickings were good. I'd set my sights on a woman named Lillian Long. Adam, however, turned his sights elsewhere. Never in my wildest dreams did I think he'd select Edgar O'Malley's ex-wife as our newest target.

The front door burst open. Wind gusted in, and Scarlett spun around, anxious to share all of her information with Logan. But it wasn't Logan in the doorway. It was Adam Grant, and for the second time that week, she stared into the barrel of a rifle.

"Don't scream," Adam warned. "Don't run. Don't even move an inch. You know I'm a perfectionist, Scarlett, and that extends to my marksmanship."

She stared dumbly at the man who'd married her mother, the man she'd been forced to call Dad. She wasn't afraid of him then; she wasn't afraid of him now. He was sick. Deranged. She'd always thought something was wrong; now she held the proof in her hands.

"Did you really plan to kill my mother?" she asked.

"I loved your mother. I've told you that over and over again, year after year."

Scarlett's eyes narrowed. "But you killed other women you supposedly loved."

"Did Edna tell you that?"

"It was in her letter."

"Ah, the letter." Adam moved slowly toward Scarlett, his finger on the trigger, the rifle aimed at her face. "The letter will burn, and no one will be the wiser." Adam tapped Scarlett's shoulder with the end of the rifle. "Do me a favor, Scarlett. Lay down on the floor. Facedown."

Scarlett tucked the letter between the sofa cushions, hoping Adam wouldn't notice, since his eyes had never left her face. Fear rumbled through her, but she tried to swallow it back as she stared at the front door. It wasn't all that far away. Maybe she could get out of the cabin; maybe she could hide in the trees.

There was no way she was going to lay down on the floor and let Adam put a bullet in the back of her head.

She stepped around the coffee table, keeping an eye on the tip of the rifle. If she ran, impulse might make him shoot, and with any luck, he'd hit nothing more than her shoulder or arm. She had to take a chance. Had to.

"Lay down, Scarlett," Adam said calmly. "Now."

Scarlett bolted for the door. If the gun had gone off, she'd been too frightened to hear it.

She grabbed the doorknob and froze when cold steel touched her neck.

"If you want one last chance to see your precious Logan Wolfe," Adam said, "you'd be wise to lay down on the floor."

Scarlett dropped to her knees.

"Not there. In front of the couch, where he won't be able to see you when he comes through the door. Because he will be coming, Scarlett. Quite soon, in fact."

Through the dread lodged in her throat, Scarlett asked, "How do you know?"

Adam moved in front of her, the rifle once more pointed at her face. "He's been in my house listening to my tapes."

Scarlett frowned. "What tapes?"

"On the floor, Scarlett. Now. Please."

She moved to the couch as Adam had told her. Her legs felt weak; her stomach was in knots, but she lay facedown. Through the legs of the coffee table she saw Toby and Snagglepuss huddling together, both of them shivering, as if they were as frightened as she was.

She heard Adam's footsteps on the hardwood floor and looked toward the sound. He stood in the bedroom doorway, a place where he couldn't easily be seen through an outside window.

"Are you going to tell me about the tapes?" Scarlett asked, breathing deeply, hoping to find some way to calm down, hoping to get out of this mess.

"Wouldn't you rather know how you're going to die?"

"Not really."

"It'll be quite painless," Adam said. "A bottle of wine shared between you and Logan, with a simple little drug mixed in that will render you unconscious. You'll be in bed. Holding each other, like the lovers you are. The fire will start in the living room, of course. It's only a matter of having a log roll out of the fireplace and onto the carpet. Your lungs will fill with smoke."

"That's straight out of *Woman in Black*."

"Exactly. Your father was brilliant, masterminding so many perfect crimes. If I'd had the pleasure of meeting him, I would have told him so."

"Then he didn't have anything to do with the murders Edna mentioned in her letter?"

"Of course not. *I* killed my wives. Not your father.

Not Edna. I did them all quite perfectly, too. No one ever expected; no one ever found out."

"And you were going to kill my mother, too?"

"I loved your mother. Falling for her was the only mistake I ever made."

"But you were seeing other women. You sneaked off during the night—"

"To listen to my tapes. Bugging phones wasn't easy, and my recording system was expensive, but I had to know what was going on in town so I could be the perfect chief of police, the man everyone looked up to and admired."

"I never admired—"

"Quiet!" His voice boomed.

Toby and Snagglepuss shuddered. Scarlett tensed, fearing what might come next.

"Logan's coming," Adam said, his voice low. "I don't want to shoot him, so just keep your mouth shut."

Adam was following *Woman in Black* to the letter. He was a perfectionist. He wouldn't stray from what he thought was the right way of doing things. That meant he wouldn't shoot her or Logan. He'd drug the wine, just as he'd said. He'd burn down the house and destroy everything. It would take time, which meant there'd be time to fight back . . . somehow.

Adam slipped further into the bedroom when he heard Logan's footsteps on the porch outside, but Scarlett could still see the barrel of the rifle aimed at the door. One shout out of her, and Adam might mess up again; might accidentally shoot. She had to be quiet for Logan's sake.

The front door opened slowly. Logan had to know she was here because her Jeep was parked outside. As for Adam's car—he may have made a few mistakes in the past, but he wouldn't leave his car out in the open. That meant that Logan would have no way of knowing a killer was lurking inside.

Unless he could hear the horrendously loud thump of her frightened heart.

"Scarlett?"

It was amazing what you could hear—or not hear—when you lay quietly on the floor in a state of near panic. The front door didn't close; had Logan left it open on purpose, in case he needed to get out fast? Each touch of his boots vibrated through the floorboards and echoed against her ears. She could almost hear her blood pulsing through her veins.

And then she saw the tip of Logan's black boots at the end of the sofa.

"How nice of you to join us, Detective."

Adam strolled out of the bedroom, rifle poised at the ready. He had a smile on his face.

Scarlett tilted her head to get a better look at the man she loved. His jaw was tight; his eyes narrowed. He looked from her to Adam. "I take it you've been listening to my conversations ever since I moved into town."

"Ever since I found out you were a cop. Or should I say a traitor." Adam grinned. "It's been bad enough having to contend with Scarlett and her sleuth friends, without having an ex detective move into town who has a bad habit of putting his nose where it doesn't belong."

"Afraid I might move in on your territory?" Logan asked. "Start listening to other people's conversations, so I can blackmail them?"

"You're wrong about the blackmail." Adam, with the rifle still pointed at Logan, went to the kitchen and retrieved a bottle of wine, plus two glasses. Obviously he'd been in the cabin earlier, getting ready for the kill. "Have a seat on the couch, Logan. You can join him, Scarlett. Might as well be comfy while you drink your chardonnay."

Logan pulled Scarlett up from the floor, and she found comfort at last in his arms. Her life wasn't going to end. She knew it. She couldn't have finally found the man she could love forever, only to have forever end just days after they met.

They sat together on the sofa. Logan kissed her brow and whispered. "We'll get out of this. You know that, don't you?"

Scarlett put all of her trust in Logan—and smiled. "I know we will. We have to."

"How nice," Adam said as he put the wine and glasses on the coffee table. "Sharing your last little chat."

Adam sat in the chair across from them, rifle aimed at his newest victims. "Why don't you pour the wine, Scarlett? I bought the best, to give you a nice send-off."

Scarlett poured the wine as slow as humanly possible, giving Logan time to make some kind of move.

"You gonna tell me about the blackmail?" Logan asked. "What you got out of it?"

"This is my town," Adam said, "my community,

my friends. There's no need to blackmail anyone when you know all of their little secrets and use them to full advantage." He leaned back casually. "Art the barber gave me free haircuts after I mentioned that I had a friend who'd gotten swindled in a land deal. Not one of Art's swindles, of course. It was a made-up friend, a made-up land deal, but it made Art uncomfortable enough that we became the best of friends. He'd do anything to stay on my good side. A gold watch here, a good bottle of wine there. Of course, I couldn't protect him after Scarlett and those old lady friends of hers got involved.

"And then there's Joe. Says his wife died when their little girl was born. That's not true at all. The man's gay; his daughter's adopted—and he's well aware that I know the truth. He wants everyone in town to think he's this big macho mayor, and I've made a point of fostering that notion in the minds of everyone in town. Joe thinks I can do no wrong, and when you've got the mayor on your side, you've got it made."

Logan picked up the glass of wine Scarlett had poured. She'd wanted to stop him, but he seemed totally unaware there was anything wrong with the wine. Even now he swirled it around and around in his glass, watching Adam over the top. "How'd you come up with that kind of blackmail scheme?"

"It's in *Betrayal*," Scarlett blurted out. "My father's first book."

"That's right, Scarlett. I'm surprised you never caught on. But then"—Adam grinned, and Scarlett wished she could punch him in the mouth—"I've orchestrated everything perfectly."

Scarlett frowned. "You made a big mistake trying to cover up Edna Grace's identity."

"Edna's a mistake I should have taken care of years ago."

"It's easy to kill a wife," Logan stated, "but not so easy killing your mother. Right?"

Scarlett's gaze spun toward Logan. "You knew?"

"Yeah. Nick left a message on my recorder saying Edna was in prison in Chowchilla. Her son visited her once a month." Logan turned to Adam. "Isn't that right?"

Adam grinned as he crossed his legs. "Not exactly."

Logan's eyes narrowed. "What do you mean?"

"Edna wasn't my mother. She was my wife." Adam laughed cynically. "If you'd found her wallet you would have known. Damn fool woman carried around our wedding picture; her in white, me in a rented tux; the old bitch and the young guy kissing in some cheap Las Vegas chapel."

Adam shook his head as if it had all been some big joke. "I tried covering her identity so you wouldn't find out I was a bigamist. If I'd left well enough alone, you might have gone on thinking Edna was my mother. The killings would have remained my little secret, too." He laughed again—short, abrupt—then glared at Scarlett and Logan, all hint of amusement gone. "I made a mistake, but rest assured I won't make another. Now, do me a favor and drink your wine."

Logan continued to swirl his wine in front of his face; he continued to stare at Adam. Scarlett picked up her glass. She held it to her lips, but she didn't drink. "Did you love Edna?" Scarlett asked, finding this whole thing hard to believe.

"She had a beautiful house. A Victorian. I've always loved Victorians." Adam's train of thought seemed to wander. Logan's hand rested on her leg, and she could feel it tighten. "My mother and father had a Victorian. I loved that house, just as my mother did, but my father made some bad investments and lost everything. When I was twenty-one I drove by that old house. I knocked on the door and Edna answered. Right then and there I decided I'd marry her so the house could be mine."

Adam's gaze went back to the wine. "Drink up. Both of you. This is a party."

Logan pretended to drink, but Adam seemed in too much of a fog to notice.

"Did your other wives own Victorians?" Scarlett asked, hoping Adam's mind would wander back to the houses he seemed to love more than anything else.

"I had to have some enjoyment in my marriages. Edna and my next two wives were hags. But they owned beautiful homes, which made living with them bearable.

"And you married my mother for her house?"

"I know it must seem impossible to you that I could love someone, but I did love your mother. Of course, I had the benefit of living in that Victorian of yours, too, making it my own, making decisions on how it should be decorated. I did buy my own place though, just outside of town. It's beautiful. Of course, so were the ones I had to burn down." Adam frowned, as if old memories had come back to haunt him. "I didn't love those women, which made killing them easy. But Edna squandered the insurance money I collected, so I often wonder if destroying those homes was worthwhile."

Adam shrugged, the dead women and the old Victorians no longer important. "Drink up. Drink up."

Scarlett took a sip from her glass, then let it trickle back in, hoping the drug he'd laced in the wine wasn't strong enough to enter her bloodstream and knock her out.

Logan, far more composed than she was, continued to swirl his wine. "Why didn't you divorce Edna?"

"It's the only way I could protect myself and all my little secrets," Adam said. "She might have come up with the idea for me to marry and dispose of a couple of wives, but I did the dirty work and I'm the one who'd get the death sentence if she talked. She promised to keep quiet if I promised to be her husband forever and ever."

Adam got up from the chair and circled the room, his finger teasing the trigger on the rifle as he walked. "She had pictures. She had diaries and dates. I didn't know where any of that stuff was—until this morning when Ida Mae stumbled across everything. When I burn this cabin down, I'll burn all the evidence as well, and then I can go back to my nice, peaceful existence here in Plentiful."

"You going to kill the Sleuths, too?" Logan asked. "They're bound to know everything. And then there's my old partner, Nick Considine. He's fully aware of what's going on. How do you propose to get rid of him?"

"Shut up." Adam stomped across the room. "I knew that bitch would get me in trouble. Knew she'd make me do things I didn't want to do." His eyes narrowed. "I knew I should have killed her. I should have done it when she called Elizabeth and told her about me." Adam glared at Scarlett. "She'd been calling your mother all along. Nine years of phone calls from that bitch—when she wasn't in jail. She never identified herself, but she planted ideas in your mother's head about me. Bad things. And then that last night Edna told Elizabeth everything. Every single thing. I've got it all on tape. If you weren't about to die, I'd share it with you."

"Maybe you could just tell me," Scarlett said. Adam was losing it, and she was hoping for extra time. "Please, I need to know."

"Your mother sneaked out of the house, past the nurse I'd hired to take care of her. She got in the car and she drove up the mountain, and . . ." Adam slumped in the chair again. "I might have been able to save her if I could have gotten there in time. I was listening to the call when Edna made it. I heard your mother crying. I started for home, and when I saw her drive by, I followed. She was swerving all over those damned mountain roads, and then some ass-hole ran her off the side and she hit a tree."

Scarlett felt sick inside, all the pain coming back. "Was she still alive?"

"For a moment or two, long enough for me to tell her I loved her." Adam looked up; tears filled his eyes. "I wanted to love you, too, Scarlett. I wanted a happy family. I wanted to put everything I'd done behind me, but I couldn't. Edna wouldn't let me."

Logan sprang from the sofa, his body flying over the chrome-and-glass table and plowing into Adam. It happened suddenly. Scarlett hadn't expected it; she hoped Adam hadn't either, but the rifle went off. The explosion was deafening. Blood splattered everywhere, a few drops hitting Scarlett's face, her chest.

The men struggled; they fell on the floor, and the rifle skittered out of their reach. Fear for Logan's life came close to strangling Scarlett as he and Adam wrestled, leaving a bloody trail across the wooden planks.

They pummeled each other. Logan hammered a right against Adam's head. It was then that Scarlett saw the hole in Logan's suit coat, saw the blood oozing from his arm. She moved close, wanting to help, but Logan screamed at her. "Get back, Scarlett."

Adam smashed Logan in the nose and more blood flew.

In the kitchen Snagglepuss hissed; Toby growled, and suddenly two balls of fur joined in the fight. Toby chomped on Adam's hand; Snagglepuss clamped four sets of claws into Adam's back.

"Get these goddamned animals off of me," Adam screamed, turning his fury away from Logan, struggling now against the dog and cat.

Logan took advantage of the upper hand and landed a hard right under Adam's chin. The chief of police reeled backward. He staggered as Toby and Snagglepuss scrambled away, then fell face first onto the hardwood floor.

Logan dropped down beside Adam and pressed two fingers against the artery in his neck.

"He isn't dead, is he?" Scarlett asked.

"Out cold, but who knows how long that'll last."

Scarlett grabbed the handcuffs from the bottom drawer of Logan's desk and ran again toward the man she loved. Blood dripped down the sleeve of his jacket as well as from his nose and lower lip. But, in spite of it all, he managed to look up at her and smile.

"Are you all right?" Logan asked, caressing a tear from Scarlett's face as she knelt beside him and snapped the cuffs on Adam's wrists.

"Adam's going to jail. I know the truth about my mother's death. And you're here beside me." She kissed Logan's swollen and bloody lip. "Except for a few raw nerves and the man I love being battered and bruised, life couldn't be much better."

Logan buried his fingers into Scarlett's wayward curls. "It can be better, Scarlett. I'll prove it to you—every moment for the rest of our lives."

Toby's tail wagged. Snagglepuss purred.

And Scarlett sighed as Logan kissed her.

Life had just gotten better. Without a doubt, to-morrow and all the tomorrows after that were going to be absolutely divine.

Epilogue

Rose petals drifted down, down, down, settling lightly on the blushing bride's breasts. Scarlett Mary Catherine O'Malley Wolfe had been married a grand total of three hours and twenty-seven minutes, but her new husband and Plentiful's chief of police, Logan Wolfe, had already carried her across the threshold of A Study in Scarlett, trounced up the stairs with her cradled in his arms, stripped away her silver-and-white star-studded wedding gown, laid her in the center of their bed, and right this very moment, smiled down at her as he sprinkled the last of the rose petals over her body.

Only minutes ago he'd been a man in a hurry, convincing her to sneak away from their July 4th wedding reception in the park, from the Sleuths, who'd graciously consented to take care of Toby and Snagglepuss during the honeymoon, from the dazzling fireworks, and from Mayor Joe Granger and his daughter, Sue. They left gum-chomping Nick Considine, who'd spent the evening dancing with Molly, a few hundred frolicking citizens of Plentiful, and a dozen or so Vegas cops who were too busy slugging down Moose Jaw to know anything else was going on around them.

Now he was a man of great patience; a man who obviously had a plan—of total seduction.

Logan turned on the music—Elvis, of course. Scarlett had expected something soft and romantic, "Can't Help Falling in Love" maybe, or "Surrender," which she was more than willing to do. Instead, pure rockin' Elvis rolled through the room and Logan began his moves.

He tore off his coat, his tie, and his shirt, his pelvis rocking and rolling in time with the music. "Shake it shake it sugar . . . ," he sang along with the King, offering Scarlett her own private floor show, one far, far better than any Vegas performance.

A lock of his dark chocolate hair fell over his brow, and his hips swiveled seductively. He kicked off his shoes, and in a strip that left Scarlett breathless, he rid his body of all other encumbrances—except one.

Surprised and delighted, Scarlett crawled to the end of the bed and took a nice long look at Logan's shiny new belly button ring and . . . well, she also peeked at another fixture on his fabulous body, one that wasn't exactly dangling.

Reaching out to Logan, she caught the golden ring, curling her finger through the lustrous circle. "Goodness, what a nice ring you have," she said, and tugged her husband, the man she loved and would always cherish, toward her gently. "A girl like me could easily get stuck on a guy like you."

The Big Bad Wolfe winked. "That's the idea, my dear. That's the idea."